# SASSO

# SASSO

James Sturz

Walker & Company
New York

To my mother and father,
in and out of time

First published in Great Britain in 2001 by Century Random House;
first published in the United States of America in 2002 by
Walker Publishing Company, Inc.

Published simultaneously in Canada by
Fitzhenry and Whiteside, Markham, Ontario L3R 4T8

For information about permission to reproduce selections
from this book, write to Permissions, Walker & Company,
435 Hudson Street, New York, New York 10014

Library of Congress Cataloging-in-Publication Data

Sturz, James.
  Sasso / James Sturz.
    p.   cm.
  ISBN 0-8027-3372-7
    1. Italy, Southern—Fiction.   2. Serial murders—Fiction.
    3. Cave paintings—Fiction.   I. Title.

PS3619.T87  S37  2002
813'.6—dc21

2001056758

Visit Walker & Company's Web site at www.walkerbooks.com

Printed in the United States of America

2   4   6   8   10   9   7   5   3   1

*Se le tue mani fossero il mio cuore,*
*il suo battito sarebbe l'applauso.*

*Ma siccome le unghie sono coltelli,*
*il bis sarà breve.*


[If your hands were my heart,
its beat would be applause.

But since your nails are knives,
the encore will be brief.]


**Giancarlo Tramontano**
translated from the Latin
by Dr Gaetano Stoppani

# PART ONE
# FALL

# Chapter 1
# Tufa

You woke me with laughter. I was dreaming of fish. But you were letting out peals of laughter, already wide awake. The bedsheets were tangled in your hands and pressed to your face to stifle the sounds. I turned to you. I said in my morning voice, 'What's so funny?' You looked at me plaintively, still full of laughs, your hair tousled and tangled from rolling in bed. You had all the covers. You said, 'I don't know. I can't remember.' That was how I woke, how you used to wake me.

It was early morning when I left. Late September. The trees were trying to flirt with every color they could muster: orange, brown, yellow, crimson, rust. The knots of the trees had come alive, wooing the breeze with open-mouthed kisses. On the ground, the fallen leaves were a soft kilim of crinkling sheets, veils promising nudity, even hinting misleadingly of sex. But inside the apartment, you busied yourself watering plants, feeding them the nutrients you mixed into the water as if you were making a broth. The night before, you'd looked at me screw-eyed, and warned: 'In the morning, slip out. *Write*, don't call. Or wire flowers every once in a while to surprise me. Everyone likes flowers, and it doesn't matter which kinds. Besides' – you pointed to a jar of peonies on the table – 'these ones are dying.'

'No, no,' I told you, 'they're just distracted.'

The trip was hard. (It was hard even before I got started. The bare skin of your shoulder attracted my hand in the morning, and I kissed you goodbye like they teach in the movies. Then as I lumbered out, weighted down by my bags, you tried to ignore me, quietly crying.) I flew to Amsterdam, and then to Rome, and then again to Bari, in a rickety Fokker 27 that actually shook. In Bari, we were supposed to catch our breaths once our group was assembled, but there were notices of an outbreak of cholera, and murmurs of the irony of dehydration so close to the sea. The old port of the city was full of old disease. It made me wince to see people clutching their stomachs from cramps, staring back at me from pools of diarrhea.

Dr Stoppani met us at the airport, and we spent the night at his home, watching the news reports on TV, as he translated to us whatever details we missed: a seventy-year-old fisherman, wanting to prove his catch was safe, had gulped down a bowl of mussels on camera, and the networks were showing the footage over and over, because now this fisherman was dead. His widow had become something of a celebrity, granting interviews in her slippers from the door to their ramshackle home on the town's northern edge, by the *frazione* of Santo Spirito. She carried a framed photograph of her husband in her hand, and wanted to know who was going to support her.

That evening, Dr Stoppani's wife served mullet that both of them vowed had been flown in from the north.

'This is Mediterranean fish, *Ligurian* fish,' Monica Stoppani said, in an accent that showed her English was studied, and not just learned. She was an elegant woman, refined. She wore jewelry. 'This is red mullet from Portofino,' she said. 'So it is quite all right.'

'My wife is beautiful,' Dr Stoppani told us after dinner, as if to make sure we realized it. 'And she is charming,' he added, implying a degree of cause and effect.

In the morning, we headed inland by car, threading south through the valleys on the barely trafficked roads that lead the way to the city of Mancanzano. There were five of us: Dr Stoppani, Middelhoek, Fortune, Linda and me, in three beat-up Fiats, carrying our luggage and equipment, rumbling past the dry range in a caravan of creaking chassis. Middelhoek went on and on about petitioning the Ministry of Transportation to have the roads repaved, and he kept leaving reminders about individual potholes on a tape recorder he'd been pulling out of his breast pocket ever since joining up with us at Schiphol Airport. But now, three hours outside of Bari, one crevice was so huge that it was more like a fissure, and a wheel of Fortune's Fiat got stuck. We had to tow out his car – the most heavily weighted down of the bunch thanks to two taped-up steamer trunks on top – by unfastening the baggage from the roofs of our own cars, just so that we could use the rope. It's a good thing I'd practiced driving a stick shift with you before I left New York. I turned up the radio when the gear-grinding got bad. The air already smelled burned. When I stuck my arm through the window, I could feel the heat from the air on the flanks of the car whenever my skin touched against metal.

It's picturesque to imagine all of us decked out in desert clothes, drinking from lozenge-shaped, dented, canvas-wrapped canteens: a regular expedition into the unknown. But Dr Stoppani wore a light blue linen suit, and, halfway through the trip, he brought out a box of individually wrapped almond cakes and a Thermos of lukewarm espresso that he poured into porcelain cups. Linda, at least, had put on a pair of khakis, and she sipped from a bottle of mineral water with a half-detached label that hung by her wrist.

Just as she finished drinking, she glanced around at the empty landscape, and, much like Ozymandias surveying his kingdom, said, 'I hope this doesn't make me have to pee. Because there's no place to go.'

But we got there, all right. We saw Mancanzano rise right out of the dust, like some Italianate Oz.

In order to describe what it's like here, I'd better start with the winds. This time of the year, they hit you in the face just to surprise you. Then they loiter around the back of your neck, like a pack of punks, before ducking inside your collar to perpetrate even more mischief. The hot breezes come out of nowhere, like they're sucked from the earth. They make you sweat. Then they give you the chills. Until you get used to them, you walk around feeling like your skin is somebody else's. The more you perspire, the more the dust clings to you, eventually turning to crust.

Just outside of town, there's a ravine with a creek that the Mancanzani visit, where they stick their bodies for as long as they can. We've only been here for a week, and already we've joined them, even if Fortune's still having trouble communicating with the townsfolk in his English-schoolboy Italian. Sometimes there'll be six or seven of us in the creek, stripped down to our underwear, lying in two feet of water. When it gets crowded, you stand up with pebbles still pressed to your skin. Then you brush them off, and the little red indentations turn white, and then smooth, and then hot like the rest of your body. Dr Stoppani has warned us: submersing yourself in the creek isn't always well regarded in Mancanzano. Doing it more than once a day is generally considered so slothful and indolent that people eye you warily when you pass them on the street. You can tell what they're thinking, Dr Stoppani says. They're thinking: *There goes the guy who can't take the heat.*

There are vast patches of rock all along the outskirts of the city. It's the stone that I told you about before I left: a calcium carbonate called tufa, the texture and color of sand. Where the tufa breaks through the earth, the terrain is covered with mottled tapestries of white, black, yellow, orange and rust. (They're almost the same colors I remember from autumn with you, transported and transmogrified.) In some remote places, pebbles give way to rocks the size of fists, which then turn to boulders, before finally the whole ground transforms to broad sheets of stone.

Where the tufa's been disturbed by any one of the local kids who come through here looking for something to sell, the fossils of Pleistocene seashells ripple across the rock. I've seen kids digging with bare hands, with monstrous calluses on their fingertips, bulging just below hardened nails. It boosts your ego to say you tore the ground apart with your hands. From what we've been told, the Mancanzano women say these guys are rough, and, yes, sometimes the guys even hurt them, but in a land where people are hardened by sun and wind, what frightens them most isn't the prospect of pain, but the absence of sensation.

But I don't know how you could be dulled to anything here. The air is full of the scent of thyme, and thistles mix with rosemary, sage and flowering asphodel. Wild asparagus sprouts unpredictably, yards away from bloating cactus. There are a few ash and olive trees folded into the thorn bushes that are home to maybe a few nose-twitching hares. There are some fig trees too, with swollen fruits draped from their branches like Christmas tree ornaments. But in desolate areas, where sparse plantlife clings to the ground, groping for cracks where it might unassumingly shoot its roots, snails appear by the thousand, sharing the terrain with darting squadrons of lizards. They get in your boots.

Here in the city, mixed into the disarray, there are eccentric homes built from the tufa. These are the cave homes that the Mancanzani call 'sassi' (even if the word ambiguously only means 'stones' in dictionary Italian). In the oldest parts of the city, the sassi are set off by tiny piazzas, layered one on top of another, and tangled along the face of two giant bluffs. Here, Mancanzano is all one intricate web: houses fold into each other like a distended urban origami, as the roof of one becomes another's floor, or a walled-in courtyard, or a neighborhood's sidewalk. Façades have been added to the fronts of some homes, but so much of Mancanzano is actually just an arabesque of grottoes. At night, it's easy to see which of them are currently occupied. Lights shine through doorways and windows, filling tenebrous streets with an eerie glow.

For hundreds of years, the people here used a system of cisterns carved into the rock to collect rainwater. God and gravity were all the town's inhabitants knew about modern plumbing. But then the same southern winds blew radio and television signals into town, and Mancanzano had to start playing catch-up with the rest of the country. Today, the Mancanzani are still laborers and farmers, but they are also bankers and architects who can languorously quote Gramsci and Proust. Sometimes you see a guy in a well-tailored suit, short slicked-back hair and callused hands. Then you think: this is not a man to be trifled with. Sometimes you see these men, and the women too, at the creek after nightfall, ties and pants and jackets and skirts folded over the stones, and a half-dozen barely clothed bankers lying still in cold water, remembering what it was like to be six years old, before money and government and religion and sex.

Sometimes it gets so hot in the honeycomb of houses that you press whatever skin you can bare against the porous, cool stone. It's a sign of great hospitality, here: offering a wall of your home against which a guest can pull up his shirt and press sweaty skin. Just short of that, what people do to keep cool when they're away from the creek is they cover themselves up with powdered tufa. They really let it soak up the sweat.

The day we arrived in Mancanzano, we visited our local contact, the High Deputy for Public Works, at her modern hilltop home. La Dottoressa Donabuoni is a woman in her mid-fifties, cultivated in dress, but with the exaggerated femininity of a gnome doped up on estrogen. She's what the Italians call a *donna prosperosa*, a woman whose prosperity is measured by the voluptuousness of her breast. That afternoon in her living room, as we sipped glasses of sweetened iced tea, we all watched intently as she took a handful of tufa from a basin and sprinkled it down the back of her blouse. So I did the same, for which she offered me a conspiratorial glance. And later that week, when I visited her office to discuss an ongoing matter of permits, I saw that she had a small ceramic jar of powdered tufa on her desk. I could barely get out a word before she reached across the giant slab of mahogany to hold the container before me. Then she dabbed a powdery finger at her cleavage, as you might a perfume. I put a few fingerfuls along my neck, which tingled to the touch.

So what am I doing in this funky spelunky southern Italian town anyway, lodged like a pebble in the instep of the Italian boot? And what am I doing here in Mancanzano, when I keep thinking of you five thousand miles away in New York?

We all have Dr Stoppani to thank. He's the one who put our team together in the midst of all the commotion here, contacting a handful of universities in northern Europe and the United States to offer positions that no one in Italy was willing to take.

Fortune, a geologist from the Imperial College of Science and Technology in London, was the first one to sign on to our group. He's been taking samples of the tufa deposits around Mancanzano's outskirts since we arrived, and already he's got a team of locals helping him: a ragtag bunch of kids from the *liceo scientifico* here, whom you catch holding hands exactly when they think you're not looking.

Joost Middelhoek, a curator at the Rijksmuseum's largely neglected Italian collection (not to mention a graduate of the Netherlands State Training School for Restorers, where he claims he showed unparalleled aptitude at differentiating among the chemical properties of yellows and blues), is focusing his attention on the underground frescoes, the ones that the police and those other kids found. Middelhoek's job is to gauge what damage there's been to the wall paintings thus far, and he's collaborating with those do-nothings from the Centro per la Valorizzazione e Gestione delle Risorse Storico-Ambientali, two and a half hours away in Potenza, whenever the high deputy can convince them to make the visit.

Linda and I, as our team's two American cultural anthropologists (and the only ones to know one another before coming here) are sticking above ground, traipsing across Mancanzano's narrow streets with a six-page penciled-in, crossed-out map, knocking on doors and gathering stories. Our goal is to get as many oral histories as we can onto tape, so that at least we'll have something if everything everyone else does amounts to a hill of *fagioli*.

Now that we're all here, it's not clear what Dr Stoppani does himself. Every few days he gets in his car and drives like a madman in the direction of Bari. He comes back in the morning, just as the sun's up, looking a lot like an exhausted teenager.

But I tell you, it's amazing they want to tear all of this down, hide away the history just because of the deaths. Essentially, Mancanzano's modern history began in the sixth century AD with the monks. They were Benedictines fleeing the Papal States and the Kingdom of Naples, and they apparently chose Mancanzano because they couldn't imagine anyone following them to so miserable a place as this abandoned cave town. With its arid landscape, dusty hills and remarkably few natural resources, the warren-like sassi would finally provide them with the insularity they craved.

Plagues, earthquakes and famine had wiped out the town's earlier inhabitants. So once the Benedictines arrived, they got to work. They dug gargantuan monasteries and churches into the tufa bluffs, excavating apses and altars, columns and naves. They chiseled vaulted ceilings and cubbyholes the shapes of enormous sunken teardrops, then they covered the chalky subterranean walls with frescoes of vibrant peaches and blues. Angels showed up suddenly, inscribed in the dust.

Smaller grottoes that had served as homes since Paleolithic times were further transformed into chapels, now connected by tunnels. The work turned the interior landscape into an even more beguiling labyrinth. But not even the Benedictines would remain. In the fifteenth century, the riches and excesses of the

Renaissance slowly seeped south, and as word spread down the peninsula of Michelangelo, da Vinci and Fra Filippo Lippi (a Carmelite monk who'd been so debauched as to marry and father a son), Mancanzano's monks couldn't help wonder why they were still living in caves, traveling their underground metropolis like obeisant armies of worker ants. So the monks, in turn, abandoned the cave churches they'd dug into stone, and they disappeared into the neighboring open-air towns, establishing a confetti of churches and chapels across Italy's south.

Soon a new wave of farmers took the monks' places, inhabiting the rock monasteries along with their livestock, herding their cattle against the frescoes, teaching chickens and pigs, and even themselves, how to live inside caves. Within the chapels, they constructed giant stone vats for stomping out wine, storing caches of their product in the cool, sunken recesses. Five hundred years ago – long before our own ancestors were born, I think – the inhabitants of Mancanzano reveled underground, drunk like stone skunks on their cavern wine.

But if this starts to sound even the least bit luxurious (as drinking stories sometimes do), you have to keep it all in perspective. Farmers feel rich if there's milk on the table and a little meat on the fire. Whereas in more urbane environments, such as those found closer to Rome, there has been the tendency to feel rich if you have the right shoes and political connections.

By the 1930s, Mancanzano's caves came to symbolize southern Italy's extreme indigence. Here, poverty was classified by how far into the earth's bowels you were willing to live. There were troglodyte Mancanzani called 'Ventimetri' because they lived twenty meters from open air. There were 'Trentametri' and 'Quarantametri' too. If the size of your home was a measure of your patience – of how long and how deep you were willing to dig – then there were families of ten and more crammed into twenty-square-meter spaces. The members would curl into balls at night just to make enough room for sleep.

Halfway through this century, when Carlo Levi's memoir *Christ Stopped at Eboli* suggested that humanity hadn't reached much beyond Naples, and that, farther south, Italians lived as wild animals or beasts of burden, Mancanzano had acquired the nickname 'Mole City'. But amid well-publicized newspaper reports of its poverty and squalor (some accompanied by photos of black clouds of flies over mounds of garbage), the well-coiffed plutocrats of Rome began to declare the city responsible for an unacceptable ill – and this one abominable in an age of mass communication: publicly exemplifying their country's worst.

As Dr Stoppani tells it, indignant legislators across the capital announced: 'It's a scandal the people of Mancanzano live this way. So let's not let them.'

Not even the town's once-legendary frescoes could save Mancanzano, for over the years they hadn't fared any better than the people. Where livestock had been herded into the sassi – and where human beings had driven in nails, chiseled shelves, and cooked over fires without so much as a chimney – the Benedictine cave paintings were so badly damaged that there wasn't much anyone considered worth saving. Smoke from olive branches and meats had permeated the walls. So had urine from burros and cows. Burnished frescoes once painted to praise God, virgins, angels and saints now looked as if they were ducking back into the stone, reburying themselves in the womb of the soft rock. By some people's reckoning, it was as though the angels had congressed and decided that Mancanzano's caves were no longer a safe place for miracles. Which might have been right. Because by then Italy was under the churn of Fascism.

In 1937, fifteen years after Mussolini took power, Rome officially declared the caves of Mancanzano a *vergogna nazionale*, a 'national embarrassment' that belittled the spirit of Fascism's copious public works. So Il Duce decreed that the cave homes would be razed and replaced with modern monolithic structures. Soldiers were dispatched to Mancanzano with orders to give the twenty thousand cave-dwellers four days to move, but few of the soldiers wanted to linger that long; so they gave the town's peasants just six hours to decide where to go next. Mussolini's Italy was caught up in ideas of modernism and conquest. His soldiers couldn't understand the appeal of burrowing into a hillside.

The soldiers also couldn't comprehend the cult of tufa, which the local Mancanzani believed then to have medicinal and even magical properties. The townsfolk would mix the powdered stone into their food, as though they were sprinkling on dietary supplements, or, better yet, freshly grated cheese. If you weren't used to eating the powdered tufa, its taste and consistency made you gag. If you poured too much of the tufa into your food (or, perhaps, into the food of a visiting soldier who had just thrust a jackboot through your door), it turned from powder to paste, and then to cement. It could harden on your plate. Or in your stomach.

At the end of three hours in Mancanzano on April 19, 1937, a half-dozen of Mussolini's troops were clutching their abdomens. But after three hours more – it was by then five o'clock, and southern Italy's sun cast fractured shadows across the sprawling sassi – the ambulatory Fascisti fired shots into the still-occupied homes. The soldiers' bullets riddled holes through flesh and stone, splashing blood and drilling deep into the tufa. According to orders, tents for the displaced townspeople were to have been put up on Mancanzano's outskirts, but the soldiers had chosen to wait until the late afternoon to erect them, once the sun wasn't so hot. So into the evening, the weeping, and now homeless, Mancanzani sat around, consoling each other and rebundling their belongings, as they waited for the awkward *favelas* to go up.

The construction was finished just before midnight. But the tents came down the following morning, just as soon as it rained. Over the next few months, two new neighborhoods were tacked on to Mancanzano's flatland periphery by an army corps of engineers. But as the war effort mounted, their energies were needed elsewhere, and most of the buildings remained half built, with beams jutting out into the still air. Some Mancanzani moved back to the caves despite warnings, lodging in the deepest tunnels and emerging at night on clandestine forays for whatever food they could find.

What the Fascisti accomplished, besides killing a few hundred people, was to create an atmosphere of lawlessness among those who remained. But Mussolini's men had other worries by then. In 1939, Il Duce signed on with Hitler, and in 1940 Italy entered the war in Europe. So the remaining troops left Mancanzano to face more pressing challenges beyond Italy's borders. After all, now there were Ethiopia, Albania, Yugoslavia and Greece to menace.

Back in Mancanzano, where soldiers had sprayed bullets with the nonchalance of gardeners spraying weedkiller across lawns, the tufa had absorbed the blood, and the walls and doorframes of the cave homes were permanently stained red. Over the next two decades most of the sassi remained empty, even once the Fascisti were gone. No one wanted to live in a place that so inescapably reminded him of death.

By the late 1960s, the sassi were still predominantly un-inhabited, and they became havens for late-night parties, cultish rituals, and sometimes both. The maze-like caves attracted teen-age boys, who would use their cubbyhole quiet to woo whichever girlfriends responded well to this kind of wooing. In the process, they littered the grounds with wine bottles, candles, magazines and condoms. Although the furniture from the homes had long since been removed, there were still some mattresses scattered throughout, and many of them had been pushed into the corners of the oblong rooms. The mattresses were tattered and worn, and consumed in a mildew that masked the dank smell of sex. Decades of wine and sweat had soaked into the cottony fiber.

So, when the carabinieri found the two missing teenagers just those six weeks ago, they saw what I told you even before I left.

Both the boy and the girl were sprawled across the cave floor, naked. There was no sign of their clothes anywhere in the nearby sassi or interlocking tunnels, and, given the far-from-impressive caliber of local forensics, it was virtually impossible to determine what route the teenagers had taken through the labyrinth of the city to get to these particular caves.

Both the boy and the girl were dead. Their teeth were chipped, and their faces were bruised and cut, especially around their cheeks, noses and chins. Their jaws were jacked open and their tongues abraded. A cobweb of lacerations followed the contour of their lips. Photographs ran in the local newspapers, and in these pictures the faces of the teenagers looked like latex Halloween masks, waxy, swollen, grotesque – the newsprint giving them an even more exaggerated pallor.

In the absence of any wounds, the earliest speculation was that the teenagers had choked on the stone. They'd eaten the tufa right from the walls, gnawing at the softest sections of the rock, biting away at powder, pebbles and chunks. But while the mystery of their deaths enveloped the town, the most startling part of the discovery – at least as far as our team would be concerned – was that the insides of the boy and girl's mouths were caked not only with white, but with a few pigments of red and peach that came from where their gnawing had uncovered the most astonishing frescoes.

So it's as I said: the High Deputy for Public Works is the one who got the ball rolling (even if we've found it rolls slowly across dusty terrain). She contacted Dr Stoppani, who, through our various universities, contacted us. There was a departmental notice at Columbia, plus another at Rutgers, where Linda saw it. And the rest you know already: one year out of graduate school and still without work, I accepted the opportunity to jump-start a stalling career.

In Italy, the carabinieri were concerned with solving (or, perhaps more precisely, investigating) the crime, and some folks along the peninsula were saying the Fascisti had been right:

Mancanzano's caves were more than a national embarrassment, they were the very distillation of southern Italy's problems – whether it was poverty, illiteracy, ill health, corruption, the Mafia, or whatever malaise you wanted to add that day. With the exception of a small nucleus of renovated houses along the top of Mancanzano's slopes, most of the sassi by now *were* in a sorry state, if not in impossible disrepair. And as for the frescoes that had been accidentally discovered at the remotest parts of the caves, indignant voices now swept through piazzas in the rest of Italy – where so many buildings were already covered in scaffolds and funds for the projects had been squandered on bribes – questioning how anyone could appreciate art that had first been covered up in a thick coating of white and that naked teenagers had then tried to eat, regardless of what the high deputy and her so-called team of 'imported experts' were presenting as the greatest find of the last forty years. After all, people said, *children had died* . . .

By the time our group arrived in Mancanzano, many of the town's residents were already gone. Others were making plans to leave. Even among the fifteen thousand who remained in modern complexes around the town's outskirts – plus a scattered thousand in the sassi themselves – there were proposals to finish what the Fascisti had begun in the thirties, and condemn the conglomeration of caves in Mancanzano's old center, detonating them with such finality that they could never again be inhabited.

If Dr Stoppani from Bari hadn't met the high deputy in Sorrento, and been so impressed – and, I imagine, enticed – by her pluck, he'd never have helped put our team together. And I'd still be back in New York with you, watching your belly quietly rise.

So will you forgive me for coming to this faraway city? Will you forgive my fascination with Mancanzano? When I said I was leaving for Italy, you asked sullenly, 'Don't you want to watch me be pregnant? Don't you want to study *me*?' But when

I told you I was leaving soon, and for almost a year, then you warned, 'If you're not here when I give birth, I won't be here either. This apartment will be empty. I'm not Penelope. I'm not going to wait.'

So would you make me one promise? Embroider it on sheets, scratch it across mirrors. Or write it on plaster wherever the wallpaper's come unglued. Don't forget I'm coming back, don't worry, I'm coming home.

Because, even here, my arm wants to wear your waist as a sleeve. And I want to picture you laughing, not flushed from tears. You've said not to call until I'm boarding a plane home to you in June. You've said that no contact would be easier than hearing my words trickle from far away. But I want you to know that in a town where razor-sharp skepticism meets all interlopers, I miss waking up and finding you next to me, and knowing that I am in exactly the right place.

I love you and miss you; the first part feels good and the other part hurts.

I'll be back with you in New York before our child is born, that much I promise. I'll be there to welcome a new us onto the earth. But for now, here I am, lost, at work, in Mancanzano. (And have I mentioned the high deputy is still trying to track down money for stipends?) What kind of anthropologist did I come here to be? A famous one? Hardly. A poor one? Sure. Here. Away from you. Lost in the sassi.

# Chapter 2
# One Last Supper

Ethnographic notes from a stone city: in the 1930s, the women in the sassi always wore black. The *miseria* in this part of southern Italy was dire enough to warrant full-time mourning attire. Around the cave homes, the poverty was so severe that local anthropologists explained the women's grieving as a self-defense mechanism for containing their sorrow before it consumed them.

In the mornings in Mancanzano, the men went to work in the fields, while the women did the washing, the cooking and cleaning. Husbands and wives saw each other only at breakfast and dinner. Each member of a family ate from the same plate, sitting in the same chair, using the same set of wood utensils. The family members would take turns eating at mealtimes following a hierarchy that was etched in blood, and then revised according to age, height, marriage, musculature and an occasional fistfight.

In the afternoons, in the spring, summer and fall, young children played soccer in the tiny piazzas outside of their homes, with balls made from socks and other rags, with rocks inside to give them ballast. The children played barefoot over rough stones. In the evenings, they'd show up at home with broken toenails and bleeding feet.

In the winter, a damp cold entered the sassi through the doors, ceilings and walls. The elderly felt this chill the most. In

February, Mancanzano was a city of sufferers of rheumatoid arthritis. During the day, anyone over the age of seventy sat outside his home in its one chair, huddling under the rays of the sun. This was the only time of the year that the women in black couldn't mortify their flesh under a searing sky. They mumbled and shivered and fumbled with rosaries. Their devotion to the Madonna was as inexhaustible as Mancanzano's fine tufa dust. Sometimes they swore that Maria herself could be glimpsed in their breaths.

When the Fascisti forced the Mancanzani out of the sassi, the townspeople couldn't stand the silence. They were used to swarming sounds all around them, of yelling and children and barking dogs and cows and chickens, and singing and sighing and clanking pots. It didn't matter now if you were the one who had left a cave home, or the one who remained. Nothing was worse, and newer and stranger, than the swallowing silence of a half-empty city. For the people of Mancanzano, the quiet was the beginning of a modern, mysterious world.

—

In Mancanzano, our own world has been forming around us. Since we've arrived here, we've been learning to call this region 'Lucania', as so many do. Long before the monks, this area was part of the 'Magna Graecia': seaport cities colonized by the Greeks from the eighth to the second centuries BC, and then by the Lycians, who had already built tufa homes in Asia Minor. When those maritime settlers reached Italy and wandered up the peninsula from the Ionian Sea, they found the hills they traversed so treacherous that they rarely came back.

In the first century BC, Cicero is known to have visited Mancanzano from the north, and to have told of a land so soft that it swallowed you in, like a body of water, or like a priceless whore. The poet Horace, who was born in a Roman military colony just eighty kilometers north, toured this part of Lucania too, and he entertained Augustus's court with stories of vipers, lizards, rabbits and bears, and the men who lived among them, all of them in lairs. Byzantines, Goths, Romans, Albanians, Lombards, Christians, Jews, Greeks, Normans, Swabians and Saracens alike all visited Mancanzano, and all of them left parcels of their cultures behind. But this was an area of earthquakes, and whatever the settlers constructed inevitably became rubble.

By the late fifteenth century, when Mancanzano's Benedictines were relinquishing their caves for life on the surface – and much of Lucania now had the modern name 'Basilicata' – the town was a fiefdom of the tyrannical Neapolitan count Giancarlo Tramontano, who was assassinated in a popular revolt one Sunday after Mass as he exited Mancanzano's cathedral. His crest was a chunk of stone under the forepaw of a griffin.

On the western edge of Mancanzano's urban nucleus, the Castello Tramontano looms ominously over the sassi, twenty-eight meters tall, constructed entirely of tufa bricks. One broad tower rises from its center, surrounded by a ring of parapets. Count Tramontano was known to have been crazy. He'd stand atop the tower, thread his penis between battlements as if it were a cannon, and see if he could urinate beyond the castle walls. He was a bad judge of distance. He always missed by hundreds of feet. But the count was convinced that one day, with practice, he'd finally succeed. In the afternoons, his servants would come out with buckets and mops to swab the grounds and the castle walls. If they passed him on the way back to their quarters, they'd tell him encouragingly, 'Next time, Your Highness! Next time you'll make it!' And the count, certain of this, would smile maniacally back at the servants.

But even with years of practice, Count Tramontano never succeeded. And, of course, there were additional indignities he showered on the town: beheadings, torture, public assaults, ruthless levies on every activity, including the mining, collection and distribution of tufa. So after more than a decade of rule, the

Mancanzani decided they'd had enough.

It was 1514, and the last Sunday of December, and the people realized they couldn't endure another year. Count Tramontano didn't get more than a few feet past the cathedral's doors before the throngs descended on him, brandishing knives. Within minutes, the count's body was heaved into Piazza Ridola (which in those days was called Piazza Tramontano), and he was hung by his ankles until his body stopped dripping blood. Then, once the stench was intolerable, the corpse was pulled down and dumped into a wheelbarrow. It was brought to a cave a kilometer from town, where it was heaped inside, still clothed and bloody. The people from town arrived one by one. They hurled rocks and stones into the cave until it was filled, and the earth had reclaimed what it had errantly proffered. No gravestone was left, and Piazza Tramontano was renamed within a few days. So was a side street behind the cathedral where the stabbing took place. Now it's called the Via del Riscatto – the 'Street of Vengeance'.

Today, teenagers come to the Via del Riscatto to kiss one another where blood once trickled from brick to brick. To refuse a kiss here is unthinkable. 'You realize what could happen?' suitors threaten. 'A throat could be cut. Things could get messy.'

A couple of days ago, I was walking this street not long after dark, and I heard a teenage boy and a girl talking in the hushed voices of lovers.

'I want to kill something,' the boy said.

'That's sexy,' the girl answered. She looked at him with wicked delight.

'You ever kill anything?' the boy asked her, seriously.

She shook her head, no. 'But I want to,' she told him. 'It's something I've been meaning to do. Is it fun?'

As I walked away from them, I could hear his voice fade, as he flirted with her again. Now he was telling her: 'I want to bury you up to your neck and kiss you until you can't breathe.' And: 'You'll never forget me. Because I'm going to betray you.' And:

*21*

'I want to eat the parts of your body they wouldn't sell even at the best butcher shops.'

This kid had all the lines; I suppose he was a real Lucanian Lothario. By the time I'd left, he was nibbling at her neck. The air was hot and enveloping, like a quilt. And he was wrapping it around her.

But can you imagine eating a fresco right from a wall, what that would do to your cheeks and to your chin, to your nose and your teeth, if you gnawed at the cave until the soft rock filled your mouth like a granitey dollop of mashed potatoes? Inside the cave where the two dead teenagers were found, the peach of the frescoes – angel heads, bishop arms, and the dwarfish hands of cherubim – mixed with blood from the two teenagers' faces and mouths. Then the tufa walls of the cave sucked back the paint like a sponge. The colors left on the walls were astonishing. Especially the reds: bloody and passionate.

After all, when the carabinieri found the couple they'd been dead for less than two days, and there were still signs that they'd been in an embrace. They'd had sex and they'd died. Gobs of semen showed up in vaginal smears. It was likely the girl had lived long enough to conceive.

Rigor mortis had come and gone. The teenagers' faces and shoulders had begun to discolor, taking on a shade of pale green and marbling along the blood vessels. Decomposition fluid trickled from their mouths and noses onto the earth, and their swollen tongues protruded between their teeth and lips, still coated in tufa. Below their waists, juices from lovemaking had dried around the shriveled base of his penis, and matted the hair and tangled the curls. Alive, both the boy and the girl had been young, handsome, healthy – nineteen years old and objectively desirable. In death, they were gruesome. But what people wondered about was the sex.

Dr Stoppani had rushed to Mancanzano when the bodies were discovered, and he'd gained admittance to the cave by showing a host of IDs, some of them even real. From his descriptions and others, we learned that the girl had been on top when the two made love: a mapwork of contusions and abrasions lined her knees and the boy's back, and a sprinkling of pebbly tufa clung to what had once been hot skin. The boy had held on to her sides tightly during the sex. There were hickeys and scratches, and finger-shaped bruises contouring her ribs. Each other's skin was under their fingernails, mixed with the tufa that had been scraped from the walls and the cave floors.

Where their flesh was reddish purple – or where it was pale – livor mortis (the discoloration of skin caused by gravity's settling of red blood cells in the body) showed that the two had died next to each other, with her arm draped over his chest. From all of the evidence, the couple had enjoyed themselves immensely before they went crazy. And before they went dead. That's what people said softly. They said, 'It must have been good, lethal sex.' They fucked each other to death. There were people who said, 'That's the way to die.'

The carabinieri made their rounds in the cave, gathering physical evidence, taking photos and making notes. They had to wait until a doctor could be summoned from town to confirm that the two teenagers were dead, even though their bodies had already begun to stink.

Then once the doctor had left (though not before recommending his brother to them as an excellent mortician at a first-rate funeral parlor that paid a finder's fee to police), one of the carabinieri glanced over the two naked bodies, and the absence of clothes, and said, 'I don't know what to do. You never undress a body before sending it to the morgue. We learned that at the academy.' Thus, what to do with the bodies became a genuine question of strategy before the officers decided they wouldn't be risking their own necks by taking immediate action. Only then did they wrap the teenagers in plastic, heave them up the bluff on body boards, and send them to the *medico legale*, two and a half hours away in Basilicata's capital city of Potenza.

The girl found in the cave had two sisters, aged five and six. At first, their parents tried to keep the facts of their sister's death from them. Their father explained tersely at dinner, 'Lucia died in an accident in one of the caves.' But the girls wanted to know: 'Did the roof fall down? Was she bitten by a snake?' Their mother, crying, just looked at them over dinner plates and pleaded, 'Why don't you eat?'

Then the girls heard the specifics from the other children at school. Their classmates whispered about what happened, folding the scenarios of the deaths into their playground games. Prepubescent couples – sometimes two boys or two girls, sometimes mixed – would collapse to the ground and pretend to bite away at the earth. It was a matter of pride to get the most grime on your face. Their teachers frantically lined up the children and tried to explain the seriousness of what had happened down by the caves. In the newspapers, the issue became a subject of fervent debate: at what age do you teach children about tragedy?

But the game continued unabated. The two girls played it too, mimicking the death of their sister, whom they only half understood they'd never see again. There was a week when nearly every child in Mancanzano under the age of eleven had to be punished to get them to stop. The mothers in Mancanzano all wept, reliving the episode as though Lucia had been their daughter, even while they were horrified at the sight of their own children tumbling to the ground, giggling.

The dead boy had brothers, all of them older. The eldest lived in Gallarate, an industrial suburb of Milan, and didn't speak much with the rest of the family. The remaining two were in their twenties and lived in Mancanzano, where, like their father, they worked as stone masons, restoring sassi. Their father had a long moustache, thick forearms and broad shoulders. He'd routinely challenge his sons to contests of strength. Against a wall of their home, a dresser was cracked at its base where one of them had dropped it.

The dead boy and girl's families barely spoke to each other, even though they were grieving in similar ways. But their mistrust of each other was public and pronounced, and each was convinced that the other's child-rearing was to blame.

The boy's mother, distraught, was overheard saying, 'That Lucia was a real *puttana di merda*. What's a young girl like that doing having sex? Didn't her parents teach her to have any shame? That's the most important thing parents can do.'

Lucia's father said, 'If that boy Giandomenico hadn't died, I'd have killed him myself. He got off easy disgracing my daughter. It so happens I have a book in my home that lists some of the things Count Tramontano did as torture.'

'A mother shouldn't have to put up with her daughter's body being autopsied,' Lucia's mother wept.

'But they should autopsy that boy,' Lucia's father added. 'They should autopsy him down to the bones.'

The preliminary results from the forensics unit in Potenza arrived in a large gray envelope covered by a hodgepodge of stamps and waxy seals. It was brought to Mancanzano by a special messenger, in a special car, with sirens blasting and lights that flashed ineffectually in the noonday sun. That afternoon, people took time off from work to linger outside the main office of the carabinieri, speculating aloud, which they found every bit as entertaining as talking about politics and sports. Because of the substantial public interest, Major Luigi Martella broke with regulations, and, after reading the report once at his desk, he came to the doorway of the station on Via Stigliano to address the crowd.

Major Luigi Martella, in his early forties, had the sinewy form of a mule that had been trained as a racehorse. His torso was broad, his complexion dark, and both his muscles and chest hair showed through his white shirt. Report in hand, he stood on the first steps of the police quarters he commanded, and he smoothed a carefully trimmed moustache past the sides of his mouth with his thumb. Then he brayed to the crowd as confidently as a thoroughbred stallion.

The autopsies, he told them, confirmed that tufa from the walls had caked the teenagers' stomachs, lined the membranes of their mouths, sinuses and throats, and had even been breathed into their lungs as fine powder. But, he told the crowd, neither of the two teenagers had choked. Neither showed signs of vomiting, or chests heaving for air. Notwithstanding the decomposition ('That's as natural a process as digestion,' he started to explain awkwardly), the expressions on their faces were so placid that the teenagers might even have died in their sleep.

So it was still a mystery how they had died. There weren't any signs of blunt-force traumas, knife wounds, bullet wounds or traces of hypodermics. And there still wasn't any explanation of why the teenagers had gnawed at the tufa-coated walls with such acute abandon, or why that gnawing was fatal, or why it should have been done undressed. Thus far, nothing unusual had been found in their blood, or their urine, or in the remaining contents of their stomachs. Moreover, tissue samples showed the teenagers hadn't been poisoned, not even by the pigments in the paint.

'No answers yet, absolutely none to speak of,' the major admitted, as he raised the report and flipped through its pages. 'Naturally, we're deciding whether to consider these deaths homicides. But while we continue our investigation, the important thing is to make sure we don't eat tufa ourselves. I've long been convinced that it's as bad for you as putting cheese on your fish.' Major Martella grimaced, and then shook the report demonstratively. 'Now, if you want more developments,' he told the mob, 'you're just going to have to wait.'

Giandomenico's mother was in the crowd that day, and when she heard the results she cried out hysterically: 'Three times a day I fed my son. I always made sure there was plenty to eat! But Giandomenico wanted to eat walls, and I only made him cavatelli!'

Since then, she has been filling bowls outside her home with the pasta in a thick tomato sauce. The food sits there until the wild dogs of Mancanzano come by and gobble it hungrily, licking their jowls afterwards with their long, tripey tongues.

# Chapter 3
## Figli di Puttana

So that's what's been happening since before we arrived here – and since the four of us foreigners got to work. In the mornings, while Middelhoek and Fortune investigate matters of art and earth (and Dr Stoppani keeps commuting four hours from Bari, sluggish from conjugal investigations of his wife), Linda and I have been combing the sassi with our tape recorders in hand, collecting oral histories.

Two mornings ago, on Via Palata, I interviewed a woman who told me she'd lived in the caves for a full seventy years. She said there was nothing in Mancanzano that would ever make her move from the sassi, especially not the discovery of two neighborhood teens lollygagging around, dead, in their birthday suits.

This was the start of October, but it was still the kind of day in the enclosed Italian town where the heat permeates your skin, burns past your brain, and encircles your lungs like an invading army. The old woman was sitting in a hard-backed, wood chair just outside her home, about halfway down the slope. She rocked forward slowly once I stood before her, and her head, camouflaged in gray, hunched into her neck and then into her shoulders. Broad hands sat in her lap, with long fingers coiling over a black dress that appeared to have been restitched many times. Her body was thickset, and her feet were wedged into a pair of flat, scuffed shoes. Up close, I could see that the skin of

28

her face was filigreed as intricately as the finest lace.

She smiled at me proudly, in a way that displayed a mouthful of teeth. Then she told me: 'The high deputy said you'd be coming. She said you'd want to see my lair.'

Inside the woman's home, iron cooking utensils hung from a wall, and a washbasin sat on a low table, its enamel badly chipped. Other than that, her makeshift kitchen consisted of a metal jug, a few glasses, some jarred spices, a heap of wood, and a large pot raised over the floor. Two bare light bulbs dangled from an electrical cord that traveled the length of the ceiling, zigzagging across the rock like a fissure. To one side of the room, there was a small dresser and narrow, wood bed. A space heater sat next to it, covered in tufa dust.

A dozen feet farther back, a bedsheet separated the tiny home from the rest of a cave, which looked to be burrowed deep into the hill. But it wasn't until we approached the sheet (the woman's gait was deliberate and fast; she almost appeared to scurry), and she held the material aside with a pinch of two fingers, that I saw how enormous her home really was: she lived in a cavern, more than fifty feet deep and at least half as wide.

Above and beyond us, the chiseled ceiling (aside from a scattering of narrow holes) looked like a matchbook mosaic, where slices of tufa had been carved away through painstaking effort. The chamber before us was barren, except for the mangled remains of an aluminum cot, two sodden mattresses, and some large chunks of tufa that had fallen from the ceiling around the holes. To our sides, the dark hulking walls of the cavern were damp – turning green at some parts from oxidation and even moss – and the temperature in the gently sloping space slipped a degree with each step we took.

At the far end of the cave, the air was fetid and cold. One wall showed disintegrating traces of a fresco, but the painting was far too damaged to make out any imagery. Another wall, in an area that seemed relatively dry, had been adorned more recently, this time with engravings. As I traced the carvings lightly with my fingers, I realized that the old woman, to my side, was now using her own fingers to cross her breast. The markings before us were not hard to decipher. Below them, a two-foot-long crypt had been dug into the earth.

'I'm too old to kneel. I used to kneel,' the old woman said, addressing me now for the first time since we'd entered her home.

'Who's buried there?' I asked her, pointing.

'Nunzio.'

'Who's Nunzio?'

'My husband,' she said. 'Those are his bones.'

Nunzio, the old woman recounted, had been dead for twenty-one years. Overwhelmed by pneumonia, he'd dug out the cave floor a little each day once he'd begun to grow sick. She'd known him since their days attending *scuola elementare* together, right after the First World War, when the city was ensnared in its worst levels of poverty. Like her, Nunzio had been born in Mancanzano, and, like her, he had never left.

'Do you want to see his bones? I wouldn't mind seeing them myself,' she told me giddily. There was a nervousness to her voice, despite her years. 'That's where my bones are going, too,' she said. The look on her face was vaguely amused and still vaguely sexual.

'You can lift off the cover,' the widow said, moving toward me ever so slightly. 'I'm too old to do it now, but I like to be around when others want to.'

I didn't know what to tell her. I was pretty confident I didn't want to look inside the crypt, even if I knew any flesh left on the bones would have decomposed long ago. The inscriptions on the wall before me read: NUNZIO LA CALAMITA, HUSBAND, LUCANIAN, THE GROUND TAKES HIM IN.

I didn't say anything, but then the woman mouthed to me: 'Please.' So I bent down, and curled my fingers around the edge of the slab covering the crypt. The piece was about six centimeters thick, hewn from a giant block of tufa. I was surprised at how easy it was to lift up.

'Do you see him?' she asked. 'Do you see my Nunzio?' The old woman's voice both crackled and purred.

Still squatting, I looked down into the hole. There were some bones by my feet, to be sure. But from what I could tell, they weren't her husband's. Some were from chickens, the others from dogs. There were the skeletal remains of an animal's snout and skull, with the sharp teeth folded into each other like a zipper. It was impossible to tell how long the bones had been there.

'Do you see them? You see them?' the woman asked again. 'Nunzio always wanted us to be together, even past death. He said having his bones here would always make me feel safe.'

Mixed in with the bones, there were also a few unraveled condoms, tied in loose knots and filled with seed. The underside of the tufa slab bore its own inscription, scrawled in a black marker: NUNZIO LA CALAMITA, HIS BONES MADE SOUP. Nunzio's widow, hovering beside me, looked at me, glazed, cheerful and beaming.

I didn't say a word about what I saw in the crypt. At first, I was just amazed at myself for not having realized that my informant (that's the term we anthropologists use in the field, no doubt to feel every bit as important as agents of the FBI) was effectively blind. But after I'd replaced the tufa lid on the crypt, I walked back with her toward the kitchen, and past the bedsheet hanging at the mouth of the cave. The temperature in the cave home rose with each step we took toward sunlight. When we reached her kitchen table, it was she who spoke first.

'The high deputy told me you liked stories.'

'That's why I came to meet you,' I told her amiably.

'A lot of people are like that,' she answered me, nodding and self-assured. 'Kids come all the time to hear my stories. And, of course, they come to see Nunzio.'

'Is it common to keep your husband buried inside your home?'

'I don't know,' she told me. 'This is the only time I've done it.'

She maneuvered herself into a chair beside the table. I went outside to grab what was apparently the only other chair she had, and brought it back from beside her door. Then I placed the hard-back seat before her, sat down myself, and pulled out my tape recorder from my shirt pocket.

'You don't mind?' I asked her.

She shook her head. 'No, go ahead and smoke.'

'No, it's a tape recorder,' I told her plainly. Then I turned it on, and she told me her story.


Back in the thirties, when the Fascisti came here, Nunzio and I were newlyweds. At least newlyweds in the sense that we didn't have any children – which some people say is the only real way to judge how long you've been married. Well, this cave we're sitting in is where Nunzio and I lived. So when the soldiers ordered us out, the only thing we moved outside was our furniture. That made our sasso look abandoned. So then we hid inside. We hid under blankets. Because, like my husband said, this was our cave. This was our home.

Of course, the soldiers fired some shots. But they didn't realize the floor sloped down. So their bullets went straight into the ceiling. They went into stone. Nunzio and I weren't hurt. That must have been unsatisfying for the soldiers, because that's not why people fire guns. I remember one soldier in particular heading toward where we were hiding, with his rifle in hand. Now he really could have put some bullets into our hides! But we were saved, because his sergeant called out to him, and said the most beautiful words I've ever heard – second only to my dear, sweet Nunzio's. The sergeant said, 'You, *soldato*! Come here! You're wasting your time in that cave!' It was like music, those words, to hear how you weren't worth wasting a teenager's time, when you knew that teenager was a uniformed kid with a gun.

So then these soldiers moved on from the sassi. They headed to the edge of town. They were going to cut down the trees. They hadn't done enough, no? Definitely no. They were on a rampage, and they hadn't shot enough people yet. So they were going to chop down the trees. To provide us with wood. To build us new homes. After they shot up our old ones. That's how they explained it. And that's what they did.

So I snuck out of the sassi, and I followed them to our little woods. That would have been difficult to do if, like I said, Nunzio and I'd had children. But without children, see, I really could dart. So I watched the soldiers, and, for about an hour, they went at the trees with axes. Until someone got an idea, and picked up his gun. So then these *figli di puttana* – these sons of bitches, if you don't mind me calling them that – started shooting at the trees, firing at them, because it was so much easier, and then they didn't even have to sweat. When you fire at a tree, wood goes flying. Trees go flying.

These soldiers were like locusts. They didn't stop until they'd shot down our forest. Also, they shot up some rabbits. And some foxes and martens. Do you like foxes? When the soldiers marched off, the area was all broken branches, splattered tree trunks, and blood. The foxes definitely didn't like the Fascisti. Neither did their cubs. Especially not the dead ones.

For the next few days, I remember, birds circled the area. They looked for their nests, and they looked for their chicks. The birds swooped those two days, and also for two nights. But they couldn't find one single tree that was left standing. When they finally gave up, they'd littered the whole area with bits of worms.

The woman stopped. The chill from the depths of the cave

had dissipated in her kitchen, and I plucked at my shirt, once again already hot. I switched off my recorder.

Then the woman said, 'That's my story. So I don't care what people are saying, and if some kids are dying, because kids keep visiting me all the time. I like kids, don't you? So, it's just like I said: I'm not leaving Mancanzano. My husband's not leaving either. He's dead, so he can't. Besides, Nunzio liked foxes. And he liked children too. So you want to know why we didn't have kids? Because watching the Fascisti in the woods scared God out of my eggs. That's how Nunzio explained it to me, and I figure he must have been right. Of course, I'd have liked to have children. Because when they're young, they're as cute as foxes. And then they grow up, and bring you things when they visit.'

I went out and returned with a loaf of bread, and a handful of vegetables. Then I left again. With the used condoms in my pocket.

I told the high deputy about the chicken bones and dog bones and the old woman's crypt. She looked at me dolefully, but also in a way that showed me she wasn't surprised.

'With all that's going on in Mancanzano,' she said, 'I suppose it could be worse.'

A new set of autopsy results were to be issued shortly by the forensics team in Potenza, and a climate of curiosity and nervousness had taken hold of the city. In the evenings, families would sit with their ears to their radios, listening to the church's one station, Radio Maria, which promised 'complete coverage of the deaths of the two *fedeli*'.

Where details were scant, local newspapers were happy to speculate, and, in the absence of evidence, everyone was free to choose for himself what to believe. Suspects ranged from deadly evil-eye hexes; to a deranged assassin; to a cantankerous assassin and his resultantly deranged wife; to a batch of tufa that had been infected at turns by neo-Fascist and then by Roman spores; and, finally, to divine retribution against the teenagers for engaging in premarital sex. In some parts of the city there had even been rumored apparitions of a blood-drained and vengeful Count Tramontano, wandering the city, his skin lacerated by knives. Sightings of the count were frequently accompanied by a sour odor, taken by some to be the astringent smell of his urine.

With all of this going on, I asked Dottoressa Donabuoni to escort me to the area where Mancanzano's trees had once stood, and we headed there late one afternoon, on foot.

On the outskirts of town, the tiny forest had been transformed in the late 1950s into a tufa quarry, and without any trees to stand in the way of the wind the area was full of powerful gusts that kicked powdered tufa into the air. Bone-colored and flat, the tract resembled a skating rink, although it was closer in size to two football fields, laid side by side. Across its surface, giant excavators and dozers mangled the earth, digging the quarry deeper and wider, while others smoothed out the ground with enormous steam rollers. The quarry had already descended sixty feet into the earth. The high deputy told me that a few people in town claimed the digging had released homicidal demons, whereas others were convinced the quarry's owners were intending to excavate all the way to Hell.

A few flatbed trucks were parked across the surface, loaded with slabs of tufa, and lightly coated in tufa powder. From wherever you stood, it was difficult to picture the area covered with trees, and the trees, in turn, filled with birds, or even the area filled with the steady report of firing guns. The cavity before us was stark and white. Inferno seemed a long, long way off; there wasn't any brimstone here, just blocks of tufa. But looking at them piled up, you could imagine that when it rained, everything here would start to glisten.

That evening it poured, and the streets of Mancanzano trickled with floes of vanilla ice cream. A small piazza not far from the quarry was covered by an inch of chalky water, and a crowd of barefoot children jumped up and down in it, whooping and splashing. These kids were too young to be troubled by the deaths of the teenagers, and they flapped their arms by their sides carefreely, like wings. A young mother sat on a staircase in front of them, a short distance away, with her feet raised just out of the water. I walked over to her and smiled.

She looked at me skeptically. '*Lei è bagnato*,' she told me. 'You're wet.'

I looked to my pant cuffs; she was right.

But before I could answer, she leaped to her feet and started shrieking past my shoulders, gesturing frantically with both of her hands. She yelled in a way English-speakers don't know how to – with volume, gesture, centuries of practice, fury, fanaticism and the terror of Roman legions fused into one. Then, when her voice was spent, she sat back down, and took a slow breath, physically exhausted from her efforts. Slowly, she smoothed out her skirt, and even smiled flimsily in my direction. Then she admonished, 'Sometimes the *bambini* have to be reminded not to drink.'

I nodded back at her to show that I empathized. 'I suppose that's true especially now.'

'Especially now,' she repeated. 'Because there's no pain on earth like a grieving mother's. I know,' she continued wistfully, 'because I lost a child once. I had to have three more before I was over it.'

Behind me, Mancanzano's barefoot children kept flapping and splashing, and leaping around the piazza. Some were shrieking exuberantly, kicking water into each other's wings.

Now the mother stood up, inhaled once deeply, and yelled out to them, '*Bambini*, fly! Flap your wings, fly! The best *bambini* can fly all the way to France!'

Somehow I thought that sounded like good advice.

The new sets of reports arrived in Mancanzano, as expected, with the same flashing lights and caterwauling sirens, and the same scarce information stuffed inside another oversized envelope covered by a new dermatitis of stamps and seals.

Once again, Major Luigi Martella came to the door to address the assembled crowd – which had doubled this time, thanks to public service announcements broadcast all morning on Radio Maria.

First he waved away a pestering battalion of flies, then he smiled to the townsfolk. Then he simply shrugged. Then, once again, Major Martella told the crowd that the forensics team in Potenza still hadn't been able to determine the causes of death of the two teenagers. In fact, now that all the results were in, an analysis of bodily fluids, stomach content and tissue samples still hadn't revealed the presence of a single toxin, much less of any narcotics, whether natural or not. As before, the two bodies showed no signs of wounds. And, as before, the two naked teenagers' ravenous appetites for tufa remained unexplained.

'I want to make it clear that these children have been split open and dissected!' Major Martella promised the crowd. He held the forensics report aloft in his hand, perhaps just to prove that it existed. 'So I don't want anyone in Mancanzano thinking the forensics people in Potenza haven't done their jobs. These teenagers' organs have really been put under the microscope!'

Major Martella pointed to a particular line of the report with the tip of his finger. 'Right here,' he read aloud, 'the *medico legale* says he used a hypodermic needle to withdraw the vitreous humor from the kids' eyeballs himself.'

A warbling voice from the crowd called out: 'Are they putting the organs back inside the bodies when they're finished?' It was the dead girl's father, who stood in the crowd with a framed photograph of his daughter, much like the old fisherman's wife we'd seen on TV.

'They're keeping some blood and some tissue on file, but everything big is going back in,' Major Martella answered, trying his best to be reassuring. 'So don't you worry, you'll find your loved ones just the way you left them.'

The two cadavers were sewn up neatly, with all the craftsman-ship of a lacemaker from the Venetian island of Burano, and returned to the city the following day by hearse. That vehicle had the same flashing lights and wailing siren of the car that had come before it, and its driver, of course, was unchanged. Around Mancanzano, posters had been affixed to city walls, announcing that funerals for both teenagers would be held that week. Dottoressa Donabuoni advised our coterie of *stranieri* not to attend them, fearing particularly that the presence of anthro-pologists might even seem a touch carnivalesque. But she met with us afterwards at our group's living quarters, and issued a full report.

Among a possible field of three funeral parlors – plus a fourth twenty kilometers away in the town of Montescaglioso – both families selected the funeral home recommended by the doctor who had confirmed the teenagers' deaths. (The officers who'd summoned him that day now appeared at the ceremonies wearing new suits.) Both funerals were held the same day; but since the two sets of mourning parents still weren't speaking, the services were staggered, with one at ten o'clock in the morning, and the other at four o'clock in the afternoon.

At the second ceremony, the high deputy told us that the boy's mother – the one who cooked pasta each morning to feed to the dogs – stood beside the open casket for more than an hour before the service, running a gentle hand over her dead son's gently embalmed cheeks, with tears cascading down her face and onto his. The room was festooned with asphodels and irises, plus a few leftover lilies from the morning's *addio* that had been allowed to remain. After the ceremony – that is, until the last moment when the bier was wheeled away – she told whomever would listen, 'My God, doesn't my son, my angel, look wonderful?'

An early dinner was held at her home after the burial. And, once again, she repaired to the kitchen to cook cavatelli.

# Chapter 4
# Torrente

Mancanzano is a city that everyone conquered and that no one kept. It doesn't matter if it was Saracens, Greeks, Normans, or anyone else. It's a city that not even the rest of Italy wants to keep.

Every few years in the conglomeration of dilapidated sassi, a roof comes crashing down. Or a cave-dweller wakes to find an ominous crack running the length of a wall. Or in the middle of the night, when even the town's wild dogs are silent, there's the muscular creaking of shifting stones. The occupied houses in the sassi are reasonably safe; for the most part, hulking rock walls don't want to come down. But the abandoned bullet-pierced caves that surround the sassi, and the caves on the town's outskirts that were forsaken in its ancient history, share much with the sticky filaments of a spider's web: they promise inattentive wanderers unpredictable risks.

Among the teenagers here, there are rumors of lovers lost in a cave – a couple perhaps much like Giandomenico and Lucia – except the way they died could be plainly understood. They died when an unstable cave flattened both itself and them. They died on a mattress, cushioning it from the rock with their mashable bodies.

In Mancanzano, there are I-beams and struts and scaffolds in some of the empty sassi, helping to keep them up while the rest of the country decides whether to tear them down. Mancanzano is a city of collapsing caves. It is the seat of a culture that beckons its own extinction, for it is a place where not even its buildings are to be trusted.

—

Sometimes, it doesn't matter where you are. This morning, I visited the open-air market in Piazza Ridola, in the center of town. The square sits on a plateau just above the two slopes of sassi, and its buildings – a mix of neoclassical and baroque – date back to the seventeenth and eighteenth centuries, when they were erected by wealthy merchants and tax collectors from the Kingdom of Naples, whose wives wouldn't consider stooping so low as to crawl through caves.

Three days a week, at one end of the piazza, fruit sellers stand together in front of cardboard trays and wooden crates. They wear old, restitched smocks, and they hit your hands brusquely if you try to touch just one pear or peach. The produce is uncovered, and there are flies on some of the fruit, and clusters of insects swarming and crawling on others. But the grocers still insist that it's unsanitary to touch their produce without wearing gloves. Some of them must have been wearing the same latex pair for four or five months, and the fingertips of them are already in shreds. I've watched the fruit sellers cough and sneeze as they bargain, enveloping their produce in a cloud of expectorated mist. Then they shine the fruit with a bit of fabric from their sleeves, selling an apple or orange from the top of a heap, saying, 'Yes, this is the best one. See how it gleams.' And: 'Absolutely no pesticides. You don't even need to wash them.'

It's been one month since we arrived here. We've gotten to know each other better, and the town has gotten to know us. I'm not going to say for a second that the people in Mancanzano trust us. As far as they're concerned, nothing' is worse than to be without relatives, and the four of us are foreigners living in Mancanzano, alone. We inhabit a city teeming with parents and children – and with grandparents, aunts, uncles and cousins – in a city where half of the population is related through marriage, if you look back far enough. When the two teenagers died here, half the city lost a part of its family.

In graduate school, we read about Edward Banfield's stay in Lucania in the 1950s. Banfield was an American sociologist who wrote about 'amoral familism'. That was his term for the pattern of behavior he saw all around him in the town of Montegrano, where all that mattered to people was how they treated their closest kin. He wrote that Montegrano's villagers were incapable of acting together for their common good. He argued that the only thing they cared about were the material interests of their nuclear families.

When Banfield published *The Moral Basis of a Backward Society* in Italy in 1961, his book was vilified throughout the republic. Critics rejected his depiction of peasants as prisoners of their own culture. Instead, they repainted the southerners' solipsistic attachment to their nuclear families as the effect, and not the cause, of their excruciating poverty. But the approach of the Italian academics made sense. Their country has always been one where cause and effect are reversed as effortlessly as they are in this town, where to build a home it has always made the most sense to dig down.

In Italy, the one great axiom is that citizens lack faith in the impartiality of their state. Contracts are granted to those with connections. Bribery is prosecuted among those who don't bribe enough. So it's clear why the poor would put their trust solely in their own families. Rome and its laws have generally proved fickle, and prickly to the touch.

But the historic problem is this: once people began resisting the state, the state stopped seeing them as compatriots. Instead, its citizens became allies or obstacles to the smooth functioning of the government's bureaucratic machinery: clients to court, or enemies better shut away. In Italy, things don't get fixed because people are afraid they'll be dangerous if they work too well.

Mussolini's regime was the perfect example of what happens when there's too much precision, and the only one anyone will need for some time. After all, who wants a hydra where all the eyes actually see? Or where every arm of government ends in a hand that can squeeze into a fist?

But whatever you believe about Banfield's account of disenfranchised peasants who care only for themselves, only one thing can be argued about Linda, Middelhoek, Fortune and me: we are loners here, in a secluded town where people don't trust you unless they know the bosom you suckled, and the womb that grew you before it was safe to see sun. So our group doesn't square with the people, *or* with its government. We're a bunch of orphans at a family reunion: awkward and pitiable, and just maybe suspect. I always remember the scene in *Christ Stopped at Eboli*, where the villagers of Gagliano mistrust Carlo Levi, who has been internally exiled to their town, until his sister visits him from the north. Then Gagliano's old women look up from their knitting to watch the two walk arm in arm, and they joyfully pronounce: 'A wife is one thing, but a sister's something more!' The snag for us four is that when we walk two abreast we only manage to seem twice as dangerous. We're hydras with clenched fists, but we're still somehow bereft of our bodies.

These days, in Mancanzano (less than a hundred miles from Banfield's beloved Montegrano) the only ones looking out for us are the high deputy and Dr Stoppani, and neither one provides much familial support. So I don't dare tell anyone about leaving a pregnant girlfriend at home without alienating myself from the entire community. People here would say I was selfish and savage and crazy to have left you. They might even wonder if that meant I were Mancanzano's deranged murderer myself. Because where kinship's essential, the only thing worse than being without relatives is to have left them behind. Doing that in a city like Mancanzano is a form of cultural suicide. And where Catholicism is the rule, that means you don't even deserve a decent burial, because it's a rejection of God and yourself and the rest of society.

42

Amoral familism is the way you act toward others in the midst of a crisis, except that with amoral familism your whole life exists during that crisis. For many of Italy's southerners, birth is the start of when life gets bad. But for the worst among them, that also makes it into a grotesque kind of an Eden.

Down at the creek, the men talk about Linda. It's a twenty-minute walk to the water from the edge of the city, where the sassi sputter out, and Via d'Addozio transforms into a serpentining path to the base of the ravine. The path down the hill is a wild mosaic of ceramic, broken bottles, rocks, wood and metal scraps. Occasionally, a butterfly takes off, flapping its wings and revealing suddenly that it isn't a stone. Or light hits a rock, and you realize it's actually a shard of brightly colored glass. Gray limestone deposits line both sides of the path, and the stratified rock looks like cracked phyllo dough and weighs practically nothing at all. You can throw flakes of it into the air, and they'll rain down on your head with a light patter. But keep your eyes closed: their edges scratch.

At the bottom of the path, the dragonflies are mouse-sized, and frogs leap from a floor of wet moss. Great patches of terrain here are splattered with cow dung – magnificent explosions that look as if they've been hurled from the top of a rock. At one far end of the creek, you can usually spot an anemic-looking herd or two of cattle. The bells at their necks play a tri-toned symphony – *lah-dah-dee* – and they sound like steel drums. But the skin of these cows is stretched so tightly against their bones that it would fill you with shame to drink their milk.

Where there are trees on the creek's banks, they generally are oaks, but there's barely enough soil coating the underlying tufa for them to grow. So, Mancanzano's oaks look more like wild bushes. These bushes, in turn, are enveloped in capers, hawthorns and flowering thistles. The lowing of the cows hides the hiss of mosquitoes. The smell in the air here is of hay, thyme, rosemary and shit.

Bathers collect at a far end of the stream, where, because of some small rocks and a further dip in the terrain, the water flows with a little more force, and the creek develops into a *torrente*. Linda's the most popular one of us here, but that's not surprising: this is Italy. Linda is a woman, and single and pretty and young. She is twenty-eight years old. Even the most conservative swimsuits don't hide the undeniable truth that her stomach is flat. When she alternates between them, the straps leave a mural of burns and white bands across her back.

The men undress themselves teasingly when Linda's by the water. When they're down to their trunks, they look at her swaggeringly and start conversations. 'Tell us,' they say, grasping at what little they've successfully gleaned, 'about this magical place you speak of, this place called "Raritan, New Jersey".'

Linda's afraid to be around many of the men alone. There are enough invitations – to breakfast, lunch, dinner, concerts, walks, theater, even weekend trips to the Ionian coast. She says no to all of the offers.

'But surely,' one man asks her, 'you'll accompany me this Sunday to *Mass*?'

She whispers to me afterwards: 'Not in his prayers. Not with God as my witness.'

It's roughly the same for her all over the city. By Piazza Ridola, at the tobacconists' shops, men offer to buy her magazines, cigarettes, even candy. They say, 'You're foreign. Perhaps you'd like a few postage stamps.' To be polite, she tells them she'll accept a glass of water. But to me she confides, 'I hope that makes me come off as bland.'

But it doesn't. Quickly Linda's become everyone's favorite water date. The men in town call her 'Sirena', Italian for mermaid. I keep picturing Linda with that funny striped scarf she used to wrap around her neck on visits to Manhattan, luring sailors to their deaths with a couple of shaky high Cs. But I don't think any of them here have heard her medley from *South*

*Pacific*, much less that Ethel Merman imitation she's so particularly fond of.

Down at the creek, they chant, 'Sirena, let's see your scales. Show us your fins!' If she gets in the mood, and pulls up her pant leg to uncover an inch of skin, the men break into spontaneous hurrahs. Slowly, they're winning her over. She likes it if they splash her, and an arc of droplets splatters her in the face and chest. She admits: 'Nothing feels better than water.' She urges them on.

Then, the other day, the bartender at the place on Via Argia was laughing. Linda was smiling and stamping her heel in a display of mock consternation. 'For *la sirena*,' the man joked from behind the counter, after handing her a glass, 'water without bubbles – *acqua non gassata* – because I wouldn't want it to tickle your gills.'

And now she's really living it up. 'You know, where I come from,' she tells them, 'when men are eighteen or nineteen years old, they swallow live goldfish. It's a rite of passage.'

'Sirena!' the men shout, offering their applause.

'Linda!' they ask. 'Have you swum with icebergs?'

'Only with little ones in my drinks.'

'It must be a magical place, this Raritan, New Jersey. Don't you miss it?'

She answers them honestly. 'Yes.'

Linda, like me, came to Mancanzano to further her career as an anthropologist, two years out of Columbia and teaching classes at Rutgers twice a week. I hardly think about our past. The past is a foreign country, is how the phrase goes. And it sure doesn't look anything like this one. Here, everything is heat and sweat and a broiling sun, while *my* past is a place where I kept my arms around you, and joked that I'd only let go if I were falling off a cliff.

Besides, Linda always tells me how much she likes you. She says that seeing you with me always convinces her to leave me alone.

Middelhoek has a different story to offer: 'I accepted this job in Mancanzano to get away from Amsterdam. Which was really to get away from Mathilde. I'm not going to say we're in love. I'll just say that *I* am. Although, once upon a time, we both were.'

The other day at the creek our Dutch friend was really baring himself, both body and soul. His shoulders were burning as he sung this lament: 'Mathilde treated me badly, but I was used to it. You see, the problem with Mathilde is you don't get a Dutch body like hers from drinking the milk from the cows around here. You English-speakers have a phrase . . . What is it? – Yes, "cottage cheese thighs". Well, imagine how supple those thighs can look when the cheese is gouda.

'But the other problem with Mathilde is I can't resist her. We were always attracted to each other in different amounts, but they were compatible amounts. I liked her passion. She respected my character. For two years, we were together. I won't pretend it was peaceful. I won't even say it always was fun. But when we fought, I'd tell myself, "Everybody fights." I used that logic three times a week. It makes me grimace in retrospect.

'But then, all of a sudden, everything changed. A friend of mine started dialing her up. I don't want this to come out the wrong way, but this friend of mine was a homosexual friend. He was a man I'd seen kissing many other men. He was a man who loved everything Amsterdam had to offer. But when he met Mathilde, he liked what she had to offer too. I was a fool. I introduced them at a party where he'd brought his boyfriend. But then he started telephoning Mathilde at work. And then he started calling her at home. Maybe I should have seen it coming. Maybe I should have figured it out. But what was I supposed to do?

'When a straight man hits on your girlfriend, you pick a fight. But when a gay man hits on her, the response isn't as certain. I'd ask Mathilde about it. But she'd say, "Don't be silly." So that's why I'm here. Because I should have been silly. I should have taken my very good gay friend drinking one night, and then let him drown in the Amstel River. Or I should have rented a small town of young men outside of Rotterdam to keep him occupied, week after week. But people don't do that. So I didn't either. And, instead, the woman I loved preferred a gay man to me. I couldn't compete. A gay man had reversed his sexuality in order to love her. I told Mathilde that if I'd been gay, I'd have gone straight for her too. But she just looked at me blankly and said, "No, you wouldn't have." And there was no way to prove it.'

Middelhoek smiled at us sadly, his shoulders reddening, along with his eyes. 'I don't know about you,' he said, 'but I'm in Mancanzano because I'm in exile.'

Fortune's story follows a similar vein. He's here to escape some part of his life in London, even if the way he recounts it is a bit more laconic: 'Fuck my home. The Imperial College can shove its rules up its sodding arse. I'm in Mancanzano because I say so. I'll be happy to discuss it with anyone who's got a problem with that.'

But he's been spending time with the rest of us down at the creek, in between his geological assays. He shows up there caked in white after surveying the ground, and his demeanor slackens as he wades into the stream. Every once in a while, he'll point to a bather, and say, 'Do you see that one over there? The one who's just removed her blouse? Now, look at that woman! *She*'s really got some flowering cacti!'

Fortune is a man who identifies sources of succor and then pursues them without any qualms. I wouldn't be surprised to learn he became a geologist because as a child he liked to throw stones. He likes earthquakes, volcanoes and plate tectonics. He carries a hammer, and likes to hit things. Fortune is drawn to this rough, rocky town like it is Mecca.

Fortune says: 'Now, correct me if I'm mistaken, but the thing about anthropologists is they're like detectives – or maybe just psychiatrists. Always trying to work out everyone's motives. Whereas what a geologist does is much closer to God. You worry about what happens to a culture over a hundred years, but when I look at rocks, I think in terms of spans of millions. I make leaps in my thinking as effortlessly as that! So, because of me, vastness can start to make sense. Whereas the best you do is bring order to a ritual like eating a meal. So it's not that I think what you do isn't important, it's just that you can't deny it's a lot like being a little girl playing house. All that focus on how to take tea and eat up your scones, instead of why the earth is round, and what in the cosmos keeps it from falling apart.'

The thing about Fortune is that his eyebrows look like Kalashnikov rifles. Whereas Middelhoek's look like two fleeing ducks shot from the sky.

Dr Stoppani's story goes like this: he's a citizen-of-the-world wannabe. The kind of man who dresses without regard for the weather. He'll guess at your shoe size, and he remembers the color of women's eyes. But he stares past your shoulder when you shake hands.

He's counting on our team to make him famous. He uses his own wiles for other things.

Dr Stoppani has been driving to Bari less frequently now. There's a girl in Mancanzano who's begun occupying his interests. Her name is Anna. She works in a bar. He says her chief features are her legs. They are like the aerial roots of a banyan tree.

'Will you answer one thing?' Dr Stoppani asked me just a few days ago. 'Why do women in short skirts always know to bend at the knee? Do they do that to spite me?' He looked at me desultorily. 'I'll have to ask Monica about that the next time I'm in Bari. Of course, I'm going to say it's your question.'

He flirts with Anna while she prepares his cappuccino. He tells her she has frothy eyes, cinnamon lips. Sometimes it gets too embarrassing to watch.

But Dr Stoppani's milking this romance for all he can get. I've caught him escorting Anna through some of Mancanzano's caves while I've been scrambling through them myself looking for people willing to talk. Anna lives in Montescaglioso, twenty kilometers away. She comes to the city in the morning by bus. Can you believe she says she's only wandered through Mancanzano's sassi once? She said it was back when she was thirteen years old, when some guy felt up her tit and chewed on her ear on one of those discarded mattresses, and word got out to a number of people, including her mother and the teenager's friends, who, as you can imagine, differed in their reactions and response.

'*Questa è la prima volta che sono stata nei sassi da quando quel Leoluca mi toccò*' – 'This is the first time I've been in the caves since that Leoluca touched me,' she is reported to have said.

At which point, apparently, Dr Stoppani kissed her.

And, so I think, the High Deputy for Public Works has begun to regard Dr Stoppani with suspicion. Which means that she is an excellent judge of character. She is a woman who wears linens and twills. With an alabaster complexion from the repeated applications of tufa to her skin, she has the graceful bearing of a marble bust. As far as I know, she has never been married and never been a mother. But I have seen her stoop down in Piazza Ridola to pick up a crying baby, and hold it aloft – with its face a contorting collage of redness and wrinkles – and say to it, 'Cry, little one, cry. Let everyone know that you are here.'

So why does the high deputy mistrust Dr Stoppani? Could it be his advances have extended to her?

Maybe it's just intuition. Yesterday she stopped me on the street as I was hustling to an interview, and asked me quizzically, 'Am I right in thinking you've left someone back home?' I smiled at first, but then decided to keep silent (half the risk of explaining is that you'll explain wrong).

But meanwhile, as I wander Mancanzano, this is how I've come to suppose: Middelhoek's here to escape Mathilde. Dr

Stoppani's in Mancanzano to cheat on Monica. Fortune's come as a retreat from London, and who knows what else? Linda, at least, has found temporary excitement as the irresistible swan-song-singing Sirena. But me? I keep wondering about the value of salvaging a culture, when I could have more easily remained where there was burgeoning life.

Now, when I go to the creek, I try to picture you with me, our bodies as big and as swollen as Paul Bunyan's. I imagine transforming your skin into goosebumps until it matches the terrain. You'd be buttes and mesas, and a body of badlands. Or I imagine the single sputtering creek here as one gigantic chasm. You'd smile approvingly, as a river splashed through it. Then, with my hands at your hips, we'd anticipate navigation.

So forgive me if I focus on sex, but sometimes I think if I can remember it and revel in it, then I can use it to withstand our separation. Then this harshness will only be a kind of foreplay. Then we'll think of this time as a period of longing, punctuated by return and relief. So better to forget all about Fortune's millions of years. Even a single one is hard enough.

# Chapter 5
# Fresco

A few days after the second forensic report arrived from Potenza, Mancanzano's town council voted to erect a series of warning signs around the sassi. The vote was thirteen to two; only Dottoressa Donabuoni and the mayor objected. Now, around the town's outskirts, especially where the stratified tufa splinters and crumbles like crackers, placards read: PER DECRETO PUBBLICO: VIETATO MANGIARE – 'By Public Ordinance: Do Not Eat'.

Linda and I pass the signs each day on our way to record oral histories. This morning we interviewed a woman in her cave home, off Via Cererie. She seemed to have the worst case of dandruff I'd ever seen. Both of us kept wondering why she wouldn't do something about it. After all, in a region like this one, and all around the Mediterranean, olive oil is an emollient for almost any affliction. But maybe it was the woman's age: past eighty, who really cares about a little flaking? The woman kept regaling us with details from her life over the past few years, but mostly it was how she ate this for lunch and said that at the market, and how the day before she took her broom and meticulously swept the floor of her house. It was the kind of conversation where your eyes can't help but roam, where you try to find something – anything – to occupy your interest.

That's when I realized that the woman's dandruff was actually tufa. The flakes on her shoulders weren't only on her shoulders. The rough skin of her ankles was caked with white, as were her toes. She bounced her feet as we spoke, and anthills of tufa formed around her shoes. The objects in her house all bore smudged white fingerprints. When she caught our gaze wandering, and thought we might not see, she'd run her fingers through the powder, stick them surreptitiously into her mouth, and suck.

As far as policework is concerned, you'd laugh at what passes here for an investigation, if it weren't also indirectly what's keeping me in Mancanzano and away from you. The carabinieri are a devoted lot, but their legendary torpor makes them the butts of jokes all over Italy. E.g., carabiniere to shopkeeper: 'What color Italian flags do you sell?' Shopkeeper: 'Green, white and red ones, of course.' Carabiniere, enthusiastically: 'Then I'll take a green one.'

Here, in Mancanzano, the police force's prowess remains a thing of archetypal beauty: criminal investigation as kabuki theater, with ornate costumes, stylized motions, and the meager success of snails chasing after a tortoise. Major Martella enjoys the recognition of reading the forensics reports to the crowds, and a few local residents have plied him with gifts to ensure his squad's continued vigilance. But while he obviously enjoys the complimentary cheeses and hams (all of them hefty and succulent), there's no changing the fact that his mother lives a hundred and thirty kilometers away in the town of Moliterno, and that, as a dutiful son, he leaves Mancanzano promptly each Friday at noon to spend the weekend with her.

In Major Martella's absence, there's not a lot that gets done here, and even less that's done well. Just yesterday Middelhoek got in a brawl with a carabiniere, a guy in his early twenties who was ruthlessly scraping samples of compacted tufa and paint from the frescoes. Our Dutch friend actually hurled himself at the officer who, trained in such situations, responded fluidly with his gun, and came close to shooting Middelhoek in the center of his very broad Dutch forehead.

'These frescoes are more than a thousand years old!' Middelhoek shouted, apoplectic with rage, even as he retreated from the barrel.

'Everything's at least a hundred years old here,' the carabiniere answered coolly, returning his gun to his holster. 'But that doesn't mean it's all worth saving.'

'This is!' Middelhoek parried. 'That's why I'm here!'

To which the carabiniere replied: 'If it were only decades old, I might understand your point better. Because then it wouldn't be falling apart.'

'But it's not falling apart!'

'Of course, it is!' the carabiniere said, banging the butt of his gun into the wall. '*There*. Can't you see it? Now, don't you realize there comes a point where you've got to stop picking up the pieces?'

But the carabinieri have finally left the paintings alone, even if they've scraped off some unforgivable elements in their otherwise clamorless search for clues.

To get to the cave where the frescoes were discovered, you have to travel fifty feet underground, first taking a convoluted path through two different tunnels at the farthest edge of the sassi and then crawling through a rectangular opening just a few feet across.

Inside the cave, the main fresco covers a wall roughly eleven feet wide and seven feet high. The whitewash that the teenagers first bit through has been stripped from its surface, and the images underneath are plain to see. At the bottom of the painting, there's a covey of cherubim on the ground, smiling, frolicking, playing music: they're an angelic orchestra of flutes, lyres and lutes. Just beside them, there's a flowing brook that has got to be Mancanzano's one sputtering creek, although there's more water in the painting than the real stream's had for centuries. On the wall, there are cattle, livestock and fatted hens, all of them waiting to be slaughtered and devoured for a raucous feast. A few of the cherubim drink from earthenware vessels, spilling red wine down their chests, and past their rotund bellies. The wine wells at their feet, painting their toes and splattering their insoles, in a marvelous marbling of drunken celebration.

The apostles are just above the cherubim, at eyelevel; but smaller, receding, farther away. They are by the town's sassi, as though they've just been mysteriously transported to Mancanzano. Properly iconic, Peter's got his fish, Andrew has his letter X, John's got his chalice with a serpent dangling, and Judas sports a debonair pucker, with a rouge to his lips that seems to have endured a full thousand years. Some of the apostles are talking and gesturing, while others appear more meditative or sedate. But Judas looks ready to kiss.

At the top of the fresco is the azure sky, the one we invariably see in Mancanzano each day. But where there are clouds, this painted sky thunders apart. There are traces on the wall of the archangel Michael once being depicted, but what's in his place now are bodies. Human figures rain down from the sky. There are dozens of them, some entangled, others falling free, arms and legs flapping wildly in the wind. The uncovered fresco portrays the first of the bodies about to hit the ground, far from the cherubim, who cavort and drink unawares, unable to conceive of any other way on God's tufaceous gray earth to have more fun. Crashing down past the sassi, the naked form of a young male points headfirst at the earth, ready to snap at the spine on impact. His expression is blurred, but it looks, quite understandably, to be one of terror. One of the apostles, Matthew, is pointing at the flow of human beings with some idle curiosity. But the others, much like the cherubim, don't appear to notice. It's as though one of them might be saying, '*Can you picture a more delightful day?*'

I've gone back to the fresco in the caves' core many times, and each time the images are equally unsettling. The insatiability in the cherubim's eyes belies the melancholy of Mancanzano's living, grieving parents, and to look at the faces of the angels with exhilaration is to forget that their discovery has entailed two mysterious deaths – not on a cave wall, but in everyday life.

After an initial flurry of police activity spent gathering physical evidence (ultimately, Middelhoek petitioned the high deputy to stop the carabinieri from chiseling at the fresco, and the carabinieri agreed once Dottoressa Donabuoni came up with enough sundried tomatoes to make her point), the investigators have lost interest in spending any more time in the caves. Instead, they've returned to their desks on Via Stigliano, where they're now making the argument that the most effective forms of policework occur at one's seat, and particularly around the hours of lunch. The upshot of this is that the carabinieri are leaving Middelhoek alone to do his work. This leaves the rest of us free to do ours when we're not too busy watching him.

With the carabinieri gone, Drs Stoppani and Donabuoni have called in a team of art restoration students from the University of Calabria to assist Middelhoek with the fresco. (They figured correctly that even if the Government of Italy wasn't interested in Mancanzano's underground paintings, there might be a few patriotic citizens in the peninsula's toe willing to help out.) So the Calabrians have been arriving in Mancanzano over the past several days, and they're in the caves now studying the pigments, and, to Middelhoek's mind, constantly getting in his way.

Middelhoek nearly quit when he first learned he wouldn't be working alone, and he had to be appeased with promises of a trip back to Holland at Christmas. One of the University of Calabria restorers actually arrived in Mancanzano with a Polaroid camera that some neighbor's cousin had purchased in Malta, and he started clicking away at the colorful wall – and at the back of Middelhoek's head – until our Dutch pal, politely, then adamantly, and then finally belligerently induced him to take a long break.

But even while Middelhoek and the crew from Calabria have been stumbling over each other, they've made a puzzling discovery from inside the caves. After analyzing the cherubim at the bottom of the fresco, and trying to restore them where the teenagers gnawed and the carabinieri scraped, they've detected additional images beneath the top layers of paint. On the surface, the laughing cherubim are drinking and spilling wine, while human beings, at the far corner of the fresco, cascade haphazardly from the sky. But underneath this top coating of color, what's dripping from the angels' mouths wasn't originally supposed to be wine. The wine jugs were only a subsequent addition. Without them, what's dripping from their faces resembles blood. It's smeared across the angels' faces and chests. Beneath a layer of painted complacency, they look to the skein of falling bodies with frantic, ravenous delight.

———

A second pair of dead teens was found just yesterday in Mancanzano, and like the first pair, both the boy and girl were naked and they'd just had sex. They were discovered in a small cave, not far from the inhabited section where Linda and I had begun conducting our earliest interviews, by a group of kids who continued playing around the bodies for another hour (a variant of hopscotch that had them hopping around the corpses), before they cut short their games to tell their parents about what they'd found. Needless to say, the kids' games erased most of the footsteps on the ground, and it was again beyond the carabinieri's means to reconstruct what had happened to this new teenage couple once they'd entered the chamber.

Through the high deputy's influence, Linda and I were permitted to survey the scene, and when we arrived at the cavern the bodies still hadn't been covered. From what we were told, each of the dead kids was seventeen years old, and both had apparently been well liked in school. The girl looked familiar. I think I'd seen her once or twice at the fruit market in Piazza Ridola. Her eyes were like agates, and her hair had the concentric curls of tiny snail shells. As for the rest of her, I remember that I'd once overheard someone saying, 'When you saw her hands, you wanted to watch her pick things up.' But now this girl's hands were clenched around the boy's upper arm, in rigor mortis.

The boy was lean, and in a fetal position beside her. The dirt around him revealed where he'd writhed before settling into a tight ball. His chin was tucked into his knees; he left this world just as he'd arrived. The group of children that found the teenagers had prodded them at first, thinking that maybe they were only asleep. (Think of the fun of towering over two naked teenagers when you're eight years old, part of a group, and fully dressed.) But the boy and girl had apparently been dead for about twelve hours – at least since the middle of the previous night – when they walked to this uninhabited cave, covered in tufa, from the furthest limits of the occupied sassi.

In this cave, as in the first, one of the walls had been painted white; and although the boy and girl's faces weren't scratched or cut, the insides of both their mouths were caked in tufa. Their clothes sat in a corner of the cavern, neatly folded, and also coated in powdery white.

It was still anyone's guess what had killed the teenagers, but by looking at them you knew they'd realized they were going to die, and you could tell that the thought comforted them and scared them at the same time, like when you dive off a cliff and first feel your hands, then your head, and then the rest of your body break the hard surface of water.

## Chapter 6
# *Natale*


Across Mancanzano, lights have been strung from building to building, crossing streets, attaching at roofs, and covering the town with a gleaming web of colored circuits. In the sassi, small children sell licorice in the hours between the end of school and December's early dusk, pocketing handfuls of fifty- and hundred-lire coins, gathering just enough to turn their licorice money into a more precious commodity: chocolate. On Via Pentolame, Signora Bitonto stays late every night in her bakery, selling the factory-made holiday panettoni, swollen and sweet, with raisins inside. (Her own breads, baked before sunup, disappear each morning without fail, grabbed by housewives for workaday lunches and dinners.) On Via Lucana, Tonio Archimede carves fragments of tufa into holiday ornaments. On Via La Murgia, Diego Gattini stocks his record store with LPs and cassettes of folk songs and traditional hymns, hoping that this year they'll finally sell.

With Christmas so close at hand, beggars come out in droves, capitalizing on everyone's sense of charity. 'Can you spare five hundred lire for a nice plate of pasta fagioli?' they plead. (The economy picks up around Christmas for everyone, the destitute especially.) It's only the licorice-selling children who don't make donations. But every once in a while even they hand out free candy.

In the dead of night, when Mancanzano is quiet, the air is

finally cool. Sometimes, I hear the wind travel through the streets, rattling hanging lamps and the leaves of trees. Then I close my eyes and I think, I want to remember what it feels like not to be hot. And I wonder if there's some way to keep the cool circulating inside me, chilling my blood like it's been poured intravenously from a pot of gazpacho.

It is two and a half months since I arrived here.

The second set of funerals took place last week, after more than a month of inconclusive forensics. Once again, the same strobe-bedecked car returned the bodies from Potenza. However, this time the lights were left off and the driver wrung his hands sheepishly when Major Martella's officers peeked inside the caskets. After a brief discussion with local morticians, a decision was made to get the bodies underground as quickly as possible.

What remained of the teenagers was to be brought to the Cimitero Santa Maria della Palomba, on the far side of the canyon, where a joint ceremony would be held. First, there would be a procession, with two mules drawing a cart with the shrouded bodies, both sets of wailing parents, and a few scattered buglers and drummers.

Once again, Dottoressa Donabuoni got word to us not to attend. 'Let them have this for themselves,' she suggested, meaning not just the parents, but also the larger, longer-suffering community of Mancanzano. 'Besides, if you go to these funerals, people will wonder why you've begun playing favorites. Of course, the flip side is that if you don't attend these, you won't be able to go to any others later on.' She bit her lip. 'That is, if there are any.'

So we watched the funeral procession from the balcony of a nearby apartment, observing the crowd as it swelled into piazzas, threaded through streets, and then headed downhill, across the creek and on to the distant plateau. Much later, in the cemetery there, we could see where the soft stone had been torn from the ground, and the bodies had been interred in what amounted to tufa catacombs. The graves were covered with asphodels and figs. Where the earth was disturbed around the teenagers' tombs, we could see where grieving parents and friends had fallen to their knees, weeping.

And so it's a somber holiday season here, one of going through motions. The second dead girl's parents had already bought Christmas gifts. Rather than return them or give them to others, the wrapped boxes were pushed up against one wall of their small cave apartment, where it seemed the boxes might stay as fixtures. Even after the girl had been buried, her father wrote out a Christmas card. 'Carissima Angela,' it read, 'may this be your happiest Christmas yet.'

Diego Gattini offered the four mourning families his cassette recordings of traditional hymns. (Word was he'd bury the rest of them after Christmas, then declare them stolen on his taxes.) Tonio Archimede tried carving effigies of the teenagers out of tufa, but the likenesses weren't convincing. The faces were blurred, like the image of the men falling to earth in the underground fresco. Archimede made three models of each teen, before giving up.

One week after the funerals, friends and family wandered back to the cemetery like ghosts. They let handfuls of powdered tufa fall from their fists, over the graves, sprinkling them like ashes.

In the days that followed, teenagers still collected on the Via del Riscatto after dusk, but their romantic entreaties now seemed laced with despair.

'I'll love you for ever, or at least until tomorrow.'

'No, love me this instant. Then forget all about me.'

'How about till the morning?'

'Only if we're alive.'

'And if we're not?'

'Then love someone else. You're all right for Mancanzano, but I'm hoping for more in the afterlife.'

'Better than me?'

'And better than *this*. Angels, saints, demons. Anything.'

Something to transform death into the positive experience that Christianity always has.

So this is Christmas. No snow. Definitely no reindeer. Little cheer. Austrian mistletoe at the expensive shops, from over the Brenner Pass, and by truck to Bolzano, and then to Milan, and then by air to Bari, and then again by truck to Mancanzano: not so different from how we arrived in this lost town last fall, when we had no real idea what we were getting into.

There are no Christmas trees in Mancanzano, but there are a few Christmas cacti – apparently from greenhouses in the Netherlands, if you believe Middelhoek, who seems convinced that his homeland is their only possible place of origin.

He pointed them out to me at the florist's shop on Via Ginosa, around the corner from Piazza Ridola. There must have been a hundred buds blooming in two dozen pots.

'These plants have seen Dutch girls more recently than I have,' he offered nostalgically.

'So buy one,' I said. He smiled. Then he bought two.

Sometimes when Middelhoek lumbers along Mancanzano's dusty streets, I think he'd have an orgasm if he just saw a tulip.

But it's tough to appreciate very much joking. Our work's going slowly. Four teenagers are dead. The deaths of the last two has extinguished the enthusiasm in nearly everyone, including us.

On Via Falciata, Angela's father started planning a surprise party for his daughter – that is, until his wife stopped him.

'Imagine if I hadn't found out!' she blurted.

It was Signora Bitonto who'd told her. She'd been asked by the grief-stricken father to prepare a cake. 'Make it sweet!' he'd insisted. 'With icing like the monument in Rome to Vittorio Emanuele II.'

'I'd have done it too,' Signora Bitonto explained to everyone. 'But first I wanted the go-ahead.'

Then, on December 13, it was the feast day of Santa Lucia. From the main cathedral in Piazza del Duomo a candlelight procession took off at dusk.

'Remember, this isn't a funeral. It's a celebration. This is a *festival*,' Bishop Giuseppe Pascoli importuned everyone. But the parishioners trudged, uninflated.

A papier-mâché float of St Lucy led the way, threatening to tip at every turn down the narrow streets, past the sassi. Like Lucys everywhere, this one held a pewter dish in her hand bearing a pair of eyeballs, and she leaked a dab of crimson from a gash at her neck. The legend is that a nobleman in Syracuse, Sicily in the fourth century AD wanted to marry the real Lucy because of the beauty of her eyes. So she plucked them from her head, handed them to him, and then asked that she be left to focus the rest of her life on God.

Naturally, when a new pair of eyeballs miraculously appeared in the appropriate sockets, this fellow denounced Lucy to the Roman emperor as a bad sport and a Christian. Since Lucy so badly had wanted to die a virgin, the presiding judge decided that having her violated in a local brothel would be the most suitable punishment. But Lucy's body became immovable, as they sometimes did in those days. So the frustrated judge now resentenced her to immolation. But, again, Virgin Lucy just could not be burned. Finally, everyone was happy when a lucky sword stab to the neck did her in, but the idea of a young girl dying for her faith quickly transformed Lucy into an early Christian martyr. She hadn't traveled much while she was alive, but her corpse got to go to Constantinople, and then also to Venice when Crusaders brought her back.

Today, Santa Lucia is the patron saint of people with eye trouble (and, also, by extension, of glass blowers and glaziers), but as her eight-foot papier-mâché mannequin made its rounds through Mancanzano's city streets, the golf-ball-size eyes she held by her chest mostly reminded me of the ones that belonged to the first dead teens, the eyes that Major Martella claimed had been personally examined by the *medico legale* in Potenza, via a hypodermic needle to the vitreous humor. Also, in light of Lucy's particular insistence on dying a virgin, her rounds through the city cast a peculiar shadow on the plights of the four decidedly non-virgin, non-married, non-living teens.

To provide some additional color to the procession, Tonio Archimede had carved figurines (this time, apparently, with more success) of angels, which rode on a carriage on another float. Adapting the story of Lucy just a little, Archimede accompanied the cart, explaining to whomever would listen that Lucy never went anywhere without a few angels in her protective tow, although it was only this year that he'd realized this fully.

But to my own taste the angels he'd carved bore a spooky resemblance to the dead teenagers he'd tried whittling out just a week before, and I think I wasn't the only one in Mancanzano to draw that conclusion. As soon as the cathedral was out of sight, one of the men pulling the second float drew some extra material from around the base of the figurines and wrapped it around them, burying the four in folds of bright red cloth, effectively keeping the carvings out of everyone's sight.

Angela's parents, the parents of the boy who had been found dead with her, and the parents of the first two teenagers to die all participated in the march because they'd come to rely so heavily on the bishop in the preceding weeks and months that they didn't dare betray him. Even Dr Stoppani stood at the flanks of the procession, although this time he was there with his wife, Monica, whom he'd shuttled by car from their home in Bari. She was nattily dressed, with her hair off her shoulders. The heels of her shoes were two inches higher than anyone else's.

'How do you like Italy?' she asked us, as we all watched the procession. 'I just love it when I get an opportunity to visit, myself.'

Middelhoek shrugged. 'To be honest, I'm more a fan of Florence and Venice.'

'Oh, me too,' Monica Stoppani told him. 'And also Paris, and the Costa del Sol.'

'That's not Italy,' Fortune objected.

'No, but they're nice,' Monica said. 'And you can't have enough nice places in the world. You need them to offset the ones like *this*.' She glanced around wearily, eyeing the troglodyte Mancanzani in such a way that showed she might have preferred them all tucked underground.

Then she said, 'I don't know why Gaetano asked me to come here.'

'You don't like Mancanzano?' Middelhoek asked.

'There are some very lovely restaurants. And they wash the dishes between each use, or so I'm told. But I suspect I'm needed back in Bari to have my hair done, or knit, or build bridges, or do something like that.' She looked conspiratorially at Linda. 'You know what I mean.'

'Oh, I'm sure I do,' Linda answered quickly. 'You can't imagine the amount of civil engineering that piles up at my door for me when I go away for the weekend.'

Led by the eyeball-carrying Santa Lucia, the procession traveled from Piazza del Duomo, to Via Lucana, then along Corso Umberto II, and then past the inhabited section of the sassi, until a giant loop around Mancanzano's center was completed, and everyone had reached Piazza Ridola, where cords of wood had been set in the middle of the square. Those with candles threw them onto the two-foot-high heap. The dry logs caught, and the flames licked up their sides, illuminating the piazza. Then when the fire was high enough, the papier-mâché Lucia and the small figurines were lowered from their carriages and launched into the flames. St Lucy was stripped of her skin quickly (fire, if you're wondering, is an excellent exfoliant), revealing a skeleton of metal inside her, like some Old World cyborg. Then we all stood around the circle and stared, mesmerized by the tarantella of flames against the stark night sky.

The fire swelled, sucking fuel from the wood. Suffice it to say the fire grew big. There must have been six or seven thousand people in the piazza at once, huddling around the bonfire, surging as close to the flames as the carabinieri would let them. A few teenagers held hands, tearing their fingers free every so often to point at the burning figure in the piazza before them, and then at the small tufa casts glowing like embers on Piazza Ridola's floor.

When the fire seemed its hottest, Angela's father ripped off his jacket, and then his shirt, and threw them both into the bonfire. I was surprised the clothes didn't unfurl in the air, but they kept to their trajectory in a tight ball. For a few moments, Angela's father looked like he was going to immolate himself. Then the expression on his face quietly slackened. He stood with his arms wrapped around his chest, shivering. The hair on his chest was gray, not singed, just aged. Someone beside him wrapped an arm around his shoulder, pulling him close. One old man huddled against another in an act of grizzled compassion.

A few people watched the flames and the burning, yet historically unburnable Santa Lucia, and said to each other, smugly, 'This year, we got her.' But I'm told they say that every year. Every year they also debate new ways to finish her off.

In the morning, the smoldering ashes were dampened with buckets of water and taken from the piazza by a small army of street cleaners. Tonio Archimede's figurines, carved from tufa, were as black as charcoal, but mostly intact. One of the men in the crew tucked them into a pocket in his coat, then they all took their mops and brushes to the scorched ground, wiping away Santa Lucia's soot.

By ten o'clock, when we had our first interviews, you could barely tell from looking that anything had occurred in the piazza the evening before. But when you took a deep breath you smelled the embers of burned cedar mixed with the wafting astringency of industrial soap.

Monica Stoppani left the following afternoon, in her husband's car, without her husband, effectively stranding him in Mancanzano like the rest of us. Apparently, Dr Stoppani didn't even realize it when she left. He was at lunch with Monica, in the center of town, at a restaurant that we've all grown to like – a simple place with sparse furnishings called the Trattoria Lucana. As Dr Stoppani tells it, his wife got up for the toilet. She was taking a while, but he guessed she was just checking her makeup. But when both of their plates were cold, he looked all around the restaurant for her. Then, once he understood she was gone, he asked for the check. The waiter told him that Monica had already paid it.

'Fifteen minutes ago,' the waiter said. He smiled servilely. 'She told me you'd want a coffee.' The waiter hurriedly brought an espresso to the table.

I don't know how, or if, Monica heard about Anna – or if she heard about anyone else. But from the tale of her departure from Mancanzano, I knew for the first time that I liked her. I used to think how everyone has fleeting moments of brilliance, nano-seconds of lucidity that are too short to take advantage of before they fade. In getting up from the table, Monica Stoppani had hers and used hers, and she did so with the greatest of flourish. It was the kind of behavior that demands an encore. I hope she comes back.

Meanwhile, Middelhoek has been working on the fresco with the students from the University of Calabria. The discovery of the blood dripping from the mouths of the cherubim seemed such an extraordinary discovery that it elicited a visit from the Istituto Centrale del Restauro in Rome.

Professor Pietro Ugolino arrived in Mancanzano in the late afternoon, and demanded to be brought to the cave at once. He glanced over the fresco for a good fifteen minutes and scribbled a few notes, and then he excused himself to Dottoressa Donabuoni's office, where he made a handful of calls (one of which seemed to be to a girlfriend, and another, less amorously, to a wife). Then Professor Ugolino went about enjoying the rest of a four-day junket to Mancanzano that the Istituto had authorized, most of which was spent visiting restaurants and eating lavishly, not always in the city of Mancanzano itself.

On the second day of his trip, he visited the resort town of Metaponto, forty-odd kilometers south of here on the Ionian Coast (where Pythagoras lived and taught when this area was still Magna Graecia, and where Hannibal fought Rome during the Second Punic War), and then he called the high deputy in Mancanzano to say he was spending the night and would have to cancel his morning meetings.

The next morning, Professor Ugolino canceled the afternoon ones too. Then on the fourth day, after what he termed an 'in-depth study of the matter and all of its surrounding issues', Professor Ugolino issued the following recommendations to Mancanzano's town council: build a better hotel, establish some better restaurants, and remove the fresco from the underground cave wall, so it can be remounted and shown in a Roman museum.

Then Ugolino returned to Rome himself. The newspapers quoted him the day he left, declaring: 'I'm sure the proud citizens of Mancanzano, from their venerable city carved of stone, will want to share their cultural heritage with the rest of Italy, particularly because their heritage is so rich, and their venerable city is so hard to get to. It's worth the visit, but only if you have the time.'

In an interview in one newspaper, Ugolino suggested that Mancanzano's town council levy new taxes to fund additional restoration and study of the fresco, which would include its transport to the Museo Nazionale Romano – 'just across the piazza from Rome's train station. Convenient for every visitor to the Italian capital.'

Professor Ugolino left for Rome on December 18, waving his hands to us at Piazza Ridola and wishing everyone '*Buon Natale*', before getting into his car and driving off.

Middelhoek muttered something in Dutch as the car disappeared from the piazza along Via Annunziatella, and into the distance. Then he rubbed his hands, and said, 'I'm going to ask if there's room for the fresco in the Rijksmuseum.'

'I hope you're not serious,' Linda said.

'Just disgusted,' Middelhoek told her.

But what Fortune said was, 'It's a shame what tufa will do to a car engine. I'll give him sixty kilometers, tops.'

That afternoon, Professor Ugolino had to call a garage in Megliofiume to tow his car from the side of the road. The High Deputy for Public Works easily persuaded the local mechanic not to reveal what was wrong with the engine.

'You know, *Professore*, I've never been to Rome,' the mechanic told Ugolino, once he'd deposited both car and driver in his garage.

Ugolino nodded at him dismissively, making a flurry of calls from a phone on the wall.

'That's it,' said the mechanic. 'I just thought you'd find that information interesting.' Then he pointed to Ugolino's BMW. 'This is going to be very expensive to fix.'

'That's what mechanics always say.'

'Yes, it is. You're right.' The mechanic glanced lazily at his watch. 'You know, *Professore*, we can spend the evening chatting. But I think you're going to need to find a hotel room first.'

'I'm going to have to spend the night?'

The mechanic smiled benignly, rubbing his hands on his coveralls, which only served to spread the grime further. Then he said, 'The information office is down the street. They're very understanding, and you can tell them I sent you.' He walked to a low stack of metal shelves covered with parts from demolished engines, and reached for a pile of fliers held in place by a carburetor. He pulled one out. 'This coupon will get you a ten percent discount on rooms at the Hotel Olivi,' he offered. 'Many of my clients stay there. Take it with my compliments. Please.'

Professor Ugolino regarded the mechanic's greasy hand with contempt. Then he said: 'If I have to spend the night in this shit hole, the taxpayers of Italy are going to pay full price.'

Dottoressa Donabuoni told us the story (as the mechanic proudly related it to her on the phone, over the background clanking of his garage) at a lunch she organized for us on December 23. The meal was held at the Trattoria Lucana, and Dr Stoppani appeared truly uncomfortable to be there. Halfway through the first course, he excused himself to go to the toilet. I almost thought he was hoping he'd find Monica in the bathroom, adjusting her mascara, and asking innocently, 'Oh, have I been that long?'

As lunches go, this one was pretty sullen. Dr Stoppani looked so tired that even sleeping wasn't going to be enough. Middelhoek, who hoped time and distance might fill up the fissures in his relationship with Mathilde, was taking the week to travel back to the Netherlands as part of his negotiated settlement with the high deputy and Dr Stoppani for bringing in the Calabrians. 'The worst Mathilde can tell me is "I never want to see you again", right?' Middelhoek said to us frankly. His logic was convincing and dangerous. We wished him luck.

Linda announced that she'd been invited to a Christmas dinner at the home of three brothers, each of whom had individually made clear his romantic intentions and then done whatever he could to belittle his brothers' amorous faculties.

One had said, 'Michele isn't afraid of commitment. He'll tell you he loves you. He's told many.'

Another had said, 'Alessandro has a problem with his back. Maybe you can't tell when he's standing. But if you want to do something requiring even the slightest bit of activity . . .'

69

The last one had told her, 'Carlo is asthmatic. I remember how scared his last girlfriend got. They'd both start gasping, but poor Carlo would be gasping for air.'

Linda's plan was to play the brothers off on one another, keeping them each as a foil and protector.

'No matter what,' she told me, 'it will always be two of them against one. Plus, it will be Christmas, and there will always be their mother to act as umpire. I'll bring her a present to win her over.'

'Just watch out for their father,' I cautioned.

Linda laughed. She ran a finger along the metal teeth of her pants zipper. 'The brothers all tell me he was injured in an industrial accident. Mangled and repaired, but completely dysfunctional. And, of course, they asked me specifically not to question him about it.'

So after the high deputy's luncheon, which had really been organized to have us all together before everything ground to a halt for the days between Christmas and New Year (and then again for Epiphany on January 6), we said goodbye. The high deputy said she was looking forward to a quiet holiday with her family, many of whom, she admitted, had moved to Megliofiume and Potenza.

Dr Stoppani said he was going to visit some relatives in Foggia, north of Bari, maybe a hundred kilometers up the back seam of the Italian boot. He offered apologies, stammering to us, genuinely chagrined.

'If it wasn't for this nonsense with Monica – I'm certain, of course, we'll straighten it out as soon as she tells me I can come home, and then I know she'll be really apologetic, and I say this because I know my wife – I'd really have liked to have invited all of you over. You know, like when you first arrived.'

But the following morning Dr Stoppani arrived sheepishly at our door, his collar unbuttoned, and his tie in his jacket pocket, otherwise dressed as we'd seen him the afternoon before. He looked exhausted.

'Listen,' he said, 'it turns out that . . . well, it's just that . . . OK, so Foggia's not an option. So if you're not too busy . . .' He motioned to Fortune and me, since we were the only ones left without clear-cut plans. 'I was wondering if you'd like to have dinner tomorrow. For Christmas. The three of us.'

'We'd love to have you,' Fortune told him.

'I mean, you are Christians, of course? You do celebrate Christmas?'

'Actually, I'm non-practicing,' Fortune answered, his hands in his pockets.

'I'm Jewish,' I said.

'But you believe in Jesus?' Dr Stoppani asked hopefully.

'For you we will,' Fortune told him. 'So, yes. Come tomorrow.'

'Come tomorrow,' I repeated.

Dr Stoppani turned around, saying, with enthusiasm, 'Tomorrow is Christmas.' But his enthusiasm seemed forlorn. I smiled. He smiled. We let him go.

December is a month of processions. On Christmas Eve, the town's boys amassed in Piazza del Duomo, carrying candles, figs, sprigs from trees, and entire palm fronds that had been brought in from the Calabrian coast, by way of Cosenza. What remained of our team trailed behind the people of Mancanzano, looping around the city and its sassi. Eventually we made our way back to the cathedral, where we stood at the back, behind the throngs gathered for Midnight Mass. We couldn't spot Angela's parents, or the parents of the three other dead teens, but there was an appreciable attentiveness that many of the town's parents seemed to be extending to their own children, as if to say, 'I don't know what's been going on here, but I'm not going to let it happen to you.'

The first minutes of Christmas in Mancanzano were spooky. Bishop Pascoli presided from the altar, dressed dutifully in a chalky white chasuble and miter, telling the town that now, with

71

God's help, the mysteries of the teenagers' deaths would be resolved. 'I promise,' he told them, 'that this will happen before Jesus's body rises at Easter.' People in the back rows turned to us, as though we had the answers, as though we were to blame, a couple of them, very possibly, clenching their fists.

That night I had a dream. A dream in which I sat at a long table covered in burgundy linen, with opulent flowers, narrow candles in brass candelabras, massive goblets and plates of brilliant bone china. The silverware, heavy at the handle, glinted in the candlelight. Arias from Verdi's *Un Ballo in Maschera* coursed through the room. The walls were covered in frescoes. A newborn baby – I don't know if it was supposed to be Jesus, a cherub, or the one that will eventually be ours – lay wrapped in swaddling clothes on the table, suckling wine from the teat of a wild dog, or perhaps from a she-wolf, like Romulus. You sat beside me, your dress open and undraped from a shoulder. A napkin was tucked under my chin. All around us, the people of Mancanzano watched.

I began with your fingers, carving them delicately from your palms, following the contours of tendon and bone, folding away the skin from your flesh. I dabbed at the blood with my napkin, concerned about spilling too much on the tablecloth. You laughed: 'No, no, use your mouth. The blood's the best part.' You caught some with your good hand and smeared it on my lips. 'See? See?' With every slice of skin, the Mancanzani applauded and the baby suckled more.

I carved all five fingers and arranged them on a plate, with the meat from the ball of your thumb in the middle, still attached just below the knuckle. It took some work to remove all of the fingernails. 'This is harder than eating lobster!' I complained. I dribbled the juice of a lemon across the plate, watching the severed fingers quiver where the fluid burned. The stubs on your hand shook sympathetically. You grimaced. Then you smiled your best.

We moved up your arm, filleting the flesh along your forearm

72

into sirloin strips, cutting around your elbow, and then continuing to your upper arm. 'You've always liked biting me there,' you giggled. I took a few nibbles from your biceps directly, and then kept carving, peeling your triceps away from the bone. Soon I had all the meat from your arm on a platter, and you helped garnish it yourself, with rosemary, marjoram and some coarsely ground pepper. We cauterized the wound at your shoulder with candle wax. We used three candles to get the job done. 'Don't get wax on my clothes!' you insisted. 'Of course not, darling,' I soothed. Then you looked at me and said poutily, 'This had better be the best meal of your life.'

'It is! It is!' I offered you a bite.

But the Mancanzani, restless, all wanted bites too, and I had to work on your leg to cut away enough flesh in order to feed them.

Soon, Verdi's arias turned into hungry gulps, and then into howls and moans. In the center of the table, our little Romolo Cristo yelped between sucks, until he started disappearing, fading away in shudders and pulses, and the wine from the wolf dribbled from his mouth and onto the table, where I later found it pooled into sweat and semen on my sheets.

—

Dr Stoppani arrived at our door the following evening. He was supposed to come at eight. He came at six. He said, 'I may be early.' He wore a double-breasted jacket, with creases along the sides, that looked like it had spent time in a box. He wore an ascot. He reached into a bag and held out a bottle of wine.

'Merry Christmas,' he told us.

Fortune and I hadn't dressed up. We'd bought a rabbit at the market, and Fortune was preparing something called 'coniglio ripieno', our little bunny stuffed up to its esophagus with veal and egg. We'd overheard two women discussing the dish at the Mercato Mater Domini on Via Argia as we were paying, and they'd been kind enough to write out the recipe for us when Fortune asked.

'You don't think there's anything insidious about cramming the rabbit with all of that stuff?' I asked him, trying to forget my own dream from the night before.

He smiled agreeably. 'It'd stuff itself if it were alive.'

Deboned and dehaired, the rabbit sat in a dish by the sink, surrounded by slices of onion and celery, waiting until it was time to be cooked.

We were three men at various levels of happiness, together at Christmas, so we could strive to be happy. At seven o'clock, we ate. The rabbit bobbed in a sauce of wine and tomato. Somehow the flavors weren't right. The flesh was chewy like squid. It looked pathetic.

'There are a lot of things going on in this dish,' Dr Stoppani said. 'Some of them are mysteries.'

After a while, we gave up on the rabbit altogether, and stuck to the veal pressed into its gullet, forking it heavily onto our plates. Then Fortune took away the empty bottle of wine and replaced it with a full one of whisky (not something lesser like grappa or a quaint *digestivo*), and Dr Stoppani took out a box of funny-looking cigarillos that seemed to have been manufactured in Tuscany with Swiss tobacco (or maybe vice versa), and we took away the empty plates and the eviscerated rabbit hemorrhaging veal, and we brought out one of Signora Bitonto's panettoni.

Then we got down to it. We started to talk, with crude handfuls of the cake stuffed into our mouths (our methodology surprised Dr Stoppani at first, but then he seemed to flourish), with cigarillos trailing smoke and with glasses of whisky keeping our throats adequately moist.

We told stories. I started.

'I could tell you what I've done every Thanksgiving or New Year's Eve since my late teens,' I told them. 'But Christmas isn't always clear. I think it's because I'm Jewish.'

'Like Zero Mostel,' Fortune suggested.

'The most important holiday in the world. And where I come

from, comedians joke that the Jews are the ones left without anything to do on Christmas.'

'Like me!' Dr Stoppani said energetically.

'Anyway,' I continued, 'the one Christmas I always remember was actually two weeks before. My girlfriend and I went to visit friends of hers in Connecticut. A couple. With a house. Which is something that always amazes native New Yorkers. Now, in a lot of places in America – I mean, not in New York City, where land is scarce, but in America, the country – where if you want a Christmas tree, an evergreen, I mean one that's real and not made of metal and plastic . . . something that was living to put in your living room' – for some reason, I felt I had to explain this to Dr Stoppani, who had begun looking at me skeptically – 'you go to a tree farm. They are acres and acres. Hectares and hectares. You rent a saw if you don't own one. Then you put on your hiking boots, and you tramp through the grounds, looking for the perfect specimen to cut down. You get on your knees. And maybe even onto your stomach. And then you start cutting the base of the trunk until your tree topples.'

'I've never done anything like that!' Dr Stoppani declared. 'It sounds like the kind of thing that requires special clothing.' Then he looked at me askance. 'Didn't one of your presidents get into trouble chopping down trees?'

'A long time ago,' I told him, 'and in another season, I think. But the main thing about cutting down Christmas trees is that I'd never done it. I was thirty years old, we're visiting some friends of Julie's, and we go to the tree farm to get them a tree. At first they're very particular, looking at blue spruces, white pines, Douglas firs, et cetera, et cetera. And we're trudging behind them, Julie and me, watching our breath fog up in the December cold. This goes on for almost an hour. We've given up on the paths, and we're weaving through the trees to find the one we want.

'But then we spot it. I don't mean that the couple sees it, I mean Julie and me. *We* see the tree. It's perfect. It's beautiful.

This tree is breathtaking. It's raised on a mound, surrounded by others, and the other trees are worshiping it. This tree is their centerpiece. It is their idol.

'So we go running after her friends. We're running, we're shouting. Julie's waving her arms frantically, motioning for them to come. Finally, they see us, and we lead them to the tree. It's a fir, over three meters tall. Not missing one single branch. And this tree is gorgeous. It's an elegant tree. It's an eloquent tree that says, "Take me, I want you. I'll be so good."

'But the thing is they don't want it. The guy says something like, "It's not the green I had as a kid." The woman says, "I look at this tree and it makes me feel fat." They confer for a few seconds. Then they look at us squarely, and they say, "No, that's not the one we want." So that's when we realize we've bonded with this tree. In fact, maybe it's better that they don't want it. Because now *we* want it. We borrow the saw, I get on my stomach and I cut down this tree.

'Now we've got this tree. Julie and I aren't living together yet. We tie the tree to the roof of my car, and we drive the three of us back to the city – Julie, me and our tree. It's Sunday evening and New York City is all traffic. But finally we get to her building. Now we have to drag the tree from the car's roof. This is heavy work. This is cumbersome work. Somehow, it was easier to do it in Connecticut, you know, maneuvering the tree onto the roof of the car in the open space of a tree farm. But on the side streets of Manhattan, double-parking the car so that you're even farther from the curb, that doesn't make it any easier.

'Still, we get the tree to her building. We're doing all of this work, and we're sweating. Now, mind you, like I said, I've never had a Christmas tree before. I've never wanted one. And I've just spent the afternoon hunting for one, sawing it, and dragging it around much of the northeast. So we drag it through the lobby, over the rugs, leaving pine needles across the floor and we get the trunk to the elevator.

76

'Now the tree's mammoth. Huge. Wide. So you can guess at this point. Julie lives on the fifteenth floor. And there's no way to get the tree into the elevator. I mean, we try. We try. We really try. But there's no way to do it. And there's an elevator man, and he's got on these gloves, white gloves, and he says to us something like, "No sap on my clothes, please." I want to hit him. Of course I do. He keeps telling us in this English that isn't right, "No way in, please. It can't because of the cones, please."

'So I start to suggest, but Julie looks at me. And she says, "We're not going to cut it, we're not going to do it." And that's it. It's over. Because you have to know with a woman when there's no way you can possibly win. So we drag the tree back through the lobby, and back to the car, and back to the car's roof, to bring it to my building, from the Upper West Side to Greenwich Village, and then back off the car, up four flights of stairs, and into my apartment. It fits through the door. It doesn't ooze sap. It damages nothing. We get it by the window. We're heaving, exhausted. But it looks great. Eventually, we figure, we'll get it decorated, but the tree is so perfect that it doesn't need glitz.'

'It doesn't make you feel fat?' Fortune asked.

'It doesn't make us feel fat. And Julie looks at me with this look on her face, and says, "Now that the tree's here, and it looks this good, which is really good, I can't ever abandon it. I need keys. Give me a set of keys. I can't leave your apartment. I don't even want to be away long enough to go to work."

'Julie didn't spend another night in her own building for three weeks. Then she was gone for a night. Then she moved in for good. I said, "If we're living together, then this is really serious." Julie offered, "I can threaten to leave you tomorrow, if that helps you relax." I said, "No, stay," and she said, "OK, then I will. But, remember, I'm a little more complicated than a tree. So you're going to have to give me more than a bowlful of water."'

'That's really very mushy,' Fortune said to us all, disgusted.

'I'm not sure what "mushy" is, but it's a happy story, which makes it inappropriate for grown men to tell at Christmas,' Dr Stoppani said, finally speaking up. He reached for the disassembled panettone, putting the last of its crumbs into his mouth. His ascot was untied and it hung from his neck. He looked at us to make sure we were listening. Then he spoke.

'My story's much different. This is how I met Monica. We were at a dinner party. Much like this one. But there were more people, of course. And there were women. I don't mean prostitutes. Actual women. Many of them were attractive.

'In retrospect, it was a very sad affair because the food was bad, and the couple who hosted it later split up. The fellow had been a minister in the first Aldo Moro government, back in 1964, but that didn't stop his wife from leaving him right after she finished redecorating their apartment. Can you imagine? She made him throw out all of their old things. Then she planned the dinner, made him buy new chairs, and left him three weeks after they washed the last dishes. And he was a Socialist too, so you can imagine the insult of having to endure such deliberate selfishness on her part. Their relationship grew terrible the moment she started picking fights. First, the arguments came from out of the blue. Then she told him she was moving out. So he wanted to know why. She answered, "Because we fight all the time."

'So then he asked her: "Where will you go?" Now, remember, divorce wasn't legal yet in Italy, so back in those days we still had Article 589 of the Italian Penal Code, which every man memorized because it said only wives could be punished in adultery cases – which, in emergency situations, was a *very, very* good thing to know by heart. But then the Socialist minister's wife informed him, "I'm going to live with your mother." The minister, flabbergasted, answered her: "*Non è possibile!*" But when she showed him it was, he just asked, "What about the chairs?"'

'You sound bitter,' Fortune told him.

'I'm not bitter,' Dr Stoppani answered. 'But I do sympathize. That much is clear.' He took a long drink of the whisky. Then he went on: 'Anyway, I met Monica at one of their parties. It would have been exactly ten years ago today in another six months. For some reason, my girlfriend couldn't make it that evening. Maybe I didn't even invite her. It doesn't matter. Monica and I spent most of the dinner in conversation. You know, talking. Like you learn in school. Then she left with a friend. I left by myself. The next morning, I awoke with a certain tumescence inside my pajamas. But for the first time I didn't know who it was for.'

'Was your girlfriend there with you?' Fortune asked.

'In bed with me? No. I went to her house after the party, since I knew her parents were away. But since they were gone, she'd done the same thing. So, we both fell asleep alone, in each other's bed. She'd given me keys. My landlady let her in.'

'So how did things start developing with Monica?' I asked him.

'First, my girlfriend and I began drifting apart. Gradually, we dwindled. The break-up didn't even require a push. Part of the problem was that she kept wanting to get married. There was only so long I could tell her, "Your mother cooks and cleans and invites me for dinner. Your father still pays all your bills. What more could either one of us hope for?"'

'Apparently more,' I answered.

'Apparently so,' Dr Stoppani said. 'But, meanwhile, I conspired to be invited to another dinner party at this minister's house. You see, he was having dinner parties now because he owned all of those chairs. So I called Monica to ask if she'd like to join me, and we spent the entire evening talking again. She was captivating, articulate. She recited poems in French. Baudelaire, Éluard and Jacques Prévert. Also, she dressed exquisitely, which is even better than declaiming a few lines of poetry. Her clothes were well-cut, very short and very tight, with those clingy materials you Americans call "space-age fabrics".

79

So the next morning when I awoke, let's just say that I knew who my swelling was for. Monica wasn't there, but I knew. I knew. And that's when I decided to make her mine. Whether she liked it or not.'

'I'm sorry things aren't working out,' Fortune offered earnestly.

I said, 'I hope you figure out what to do.'

Dr Stoppani sighed. 'With this year's referendum and the changes in law, divorce is becoming very fashionable in Italy. And the problem with Monica is that she's an enormous slave to fashion. But I'm hoping to convince her there's another way. Because if all she wants is for me to promise fidelity, that seems so easy. I can promise her anything without thinking about it twice.'

Then Dr Stoppani sat back. He seemed in good spirits. He actually beamed.

'Now, *that's* a Christmas story,' Fortune said.

Dr Stoppani nodded his head agreeably.

The whisky was gone, and I was hacking on the cigarillos when Fortune started talking. Dr Stoppani was retying his ascot and flicking crumbs from the panettone off his clothes with his fingers. Fortune stood up, walked to the sink, poured a glass of water and brought it back with him to the table. Then, straddling the chair, he began.

'I want to talk about my father,' Fortune said. 'I want to talk about him because I miss him.'

'He's back in England?' I asked.

'Back there and buried,' Fortune said. 'You all call me by my surname, so it won't mean much to say I was named after him, but I was. Of course, I mean my first name. Which is Winston.'

'Like Churchill?' Stoppani asked.

'Actually, like the cigarette. My father's name wasn't really Winston, but he called himself that and then he called me that too. He loved to smoke, so it wasn't to anyone's great surprise when he died two years ago of emphysema. You see, he was one of those buggers who say, I've got the right to treat my body how I like, it's a quality-of-life thing, so don't you tell me to think about quantity.'

'I think about quantity,' I said.

'I think about quantity too,' Dr Stoppani said, smiling sheepishly.

'Anyway,' Fortune said, 'he was a good man. And he loved me. It was December. The day he died, he'd been coughing and coughing, and by this time he was coughing up blood. In between heaves, he'd say, "I know this blood stuff doesn't look good." He still had his sense of humor. He'd sputter blood from his mouth, and say, "It sure doesn't look good. Especially on your new jumper." He made me laugh. He was in hospital. I was visiting, and he said, "Open the window, and smoke a cigarette. I can't do it myself, but it might be nice to watch."'

'Ah, your father was a voyeur,' Dr Stoppani pointed out.

'Strictly speaking, smoking isn't completely recommended in hospital rooms, but I went to the window anyway, and I wrenched it open, and I got a cigarette from a stash that my father had kept, and I lit up by the window. I dragged on the cigarette, good and long. And my dad started to smile. And that was all right. Better than all right, seeing my dying dad smiling. And I swear, I was there by the window, surreptitiously smoking the fags, and my dad, on the other side of the room, was sniffing the air and twitching his nose like a rabbit, trying to get a scent of the smoke himself. But that's also the point when my dad started to wheeze, and I had a presentiment of him giving up the ghost, right then and there. So I pulled the cigarette away from my mouth.

'But the fucker objected. Can you believe it? My father, with his nose still twitching, and his coughs interrupting his words, is saying to me, "Smoke it, you cunt. Smoke it! Let me watch."

'"Dad, these fags are killing you!" I tell him, and by then I was shaking. "I can't do it!" I tell him. "I'm not smoking it!" I tell him. And he says, "I'm the one dying, and you're trying to teach me a lesson? Is that it, you bastard? Then maybe *you* should be the one dying. Maybe you'd like that, you fucking wanker," my father says to me.

'By this point, I've walked over to him. My father's propped up in the hospital bed, wearing one of those flimsy gowns, but he's got it on backwards because he'd been saying for days, "I don't want them nurses grabbing my bum." My father looks haggard as it is, because he hasn't let them give him a shave for three days, but now he's starting to snarl in a way that I don't know.

' "This isn't you, Dad!" I tell him. I'm shaking all right, like I said. And I feel sick. I'm a geologist – but you know how the earth sometimes transforms into a giant bowl of bread pudding?

'Well, my dad grabs the cigarette from my hand. And, of course, it's still lit. And immediately I'm thinking I want to be careful he doesn't get burned. But he takes it and puts it to his mouth, and sucks on it slowly. But with this wild-animal, fuckawful determination, like I'm barely even in the room. It's just the fag and my dad and his hospital bed.

'And as he's sucking on it, he's smiling like a real fiend. His eyes are on fire. And the fag falls from his mouth and onto his chest. Which is bare now, because of how he's wearing his gown. And I say to myself, "I don't know my father's chest." It sounds rather funny, but that's what I mean. Because I can't remember the last time I saw my father without his shirt. Because, as I look at my father, I see he is covered with burns. Small cigarette burns, over a dozen, on his pecs, by his shoulders, at his armpits, a lot more trailing down his abdomen. Enough of them so that they had to be on purpose, in some strange, curlicue pattern pointing to between his legs as their ultimate goal. Like something from a torture camp, maybe. But then when I looked back at him, I mean at his face, I saw that my father had stopped breathing. And he was dead. This is how my father died. Sixty-five years old. I mean, I don't know if he got those burns with my mother when she was alive, or with other women, or with prostitutes, or what. I closed his eyes. What else was I going to do? When I took my hand away, it smelled like stale smoke.'

Fortune looked at us and drew on his cigarillo.

'That's really a Christmas story, Winston,' Dr Stoppani said amiably.

Fortune's face was flushed. 'I suppose it is,' he said. Then he said, 'Hey, you two told a pair of decent stories. I hope I haven't sucked the Christmas out of everything with mine.'

'No,' said Dr Stoppani. 'It's already a tragedy about the dead kids, anyway. Not to mention Monica.'

'Which is so recent,' Fortune said. 'I'm sure you think about her all the time.'

'You know, I'm not such a big Christmas person myself,' I told the two of them.

'The Jewish thing,' Fortune said.

'Well, merry Christmas,' Dr Stoppani told us. He pushed his chair back from the table and stood up. It was a little after midnight. He had retied his neckgear, and made toward the door. 'Perhaps now I'll leave. I mean, unless you want me to stay.'

'No, that's all right,' Fortune said. 'But merry Christmas. Thanks for coming.'

'Yes, merry Christmas.'

'Get home safely.'

'I'll keep on my clothes,' he said. 'That seems to be half of the trick.'

Then Dr Stoppani buttoned his jacket, smoothed the creases that had almost disappeared, and then disappeared himself into the dark. Mancanzano was quiet. You could hear his heels against the pavement even after he'd turned the corner. Then everything was silent again, except for the sound of Fortune breathing. And peaceful again, except for the disemboweled rabbit, which looked up from the counter from what remained of its head.

## Chapter 7
# Underpainting

After consultations with the Centro per la Valorizzazione e Gestione delle Risorse Storico-Ambientali and the Soprintendenza per i Beni Culturali ed Artistici della Basilicata, both in Potenza – and locally with Major Martella of the Mancanzano carabinieri about the possible implications to his investigations of the four deaths – a decision was made to remove more of the top coat of paint from the cave fresco, and finally liberate its underpainting.

It was January 7, a Tuesday, and Epiphany had come and gone without a single revelation.

Middelhoek was back from Holland after a bittersweet visit with Mathilde ('She said she'd have sex with me,' he recounted morosely, 'but nothing else'), and his demeanor had now grown more irritable than ever. He'd scurry around officiously, berating others for getting in his way. Formally speaking, Middelhoek was against removing the paint. But eventually everyone's curiosity, including that of our Nederlander frescologist, overcame his better judgement. And since Middelhoek was in charge of the crew studying the thousand-year-old cave painting, it was only natural that he should take the lead.

What Middelhoek and his group were going to do requires some explanation, beginning with how a fresco is made. The first thing you do, of course, is find a wall. (In the case of Mancanzano, you choose a wall in an out-of-the-way cave, where it will take a few deaths to attract any interest.) Then you prepare a rough plaster base. A sketch, the *sinopia*, is outlined on top. And then each day, until the fresco is completed, a fine layer of lime plaster called the *giornata* is spread over the surface. The evolving expanse of wall, ready to be covered with pigment, is the *intonaco*. Like this, you turn a cave wall into a canvas.

Now, there are two principal kinds of fresco. *Buon fresco* is the pure stuff. Pigment, mixed only with water, is applied to the lime-gilded *intonaco*. The lime is made by burning materials like marble or limestone, or in the case of Mancanzano by burning tufa. All of these stones contain calcium carbonate. Burning them drives off carbonic acid, which converts the calcium carbonate into calcium oxide. Then, with the addition of water, the substance becomes calcium hydroxide. As it dries, the compound reabsorbs carbonic gas from the air and becomes calcium carbonate again. But, by this time, it has been covered with paint. So now the pigments themselves become part of the wall. These are mineral-based colors: the reds are ocher, and the greens are all oxidized ferrous silicates. The blues are usually lapis lazuli or pulverized cobalt glass, with the piercing blue of a clear evening sky just before dusk (if you'll pardon the fancy description to help us waltz through the dry stuff). As the *intonaco* dries, it is transformed into a crystalline surface, chemically identical to marble. The fresco is rock-hard and washable, built to last.

The other frescoes are *freschi a secco*, or frescoes done in the dry. Once the wall has carbonized, more paint is added to embellish the design. This can happen right away, or decades later. Because this paint never becomes part of the wall, it has to be mixed with glue, egg or oil to make it adhere to the crystalline surface. But as the *a secco* paint ages, it can also harden, crack and flake away. Sometimes it puckers or starts to shrink. Scabs of glue can fall away, pulling intricate details with them.

One of the best-known examples of working with the two

kinds of fresco occurred during the restoration of the Brancacci Chapel in the Church of Santa Maria del Carmine in Florence. Moisture had been seeping into the walls, and a thin blanket of mold was consuming the art. By the mid-1980s, the frescoes looked bad, and only promised to get worse. At some unidentified stage, Adam and Eve's genitals had been given new leaf covers. That is: at some point, *a secco* paint had been added to Adam and Eve's groins, covering them up with bits of lush greenery. But now the decision was made to remove the layers of paint. (Amidst the controversy this roused, the English-speaking artists in Florence joked that Eve, minus the foliage, would only be relinquishing one 'bush' for another.) The frescoes in question were Masaccio's *Expulsion of Adam and Eve from Paradise* and Masolino's *Fall*, where there weren't any conveniently placed hands to protect Eve from inappropriate glances to her pubis.

But the issue, of course, wasn't really their nudity, even if the idea of exposing Adam and Eve publicly titillated many. The question was whether Masaccio and Masolino had applied the leaf coverings as adjustments to their paintings once the frescoes had dried, or whether later restorers (perhaps in the seventeenth or eighteenth centuries) had added them to help keep prurient eyes focused forward during prayer. Because old frescoes are frequently made up of so many layers, it is difficult and often impossible to date the layers of glue that compose the *a secco* paint. It is also close to impossible to separate the different layers from one another. So while the top layer of leaves in the chapel had clearly been painted after the first *buoni freschi*, there was no way to know whether Masaccio and Masolino had made the alterations themselves. The question was whether the leaves belonged in the paintings, or if the Garden of Eden's original lovebirds were better rendered *au naturel*.

Of all the restoration done in the Brancacci Chapel, nothing superseded removing the leaves. Nothing was more important than deciding whether Adam and Eve should be bared, and nothing was more appealing to the restorers than to be the one to do it. It was the artistic counterpart of emceeing a celebrity strip show.

It took Middelhoek two weeks, even with the high deputy's assistance, to get hold of the ingredients to mix a batch of AB57, a cleaning agent which had first been developed by the Istituto Centrale del Restauro (God bless Ugolino) in the early 1970s for use on marble, and was later used, with mixed reviews, in various restorations in the Sistine Chapel. As Middelhoek explains it, the compound is a mix of ammonium bicarbonate, sodium bicarbonate, distilled water, an antifungal named Desogen, and carboxymethyl cellulose, which adds just enough roughage to the savory fluid to turn it into goo.

You dab the AB57 onto a fresco for three minutes, remove it, let the wall air-dry for a day, and then you repeat the procedure a second or third time, as needed. The compound's not safe to use in the sense that restoring frescoes increases their luster at the cost of removing shadows and delicate design, but it's the best way of removing anything more complicated than dust and dirt. (For *those*, the art restoration students from the University of Calabria have been insisting all along that nothing is better than handfuls of water-moistened bread applied to the veneer. Signora Bitonto, exuberant, is ready to do her part!)

So after the AB57 was mixed and its consistency checked, Middelhoek got down to work. Floodlights were set up around the cave, with thick black rubber cables trailing a full kilometer through the labyrinthine neighborhood, connecting the lamps to the closest municipal electrical outlet, which turned out to be not close at all. Middelhoek instructed the Calabrians to monitor his work and act as guards, thus effectively keeping them out of his way. But, having just returned from dealing with someone who didn't want to deal with *him*, he'd appease the students by thanking them effusively every time any one of them did anything to help – as long as it was unrelated to the actual restoration.

'I'm so thrilled you are here, *grazie, grazie*,' I've heard him say dozens of times, particularly if one of them quiets onlookers or goes out to fetch coffee in the afternoon.

'What's so impressive about you,' he'll tell another, after checking the amount of sugar in his espresso, 'is both your initiative and your precision.'

Middelhoek eats *biscotti* like he is your best friend. But adjust one of the lamps or make a suggestion, and then he goes haywire.

'Don't forget this is their country,' Linda tells him.

'You have to remind *them* of that.'

'I think they know. Do you want me to ask one?'

'Don't say anything to anyone unless you begin by thanking him first,' Middelhoek answers. 'You see, I'm trying to provide an environment where everyone here feels truly wanted.'

Which brings us, I suppose, to the subject of Mathilde. Middelhoek came back from the Netherlands with a stack of photographs. Not new ones, which would really have been maudlin – can you picture Middelhoek in Amsterdam snapping away at the woman he loves, who's also the woman who refuses to be with him? – but old ones, pictures from holidays, summer scenes, the kinds of photographs you're supposed to file away at the back of a closet and not take out again until your new girlfriend demands a survey of past competition.

The week after the ingredients for the AB57 arrived, Middelhoek sat down to show me the pictures. He pulled a stack of them out of a large envelope, and scattered them over the table like a worn pack of playing cards. Then he started fishing through the photos, pulling ones out almost at random. He settled on two from the seaside somewhere. Mathilde was topless in both. It was a peculiar first choice.

'Mathilde has beautiful breasts,' he said, his voice warbling like a trapped wren's. 'You realize I'm saying this objectively.'

'It's the scientist in you that everyone respects.'

'But I miss them,' he told me. 'It's shallow, but true.

Sometimes I think it would be easier to find someone else. Not someone to love. Just someone to sleep with.'

'Yes?'

'And then I'd betray the woman I love as best I can. Then I could say I'm not worthy of Mathilde. And then I wouldn't miss her. Then I could find other breasts.'

'You might even enjoy that,' I told him. 'Half the people here have them, and the ones who do all have two.'

'But I'll tell you a story,' Middelhoek said. 'I had a nightmare last night. It was the kind where you wake up from it disoriented. I was with Mathilde, in her Amsterdam flat, and she was telling me that she didn't want to see me anymore. That's what startled me out of my sleep.'

'That was your nightmare?'

'That was my nightmare. A reality nightmare. When you're shaken awake by the way things actually are.'

'Your idea of betraying Mathilde sounds perfect. Betray her for me, if you won't do it for yourself. You're making yourself miserable. You told me yourself that Mathilde doesn't want you.'

'I know she doesn't want me. She says she doesn't want me. She acts like she doesn't want me.'

'Yes?'

'But I can't get it through my head that she doesn't want me.'

Middelhoek showed me more photographs, including ones where Mathilde and he looked unmistakably happy. 'I was visiting her in Amsterdam, and right after she told me it wouldn't work out between us, she said that she loved me. And she told me, "I miss you."'

'That's a nasty thing to say.'

'It's funny,' Middelhoek said, 'you can have a relationship without love, but you can't have one without wanting to be together.'

'Yes, that's funny.'

He showed me more pictures of the two of them.

'No, it's not funny,' he said.

'No, it's not.'

'I'm not ready to let go of her,' Middelhoek said finally.

'I know,' I told him. I took some of the photographs from his hand and laid them on the table. 'But try relaxing your grip on her a little. At least then you'll know you won't cramp up.'

'Like this?' he asked me. He swept the images to the floor with the back of his hand. He smiled at me sympathetically. Then he kneeled down and gathered them to his breast.

And Linda, by the way, had her own holiday odyssey.

'So I go there for Christmas,' she said. 'To Michele, Alessandro, and Carlo's house. And to their mother and father's. And, as it turns out, also to their uncle's. And a cousin is there too. And he's also male. And all of them are flirting with me. That's right, you guessed it. Except for the mother, who spends most of the time shuttling plates back and forth from the kitchen. And when I go in to help her, the men come in too. All of a sudden, there are two or three of them in the kitchen with us. I mean, one of them will be carrying a fork – a single fork – and he'll have the excuse that he's trying to help clear the table. Another will be carrying a bottle of wine that's still half-full, and the mother will say, "That should stay on the table," and he'll say, "Oh, you're right, of course it should." I mean, whoever it is. And then he'll just stand there in the kitchen, talking away, with the wine bottle in his hand. So that was Christmas.'

'It sounds like you loved it.'

'I spent the whole night. I know what you're thinking . . . no, I didn't sleep with any of them. But I was the belle of the ball, the demoiselle of the dinner. And that's the best part of any play. So we stayed up all night, even the mother. And we watched the sun rise. You should see the sun coming up over the sassi! It blossoms out there like a gigantic marigold. It's like watching the petals burn into the sky. So that's what I did for Christmas. In the morning, I left. I came home. It was six o'clock! I went to sleep. I dreamed of elves. *Little elves!* Tiny men scampering around, wishing me, *"Buon Natale. Buon Natale, signorina."* I woke up in the afternoon, and I dreamed Santa Claus was burying his head in my lap. Burying and burying! My best Christmas ever. God, I love his belly!'

'I get the idea there was a tiny bit more to the dream than that.'

'Oh, there was, there was. I got Santa's clothes off. Even the red long johns. You should see his little prancer!'

'Not more like a blitzen?'

'No, his superior attribute was higher up. But let's just say he knew what to do with his mouth once he got rid of the pipe.'

'You're absolutely certain I needed to know that?'

'Yes. Yes, you did. Because I'm your friend. Now, are you really going to spend all your time here faithful to Julie?'

And me? The rest of my Christmas? While Babbo Natale busied himself with la Sirena, and I made do with more tepid memories of carols and hugs? After Dr Stoppani headed home, Fortune and I stayed up for a while, drank some Amaro Lucano because there wasn't any more whisky (and it wasn't time to stop drinking yet), and then stumbled quietly to our own rooms. In the morning, I saw he'd fallen asleep with his clothes on, with his arms and legs folded awkwardly into themselves, like a foal.

But that night, I slept. And for the second night, I dreamed of you. We were both laughing. We were in our apartment, and we were happy in a way I haven't been since I came to this sullen place. Surrounded by your things and you, I felt rich. And that richness was expressed in our laughs and the quantity of them. We looked at each other and said, 'I can't stop laughing.' These were belly laughs we were producing, and guffaws. We kept on laughing. And laughing and laughing. Then finally we had to ask: 'How long do you think we can keep this up?' It was a serious question. Because the body starts to ache after a while, and now this was getting to be a reasonable worry. But the two of us were still doubled over. 'I don't want to stop, I'm not going to,' I swore to you. 'Smiles are good,' you suggested in between chortles. 'It can be smiles, not all laughing, that might be OK.' But in this dream, there was only laughing.

In the morning, a ragged Winston Fortune came into my room, still dressed in his last evening's clothes, and said, 'Your laughing kept me up the whole fucking night. Let me remind you: you're lonely and tired. Your work's going slow. Your girlfriend's in New York balling every fucker she knows. There. Now be miserable.'

I lunged at him, half-assed.

But he said, 'No, you don't fucking get it. I'm too *tired* to fight.'

—

Middelhoek and his team have begun the applications of AB57, and the fresco has really started to change. The AB57 is stripping away the *a secco* paint. The transformation in the cave is alarming and freaky. You can really see the blood on the cherubim's faces, splattering their stomachs, dripping down their necks, and staining the earth all around them. On their faces, avarice is painted around their eyes with the creasy exactitude of little crow's-feet. One of the cherubim, in the center of the group, has hands that are stained red, as though he's just pulled them out from a carcass. The color makes them leap from the wall, suspending themselves right before you, full of sinister portent. A few of the Calabrian students crossed themselves once enough *a secco* paint had been removed to establish the scene.

Middelhoek asked them skeptically, 'Does that work?'

'Of course, it does,' the students answered. They seemed very certain. They demonstrated the crossing again, dotting their chests rhythmically with their index fingers, while they gaped at the image of the cherub's hands, bathed in the brightest, most beautiful, most brutal red.

Now the AB57 is being spread over the entire fresco. The appeal of the compound is almost like a drug; using the AB57 is addictive and irresistible. You only wait three minutes to get an immediate effect – a rush of change and drama to the images on the wall. Put it on, take it off. It's too easy.

Middelhoek goes on and on about how restoration work requires immense skill, sensitivity, intuition, patience and judgment. It pleases him no end to liken himself to a medical doctor.

'If I make a mistake,' he says grimly, as he points to the fresco, 'my patient may die.'

By now he has stopped expressing any aesthetic objections to using the cleanser. And the Calabrians don't bother talking about dabbing the fresco with moistened bread anymore. They talk about AB57 like it's wine, or the purest drug (the way the rest of the people in Mancanzano talk about tufa). Middelhoek has to keep the bins with the ingredients for the mixture under lock and key. He says that bottles of Desogen have already disappeared. He says this lustfully. But at least his new passion for the solvent is distracting him from Mathilde. All across Mancanzano, I can picture people spreading contraband AB57 across their faces and torsos, as an exfoliant, as if they were lolling at a sumptuous, self-restorative spa. And watching Middelhoek, who concentrates on his work as a practical defense against everything else, I can imagine him hoping the AB57 will slough off whatever sadness is only skin-deep.

But at the bottom of the fresco, beside the cherubim, there is now the image of a body. It's clearly human. It's a dead boy, maybe thirteen or fourteen years old, naked, twisted on his side, sprawled with his arms apart, his legs splayed, with curly brown hair covering his head.

His body has appeared in the fresco over the last several days, as the *a secco* paint has peeled away, and the painting has been transformed more and more into a medieval palimpsest. A gash runs up one of the boy's flanks, starting at his stomach and extending past the ribs to his chest. You see piano-key ribs, sliced muscle and gristle folded together inside the wound. It looks a little like baked lasagna. At the feet of the cherub – the one with the ominous and awful hands – there are internal organs, lungs, a heart, a pool of sadness, a heap of flesh. The dead boy's eyes drip blood, which well in the unmistakable shape of tears, and then puddle deliberately down his cheeks.

The parents of the dead teens have come to watch the restoration. They stand at the edge of the cave, rarely talking. You nod to them in acknowledgement, but there's nothing to say. They stand there, bundled in winter scarves, hands thrust into their pockets, crumpling their noses a little at the smell of ammonia. They're waiting. But waiting for what?

The parents look at Middelhoek and the Calabria students with wry curiosity and disdain. Every once in a while, one of the parents kicks at a wall. Fragments of tufa cover the tips of their shoes like gritty bird droppings. Sometimes, friends of their children stand beside them, flanking the parents as living reminders of what they've lost. But their presence is ghostly, and the parents wonder, why wasn't it you? The teenagers, in turn, keep their gazes fixed forward, as though only the grisliest images will shield them from glares.

Dr Stoppani comes to watch the restoration too. He's the only one who says anything to the dead children's parents, standing beside them, usually silently and then just barely whispering, at the entrance to the cave.

Dr Stoppani still hasn't reconciled with Monica, but I think he's reconciled with *that*. Misery loves company, and Dr Stoppani finds company among these mourning parents. Finally, they are like kin.

But to us, Dr Stoppani says, 'When I was younger, I had a clearer sense of the tragic. It was easier to appreciate. I felt it everywhere. The goalie slips, and a missed ball was tragic. A wine goes bad, and that's very tragic. But now to feel tragedy, I really have to concentrate. Ask me if I'm happy.'

'Are you happy?' Linda and I ask him.

'No,' he says. 'Right now, I can't be.'

'What about the parents? You talk to them?'

'The parents won't ever be happy again,' Dr Stoppani says. 'That's the difference between them and me.'

The thing about happiness is that it fades at disaster. It is ephemeral and delicate; it has weak seams. In the name of romance, Dr Stoppani is stuck in the pursuit of farce. But I hope Monica takes him back, I really do. He says she's in Venice, or Rome, or maybe in France. Perhaps she's in a villa in Tuscany, hiding away in a four-star room with a view. He doesn't know. I imagine him sending telegrams blindly that say one thing: 'Stop. Stop. Stop. Stop.' Loss is a fungus. You have to scrape out every crevice before it is gone.

But, here in Mancanzano, the more you scrape, the deeper the crevice grows.

Middelhoek wanders through our apartment in the dead of night. He walks to the kitchen (where, perhaps, he meets up with the specter of the rabbit in search of its gullet), then through the living room, back to his bedroom, back to the kitchen, and then again to the living room. We hear the aimlessness of his footsteps, and the squashing of cushions. In the morning, glasses of water and juice populate the apartment.

'This is why we need a TV,' he says. 'So I have something to do instead of pretending to sleepwalk.' Middelhoek's expression is sullen and dour, as though the fleshy parts of his face have surrendered to gravity.

It takes him a day to find a discarded black-and-white set. The picture keeps sliding up the screen like a rollaway window shade.

'These problems with the television are going to stop,' he says. 'I have to have faith.' He shakes the whole box in the air, sometimes snapping the cord right from the socket.

Fortune looks at him and shakes his head wearily. 'You know, *amico*,' he says almost tenderly, 'the next step will be flagellating yourself with the antennae.'

But Fortune surprises us, himself. One afternoon, when we're all at our quarters, he tells us out of the blue: 'I was in love once.'

We look at him skeptically, especially Middelhoek and Dr Stoppani, who's visiting.

Then Fortune says, 'I'm thirty-six. Did you really believe I'd spent all these years tossing off?'

Linda says, deadpan, 'Actually, I did.'

But Fortune ignores her. 'No, the woman I loved was an Australian,' he says. 'Real commonwealthy. Her grandparents were British. She had a way about her that Australians often do. She called her cat a lush. I was her tart.'

He stands up from the table and takes a sip from one of Middelhoek's half-empty glasses. Then he tells us: 'At the end of our first date, I walked her back to her flat. Across from the Imperial College in Kensington, where both of us worked. When we got to her door, she said, "I like you, Winston. So I want to see you again." You see, her maths was exquisite. That alone drew me to her.

'Now, Valerie was a draftsman. Or a *draftswoman,* I should say. Whichever it was, she had sexy penmanship. And, understand when I tell you, that's rare. I'm not talking about dotting her "i"s. That's for children. I mean, her cursive, the tails of her letters. Her letters said, "Fuck me." And so I did. But, mostly, I'll tell you, we made love. Which can be better. So you want to know what happened? After six months, she said, "You treat me too well, Winston. I don't deserve it." I was stymied at first. That surprise lasted two days. So then I hit her. I gave her a black eye. It was because she refused to go out and get more milk. That made her furious, so we were married that summer. We honeymooned in the Canary Islands. Have you been there? Really beautiful. Lush, like her cat. But the problem was I couldn't keep up the bad treatment. I brought her flowers.

I kissed her gently. I wanted to make sure she was happy. By then, I was in love. So we split up.'

'Are you still in touch with her?' Linda asked.

'She's remarried in Brighton, the mother of three. All the kids yell. I understand she's ecstatic.'

'You're better off without her.'

'You know how you get over a woman like that?' Fortune said.

'How?' I asked.

'Yes, how?' Middelhoek and Dr Stoppani said, almost in unison.

'You find a place where people are getting murdered, and then you go there and throw your heart into it.'

'I don't think that's it,' Linda said.

'But it's worth a try,' Fortune answered. 'At least until I come up with something else.'

The restoration work goes on. Middelhoek, in the cave, continues stripping the fresco of its *a secco* paint, forever surprising us with the new imagery. In town, the carabinieri continue their sluggish investigation of the deaths – *l'omicidio quadruplice*, as it's now being called, even if there's still no rugged proof these are homicides yet. But it seems obvious to everyone in Mancanzano, carabinieri or not, that the two sets of deaths are inextricably linked. Wandering around naked and copulating in caves – regardless of whether this activity results in premature death and consequent decomposition – just isn't done in southern Italy. Not in a place where elderly women still dress in black, and spend their days conspiring with saints. And not in a town where chastity's still considered a virtue for unmarried teenage girls, even if they *do* veil their newfound femininity with powdered tufa.

So this is when Major Martella began talking about Cesare Lombroso. Lombroso was a physician who ran an insane asylum in the Adriatic city of Pesaro at the end of the nineteenth century. He was also someone I'd studied in graduate school because he had been a professor of 'criminal anthropology' at the University of Turin before that.

In the 1880s, Lombroso's home in Turin was a salon for many of Europe's leading writers and thinkers (the sociologist Max Weber most notable among them). As founder of the field of criminal anthropology, Lombroso had added his own rococo twist to Darwin's theory of evolution: he reasoned that criminals suffered from atavistic or degenerative traits. Atavists, he argued, could be recognized by subhuman physical characteristics reminiscent of apes. Degenerates, on the other hand, had already begun regressing along the evolutionary line, and could thereby be distinguished by congenital weaknesses and an overall unintelligent look. The beauty of Lombroso's theories – at least according to Professor Lombroso – was that physical anomalies would make it possible to identify criminals even *before* they committed offenses. Lombroso used the various anthropomorphic techniques that were the rage in his day (and were later deployed with great fanfare by the Nazis) to compile a handbook of measurements of criminal types. As a prison warden, he also shifted his focus from crimes to the criminal, arguing that sentences needed to fit the characters of the condemned. Even misdemeanors would be punished severely if the perpetrators' body types indicated a penchant for violence or sexual perversion.

Lombroso remained in excellent repute in Italy until the start of the twentieth century, when he began to contend that genius was merely another form of degeneracy. But before his essays and books were removed from the local curricula, his colleagues and students filled most of the posts in Italy's police forces and prisons. Right up until the First World War, being able to quote a few lines of Lombroso was a sign of erudition.

Now, Major Martella (despite whatever I'd assumed he'd learned at majoring school) was an ardent supporter of the warden's criminal anthropology. Soon, he began talking publicly about taking cranial measurements, along with limb length, finger length and earlobe comparisons, just to see if the four dead teenagers all had something sinisterly anthropometric in common. He even telephoned the forensics unit in Potenza to ask if such calibrations had been made while the bodies were laid out in the morgue. Reportedly, the major received such a hearty laugh in response that, to save face, he vowed to have nothing more to do with the *medico legale* in Potenza 'no matter how many people die here, no matter what'.

At first, I couldn't figure out Martella's modern-day allegiance to Lombroso. Who wouldn't consider his theories outdated and outrageous? Didn't the major realize he was wasting his time? But that's when I understood that the longer he took to unravel the deaths, the greater the number of gifts he'd be amassing. And that's when Major Martella's logic was revealed as calculated as anything Machiavelli had devised for his prince.

Since I'd arrived in Mancanzano, I'd been noticing a penchant for gift-giving among the townsfolk. I'd seen this when Dottoressa Donabuoni used sundried tomatoes to persuade the carabinieri to stop chiseling at the fresco, and learned about it when informants told me they brought gifts to their doctors to get better prescriptions and to Signora Bitonto to make sure she sold them the freshest bread. So it wasn't difficult to understand Major Martella wanting to solve the crimes in Mancanzano at a leisurely pace. After all, homicides put him at the top of everyone's lists. He just had to go about finding the town's murderer without aggravating anyone by appearing to do nothing – because then he might be expected to give some of the gifts back. Clearly, Cesare Lombroso's ideas were perfectly suited for Major Martella because they wouldn't jeopardize his investigation at any point by actually working.

Both Banfield and local Italian anthropologists had written about *furbizia*, this southern cunning, in their ethnographies of Lucania in the 1950s and 1960s. But now it was my chance to witness it first-hand. Should I have been surprised that the local head of the carabinieri was so adept? It wouldn't matter to anyone here if Cesare Lombroso was a relic from long ago. All Major Martella had to say was, 'Like Jesus and Paul – or, like da Vinci and Savonarola – our best teachers have lived in the past.' That alone would be enough to win the Mancanzani over, who, thrilled at the idea of having their police chief be a shrewd man of action, would quickly canonize him into one.

After his inevitable break with the *medico legale*, Major Martella announced that he would take the measurements of the four teenagers himself, and he soon issued orders to his officers to exhume the bodies. He was full of sound and fury and all the accompanying ghoulishness, and readier than ever to show the people of Mancanzano that he meant business. In fact, it was only after a full day of pleading on the part of Bishop Pascoli, who finally appealed not to God but to science – and pointed out that the bodies would already be partially decomposed, and that that might upset a lot of people – that Major Martella relented and dramatically proclaimed that the four graves would remain intact.

But Major Martella wasn't ready to relinquish his leverage. The next morning parents all around Mancanzano received notices that their children were to report to the carabinieri for 'precise, life-saving measurements'. So that night, consequently, the city's children ate well. No one wanted his kid to show up at the station house on Via Stigliano looking gaunt. In dining rooms across the city, the meal was referred to as the *Ringraziamento al Maggiore Luigi Martella*, a one-time Lucanian thanksgiving to the remarkable major himself. Some mothers used the occasion as an opportunity to cook Mancanzano's traditional dishes, preparing 'cottorieddu', vegetables and lamb baked for an entire day in a terracotta pot, and 'capuzzedde', a delicacy which, as best as I can describe it, is the head of a kid cooked on a spit. Many of the parents sent their children to the carabinieri the following morning carrying small edible offerings with the vague hope that, as one mother put it, 'the measurements would come out "well".'

A full week after the children lined up and their measurements were taken, Major Martella reported that he was still 'manipulating his numbers', which seemed like just another way of indicating that he wanted the stream of culinary gifts to keep flowing in. Radio Maria, steadfastly displaying the alliance between Church and State (or, at least, between Church and police) would alternate between broadcasts of utopian messages and more cryptic ones, where aphorisms like '*Chi conta senza Dio, non conosce l'aritmetica*' – 'Whoever counts without God doesn't know arithmetic' – would be regularly repeated.

Two days after the broadcasts reached full swing and we'd begun discussing the anthropometric techniques in some of our interviews, Major Martella arrived at our door with pages of his hand-scrawled numbers.

'Can you make sense of these?' he asked, holding the sheets before me. Linda, Fortune and Middelhoek were out.

I glanced through the pages to show I was serious. Then I shook my head, no.

'So you look at these numbers and you don't understand them?'

'I don't,' I told him.

'And you admit that?' he asked.

'I don't know what else I can do.'

Major Martella flipped through the pages, circling numbers intently without saying a word, until I began feeling truly uncomfortable. Then he looked up from the sheets, and took a slight step forward so that he was standing halfway through our door and halfway in my face.

Then he said, 'I want to tell you something from the history of our city. Two decades ago, when my father was *colonnello*, he could arrest people whenever he wanted and throw them in jail. Now, the more scientific everything gets, the less certain they become. Now there are inexhaustible possibilities for me to consider, and anyone could be considered guilty if I look hard enough. Unfortunately, we don't have the jail space for that.'

Major Martella smiled emphatically. The sheets in his hand hung by his side, where they slashed through the air like a broadsword. 'I'm sure, as a scientist, you'll agree that your failure to grasp something doesn't mean it doesn't work. After all, no one knows everything, besides God. That's true in Italy, at least.'

'At the very least,' I said to him.

'Good,' Major Martella said. 'So you accept the possibility of things being beyond your level of comprehension. Now, about Cesare Lombroso . . .'

'Yes?'

'It's been explained to me that you may have studied other things in other places that may not entirely match with my techniques.'

'You came here to tell me that?'

'I did. I came here to talk to you about my methodology. And since you are a guest in our country, and a guest in our city, I thought it would be gentlemanly of me to come to you. So this visit is a *piacere*, a pleasure for us both. We both know I could have asked you to visit me, but that's never as cordial.'

Major Martella took a measured step backwards now, so that he was standing just beyond our door. 'Now, I think we can hold off on any more pleasantries until it's your turn to do the explaining,' he said. 'We can save that for when it's *your* methodology we need to discuss. In the meantime, let's just hope there aren't complications. Because complications only remind us of our need for order. And of how my officers are going to have to tighten their grips until everything runs the way it used to, back when people were still scared to die. Are you scared to die?' the major asked me.

'Not right now,' I told him.

'Well, there's always tomorrow,' he said.

'Yes, there's tomorrow.'

'Well, then, that's when I'll see you,' he said.

Then Major Luigi Martella turned, and headed back to the station house on Via Stigliano.

Did I feel threatened by Major Martella's visit?

Of course, I did.

But it wasn't as though his visit was the only element of life in Mancanzano that had started me feeling uneasy. Just as the major had predicted, no one in town minded going to the station house for a half-hour calibration with a tape measure and calipers. For the children of Mancanzano, the visit had even seemed like awfully good food and fun. For many people here, Martella's measures bolstered their sense of hope. It diluted their *miseria* with the idea of possibility: he left the impression that progress in the investigation was being made, even if it took a great leap of faith in order to believe it.

But while the major continued accumulating gifts, and the people he protected happily gave them, anyone in the city had to suspect that the growing level of malaise in Mancanzano couldn't be masked for ever. There was enough going on in the city to make you feel anxious and leery wherever you went, and much of it seemed as odd and appalling as the deaths and the threats and images in the underground fresco.

So, meanwhile, I'll report there's a small church that sits at the foot of the sassi, on the northern bluff of the town. A path leads uphill, from the Church of the Madonna della Virtù – where the hint of immaculate honor seems anachronistic and cruel – past a lone café with rock benches and weathered picnic tables, and then along a twisting route through the beehive of restored sassi. Standing from a distance, you can see where the path peeks out from the caves, emerging into the open, almost like the flank of a snake, momentarily visible in spite of the camouflage.

Halfway up the bluff, there are the remnants of a piazza and the leftovers of a crumbling rectangular tower, about half the height of the one at the Castello Tramontano. Dilapidated battlements jut from the ground, each of them three or four feet high, with a few fallen stones scattered at the base. The piazza's about the size of a basketball half-court, and sometimes kids arrive in the afternoon, to play soccer in the open space, far above the creek, where it overlooks the precipice. You could watch the children playing there – their moves both oblivious and deliberate – and have no idea that anyone in Mancanzano had died, or that each of these kids had been so extensively measured, inventoried and itemized by the carabinieri. Occasionally, a ball gets launched off the bluff, to bounce its way down past the sassi. At the foot of the homes, by the Church of the Madonna della Virtù, Guglielmo Caduta, the parish priest, spends an hour or two every few months combing the nearby rocks for scraps of punctured balls, looking for ones that careened through the battlements, but weren't so lucky to roll all of the way down to the creek.

But it's not all so innocent with the ball players. One of them comes to the piazza with his dog. In the afternoon, I've seen the dog by the web of the sassi, gulping cavatelli all'arrabbiata out of the plastic bowls that Giandomenico's grieving mother puts out. But at night, when floodlights bathe the crumbling edifice of the tower in white, the boy returns to the half-court piazza with his dog, saying, '*Bravo, bravo*. This is for you, *caro*, take,' with one hand on the dog's back, stroking the fur, and his other hand lower, between the dog's legs, wresting the penis until it comes.

Beasts come ferociously. There is no tenderness. No licking behind the ears. Animals already wear leather and furs. After they ejaculate – in species where they are not devoured – the males, indifferent to their lays, get up and walk away.

After the incident, the boy takes hold of the dog's collar and reattaches its leash. Then he draws the animal away from the tower, and from the piazza, leaving the spilled seed on the ground, where, by morning, it will have been absorbed into the tufa or eaten by insects. The chain links of the leash clink as the two of them walk away. The dog barks, its voice bursting the quiet. The boy says nothing for a time, then breaks his own silence, saying, 'Good dog, good.' He tells the animal that both of them are brave, as the dog walks beside him indifferently.

The boy's name is Flavio; he's a student at the *liceo scientifico*, and once again he's back at the piazza with his dog. This is the third time I've seen them, always watching them from a distance; I count the pair of them as my informants. This time when Flavio reaches, the dog snarls, then bites. The dog sinks its teeth in at his wrist. Falvio looks at him, bewildered. He's just barely seventeen years old. '*Non capisco*,' he says. 'I don't understand. Why? Why?' Then the dog licks at his forearm, where there is a trickle of blood.

Other times, the dog just whimpers. It cries. Then it humps whatever it can find, even if it's just a patch of dry earth. Eventually, the dog wants the boy to do it – that is, to help it come. So first, Flavio takes out a crudely made muzzle, with scraps of leather from the shoemaker on Via Galileo Galilei. The dog is so desperate that it actually helps the boy put it on, fixing the leather against the ground and threading its own snout inside the muzzle.

From what I can tell, the tradition only takes place at night, and only at that one tower. Sometimes, I'll see the two of them heading through Mancanzano's streets after dusk, with the dog straining against the leash, doing whatever it can to get to the piazza faster. Pulled along by his dog, it is all Flavio can do not to run. As a matter of curiosity, I can report that he chooses other places for his own relief.

The last time I saw them was three days ago at the tower. It was evening, the lamps were on, and the whole piazza was glowing, bathed in the floodlights' eerie embrace. Flavio removed the dog's leash, reached into his jacket, fumbled for something, maybe the muzzle. Then the two of them stood at the battlements, and the boy leaned over, watching the sassi-checkered hill descend the two hundred feet down. The evening was quiet. Flavio smoked a cigarette, then flicked the ashes into the air. The dog sniffed at the ground, and pawed at it a little. Then it backed up, shifting most of its weight onto its hind quarters, emitted a yelp, and lunged forward. The dog passed Flavio between two of the battlements, leaping from the piazza, over the cliff. Its paws scrambled in the air. But still it didn't bark. It was only seconds before the brown mass hit heavily down, the dog's side landing on the edge of a roof, puncturing, collapsing on impact.

In the morning, Padre Guglielmo Caduta looked up the hill, and then into the air, as though his glance might travel all the way to the heavens, wondering why now this beast should come plunging down, all the way to his church. He recognized the animal, and carried the dog's broken body to the boy's home. There, he found its teenage owner sitting in the living room alone, holding the leash in the dark. The teenager said thank you for bringing his pet, the body of which was now wrapped in a damp red towel to hold it together. Padre Caduta comforted the boy, as the boy cried, whimpering with the same timbre as his pet.

That night, a few hours after the lights in the piazza switched on, dogs all over Mancanzano began to wail. In the morning, you could find them wandering the streets, sniffing at buildings, and licking the walls.

## Chapter 8
# Racconti d'Amore

Does it surprise you the people here talk of baptized meat? *'Carne battezzata'* – that's what they call themselves. Sacraments performed directly on sirloin. I suppose it's no different from what Carlo Levi found back in the thirties, when he described Lucania's peasants as beasts of burden. Or what Count Tramontano found as he looked down from his battlements. Except that the baptisms he offered were by his own holy water.

In this desolate landscape, the maples and oaks of America are no larger than bushes, and people's expectations are held to the same dimensions. So, forget about Banfield's 'backward society'. This is a community that refuses to sprout and grow. And while it's true that life in Mancanzano is much better today than when Mussolini's troops were riddling it with bullets, there's no cultural logic guaranteeing that the process of amelioration will continue. If anything, the deaths of the four teenagers has underscored that.

Afforded lives in a region of earthquakes, the Mancanzani have never been simply buried in rubble, but entombed in the earth. That is how they deal with disaster. They live in crypts. They die in crypts. Earthquakes merely shut the doors, swallowing them up as though they'd never existed. The earthquakes have smashed at this region every hundred or two hundred years, erasing generations and history and, in certain spots, proof that there has been anything or anyone here at all.

But I understand now why people stay where they're from. And I understand why they cling to their earth, and fight to the death rather than leave. The familiar is a cocoon, where people think like you, look like you, and want the same things. No one in Mancanzano will ever trust us completely, no matter how hard we try to earn their friendship and confidence. The Mancanzani are amused that we've visited, but not so glad we've remained.

Back in the thirties, the Fascisti underestimated the intransigence of these tufa-eaters. They thought they could wipe them out with a few spartan decrees and a few more fired guns. But the only ones to wipe out the Mancanzani will be the Mancanzani themselves. In this town of tombstones, they'll bury themselves up in the earth.

And you and me? What becomes of us now, separated by this time and this distance? Here teenagers are dying, and I promised you I'd be home before our own child was born in June. So I do not understand how Odysseus took off for twenty years, or how Neil Armstrong and Buzz Aldrin took off for some two hundred and fifty thousand miles, into the impossible distance, the absolute severity of the unknown. My own wrong turn was in Bari, not at Troy or Cape Canaveral.

At least in Mancanzano, my feet are on earth – or *in* the earth, if you think of the malleable ground of caves. But when measuring distances, there are only two gauges: near and far. And I am far. Can you still see any part of me when you shut your eyes? Our child's in your womb, but what's left of me in your head? When you linger in one place, as I'm doing here, every place starts to feel as long-off as the moon.

Sometimes distance is the most palpable threat.

———

The exodus from Mancanzano quickened once the second half of January arrived, and the townsfolk had already surrendered what paltry largess they had to Major Martella. Now the

Mancanzani began coalescing outside their homes with the same wintry insistence as breaths escaping from open mouths. Perhaps there had been reason to stay in Mancanzano through the winter holidays (while the major, like St Sergeant Nicholas, kept to his lists), but once the kings came for Epiphany and left with their gifts still tucked in their robes, a lot of people figured it was time to give up on the city too. If there had been any doubt in their minds about whether to stay in Mancanzano, a few wayward tremors – so low on the Richter scale that Fortune dismissed them to us as 'pussy quivers' – pushed the undecided beyond the brink. Now, every few days, all throughout Mancanzano's dead, dry winter season, people have been gathering their belongings, to haul their furniture and clothes up the town's two bluffs, before heading for cars and buses, and even the occasional dilapidated flatbed truck, rented at outlandish prices from the owners of the tufa quarry.

The defecting townsfolk say they want a city where there won't any longer be the specter of the dead. Where they can live without the history of calamity and suffering in conventional apartments. And where there will always be plentiful hot and cold running water. And consistent TV reception, with Pippo Baudo and Adriano Celentano beamed into their homes every Sunday afternoon. Potenza. Megliofiume. Pisticci. Irsina. Ferrandina. Bernalda. These are all cities where Mancanzano lives might begin anew. Miglionico. Taranto. Bari. Brindisi. Napoli. These are all places where people live above the land. And boast, when you ask them, of inhabiting the present.

This gloomy winter, it turned out there were two kinds of people left in the city: stalwarts for whom tufa was more important than bread (if only Bishop Pascoli or Padre Caduta would replace the Host for them with bits of stone!); and another wearied community who had been waiting patiently in the town for so long for a satisfactory excuse to leave it, but found that no excuse ever arrived there because nothing else ever did.

But now residents were leaving the city at the rate of five or six every week. And each time a new squadron abandoned the city, the remaining Mancanzani had to wonder if one of their departing neighbors might be a murderer: the *omicidio quadruplice*'s author, now on the oblithic lam. On the one hand, the idea of an absconding killer provided a particularly amoral familist sense of relief. If the four teenagers' deaths actually *were* homicides, Mancanzano's own miseries would now have come to an end, and other police departments in Italy could solve any successive murders. But, on the other, Major Martella knew that a serial killer's escape would only too clearly emphasize his own lethargic efforts at preventing more casualties.

To play it safe, the major established a series of checkpoints along the principal roads leading from town. To this end, his carabinieri interviewed Rino Ruggiero and family, with plans to open a shoe store in Potenza. They interviewed Umberto Curcio, going to live with his nieces in Taranto. They interviewed Aldo Padula, moving to Miglionico, where there had been the promise of factory work (a letter to this effect was withdrawn with great fuss from Signora Giovanna Padula's bust). The carabinieri even interviewed Dr Stoppani every time he headed to Montescaglioso to visit Anna, and, again, every time he headed to Bari to try to woo back his wife.

'*Come sta, Dottore?* How are you?' the officers would ask amiably, accustomed to his recurrent trips.

'Working,' he'd answer. 'I've never had so much to do. I've never been busier.'

'Well, we'll expect full reports,' the twenty-year-olds would laugh. 'You can't expect us to let you pass through our roadblocks this quickly unless you're willing to keep us entertained! You don't want us to get bored out here, do you?'

'I'm sure I would hate it.'

And so the carabinieri would solicit tidbits about Dr Stoppani's amorous affairs. And then, at the first chance they got, they would pass that information to everyone else in town.

So this is the setting against which I was now at work. With every motion the officers made to interview someone abandoning life in Mancanzano (and to amuse themselves at Dr Stoppani's expense), I'd redouble my own efforts to interview someone who was staying put. The map that Linda and I had acquired of Mancanzano's sassi when we first arrived in town was slowly succumbing to the crosshatching of pencil marks, Xs and indelible circles. Now, when we held the white sheets up to the sky, pinholes of Lucanian sun shone through the paper at creases.

I conducted an interview with a Signor Federico Freccero. It was a Saturday afternoon, and he was sitting outside of his home in the sassi, chewing a licorice stick he'd bought from one of the local kids when I arrived at his door.

He said, 'I'm going to tell you about cheating on my wife.'

I said, 'I thought you were going to tell me about life in the sassi.'

He said, 'I'm going to tell you about cheating on my wife in the sassi. Now, *zitto*, listen.'

Federico Freccero was forty-seven years old, with the first strains of gray starting to show in his hair. His jaw was square, and his look was smug. He said he'd been married for twenty-five years to the same woman who went away on weekends to visit cousins he refused to visit himself. After one such weekend, she came home to find a pair of earrings on their bedroom dresser: the remains of an afternoon encounter between Signor Freccero and a zaftig, neighborhood friend.

'My wife saw them before I did. She picked them up in her hand. And she wanted to know where they'd come from,' he told me. 'Now, this was a pair of earrings that were obviously not hers. Well, if you're going to cheat on your wife like I do, you've got to be quick on a lie. And it's got to be a solid lie. And you've got to stick to it no matter what.

'So here's what I told her: I said I'd found them in the train from Ferrandina to Potenza, where I often pretend to go for work. I told her I brought them all the way home to see if she wanted them. And I told her: "I put them on the dresser so that you'd see them." Then I asked her: "Do you want them? Do you want them, *amore*?" Well, my *amore* said, "No." So I grabbed the earrings from the dresser, and I threw them into the trash. The important thing is that my wife saw me do this. She watched the little baubles land in the garbage. Needless to say, later that night I was on my knees, fishing around for them in the kitchen. And I gave the earrings back to the woman who left them, and I told her: "Wear them wherever you like. But never wear them in Mancanzano."'

'That's an interesting story,' I asked him, 'but why are you telling me?'

He shrugged his shoulders, and then took another bite of the licorice stick. 'Everyone else in Mancanzano knows the story already. That is, except for you and my wife.'

I interviewed another man who told me, with the greatest of relish, stories of two decades of infidelities. To no great surprise, he was an old friend of Signor Freccero's. He said, 'If you're going to want to tape this, bring an extra cassette. Because you're going to need hours for me.'

A month before, Pier Paolo Sofri's wife had finally left him. He said: 'I met Bettina when we were in *liceo*. We were together from the age of sixteen. In some ways, we were just like the rest of the kids running around here. Some of those condoms you see littered in the caves may even be my own. Now I'll tell you a secret: I don't believe in God. But I believe in the Church. Because that's where I meet the women I sleep with.'

I sat in a hard-backed chair before Signor Sofri, rapt. He wanted to make sure my tape recorder was rolling. It was.

Then he said, 'Ah, religion! *Grazie, Gesù*! You know when the women say, "*Guardami, Cristo, riscaldami e infiammami col tuo santissimo amore*"? Well, that really gets me going. I'd love to meet the *suore* who wrote that! And you know when we line up for communion? That's really wonderful. Because that's

112

when you get to see the women, one on one. That's when you get to see them *chew*!

'Now I've always been very consistent,' Signor Sofri continued. 'I cheated on Bettina before and after we were married. So it's not like, all of a sudden, I did something different! Sure, sometimes I slept with her friends, but she was always so happy that I got along with them so well. Sometimes, she'd go on and on about this friend or that whose husband wouldn't let her girlfriends into the house. Well, I was never like that. Our door was always wide open to every last one of them. Whatever the time of the day.

'Now, don't get me wrong. When I was in my early twenties, I actually experimented a little bit with being faithful. So I know what it is, and I know what I'm talking about. But like I say, I am a Catholic. So when I go to church and watch the women kneel at their pews, how am I supposed to stop looking at their ankles? I mean, the young ones, the pretty ones, the ones who don't wear any stockings! The hardest thing about being in a committed relationship like I am, is I always have to hurry up Bettina on Sunday mornings if I don't want us to be late for Mass. And I always have to remind her, if she passes Bishop Pascoli on the street, to stop and chat with him. To say hello. Because that man truly has the keys to the kingdom of God.

'You see, when I was younger,' Signor Sofri went on, 'I even thought for a while about studying for the priesthood. To be closer to the Virgin Mary, of course. But then I realized I'd be able to find bounties of virgins in other places too. I suppose as far as Bettina was concerned, the obvious thing would have been not to have married her once I knew I'd never be faithful. But I also figured what she didn't know would never hurt her – so it's her fault, not mine, that she found out. After all, the Vedova Ruspoli always gave me a hunk of pecorino for Bettina after our trysts. And Elena Mazzone always gave me a liter of milk. So I was a provider! You can't say I didn't treat Bettina right!'

Here, Sofri paused. 'Now, the Church, as you know, frowns

on divorce. Even if it's legal in Italy now. So that's another reason I love the Church. And the Pope. And Bishop Pascoli. And even Padre Caduta. Because otherwise I understand my behavior could start getting costly, and I want to save my money for charity. But if you want to talk to Bettina – you know, to get her side of the story – you can find her in Potenza. She's living there now. That's what I'm told. One of Major Martella's men interviewed her as she was driving there the other week. Poor Bettina. She swore to the officer that I'd killed those kids they found in the caves. But as everyone knows, I'd never hurt anyone. Not a soul. The Church is my witness.'

I interviewed a man who'd worked as a management consultant in Turin, a *consulente di organizzazione aziendale*. I met him at his office, around the corner from Piazza Ridola.

He offered me coffee, and then he said: 'This is what I learned after spending four years in the north. When you work with manufacturers, one of the issues you tackle is supplier-customer relations. Let's say, for example, that a manufacturer has a supplier. Fiat needs parts to put in its cars. Well, over time, that supplier becomes critical. It's been meeting Fiat's needs, it's customized its own factories over the years, and beyond that there's a certain amount of loyalty the two of them feel. But, now, let's say that Fiat gets a reference from a colleague about another supplier – with better quality to offer, or better value. Let's say that Fiat finds that there are all sorts of parts available to it in France. Well, if Fiat is smart, it doesn't go and drop the first supplier right away. But it tries out this new one at the same time. And maybe it does business with both of them for a while. So it's like that with women. When you're comfortable with one, and she's meeting your needs – she's a great companion and you're having a great time – you still want to try out other suppliers. And that's what the south of Italy needs to learn if it's ever truly going to be competitive in business.'

'What does that have to do with the sassi?' I had to ask him.

'I'm thinking globally.'

I interviewed a man who told me how he came home one morning after spending the night at another woman's house. It was nearly a year ago, it was spring, and the local flowers had begun to bloom. So he paused at the market in Piazza Ridola and bought as many bouquets as he could hold in his arms. When he got home, he festooned the flowers around his house. Then he went to sleep.

When his wife arrived home later that day – she'd been away – he said she looked around their apartment and saw all the flowers, and she told him, beaming, 'At last, you've figured out how to treat me!'

In each of the crevices, in each of the hills of Mancanzano, there is a story to be told, and another waiting to unfold. The stones keep secrets until they're turned to dust. Then they spread their words into the wind.

These men talk about cheating because it's unimportant. But the essential tales they keep close to their breasts.

I asked one man if he'd ever cheated on his wife. 'I only cheat on my mother!' he shot back. Then he pressed a framed picture of her to his chest.

# Chapter 9
# Pica and the Madonna

In the mornings and afternoons, our interviews continue.

On Via delle Belle Pietre, Margherita Bianchi says no greater pleasure exists on the planet than to share a peach for the first time with a tiny baby who before that has only tasted milk.

On Via Folletto, Filippa Grossoglio sits on her sasso's roof, plucking her leg hairs with a pair of tweezers. She says the wispy hairs dust the entire city. She loosens her grip until the hairs are aloft, marveling, 'When I was a girl, the only thing growing on my skin was fuzz. So I never imagined this swelling, these curves. Who knew getting older would mean getting equipped?' Today, the teenager's hairs are intimations and keepsakes. The wind carries them farther than the most carefully applied scents.

Across the street, Nino Gabrieli stands on his own roof, practicing his bird calls. He flaps his arms like wings for emphasis. A hundred meters away, Fedelina Soppresa hangs the wash from her balcony, with the pants and shirts pinned together, populating the sky with an army of headless soldiers. One day, while passing underneath, Tonio Archimede, the tufa craftsman, gets it into his mind to design faces to place at the top of each laundry body, and he carves them from stone to resemble the four dead teens. Next, he convinces Signora Soppresa to let him affix the faces to four good clean shirts.

The effigies of the teens now watch over Mancanzano, their

flimsy cloth bodies flapping in the wind.

'Have you seen my daughter?' Angela's father asks, and boasts, pointing to the clothesline, where his daughter's face sits atop a flowered blouse. 'She's still the prettiest girl in Mancanzano!'

Meanwhile, there's still a city to discover. We keep to our interviews, gathering information wherever we can.

On Via Argia, Lilliana Alberghetti keeps the mirrors inside her home covered with newspaper. She doesn't want her guests looking at anyone but her. You sit in her apartment, trapped in time. She talks about the 1950s like they were yesterday. But last week exists for her in the impossible future: it's a time that can't be recalled because she's not so sure it even existed.

'Certain lies have been passed off as fact,' she avows.

The magazines and newspapers in her living room have been published decades apart. The first lunar landing is still bigger news than last week's parliamentary debates. But aside from a few atemporal idiosyncrasies, Signora Alberghetti is a good host. She keeps enquiring: 'Can I offer you coffee? Can I get you some tea?' True, she hides visitors' shoes because she doesn't want them to leave. But once you manage to spot them, you'll see they've been polished until they gleam.

On Via Sant'Isaia, in the midst of the sassi, Gianluca Porfiri looks at tattered advertisements from a back issue of *Life* that he must have swiped from Signora Alberghetti. He admires the photographs. He looks at them wistfully, and laments: 'I wish I had a lawn mower. I wish I had a refrigerator the size of skyscrapers. I wish I owned a cowboy hat.'

And on Via Incertezza, Giulio Nardo sprays insect repellent throughout his house. We've been told that he's been doing it for years. One day, he saw a spider. The next day, ants. The next day, something snapped and he went ballistic. He's been spraying the repellent for so long that he's begun to absorb the poison himself. He's like a distant relative of Rappaccini. He opens his mouth. Insects flee.

Of course, the four dead teenagers' appetites for tufa still had to be explained. The autopsies hadn't identified anything unusual in their blood – neither narcotics, toxins nor man-made poisons, not even a slight mineral deficiency that might have provided a useful clue. The causes of death were still a mystery, as were the related mechanisms of death (a separate forensic category addressing the physiological changes a body undergoes after injury or disease; a car crash is a 'cause', while internal hemorrhaging is the consequent 'mechanism').

But while the major's Mancanzano-based inquest possessed noticeable structure, if not any fact-finding flesh, at least the Potenza pathologists had been able to attribute the teenagers' craving for stone to acute cases of 'pica', a little-known eating disorder with both psychological and nutritional roots. So the high deputy and Dr Stoppani (now working in tandem with Major Martella, who by late February had begun expressing interest in exploring more commonly accepted investigative routes) co-ordinated for a new expert to visit Mancanzano from beyond its city limits and offer a lecture on the strange culinary indisposition.

This visit was to be nothing like the one before it by Professor Ugolino of the Istituto Centrale del Restauro in Rome. Dr Benedetto Biaggi, with a private practice treating eating disorders in Messina, Sicily (plus seasonal dermatology in Taormina), arrived in Mancanzano, having hitchhiked all the way from the Calabrian town of San Giovanni in Fiore, where he'd stopped to conduct field research on a family of three girls, all of them suffering from bulimia nervosa.

Dr Biaggi arrived in Mancanzano onboard a truck delivering timber to Foggia, and jumped from the cabin with a single leather bag slung across his shoulder. He wore a broad hat, turned down at the brim. His shirt was covered with food stains – what appeared to be splatters of tomato sauce, olive oil, coffee and peas.

Our specialist was by no account a trim man, and it had been a minor spectacle to watch Dr Biaggi leap from the truck and onto the road without toppling over. Waddling before us, he possessed the lumbering grace of a seal on land. Linda and I had accompanied Dottoressa Donabuoni, Dr Stoppani and Major Martella to Via Annunziatella on Mancanzano's outskirts, and we'd waited there for Dr Biaggi for a half-hour – during which time the major kept shooting me menacing glances whenever he thought the high deputy wouldn't see. But our attentions were all focused on the doctor from the moment he stood before us. We saw that his stomach extended substantially past his belt, and that he had the unsettling habit of flitting his fingers nervously as he spoke. Which now he did.

'You should have seen those crazy girls, I tell you!' he gushed, fingers aflutter. '*Dio, che malattie*! There were three of them, all in their late teens or early twenties. And all of them single and living at home. And without a *mamma*, which tears the heart into pieces all by itself! So the girls would take turns cooking. And they'd spend all day talking about what they were going to make. Agnello alle olive. Penne al forno. Braciolette piccanti.' Here, he pointed to the green on his shirt. 'And they really could cook! That's piselli con le uova. A savory dish, let me assure you.' He patted his stomach with a look of fond reminiscence. 'So I said to them – I mean, after witnessing the vomiting episodes myself – "If I'd known you were just going to spit the food out, then I'd have helped myself to seconds."'

Now Dr Biaggi paused long enough for the rest of us to speak. Even if, for the moment, we were all equally flabbergasted.

The High Deputy for Public Works tried first. 'Welcome to Mancanzano,' she said guardedly, but warmly, before extending a hand.

Dr Biaggi sized her up, licking a fingertip with uncertain intent. '*Dottoressa, piacere*. I am very happy to meet you. Very happy, indeed.' He paused, still sucking. Then he added: 'After

119

so much time in San Giovanni in Fiore, let me add that your matronly heft comes as a refreshing surprise.'

Dottoressa Donabuoni blanched, obviously taken aback. Major Martella, and the rest of us, offered our hellos as shrewdly as possible.

'Hello,' I told him.

'Hello,' said Linda.

'Hello,' said Major Martella. 'We spoke on the phone.'

'Hello,' said Dr Stoppani. 'Nice bag. Nice hat.'

Dr Biaggi considered the remainder of our group; I wasn't at all certain he was pleased. Then, as we began the ten-minute walk toward town from Via Annunziatella, he returned to his story, perhaps now showing moderate strains of annoyance at having been interrupted by our greetings.

'You see,' he continued, starting off slowly, then quickening his phrasing into an air-guitar arpeggio, 'I'd never have gone to San Giovanni in Fiore to check into the bulimia if two of the sisters hadn't been arrested after a bout of kleptomania. I know what you're thinking! You're thinking, it doesn't get any more symptomatic than that! But the most colorful part of the story is the sisters were caught stealing a ten-liter tub of chocolate-hazelnut gelato. Can you picture these girls, these wispy little rascals, not much more than forty kilos apiece, bent over like broken celery stalks from the weight of the tub! Well, when the store manager tried to stop them from hobbling away with their booty, they made a scene. In fact, they made so much of a scene that a small contingent of carabinieri had to come. Then one of the sisters called a police officer "a fat-sucking bastard", and actually tried to bite him. So that's when the carabinieri escorted them to jail.

'But that's also where everything got even more interesting!' Dr Biaggi continued. 'The girls' father fumed when he learned what his daughters had done! So he insisted they spend a few hours behind bars to teach them a little lesson. Now, he'd been promised his daughters would be kept in a cell by themselves, which they were. But what happened is that all of the jail cells were attached, so it didn't take long for the other prisoners to start clamoring. They were screaming and shouting, and rattling the heels of their shoes against the bars! It was a lot of noise. Even for a town in Calabria. So a guard came back to see what was preventing him from taking a few hours' nap. And it was obvious from the moment he got there. The girls had swallowed a load of ice cream back at the shop, and with all the ruckus they hadn't been given a chance to purge. So they were petrified about absorbing the calories, and they figured the time was now.'

Here Dr Biaggi broke off. We'd all been walking beside him as he produced his story (the same way, perhaps, a squirrel produces nuts from its cheeks), and by now we'd arrived from Mancanzano's penumbra to the heart of the sassi. It was six o'clock, and the late winter evening had sneaked up around us. The light from the cave houses perforated the darkness, limning the shadows with an eerie glow.

We stood at the overlook at Via della Vergine, not far from Padre Caduta's parish church. For a moment, Dr Biaggi startled us with his silence. He leaned against the rail that separated us from the deep, dark slope – watching the beehive of cave homes that piled before him, rising from the foot of the canyon, which was already swallowed in black. But then Dr Biaggi straightened, and his fingers danced and clinked nervously against the metal rail. He took a step backwards, and then licked his fingertips once, as if to indicate that he was going to speak.

'But enough about the girls,' the doctor said finally. 'I've been to San Giovanni in Fiore several times, and bulimia's the kind of thing I run into every day. You might even say that it's my bread and butter. But this is my first time visiting Mancanzano, and the problems here, as your major explained them to me on the phone, are completely different. And pernicious. And, I don't mind saying, completely weird.'

'Is that your scientific assessment?' Dr Stoppani asked skeptically.

'No, my scientific assessment,' Dr Biaggi replied, 'can only be based on what I witness first-hand.'

'But it *is* weird,' Linda told them.

'I'll tell you right now, it's as weird as it gets!' Dr Biaggi exclaimed. 'But eventually we'll devise some other nomenclature for it. Now, in the meantime' – here, he looked to his watch – 'let's do something really useful. I base this on research. Let's eat.'

And so this was our introduction to Dr Biaggi. We accompanied him to the Trattoria Lucana, where Dr Stoppani hadn't returned since our pre-Christmas dinner. Linda, Dottoressa Donabuoni and I piled around a table, with our Messinese expert sliding unhappily with his back to the wall. Dottoressa Donabuoni sat across from the doctor, looking flummoxed and annoyed; Linda, in more jovial spirits, tried on the doctor's wide-brimmed hat, which swallowed her head as capaciously as a giant anaconda.

Dr Stoppani hadn't been able to resist checking the ladies room for signs of his wife when we'd arrived at the restaurant, but once he reached our table (haplessly unescorted), he ordered wine and gallantly led us in a toast: 'To Dottor Biaggi, may you be our *deus ex machina*. May you help us find the things that we lack.'

Major Martella didn't stay for dinner, but he seconded Dr Stoppani's toast before he left. 'Yes,' he told Dr Biaggi, 'may you be the one who helps solve Mancanzano's mysteries, but not one who takes too much credit for it.'

'Oh, don't worry!' Dr Biaggi answered the major. 'Even if I *do* take credit wherever it's due, I always make sure there's an ample chance for people to congratulate me on their own.'

Then Dr Biaggi drained his glass, filled it again, and took it with him as he began circling the restaurant. Before we realized what was happening, the doctor had removed a handful of embossed cards from his bag, and he was handing them out to waiters and patrons alike, telling them, 'I'm giving you my telephone number because I see that you take your food seriously. So feel free to call me, day or night.'

He didn't sit back down with us until he saw the tray of plates arrive at our table.

The following day Dr Biaggi made his presentation in the second-floor auditorium of the Seminario Lanfranchi, in Piazza Ridola. I think everyone who had caught sight of him the day before was gratified to see that he'd changed his shirt to one without stains, and that he had even gone so far as to unsling his bag and remove his hat – which was really much more than anyone had hoped for.

The lecture on the enigmatic eating disorder known as 'pica' was open to the public, and about two hundred people from around Mancanzano filled the room, including the previous night's diners, the Calabrian students, Major Martella's carabinieri and assorted officials, like Dottoressa Donabuoni and other high and mid-level deputies. Even Mancanzano's mayor, Luciano Taciuto, who'd been re-elected term after term on a vigorously anarchist platform of forswearing both gifts and accountability, came to hear the doctor's presentation. Various citizens now tried to greet the major with handshakes. He regarded them suspiciously, consenting to only a few gingery clasps. Leery of making any easily misconstrued signs of electoral co-operation, Mayor Taciuto would lower his head and thrust his hands into his pant pockets the moment his well-wishers stepped away.

But at the front of the auditorium, Dr Biaggi reigned over the podium. Whatever energy there was in the room (somehow it felt palpable and real, since it was born out of our mass expectation) channeled its way from the audience into the doctor's hands, and, from there, into the rest of his body, which shook sympathetically. Then, once the crowd had quieted, the doctor began.

First, he described pica as a compulsive eating disorder where sufferers crave substances that anyone would be hard-pressed to classify as food. (As Dr Biaggi explained it, the name for the disorder comes from the Latin word for 'magpie': the bird's genus is *pica*, and magpies are famous for their omnivorous appetites.) Then the doctor told us about the two most common manifestations of the obsession: 'geophagia', the eating of mineral-rich clay and dirt, usually by pregnant women in Africa; and what he called 'apokoptophagia', the nibbling of paint flakes by children around the world, which is still the pre-eminent cause of lead poisoning today.

But there are plenty of other kinds of pica, Dr Biaggi explained, now really beginning to savor his talk. (He had a heap of breadsticks with him on the podium that he'd pocketed from the Trattoria Lucana, and he ate them as he spoke, now crunching hungrily.)

'Pica is a wretchedly misunderstood disorder!' Dr Biaggi told the audience. 'And there are plenty of psychosocial implications accompanying the obvious nutritional concerns! People wonder why their loved ones have begun hoarding toilet-bowl fresheners! A husband one day came into my office and confessed that his wife had taken to licking the dust from their window blinds. You can imagine how this fellow was beside himself with anguish! First, he threw up his hands, then he pointed a finger just below his waist. And then he confided, "Somehow, my wife still has the nerve to say I'm disgusting when I suggest she lick me *there*!"'

Dr Biaggi took another bite of a breadstick, and smiled appealingly while his fingers cha-chaed across the lectern. 'Excuse my frankness, but I am a doctor. And I am an expert. And, above all, I am objective. I just want you to understand the peculiar nature of what we're confronting.'

Then Dr Biaggi offered a laundry list of documented substances that pica-sufferers have eaten with ravenous delight. The examples began with the vaguely edible, like toothpaste, salt, uncooked rice, whole coffee beans, baking powder and freezer frost shavings – until they turned into the recipe for a

124

genuinely gruesome diet: chalk, coal, unhardened plaster and cement, foam rubber, mothballs, sand, soot, soap, toilet paper and matted balls of human hair. Some of the manifestations had elaborate names: 'amylophagia', 'pagophagia', 'stachtophagia', 'xylophagia'; that is, picas for starch, ice, cigarette ashes and wooden toothpicks.

'Now, as I understand it,' Dr Biaggi said, 'there has been an epidemic in Mancanzano of lithophagia, which is the eating of stones, pebbles and rocks. Sometimes, picas are linked to an iron deficiency in the blood – at least, that's what the scientific literature tells us. But the forensic reports from Potenza so far haven't demonstrated that. So if the teenagers were eating the stone, it wasn't because of anything wrong with their diets.'

'That's because people in Mancanzano have always been eating tufa,' a voice called out from the audience. It came from a man who appeared to be well into his eighties, and who was quietly gnawing a chunk of the local stone.

But the old man's observation did little to rattle Dr Biaggi. 'Ah, there's a subtle distinction there!' he cooed. 'There's a difference between . . . now, how do I put it? What's done because it's folk medicine or custom, and what's done because the subjects are so out-of-their-minds *pazzi* that they are willing to eat rock from a wall. And they don't mind grating their faces like hunks of parmigiano reggiano to do it! You understand, I'm speaking non-clinically, of course.'

Dr Biaggi leaned forward on the lectern, his fingers atwirl on its outer edge. 'Now, don't think me naïve,' he continued to the audience. 'I've read all of the reports! The trip from San Giovanni in Fiore to Mancanzano is a long time to spend in a truck! So I know that the victims found in the caves exhibited their picas in the most exhibitionist fashion. Which was without their clothes. Which adds a psychosexual element to the disorder that not even my trio of motherless bulimic sisters could have imagined! And I don't mean just sexual! But fetishistic and scatological too! Because I don't want to have to tell you right here, while so many of you are wearing your finest clothes, what eating rocks will do to your digestive tracts. Although, if pressed to explain, I will.'

During this last segment of his speech, Dr Biaggi had begun to perspire. The fabric of his shirt had become stuck to his chest, and the sides of the apparel were now pulling away from each other at the buttons. Towards the back of the auditorium, the elderly gentleman who'd launched Dr Biaggi on this latest diatribe gnawed again at the piece of tufa. He smiled amiably. You could see that his teeth were bad. Many of them were chipped. A mummified woman next to him, most likely the walking remains of his wife, elbowed his side, irritated. The man took a final lick of the stone, then tucked it into his shirt pocket. Dr Biaggi plucked at his own shirt, separating the damp cloth from his skin, while he stared back at the couple with a flushed face and dilated eyes.

Then he continued, 'Look, all I am saying is that for some reason teenagers in your town were eating the walls. Which maybe wasn't so good for them, if you give it some thought! Now maybe that's what killed them, and maybe it's not. And maybe, like the gentleman in the audience says, eating tufa is good for your body, if not exactly for your teeth. But it will take more investigation until we know for sure! It will require a little more research until I can predict if more of you are going to die. So, in the meantime, I want you all to relax. Take comfort in knowing that I'm here. Just think of the advantages of having a doctor of my stature among you!'

The roomful of Mancanzani looked at Dr Biaggi, nonplussed.

'Now, before I go,' Dr Biaggi offered finally, 'I want to say one last thing about pica, which is about this fellow with the wife. The one who licked the blinds, as I'm sure you all remember. And now I'm going to ask everyone in the room to close their eyes and picture her doing that . . . There, can you picture her tongue? The dirt? The grime? Well, when this man learned that his wife's condition was diagnosable and treatable,

126

he was very relieved. And the problem *was* treated. And she was cured! And I want you to know, I have seen this man kissing his wife, and it is an awesome sight. It is a powerful sight! And, most importantly, it is a hygienic sight. The raw beauty of their kisses fills me with joy. It is a physically stirring kind of joy. I've shown films of it to colleagues, and even they ask for copies. So when I think of this joy, I want you to know it makes me ecstatic. Because it reminds me how much I've been of help!'

Dr Biaggi took a final bite of his breadstick. More crumbs spilled down his shirt, and stuck to the damp cloth. He smiled toothily, and said, only, 'I'm here to help.' But with his arms and hands jiggling, the skin of his face glistened with excitation and sweat. He wiped at his forehead with the back of a hand. The writhing fingers looked like a clump of maggots.

At the front of the room, Dr Biaggi surveyed the audience with a look of entitlement. The Calabrian students, scattered teenagers and Major Martella's carabinieri mixed in the room with the much-older residents of the city. But ripened or fresh-picked, the doctor scrutinized them all as if they were dinner.

The following day, Major Martella brought Dr Biaggi to the caves where the teenagers had died. Fortune accompanied the pair in his official capacity as the only university-trained geologist in Mancanzano who routinely worked for free, and he helped Dr Biaggi take samples of the walls and earth. As soon as Fortune knocked a few shards of the stone loose, Dr Biaggi touched a fingerful of tufa to his tongue.

He spat it out with a look of disgust.

Then Dr Biaggi glanced at Major Martella, and said, 'Don't worry. I've treated anorexics in Capri who were afraid to swallow their own saliva. So I'm sure whatever's going on in town will turn out to be nothing.'

'It's something already,' the major offered.

Dr Biaggi shrugged uneasily. As if to satisfy both Major Martella and himself, he stuck another finger to the wall, and he

127

tasted the powder a second time. Dr Biaggi spat again. 'There's definitely no confusing this with anything generally regarded as tasty!' he exclaimed.

'No,' said Fortune, touching the fragmented stone to his own lips. 'It's not even as flavorless as leftover porridge.'

But Major Martella took a more judicious approach. 'The problem in Mancanzano,' he told the two, 'isn't people eating bits of tufa. The *real* problem is that the dead kids aren't coming back to life. Because if they were, there wouldn't be a single unsatisfied person left in Mancanzano – except for maybe the dead teenagers themselves. But I'd hardly have to worry about them complaining!'

Dr Biaggi took a final taste of tufa, perhaps just to make sure there wasn't something he was missing.

Meanwhile, in the first of the caves, where the initial set of teenagers were found, Middelhoek and his Calabrian assistants have been working steadily at restoring the fresco. They've removed more whitewash, dirt and soot with moistened slices of Signora Bitonto's bread, and they've stripped off more layers of paint with AB57. Now, the imagery has further metamorphosed on the wall. As part of their field trip, Dr Biaggi, Fortune and Major Martella found themselves standing before the painting and gawking.

With the *a secco* coloring removed from the surface, the apostles have disappeared from the wall, transforming into apparitions. In their place, just above the anthrophagic cherub devouring human flesh, there is a new scene of the castigation of sinners. A herd of men and women have been shackled to one another at their wrists and necks, and they are being escorted into the underworld by a group of obsidian-colored demons. The penitents' clothes have been stripped from their bodies and strewn on the ground, and their expressions combine hysteria with dread. As Middelhoek recounts it, the pictures triggered twitters from the Calabrians when they were first revealed, and also prompted a second wave of them to cross their chests.

After the influence of the Greeks, the demons on the wall all sport enormous phalluses. Some of them have already employed their organs to drill an array of holes into the ground. In turn, the penitents have been planted inside up to their necks, and the cherubim loom above with their same insatiable expressions, ready to smash chunks of tufa down on their heads. At the base of the holes, where the human beings are buried, their bones and their flesh have begun transforming into tufa, to fade into the earth like dust over sand. An epitaph of three words appears beneath the scene, reading simply: *HOC EST PURGATORIO*.

The fresco, according to Middelhoek, is older than anyone originally thought. Perhaps it dates back to the third century AD or even earlier, when Magna Graecia could still be remembered, when the lairs that Horace reported on were still full of vipers and bears, and the people of Mancanzano knew they had warnings to tell. In any case, it predates the sixth-century arrival of the Benedictines to Mancanzano. Those monks' parables were of asceticism and grace, not of cherubic bone- and brain-smashers, and penises as potent as pneumatic drills.

So is that why the Benedictines fled? Is that why they left their city to a new wave of residents? Upon discovering the frescoes where they sought to pray, the monks must have understood their home as a refuge for stone-cold angels of death. And then done whatever they could to cover the images in the fresco quick.

But today the pica of Mancanzano isn't limited to a hunger for stones. It's a pica to unearth, to find things that are new without leaving your city. To do that you dig, wherever you are. Explore the unknown by exploring one another.

Discover a hole. Then try to fill it.

I walk through the sassi, looking for stories. Via Bradano. Via Argia. Via Sant'Isaia. On Via Folletto, a cluster of teenagers are outside a home. Someone has a radio, and the group of them are dancing. '*Ventiquattromila baci*', goes the music. 'Twenty-four thousand kisses', goes the song.

Three boys shimmy, grinding their hips under the sun. A girl dances beside them, barely willing to face them: proximity's all that she's willing to offer. Her hair hides her features, shaking as a veil. The ends of it lick at her chin and neck.

Another teenager sits on a chair, dandling a baby no more than six months old. It's Filippa Grossoglio, the girl from the roof – only a baby's legs have less hair than hers do. As the radio plays, Filippa's own legs fan out beneath her, bouncing, stepping and gyrating at the ankles, the taut skin of each catching reflections of sun. Is the baby her brother or sister? A niece or nephew, a cousin, what? Filippa moves the infant's arms to the music. But she isn't careful. The baby cries. Then she tries to calm it in ways the teenage boys like. Good things happen when Filippa moves her arms together. There's an appreciativeness in the boys' faces just beyond the infant's own.

But the boys want more. Boys usually do. They want Filippa to join them on her feet. You know this because without interrupting their dancing, they have left the other girl alone. Now all six of their eyes are on Filippa. 'Dance, dance!' they urge her spiritedly. She shakes her head, smiling. 'Dance, dance!' they shout. Then they use their own bodies to demonstrate how. Hips swivel. Pelvises sway. Torsos quiver. Faces take on a series of rhythmic expressions. 'Your toes are a tease,' one of the boys says to her, grinding.

This is too much. The other girl stops dancing, and sits down huffily. The boys still ignore her. So she walks to the radio, and shuts it off. But she's messed with the music. That is wrong. One of the teenagers switches it on again, increasing the volume. '*Frasi d'amore appassionate!*' the metal box squeals through the sassi. The baby starts crying again. Filippa's unbothered. The other girl says something crude to them all, and takes off.

I catch up with her on Via La Murgia. She's in a foul mood, but appreciates my attention. 'Whose baby was that?' I ask her.

'Was it the other girl's family's? A sister or brother?'

The teenager scowls. 'What does it matter? Why should I care? I don't know why Filippa insists on keeping them around!'

⁓

Discover a hole. Then plumb it deeper. As our work compiling ethnographies continues, I've gone back to visit the Vedova La Calamita, the woman I interviewed when we first arrived in Mancanzano, whose husband's bones were swapped for the detritus of afternoon trysts. I think I am drawn to her because she is a victim; because in a city of hidden agendas, emotions and houses, I see her as frail. So now I have come to her to ask her how she lost her sight. Because in a city of subterfuge, I want to know how she became weak.

The old woman was seated outside her cave home the last time I saw her. Like all old women here, she was dressed in black, relying on the old restitched garment to absorb whatever heat it could from the sun.

Now, when I brought up her blindness, she pointed a finger toward her eyes, and then she told me, 'This is the work of Santa Maria.' Her head bobbed back and forth naturally from her shoulders, and she continued, telling me candidly: 'It was the Madonna. Santa Maria of the sun. I'd look for her when I was still trying to have kids. Sometimes, she'll appear in the sun if you look for her long enough. Have you ever seen her?'

I told her no.

'But your mother has seen her? Or other people you know?'

'I don't think so,' I answered. But it was what I'd suspected. There were stories I'd heard, and tales I had read, of women so devout that they burned their retinas in search of God. This was the work of Maria, alas, and not of Santa Lucia. The old widow's eyes were eggs that had sizzled in their shells.

Then she asked me suspiciously, 'You mean, in America, people don't see the Madonna in the sun? But Maria is everywhere! She's all around us! So why don't you see her?'

131

'I don't know,' I told her. I didn't know how else to answer her.

But the old woman knew. 'No, I'll explain it to you,' she replied, and now her face had the sort of chiseled certainty that you see in a statue that will exist unchanged for a thousand years. 'It's what you Americans do to yourselves,' she said. 'You can't see the Madonna because there's too much pollution.'

The old woman was convinced. So it didn't matter if she couldn't see. Her conviction was what gave her strength, even if it was also what had taken part of it away. But better to surrender your vision searching for God than to lose it looking for flying saucers. Or by watching a mere solar eclipse. The old woman's certainty afforded her spirit, and it gave her as much moxie as the stone-hurling cherubim in the underground fresco. She had the tenacity of a woman who had been fired upon, and who had been blinded and barren, but had not yet given in to the throttlehold of frailty. Or to the monotony of life slowly creaking on as a widow.

Then the old woman said, 'The beautiful thing about Maria is that even if I can't see much else, I can still see her. I can see her hair.'

She smiled and she laughed, and when she did, there was a vibration to her body that reminded me of Dr Biaggi on the podium, and as this shimmying spread to the woman's legs and to her breast, it reminded me too of the rhythm of much younger girls dancing. Unlike the old couple at the doctor's lecture, with decrepit teeth that resembled mouthfuls of gravel, when the widow laughed I saw that her own teeth were as strong and resilient as small blocks of marble, and as durable as the terrible, wonderful fresco.

As I left the Vedova La Calamita in front of her sasso, the impression that stuck with me was one of persistence. A persistence that maybe it took a pica-sufferer to know – someone who would eat the inedible despite everyone else's grimaces. That perception of relentlessness stuck with me as I went back to the caves to look at the fresco, and when I met Dr Biaggi in town, dissecting and decrying the local cuisine. And it stuck with me as I interviewed more of the Mancanzani.

As the days followed each other in this southern town, and February flittered and wiggled like Dr Biaggi's fingers into March, I found myself thinking more and more of picas of bone, and of stone, and of stories, and of hair. Sometimes, I'd think of the Madonna's hair, now mixed with airborne wisps from the calves of Filippa Grossoglio (or from the long locks of her friend), and I'd see them in my mind, growing beyond blindness and beyond death. Then, I'd even look casually through my sunglasses at the sun for signs of a flaxen cable, a perfect coif, a wild tangle, a gorgon's hair, a bob, or a braid with a ribbon encircling it like a phylactery or like a whip – and then I'd look for these in the women of Mancanzano. But mostly when I was alone in the city, or when a young girl scrambled across my path, I'd remember the plush touch of tresses across my face, fondling my features and caressing my chin, helical and heliacal, smelling of chamomile and mint, and I'd think of the grizzled Vedova La Calamita, instantly reborn, telling me the only thing she sees now is Maria. Blessed Maria. Blessed Godiva Berenice Rapunzel Maria. Maria for whom no sacrifice is too great. Or remotely unnatural. Or unexpected.

Maria for whom one should be willing to take a bite of a rock.

# PART TWO
# SPRING

# Chapter 10
# The First of Primavera

Last night, in a howling storm, Tonio Archimede's effigies came crashing down to the street. The faces he'd carved from the chunks of tufa split into shards, and before the wind and rain gave up in the early morning, they'd washed away every vestige of the faces of Mancanzano's four dead teens.

In the morning, Tonio Archimede, the parents of the teenagers, their friends, and Fedelina Soppresa (whose clothesline and clothes had provided the suspended gallery space), gathered on the sidewalk to wonder why the little that remained to them had now been flushed away too.

Angela's father – the grizzled one we shared our doubts about, who'd stood with his shirt off at the fiery Festa di Santa Lucia and had tried, even before that, to order a birthday cake for his dead daughter – placed an arm around Tonio Archimede's shoulder, commiserating the loss of their respective progenies.

'I know how you feel,' Angela's father told the craftsman wearily.

But others in Mancanzano said the storm was a sign to look forward. Padre Caduta took part in the gathering, making the trip to the piazzetta outside Fedelina's house from his parish church, halfway down the slope. If people wanted a benediction, then he'd be the one to give it.

'Maybe,' he told the group, 'last night's storm was a sign for us to start over. Maybe it was a sign for us to forge ahead. Or maybe it was just a sign from Heaven above us that we badly needed some rain. But, whichever it was, look around you.'

Here, Padre Caduta pointed with one hand across the creek, to the other side of the canyon. The caves and the crags were covered with asphodels, poppies, jasmine and clover. Even on the town's side of the stream, where the sassi lined the bluff, there was the unmistakable scent of thyme impregnating the air.

Somehow, in Mancanzano, spring had arrived. The season had slipped in while everyone was busy thinking about murder. But now March was here, and it had sneaked into the city overnight, arraying the bushes and trees with the gloss of colored blossoms and flowers, and festooning the ground and stone with great green swaths of mosses and grass. The storm had swept into Mancanzano, and brought the spring with it.

So spring had arrived. But what of it?

With the ides only days away, Major Martella was back talking about his favorite Caesar: the otherwise discredited criminologist Cesare Lombroso. Now that a new scientist was in Mancanzano – meeting the size, shape and stature of Benedetto Biaggi – the major was busily plying him for endorsement of Lombroso's anthropometric ideas. But the doctor's response was always the same (and unchanged from what the *medico legale* in Potenza had communicated to him from the very beginning): '*Non fai mica sul serio*'; that is, 'You've got to be kidding.'

But for his own part, Major Martella had grown so adamant in his support of Lombroso's ideas that we could only assume he'd come to believe in them himself. Which would have made sense, since Lombroso's techniques had already netted the major a smorgasbord of culinary treats; whereas his checkpoints, interviews, routine policework and co-ordination of Dr Biaggi's arrival in Mancanzano had yet to accomplish a single thing. So now the major began recommending that parents take routine measurements of their children, just to make sure no criminal tendencies unexpectedly popped up.

'A single stray millimeter!' he warned them all, direly. 'Just one extra millimeter can signify something really insidious.'

But the lesson of spring, no matter where you are, is always the same: renewal. Even if the current of a town's life is interrupted by death, eventually there's no choice but for it to move on. Not surprisingly, life then continues unchanged because there's no new model for it to rely on. True, in the last two weeks, assorted townsfolk have been continuing their exodus to neighboring towns, cramming into their cars like pioneers into spaghetti-western covered wagons, but others here have been re-exerting their roots to the town with the same insistence as the priapic demons. Because here is a fact that's as undeniable as the flow of seasons: when the hills turn verdant, and fertility returns to people's minds (inducing individual maypoles to stir in their breeches), not even the memory of death can paralyze all human passions.

In the last several days, Linda and I have returned to our ethnographies with a restored ferocity. In the face of death, what choice is there but to pursue the things that remind us that we are still alive?

On Via Ionico, the people of Mancanzano have been visiting the newly *signora*-ed Federica Bellini. She's twenty-three years old, and a new mother now. Friends arrive at her door with bundles of flowers. The wealthier ones come with bouquets of tulips, snapdragons and lilies bought on Via Ginosa and at the open-air market in Piazza Ridola; others bear rugged clumps of asphodels and grasses newly sprouted and plucked from the outskirts of town. Federica uses all the vases she owns, then she lets the flowers pile up on her mantel. She sticks them into bottles. She feeds the stems halfway down the drain of her kitchen sink.

'But aren't you going to want to cook there?' a friend asks judiciously, eyeing a bouquet that rises like weeds from under the water faucet.

Federica glances back with a look that hollers, *Are you crazy?* 'Cook?' she exclaims. 'I just gave birth! It's someone else's turn to do the work!'

Spring is here. But what of it? Our note-taking continues: on Via Bonifaccio, there is a girl who wears a red blouse because she has begun to menstruate. The shirt is a gift from her mother. She wears it as a badge of honor, incontrovertible proof of the arrival of womanhood. Now she knows she's a force to be reckoned with: men will want her. The girl doesn't want to wear tampons; she wants to bleed. Let it get all over everything, streak the couches, splatter the floors. What's a little cleaning in the awesome face of adolescence? She wears the blouse like it's a red ribbon for winning a race.

Spring is here. With a vengeance. Even the Vedova La Calamita would be proud. The Sunday before Easter, many of the town's residents – the women particularly – are making a pilgrimage to Count Tramontano's tomb, even if no one is certain precisely where it is. But on March 23, people collect in Piazza del Duomo after Mass. This gathering has all the trappings of a religious procession: the women carry wood rosaries, some go barefoot, others wear burlap sacks over their clothes, even if they're dressed to the nines underneath, with designer labels and their finest jewelry strung from their necks and pinned to their lapels.

Then the group walks the kilometer from town on the lookout for saints. Apparently, their chances of success are considered good; when you dress as they do (religiously fashionable and fashionably religious), I'm told you can spot a saint any second without having to stare at the sun. When the procession reaches the cave, the women pull off their sacks, put on their shoes, and they return their rosaries to their pockets or purses. Then they laugh. Then, after a burst of commotion, they hold a picnic.

'We're here because of Count Tramontano!' the women shriek frantically. 'Not someone we care about. So we don't have to mourn!'

A few in the group have visited the site the night before, and hidden bottles of wine in the bushes. Four hundred and sixty years later, the count's death is still something to celebrate. One of the few things in Mancanzano to celebrate. In spite of the season.

For the first time that anyone can remember, the March rains and warm weather have brought birds to Mancanzano. Kestrels are swarming over the canyon, building nests in crevices and depositing eggs in the miniature windows of the uninhabited sassi. The diamond-shaped openings of the stone houses and churches are lined with twigs and grasses, and filled with discordantly chirping chicks. There must be hundreds of the birds, or even more. Some townspeople say there haven't been so many winged creatures in Mancanzano for forty years, since before the Fascisti razed the town's one little forest. Now when you look out the window, the birds swarm through the air as thickly as schooling fish. But their voices fill the sky with a rapid, high-pitched *klee klee klee*.

The birds surprise everyone. In the evenings, when the Mancanzani take to the town's principal streets, on their *passeggiate* (and slightly briefer, microscopically more genteel *passeggiatine*), they don't know whether to look in front of them or to look down. These walks are a time for smiling and greeting, and, above all, for cutting fine figures and making dashing impressions. But now all that is in theory. Because, right now, the townspeople spend half of their wits looking out for droppings: indiscriminate splatters of white, green and black that show up on the soles of both the finest and flimsiest shoes alike. To some of the town's residents, this turn of events is more than upsetting. It's tantamount to destroying a culture. Because how can you stride when your gait is turned into hopscotch? How can you flirt with shit on your shoe?

Dr Stoppani, normally a fan of these evening strolls, customarily a man who operates at his best in such social situations, savvies the kestrels overhead and their effluvia splotching the street, and says only: '*Porca miseria*, these birds are cramping my style!'

But as far as the springtime *passeggiatine* across Piazza Ridola still remain feasible, Dr Stoppani's favorite companion for them is Dr Biaggi. (The gallivanting Barese says the rest of our group shuffle around clumsily; it's just not in our Dutch-Anglo-Saxon cultures to know how to saunter.) So when Dr Biaggi's not busy rejecting Major Martella's requests that he measure some part of someone or some detail of some thing, he joins Dr Stoppani on the early evening walks. The two of them stroll arm in arm. They laugh like two schoolgirls. They actually snigger.

It's been two weeks now since Dr Biaggi arrived in Mancanzano, and somehow Dr Stoppani and he have managed to acquire matching clothes. Linda noticed it first with their shoes – calf-skin moccasins of the very same hue. But it didn't take long until corresponding apparel had spread up their legs to their waists. Then it was only a matter of time before the two of them had matching blazers, which in Italy really means something special. Dr Biaggi's shirt still comes untucked from time to time, but now Dr Stoppani and he are like an old married couple, and Dr Stoppani doesn't mind scolding him about taking better care of his appearance.

'I have a reputation to uphold,' Dr Stoppani says earnestly, squeezing Dr Biaggi's arm tightly and pulling him close. 'So whatever you do, don't make me look bad.'

In the evenings, the two of them stroll Mancanzano's streets, drunk on prosecco. They point to the girls. Threesomes and foursomes comparing hair, shoes, boys, overbites, the shortest skirts. *Belle o brutte, si sposan tutte*. Pretty or ugly, all the girls marry.

'There's a chance for me yet,' Dr Biaggi says, hopefully. He sucks a finger lasciviously.

But the obviousness of the gesture casts Dr Stoppani into a lament. 'I had a chance once,' Dr Stoppani says. 'I had

Monica. But she always insisted that if I said I'd do something, then I actually had to do it. After a while, that became really unbearable.'

But Dr Biaggi answers him, still on their stroll, 'You know, Gaetano, there are plenty of chances. There are as many women as meals. So there's no use starving yourself.'

When they have finished their walks, you can spot Drs Stoppani and Biaggi in the trattorias, one of the several overlooking the sassi. The two of them sit wearing matching gabardine trousers, with their legs crossed. Dr Stoppani picks at his meal, fiddling through a bowl of spaghettini with the tines of his fork. But Dr Biaggi is another story: he progresses quickly to a plate of roasted venison, with a side order of oil-drenched artichoke hearts, plus potato gnocchi dripping with butter, peas with prosciutto, onion focaccia, plus an extra carafe of robust wine. It's a cornucopia spread out before him, with a full season's harvest and a hunting expedition's kill dumped onto his plate. At the other side of the table, Dr Stoppani smiles languidly, still picking at best from his bowl of cold pasta.

'Darling,' says Dr Biaggi, shaking his head, 'eat or you're going to lose muscle tone.' Then Dr Biaggi cuts a forkful of meat from his plate and chews it, enraptured. 'You know, it was the bulimics who taught me to enjoy my food,' he says. 'They're the ones who showed me that a good dinner was always worth suffering for.'

—

Which brings me again to the subject of spring, and the theme of renewal. By way of ethnography, here's what I've got.

Picture a town of stone, grown from the earth, like a busy beehive, teeming with conversations, aromas, love stories, intrigues, ancient frescoes, ancient churches, sex. Once upon a time, in this town, there is a boy. He grows up among friends. He becomes a man. This is Italy. Indeed, this is Italy's south. He learns to plant, to hunt, to eat, to smoke, to make wine – and, yes, especially to drink it. One day his brothers take him to the fields on the far side of the creek, and during the course of three hours, he learns to swear. The easy stuff comes first, words and phrases meant to insinuate a point or call the Madonna a million memorable names. But then the moment for hand motions arrives. Fingers, at first. Then whole hands and arms (enough to make any conductor before any symphony in the world feel proud). Until this boy, in the midst of these fields, is gesticulating wildly, speaking a language more powerful than idioms and conjugations and declensions.

At the age of sixteen, this boy meets a girl. She is his age. And she is pretty, yes. But mostly, he thinks, she is desirable. Her hair is soft. It has never been short, not since she was a baby and it started to grow. Her body is soft also, where he wants it to be, where what little bits of it he sees are occasionally exposed in a breeze.

At home, adolescent hormones well up in his throat, stuck there like bouillon cubes in saliva. Thanks to his brothers, the only thing practical he knows how to gesture is 'Let's screw'. High on efficacy, but not particularly romantic or persuasive. So he waits for the night like hungry workers wait for their dinner. Then, once everyone else in the house is asleep, he gesticulates alone, pumping a direct course from his heart to his fist to his groin.

But the girl likes him, he thinks. He has reason to believe this. When there are opportunities to approach her, she doesn't run. And it's not because of bad shoes either. Her father is a cobbler, so it would be a family disgrace if she had to run because of her shoes!

One afternoon he arrives at her house with a flower, an asphodel picked from a field on the town's sleepy outskirts. He holds it in his hand like it is a scepter. She reaches. She takes it. He thinks, *She's perfect this afternoon, in the four o'clock light, with the petals of the flower touching her nose like the wings of a bee.* He's a trained master at hand movements, but all of a sudden he feels like a mute. But is this surprising? Any more surprising than a heart, all of a sudden, beating fast? At sixteen years of age, one needs darkness for courage. (The better part of his own gesticulating has been practiced in isolation, and after dark.) So he puts his hand on her shoulder, the shoulder nearest to him. The girl looks at it and smiles, appreciating both awkwardness and intent.

This is a story an old man tells me. It's a story he wants me to hear because it is his own, and because it is spring. He says it's the story of how he courted the girl who became the woman who became his wife. It's the story of how they fell in love in Mancanzano's impoverished fields in the years long before our gang arrived in his town. He looks at me seriously, and says, 'It's a serious story.'

'It's a love story,' I tell him.

He says it is. But he laughs. 'It's also a story about sex. In my day, love stories were what you told when you wanted to talk about sex. But mostly, I suppose, it's a story about spring.'

'Why spring?'

'Because sixty-four years ago, it was spring when I met her. And eleven years ago, it was spring when she died.'

'What happened to your wife?'

'She died in her sleep. In my sleep too.'

'But what happened?'

'Oh, how? The way the doctors explained it, demons came through our floor and stopped her heart beating.'

'That's what the doctors told you? I'd like to meet them.'

'Well, they're not medical ones. Because you can't trust the medical ones.'

'No. Of course not. You shouldn't. So which ones are the good ones?'

'The barbers. *I cerusici*. You can tell if they're good if they cut your hair afterwards. That's what you look for.'

'The medical ones don't do that.'

'No. They're lazy. *Bastardi*.'

'And you can't trust them.'

'No, never trust them, no matter what, never. After all, they said my wife died of a heart attack. Which was really unbelievable.'

'Impossible?'

'Completely impossible. Because then there's the question?'

'What question?'

'The obvious one. If it's a heart attack, then who attacked it? I thought it very suspicious the police wouldn't investigate.'

'No?'

'But that's because they are corrupt. So it took the barbers to explain it to me.'

'And the barbers told you about the demons?'

'No, everybody knows about the demons. Everybody who goes to school, at least. But the part I didn't know was just the way they can stick their hands through your chest without even breaking the skin, and then squeeze your heart like it's a carpenter's vice until it stops beating. Did you know that?'

'I didn't,' I tell him. 'But that's good knowledge to have.'

He looks at me, squinting. 'The best. And that's not information everybody has either. Because not everybody has the barbers we have. Or the schools.'

We walk a little along the outskirts of town. Then he says to me, 'I'm going to show you something. I'm going to show you the demons.' I wonder if these are the same pendulous ones that Middelhoek has uncovered.

We go slowly. The man is eighty years old, and his gait is unsure. I follow him to the fields where he must have picked flowers for his wife so many years ago. We walk there past forsaken rock churches on the edge of the grasses, caves tucked away into the stone, where spring's green gives way to dust. In these ancient churches, there are dozens of frescoes in disarray, shards of mostly disintegrated pictures that have succumbed to a millennium of various elements – moisture and vandalism chief among them.

We stop beside one, my barber-lover's favorite. I shouldn't kid him, of course: the barber-surgeons, the *cerusici* as they're called, played an important medical role in southern Italy until just a few decades ago, particularly when this part of Lucania was considered so remote that there weren't any real doctors available. So when the barbers weren't shaving beards or trimming sideburns, they passed out quinine and mandrake and various philters. They bandaged wounds, pulled teeth and drew lots of blood, and handled – sometimes ably, sometimes not – a wide range of medical conditions. They were quacks, of course, but sometimes even quacks get it right.

I hold on to the old man's biceps to steady him as we enter the cave's mouth, overstepping rubble and rubbish. At first, I can barely see. But then my eyes adjust, and I kick a few branches out of my way. The room's walls are covered with fragmentary images of serpents and demons, probably some of the ones who massacred the man's wife's heart when it was still in her chest. The frescoes here are in ruinous disrepair so it's not surprising that once they reached their current condition, people stopped thinking about them or visiting them anymore.

But then the old man reaches for my arm and pinches the skin lightly. Across from the illustrations of demons – scratched-out skeletons akin to the savage forms that Middelhoek has uncovered – a Madonna with child suckles her son on an opposite wall. It's only once I've seen that picture too that the old man speaks again.

'I used to come here as a boy,' he tells me, 'when I was ten. This is where I first saw the demons. You know, I was a little afraid, because I'd heard even then that they chewed on souls like they were licorice sticks. Then I came to this cave again as a teenager . . . but how can I put it? I'd moved on from demons to demon ladies. In those days, I admit, I was more interested in seeing Maria's breast. See how it pokes out of her blouse, like a turtle popping its head out of its shell? Not even my great-granddaughter has breasts like that!'

147

'You've seen her breasts?'

'No, but I'm willing to imagine. So I have to figure, it's like the *cerusici* said. That's why the demons killed my wife. Because when I'd come here back then, I'd get so excited I'd do whatever I could just to get ten minutes of relief.'

The man lets out a gasp, half-sigh and half-whimper, an audible amalgam of nostalgia and relief. 'Now, look at me,' he says.

'I'm looking.'

'I hope you don't mind my being blunt. But I couldn't get worked up like that today, not even if I wanted. And if I could' – he holds up a hand that trembles in the air like a leaf in the breeze – 'I couldn't do anything about it. But I don't miss that.'

'No?'

'Because I don't miss that need. But you? You must be going crazy. Are you going crazy?'

We're standing inside the mouth of the cave, just beyond the lip of its floor, which is scattered with twigs, leaves, beer cans and cigarette butts: refuse from nature mixed with refuse from man.

'Yes, I'm going crazy,' I say. 'Do you think it's the demons?'

'With you? You? No, your problem is you're still young.' Then he blushes a little, even if the reddening is barely visible against haggard skin. 'My problem's the opposite. If the demons got involved with me, then I'd be hard all the time. Swollen like a windsock. Now only my feet swell.'

'Yes, I am going a little crazy,' I say again, now that it's been said and now that I know it.

'I figured you might be. You got a girl back home?'

'Yes.' This is the first time I've told anyone beyond our group.

'Then you're as stupid as the medical doctors,' he says. 'Because if I still had a girl back home, I promise you I wouldn't be here with you in this cave. And especially not if I were young.

Now, could you help me a second?'

I've released my grip on his arm and he wants me to take it again. I do. He smiles at me benignly, and then all of a sudden, I see he's unbuckling his pants, unzipping them, and then letting them slide down to his ankles.

His underwear comes down too. They're prodigious shorts, with enough girth at the elastic to fit over a tree stump. He looks at me beseechingly, once the pants and the underpants are clumped at his feet, with the tops of his socks stretching up from the heap like a pair of maple saplings.

But he redirects my gaze. 'My calves? No, no. Look at my prick. Look!'

And I do. Because he asks. And because young people always want to know what they're going to turn into, once the decades play catch-up. Below his belt, he looks like my father, whom I last saw like this when I was twenty-five. But this man looks at me agitatedly. He's so much older, and uncircumcised.

'Look, look!' he says again, and this time he swats at it with his knuckles. 'See, it doesn't get hard. See, the Madonna on the wall is nothing. And when I use it to piss, it leaks for an hour.' He frowns. 'It's useless. I'm useless. Like a broken donkey tail.' He kicks his feet until his trousers and underwear are in even more of a compact clump.

'Now will you hold me?' he asks.

'OK . . .' I tell him, as ambivalently as I can, and then I'm grateful when I realize that all he means is for me to grab below each of his arms. I hold him from the front, momentarily looking him in his eyes, before he lets his weight sag backward.

'Don't lose your grip!' he warns.

'I won't!'

'Don't!'

'Why am I holding you like this?'

'Shhhh!'

I feel his full weight in my arms and shoulders, slumping like that until the old man takes a crap.

That's what it is. A crap. A mass slides from his rear, dropping to the floor of the cave, where it then steams in a heap.

'Don't drop me!' he says again. And, of course, I'm tempted to let him go. If only to watch the mound splatter against his backside like an overripe tomato. But instead I pull his body toward mine. I hand him some leaves from the branches that have been kicked into the cave. And he wipes himself with them.

'My pisser is old, but my ass works fine,' he says now with satisfaction. He pulls his trousers up halfway, then pauses to look at his bowel movement on the ground beneath him.

'I shit on the demons! I shit on them, *shit on them*! With America and Maria as my witness!'

Then he looks at me, with his pants and his underwear still at his hips. 'Now, do you want to know who's killing Mancanzano's kids?'

'Sure,' I tell him. 'Yes, I do.'

'Spring is doing it. The seasons are doing it. It's the natural order of birth and decay. Our little town is killing them. It kills everyone who dies here. It killed my wife.'

'I thought you told me the demons killed her?'

'They did,' he says. 'But *in conjunction* with spring. Because spring is death.'

The man reaches down cautiously, and he picks up a rock. It's a piece of tufa that looks like it's been kicked here from cave to cave by playing kids. He takes the stone in his shaky hand, and pulls his penis out from his underwear, and hits the stone down on its head.

He smiles amiably. 'No, don't be alarmed,' he says. 'It's what I told you. I don't feel a thing.'

I figure that's got to be true, at least as far as his prick is concerned. But then he takes the same rock and drops it purposely on his foot. 'I felt that, at least,' he says. 'I can't say that it feels good. But the sensation's important. It means I'm still alive.' He breathes in deeply. 'Ah, spring. *Ah, primavera!*'

Then he reattaches his belt, and I follow him out of the cave as he walks back to town limping.

&#10148;

A new room has been discovered in the cavern where the second teenagers died. A wall had been built, for ever sealing the room from the rest of the chamber. Just as the original inhabitants of Mancanzano burrowed into the town's bluffs to excavate their homes, at some point they'd reversed the process and returned loose stone to the hollow, building a rock wall back into the rock.

One of the art students from Calabria made the discovery. Layers of AB57 had been applied to a rectangle of paint covering one wall, but once the compound was removed, there was nothing under the whitewash except the crude masonry of tufa blocks.

Middelhoek sent the student to get hold of the rest of us right away. Linda and I were the first to arrive; Fortune, who'd been inspecting fault lines and tufa strata not far from the caves I'd visited with the old man, followed immediately after. We purposely left the high deputy and Dr Stoppani in the dark. Telling them about what we'd found in the cave would have meant applying for permits as numerous as the underground pathways in this hillside city. No one bothered for a second with Dr Biaggi. It was clear that all he'd provide were filibusters and distraction.

But once the four of us were there, it didn't take long to clear an opening in the wall large enough for each of us to pass through. Middelhoek dragged his floodlamps to the hole, and they shed enough light to illuminate the new chamber without any more effort.

The air inside the space was stale, and we worried immediately about how much oxygen there was. So we waited until fresh air had flowed into the room, even while each of us also wondered if that might somehow alter what we'd find

151

inside. But once we'd climbed into the new room, we realized that what we found would stay intact. Then we all let out a series of sighs. First, for what we hadn't ruined, and then for what we had found.

The walls of the new chamber were covered with frescoes. The paintings adorned two walls surrounding our makeshift entrance, wrapping the room in a wide swath of brilliant color. This time, unlike in the cave where the one great fresco depicted ravenous cherubim – or in the cave we'd just left, where the walls had been covered in white – the crystalline surface of the frescoes had been left untouched by later applications of paint. And because they'd been protected for so long from environmental and human havoc, they were in almost pristine condition. In this cave, the colors were powerful: bright garnet reds, lapis lazulis, and greens so lustrous they could have been emeralds. The walls here actually glistened. They actually sparkled. They shone.

So what did we find? What had the cave-dwellers wanted to hide? The walls in the cave were covered with images of lovers – men and women, naked, entwined, endlessly and effortlessly enwrapped. We found picture after picture of these lovers in an eternal embrace. We found bodies adorning the walls, wrapped around each other like shawls, copulating, kissing, stroking, investigating, eyes that were open, eyes that were closed, bodies that could not tire of one another, bodies that had remained untouched for a millennium or more, when they'd been captured in a frenzy and frozen for ever in the moments when one body finds another and is convinced of the inexhaustibility of physical attraction.

Were these pictures the Benedictines had tried to conceal? Or were they images that they'd painted themselves, when they weren't otherwise engaged in the monkish mortification of their flesh?

We should have telephoned Rome for help. We didn't. We

should have called the Istituto Centrale del Restauro. We didn't do that. We should have contacted the carabinieri. Those were our initial mistakes. Then we made others. I admit to all of them now.

Once you break down one wall, you're willing to break down another. It's like that when you cross any threshold. So no one contacted Major Martella. No one got hold of the high deputy, Dr Stoppani or even aloof Mayor Taciuto. No one worried about contacting the Centro per la Valorizzazione e Gestione delle Risorse Storico-Ambientali or the Soprintendenza per i Beni Culturali ed Artistici in Potenza. It was a conscious decision: we just didn't want any of them around. Without saying a word, each of us had agreed to our course of action, and there wasn't any need to articulate it outright.

Fortune went to our quarters, and returned to the cave with a broom and the largest blanket he could find. We hung the blanket at the mouth of the most exterior cave to keep onlookers away, hoping at the same time that we wouldn't attract the attention of the carabinieri. Two of the Calabrian art students were sent to stand guard outside, even if they didn't know what they were guarding or what to do if somebody wanted in. Then, while Middelhoek and Linda began documenting the images in the new frescoes with cameras, I started tapping on other interior walls to see if they were soft enough or thin enough to have been constructed to hide something else.

I found a wall quickly with a hollow space behind it. While this barrier wall looked real enough, there was an obvious seam where it met the ceiling. I knocked at it a few times with the back of my fist. Then Fortune came over with the broom, and he made a few hard jabs with the end of it, creating another opening in the cave, restoring to view another womb that had been hidden in the depths of the hill. Each time Fortune struck the wall with the broom, there was a moment of resistance and then the sounds of stone crumbling, as the end of the broom disappeared inside the wall, effortlessly threading through open air.

But this time the smell overtook us immediately. The stench was unbearable; we almost started to gag, and I fell to my knees and I thought I was going to vomit. Somehow Fortune kept up his hammering, and he broke away a large enough crevice for us to look inside.

To see through this opening, we needed the lamps. We tried a flashlight that Middelhoek had on hand, but we could barely see anything with it. So we dragged one of the floodlamps over, repositioning it so that it tilted on its base, held by its neck at an angle in front of the opening. Then with our noses and mouths cloaked in our shirts, we looked inside.

We saw bodies. A heap of them in various states of decomposition. Linda shuddered, and bit on her shirt. Fortune later told me he kept his composure by picturing his father's cigarette scars. Holding my breath, I entered the space and approached the bodies, which were clumped together without any clothing. From what I saw, the bodies had been left there in twos, piled on top of each other. This was a cavern of flesh, matted hair, sagging skin, frozen expressions.

Two of the bodies had barely decomposed, and from what I'd learned since I'd arrived in Mancanzano, they couldn't have been more than a few days old. The abdomens were greenish, like the grasses outside that had arrived with the spring, and this discoloration had spread to the necks and the shoulders, where the green then gave way to a matting of blood.

Another two bodies bore a more definite marbling, suggesting that they had been dead longer. Here, the blood vessels had turned a greenish black, and the bodies themselves had begun to putrefy, even as decomposition fluid drained from the faces, past the dried blood, and down to the soft earth.

A third pair of bodies had obviously been inside the cavern longest. The corpses were bloated. Their eyes were bulging, and the tongues protruded from between bloodied teeth and lips.

These bodies were teeming with flies, and their various orifices squirmed with maggots.

At the top of one wall, there was a small opening that looked as if it had been patched with stone. But the repairs had been knocked out by Mancanzano's howling storm. Just beyond the hole, there was now a view of the sky.

I headed to the opening instinctively to get my bearings, but mostly to take a fresh breath. I stood on my toes and stuck my mouth to the aperture, and I breathed. I breathed hard, as though, right before, I had been drowning. Then I pulled my mouth away, and I stuck my eye to the hole. Beyond the opening, there were hundreds of birds. They were the kestrels that had descended so recently on Mancanzano. A few were perched just beyond the opening, some with hair in their beaks from the dead bodies that were on the floor just behind me. The kestrels had come to feed on the flies which had, in turn, come to feed on the corpses.

Inside the cave, there were six men and women, all of them cadavers, all of them unclothed, and all of them, from appearances, under the age of twenty. These were the remains of townsfolk who had never been found – and perhaps were so isolated that they hadn't even been missed – but whose bodies had been entombed in the catacombs of the city, without a funeral, without a memory, with nothing more left to them than a final embrace.

At the corner of the cavern, there was an inscription traced out on the floor in tufa dust. It had probably been scrawled there with a finger. I wondered if it had been scrawled with one of the fingers of the heaped dead. The words on the floor read: HOC EST INFERNO. Kneeling before the epitaph, I could see it, the bodies, and the sky in a single wide-eyed glance.

'Are you all right in there?' Linda called out. 'I hear birds.'

A kestrel had come through the hole, and it was pecking at the mouth of one of the cadavers.

'Are you all right in there?' Linda asked again.

The feathers along the bird's crown and around its bill were coated in tufa dust. As was everything else in the dead teenager's mouth.

Immediately, I thought of Dr Biaggi. I wanted to ask if his eating disorder could be renamed after kestrels. And I wanted to know if magpies had ever descended on a city like this, with a ravenous pica for the life that starts as soon as there is death.

## Chapter 11
# Domestic Pathology

On April 2, this is how the forensic report from Potenza began: '*Tre uomini, tre donne, trovati per caso tutti morti in una caverna alla periferia di Mancanzano.*' Three men, three women, found by chance, all of them dead, in a cave on the outskirts of the city of Mancanzano.

Beyond everything, the idea of discovery through happenstance was what struck everyone most. Three men, three women, six people, all of them dead: relegated to a place that no one can identify, like pieces of a board game that have for ever fallen behind a couch.

The frescoes we'd found in the cave resuscitated interest throughout Italy in the city and history and the art and the dead of Mancanzano. But now there was also plenty of talk regionally about taking legal action against the members of our group, for:

1. seditious meddling
2. damaging a potential national monument
3. disturbing a crime site
4. not immediately reporting our findings to the ever-oscillating bureaucracy of authorities
5. consuming more electricity than we'd been granted a permit to use (our phalanx of floodlights had lit the caves like a disco), and,

6. whatever else you could think of, which someone *would* think of, if only given adequate time.

Of course, a few news reports from around the peninsula depicted us in more favorable light. In certain circles – some of them apparently official, some apparently in Rome – there was even talk of giving us medals for unearthing the dead.

'These people are heroes for finding our children!' a few Mancanzani and neighboring Lucanians pledged. 'That's assuming, of course, they didn't kill them themselves!'

But needless to say, no medals were proffered, and commendations never came. To have nudged that possibility anywhere beyond the realm of idle chat would have been to endow us with more authority or importance than anyone dared. Because although we were in Italy, we were not Italians (and not even members of the related phylum of Mediterraneans). And, ultimately, we didn't belong in Mancanzano any more than Il Duce's men had when they fired on the sassi, or Count Tramontano had four centuries before that, back when he was the Great Urinator.

So the immediate consequence of our discovery was that we became marginalized. Somehow the presumption was that we'd drift into the hillside like the Benedictines before us, and countless others – the Lycians, Swabians, Saracens, Byzantines, Normans, Greeks and Goths. In the City of Mancanzano, our destiny now was to become the lost. In this tufa town of Lucania, stuck way up on a hill, all of a sudden we were no more important than the dust.

Slowly, the bodies we'd found in the cave were identified; only the two most recently killed came from Mancanzano. The remaining four were from the Lucanian towns of Irsina and Montescaglioso (where Dr Stoppani's sapling and strapping mistress Anna lived). Once we notified the carabinieri about unearthing the bodies, we were ordered to suspend our research until additional policework could occur, and even her *éminence grise*, the High Deputy for Public Works, visited our quarters to tell us herself that we should hold back from conducting more interviews, restorations or seismologic studies until we received further word. What stones were unturned, she said, would be better off left that way.

In the meantime, we were also instructed not to exit the country until a final decision about our missions in Mancanzano could be made (apparently, we weren't as close to receiving official accolades as previously thought). The only thing official to arrive at our door, in fact, was one of Major Martella's men, who confiscated our passports to show us that the Region of Basilicata and the Republic of Italy were now really serious.

'I'm sorry to do this,' the carabiniere told us aloofly, not sorry at all. 'But we wouldn't want you heading those nine hundred kilometers north, and trying to escape over the border to Switzerland.'

In the jittery days that followed the change in our status, I took notes vigorously, but also discreetly. (I amused myself by thinking that Martella's man, a kid in his early twenties, would have taken our pens away too, if only he'd thought of it.) So I wandered the city to see what I'd find, without necessarily having to look. And I kept my ears open too.

On Via Lucana, I learned that Tonio Archimede was considering carving a slew of effigies of the newly discovered dead to join the ranks of his first four, who now existed only as memory and dust. He visited a tufa quarry, acquired some stone, but then lost his enthusiasm when he realized no clothesline would ever support so many rocks. On Via Pentolame, I saw that Signora Bitonto had closed down her bakery. I overheard her explaining to a customer: 'I'm sorry I can't help you. But the thought of baking bread right now makes me sick.' And on Via Falciata, I passed a crowd gathered outside the home of Angela's parents, who were inside their sasso with the parents of the other Mancanzano dead, debating whether the anguished parents from the other towns should be allowed to share in their grief.

Elsewhere in Mancanzano, while teenagers brooded, fretful and suspicious – and even the Calabrian students started to wonder if they were at risk – more people than ever now packed up their belongings and headed for the city's borders, intent on putting as much distance as possible between them and their tufa town.

As far as we four were concerned, there was no way to know how long we'd have to wait before we could return to work. But our uncertainty was based on much more than governmental interdiction. There were additional issues of empathy and good taste. Because how do you argue that you want to look at naked bodies on a wall, when there are actual naked bodies at your feet in a heap?

The *medico legale* in Potenza had sworn never to work with Major Luigi Martella and the Mancanzano carabinieri again. So when the six teenagers were discovered, phone calls had to be made from as far away as Naples and Rome before he consented to make the first initial, essential cuts.

From the start, livor mortis had shown that the teenagers, like their predecessors, had died side by side, on the ground, naked. The pebbles and powder that stuck to their skin – and the reddishness of their flanks that provided the only chromatic counterpoint to their cadaverous hue – demonstrated beyond any doubt that the bodies had been moved at least twelve hours after death. Which meant that it was only after the transformation from sentient creatures to corpses that the six teenagers had been piled up inside the cave. That was one piece of information that the *medico legale* stressed from the start. It comforted people to know that their loved ones had died in peace. Because in even the grisliest of deaths, there could still be an element of civility.

More information about the fatalities soon followed. Once

again, the couples had had sex before they died (at least that was certain in all of the bodies, save the two most badly decomposed ones). Once again, there were no signs of drugs in the teenagers' tissues or blood, much less any wounds or blunt-force injuries that might have pointed the way toward a mechanism or cause of death. So, these deaths were as much mysteries as the ones before them. Once more, the same pulverized tufa had been scraped from the town's walls and into these teenagers' mouths, although it was still impossible to know from which walls exactly. But, sure enough, this tufa had been served to them as a most puzzling and most definitely last supper.

However, this time the *medico legale* did find something peculiar. The blood matting the faces of the six teenagers hadn't come from their own bodies, or from each other's. The blood seeped from their lips. The blood spilled down their throats, but under a microscope, this blood hadn't been difficult to classify at all.

The *medico legale* in Potenza called Major Martella in Mancanzano as soon as he made the identification, notwithstanding his ample ill will.

'OK, listen, *Maggiore*,' the forensics examiner told him. 'The blood on the bodies comes from a dog.'

There was a long pause on the line from the Mancanzano end of the conversation. 'We have a lot of dogs here,' Major Martella said uneasily. 'They roam Mancanzano's canyon. They're wild.'

'Well, now you have one or two fewer,' the *medico legale* told him matter-of-factly.

By Major Martella's own account later to Dottoressa Donabuoni, a sickening feeling swept through him the moment he hung up the phone. First, he likened the sensation to realizing that he'd gulped down a glass of dog's brackish blood himself. Then Major Martella said he recalled, with the same surreal visual acuity one has of a dream, how just the other day he'd been watching a boy play with his dog in Piazza Ridola, and how the puppy's jaw had rested serenely on the boy's knee afterward – with its puppydog ears drooping like peeled husks of corn – and how this image was now fixed as indelibly into his memory as the face of his own mother. The major told the high deputy: 'This made me realize humanity's something we all have to grab on to by the throat.'

Then Major Martella told Dottoressa Donabuoni that he understood the *medico legale*'s call from Potenza as his own call to action. If dogs were involved, he explained, then animal rights groups in the country's north might now get involved, and *that* sort of exposure could bring his investigation additional resources (although it wasn't clear if he meant the traditional kind that saved the day, or the other variety that merely augmented it the way Cesare Lombroso's criminology always had).

So now the major asked the high deputy if she could start contacting animal rights groups for him in Florence and Milan.

'I'll get on it immediately,' she answered him, as she tried to mask her own frustration. 'But do you think in the meantime we could focus on people?'

'I'll have to,' the major replied stubbornly, 'because that's exactly my point! There won't be resources for anything else until you get on the phone.'

Meanwhile, as the town got used to the idea of more dead – and our group to the idea that our professional lives were to be put on hold – I set out to conduct more interviews. Of course, since I'd been ordered to stop working, I knew these ethnographies would have to be so clandestine and cagey that not even my informants would realize they were occurring. So I feigned a few ailments; then I sought out a barber-surgeon.

Here is the transcript of my interview with Antonio Montefalcone, held on Via Bradano (tape recorder in bag):

ETHNOGRAPHER: I don't feel well. It's a vague, undefined sort of malaise.

162

INFORMANT: That sounds serious. Often there's nothing worse. At least, you've come to the right doctor, thank God! Not that charlatan from Sicily. Now, moan for me.

ETHNOGRAPHER: *Ooh-aahooh.*

INFORMANT: Better.

ETHNOGRAPHER: *Ahh-ahooohah.*

INFORMANT: Tell me, do you eat a lot of meat?

ETHNOGRAPHER: Yes. Sometimes, I do.

INFORMANT: Then it may be the meats. They're hard to digest. Because of the fats. That puts a strain on your liver, which lets out the goblins. The poor have it easier.

ETHNOGRAPHER: They do?

INFORMANT: The really poor only *talk* about food. I was that poor, growing up. That's why I became a doctor.

ETHNOGRAPHER: Tell me about the goblins.

INFORMANT: No, no. To say more is to invite them into your intestines. So, don't insist. Anyway, my guess is you're too well off to be as lucky as the poor.

ETHNOGRAPHER: Actually, it's a much deeper aching that I feel now. Maybe it's somewhere around my chest.

INFORMANT: Be especially careful if it's by your heart.

ETHNOGRAPHER: Any specific recommendations you can give me?

INFORMANT: I think just the usual. Exercise. Healthy eating. Never smoke more than the people around you. Respect your emotions.

ETHNOGRAPHER: Respect them? How?

INFORMANT: Your friend Middelhoek? The so-called 'art restorer'? He speaks several languages. I've heard him in the caves, while he's stripping off paint. Italian, English, Dutch. I think also German and French. Very smart man. Very learned. He speaks all those languages. He's not happy in any of them.

ETHNOGRAPHER: No.

INFORMANT: Definitely, no. He should try staying quiet.

ETHNOGRAPHER: But he has to communicate.

INFORMANT: There are lots of ways. Mourn with movement. I tell the old women who consult me about their asthma to keep piling on more black clothes if they don't seem sad enough.

ETHNOGRAPHER: You want them to be sadder?

INFORMANT: No, *they* want to be sadder. Sometimes, a dress isn't enough. They need to add a shawl, a kerchief, ebony rosaries, a black pair of gloves. Then their sadness can be contained. Then they can get their fingers around it. I'll tell you something. You know why those women are so religious?

ETHNOGRAPHER: They believe in God?

INFORMANT: Nowadays? No. People believe in the saints. The Virgin Mary, sure. Demons, of course.

ETHNOGRAPHER: And, like you say, in goblins.

INFORMANT: Yes, in goblins. But the reason the women are so religious is just because there's no cooler place in southern Italy than inside a church. The priests figured it out first, built them from marble, and then got the old women wearing black. I merely follow the priests' lead. This gives me room to operate.

ETHNOGRAPHER: I'd imagine that's important for a barber-surgeon.

INFORMANT: Then you understand me exactly. So we might as well talk about you.

ETHNOGRAPHER: I'm just not feeling well. My skin itches.

INFORMANT: Then try scratching it lightly. That's usually what I do.

ETHNOGRAPHER: Also, it flakes.

INFORMANT: Listen to me, let the flakes fall off! Don't try to keep anything that separates from your body naturally. But it's more than that, isn't it? You've talked about malaise, aching, rashes, your heart, what else?

ETHNOGRAPHER: Sometimes I've been having trouble breathing.

INFORMANT: I don't suppose you want the advice I give to the women with asthma?

ETHNOGRAPHER: Maybe something else, if it isn't too much trouble.

INFORMANT: If you suffer from allergies, stay away from flowers and cats. That's other doctors' advice, but I think it sounds reasonable.

ETHNOGRAPHER: Sometimes my stomach hurts too.

INFORMANT: At some point or another, everyone's stomach hurts. Even those who don't eat regularly. You've come here worrying about not feeling well. There are some people in Mancanzano who haven't felt well their entire lives. Very sad.

ETHNOGRAPHER: I'm not comparing myself to them. I think the parents who lost their kids won't feel well again for a long time.

INFORMANT: You worry about their stomachs?

ETHNOGRAPHER: No. Their hearts, *their* malaise. Universal ailments, I guess.

INFORMANT: At least the teenage girls who died relieved their parents of worrying about what to do with them if they turn into spinsters.

ETHNOGRAPHER: That sounds severe.

INFORMANT: It can be a very acute disorder.

ETHNOGRAPHER: What about the boys? They wouldn't have ever become spinsters.

INFORMANT: There are many dead in Mancanzano. Just a month ago, I washed a woman's hair. She was already too sick to stand. So she lay on her back, and I pulled her head beyond the edge of the mattress. Then I poured warm water over her scalp. It coursed past her face, and it puddled on the ground. Next, I used shampoo. Then, I washed out this shampoo. Now suddenly she was beautiful, this same old woman, with her gray hair sparkling for the first time in over a month. Gravity pulled it away from her face, like a loose handful of curtains. You saw her cheekbones. *I* saw her cheekbones. She died last week. My point is the teenagers aren't the only ones dying.

ETHNOGRAPHER: The teenagers were young.

INFORMANT: I haven't said it isn't sad. Respect the dead, along with your emotions. Now, let me ask you a question.

ETHNOGRAPHER: Please.

INFORMANT: You don't wear black.

ETHNOGRAPHER: No, not usually.

INFORMANT: Still, you describe yourself as sick.

ETHNOGRAPHER: Recently, anyhow.

INFORMANT: Still, I'd say pretty sick. So what contains your desperation?

ETHNOGRAPHER: I don't know. Are you asking me to be helpful or hurtful?

INFORMANT: I haven't decided. I'm trying to see what's in your head.

ETHNOGRAPHER: Respect my emotions.

INFORMANT: Forgive me. But a doctor needs to look at every part of the body. Even the parts that are generally invisible to the eyes. Now, is there anything else that you'd like to discuss with me?

ETHNOGRAPHER: No, maybe this has been enough.

INFORMANT: OK, then let's see . . . Normally, I'd charge you ten thousand lire. But I'm going to give you a discount because not all of my prescriptions have been precise. So just give me seven.

ETHNOGRAPHER: Here are three. Four. Five.

INFORMANT: No matter, you'll pay me the rest later. Otherwise, you know that I'll call the carabinieri. Now, come back at four with the money.

ETHNOGRAPHER: It's four-thirty now.

INFORMANT: Oh, don't be so quarrelsome. I meant four o'clock *more or less*. Anyway, come back then. Not before. Then, maybe I'll even be able to show you something special. One of my patients. Now, don't forget.

ETHNOGRAPHER: No, I won't.

INFORMANT: No, no, you mustn't. There's an important medical difference.

When I return two hours later, Montefalcone meets me at his door, and motions for me to walk with him. We follow Via della Vergine into the sassi, then we take Via Sant'Isaia; then we go past the small half-court piazza where the teenage boys sometimes play at ball. Finally, we arrive at Via Folletto. Antonio Montefalcone points up.

Filippa Grossoglio is seated on her roof, astride the terracotta tiles lining the top of her sasso. The other teenagers are gone, as is the baby. The radio's gone, too, and right now the only sounds are of Filippa crying. Tears stream down her cheeks, marking her blouse with dark, wet splatters. She shifts around. Her clothes don't know what to make of her body; it wasn't so long ago that her integral parts were easy to cover. Now she hugs herself, arms pressing just below her breasts – hands clutching at fabric as they try to find a place to hold on.

I look at Montefalcone, to make sure she's what he intended to show me. He nods his head, yes.

I ask, 'Do you know why she's crying? Look at her crying!'

Montefalcone nods again, and says smugly, 'She has a date.'

'She doesn't want to go?'

'She's getting ready. She's opening ducts.'

The teenager wails, turning red. Her whole body quakes. Montefalcone says, 'Tears are the best lubricant there is.'

I shake my own head. I start to walk off.

Montefalcone tells me, 'Maybe it's not true, but I know you believe it.' I try to smile back at him. He says, 'Now give me the money.' I do.

Above us, the teenager's chest rises and swells like a wet membrane.

## Chapter 12
# Seminario Lanfranchi

In Italy, priests mediate between man and God. Others, like witches and magi, connect religion and magic. Barber-surgeons then introduce bad science. I knew which one Antonio Montefalcone was. Now I wondered about Dr Biaggi.

And also I wondered about me.

After what turned out to be a three-day absence, Drs Biaggi and Stoppani reappeared in Mancanzano. Apparently, the two had traveled to Bari together to try to woo back Monica. Their strategy was to show her that she'd starve spiritually and emotionally without her husband, and Dr Biaggi was just the man to make the argument sound convincing: in Bari, he'd spewed out enough professorial mumbo jumbo to keep a woman even as sharp as Monica off her guard.

Now back in Mancanzano, Dr Stoppani held on to his smile even after we told him that our research team had been forced on hiatus. The constancy of his smile could only be emblematic of his success. Like Troilus, Dr Stoppani carried a tidbit of cloth from his love that he kept clutching nervously. Dr Biaggi, sans the scrap of embroidery, bore the satisfaction and radiance of a doctor who'd saved yet another patient.

Fortune, Middelhoek, Linda and I had all 'formally' suspended our studies, but Dr Biaggi still enjoyed outright permission to work. Perhaps this was because he was Italian;

perhaps it was because he wasn't an official part of our group. Or perhaps it was because he hadn't been among us, or even been in Mancanzano, when the new bodies were found inside the cave. But whichever it was, we soon discovered that Dr Biaggi had been preparing another discussion about eating disorders while away. So now, when the doctor learned that another six teenagers had died in the city after eating more tufa, he was determined to deliver his new lecture posthaste.

A second town meeting was scheduled for the auditorium of the Seminario Lanfranchi, and once again Dr Benedetto Biaggi took to the podium before a roomful of Mancanzani, who were now joined by a new sprinkling of mourning Irsinesi and Montescagliosi. Dr Stoppani sat in the front row, dressed in the same clothes as the force on the stage before him. Nearly three hundred people filled the room.

Once again, Dr Biaggi flicked his fingers across his pantlegs. He smiled portentously. Then he spoke.

'Food is love,' he instructed the audience. 'I don't have to tell any of you about spaghetti alla puttanesca. That's not love! That isn't intimacy! That's the alimentary counterpart of what American sailors do during their shore leaves in Naples.' He glanced at Linda and me. 'No offense intended.'

Dr Biaggi continued: 'We talk about soppressata, salame and mortadella. We say they're delicious. And, oh yes, they are! But that's not love or intimacy either. That's forcing meats into what they are not! Love has to be simpler, without so many preservatives or ingredients. Prepare it right, and love won't upset your stomachs. Treat it right, and it won't oppress your hearts. Love is good wine, good food, good company, good bread. Fresh and thick, and warm and moist where it really counts. Love, above all, is feeling alive.

'So now do you want me to tell you what love isn't?' Dr Biaggi asked the room. 'Love isn't eating rocks from a wall, stripping, and fornicating inside a cave. Maybe *that* kind of romance is appropriate for lower species – and I don't want our

American friends to get offended if I repeat that it's exactly what's expected from their aforementioned sailors – but the rest of us are Italians, and this is Italy we live in! Mancanzano is Italy! The homeland of Puccini and Casanova. Here, our love affairs are fit to be conducted among the clouds. Our banquets are famous for their excesses, not their isolation!'

Dr Biaggi paused long enough for his last semi-glutinous words to congeal. Our expert on eating disorders wasn't about to miss this opportunity to milk his crowd. Signora Bitonto sat in the third row, by now weeping steadily. A neighbor comforted her. Then when she kept crying, he frantically asked her to hush. Dr Biaggi spoke again.

'Now, ten of our loved ones aren't alive any longer,' the doctor told his audience. 'And now the newest dead aren't just from Mancanzano. They're from Irsina and Montescaglioso too. Both fine towns, and both of them in Italy! So, all of a sudden, it looks as though we have an epidemic. It's the globalization of isolation that's doing us in! Because what does it mean to seek solace and tenderness from the cold flanks of a stone? Because what is a stone, if not a part of the wall we construct to keep ourselves from each other?'

So this was Major Martella's *deus ex machina*. This was the man who was going to save the day. Standing before us on the podium, our Sicilian expert implored: 'You have to feed your hungry hearts! You can't eat stones just to impress your neighbors with the weight of your words! And you can't eat rocks to get inside the bowels of the earth!' Dr Biaggi took a few steps from the lectern, pacing now in front of his audience. 'We are not moles,' he told them. 'We walk on our hind legs. Upright, proud and even angelic. So if you've heard the latest results from Potenza' – here, Dr Biaggi looked towards Major Martella with a startling measure of seriousness – 'I can assure you that none of us belongs to the charmingly quaint species of *canis familiaris*!'

Dr Biaggi smiled, opening his mouth wide enough to display

171

a heaping section of tongue, teeth and gums. 'Sometimes, people think that drinking a dog's blood is like having a pet. But it's not! People think: Ah, now, if I drink this dog's blood, then he'll stay with me for ever. Well, he won't – although maybe it's true that you won't have to walk him. Or people think, like these teenagers did, perhaps looking for something to help wash down the rocks: Ah, if I drink the dog's blood, then I can be as fierce as the dog is. Our anthropologist friends from America can support what I say; that is, if they're not too busy studying their own kind down by Naples's old Spanish quarter. Then, just like I've said, they'll be able to tell you about cultures around the world where people believe they assume the characteristics of the animals they devour. But, ladies and gentlemen, I can assure you, that is not science! That is just folklore! And this is modern Italy! This is a culture that has never given in! Here, we don't put magic and superstition before science. Here, the only thing we place before science is religion!'

Dr Biaggi finished his speech to a standing ovation. Signora Bitonto's grief had turned into conviction and strength, as formidable a transformation as water into wine. She resolved to reopen her bakery and give her loaves away free. She left the Seminario Lanfranchi at the end of Dr Biaggi's talk, saying, 'I bake my breads hard. But they're not as hard as rocks.' It wouldn't be long before people began seeing the faces of saints in her crusts.

For his own part, in the handful of weeks that Dr Biaggi had spent in Mancanzano, he'd transformed himself from an eating disorders expert into a culinary demagogue, and then into some hybrid gastroevangelist. The 'biaggification' of foods – in which nutritional staples became the elemental morsels of spiritual love – promised to be every bit as awesome as the phenomenon of transubstantiation. But, what's more, it promised to net Dr Biaggi the same culinary treats that Major Martella's stewardship of the local carabinieri had. So now the only question remaining to Dr Biaggi was where to go from here.

Around town, people began stopping him on the street. (Now that the bodies had been discovered, the kestrels had dispersed. There were no new droppings, and pedestrians were no longer quite so rushed.) People would ask Dr Biaggi questions that ranged from what to do about a colicky baby who wouldn't eat; to what to think of the burgeoning terrorism of the Red Brigades, or the equally terrifying movies of Pier Paolo Pasolini; to whether anything as highfalutin as 'one hundred percent literacy' could ever be as important as knowing how to cultivate crops. But people believed what the doctor told them, regardless of any coincidental grounding in facts. Much of the time, credulity isn't anything more than a matter of choice. And Dr Biaggi wasn't a man to tire of talking. He was always able to come up with an opinion on the spot.

Some *deus ex machina*. Expertus ex truckum de insula Siciliae. More than seven months had gone by since the first two dead teenagers had been discovered in a forgotten cave on the outskirts of Mancanzano, and the residents of the inskirts had since grown desperate. There was a gullible mournfulness you saw in their eyes, or that you could gauge in the cadences of the questions they posed. Those who hadn't given up on the town – the ones who hadn't packed up their belongings and moved away – were needy enough to put their faith into a rotund expert in eating disorders who they were now ready to believe was an expert in everything else. There were those who said, 'If Mussolini had had the charisma of Dr Biaggi, people today would be speaking Italian in Munich.' But the ones who didn't agree admitted, 'At least, that would be true as far north as Innsbruck.'

Still, it wasn't only the people of Mancanzano who were convinced of Dr Biaggi's stature and smarts. The parents of the four dead from Irsina and Montescaglioso had also become avid supporters. They wept and revered. They mourned and admired. The only way to understand the limitlessness of their ardor was to explain it in terms of the extent of their grief: they suffered as penitents, and they sought absolution from whomever they thought could provide it.

Two days after Dr Biaggi's speech, those parents asked him to help them plan appropriate funerals for their decomposed children, and when they offered to accept whatever Dr Biaggi proposed, his eyes really lit up. They won his interest by endowing him with omniscience, and then following up with an equal amount of unadulterated homage.

But what Dr Biaggi proposed was more barnstorming than memorial, and, ultimately, his ceremony was to resemble a political demonstration (although, fortunately, one without bombs).

Major Martella came to the week-long organizing meetings, and took notes. So did a contingent of barber-surgeons. They shouted disruptively whenever they could. But they were twice as disgruntled to find that the crowds quieted them down.

The funerals took place nine days later, as soon as the bodies were recovered from Potenza, stitched up and made to look as presentable as possible – or even better than new. At Dr Biaggi's direction, coffins were constructed with an additional checker-board lid of wood and clear plastic: this way, whatever parts of the corpses were fit to be viewed could be displayed to the collected mourners, who had traveled to Irsina from all over the region of Basilicata, as well as from Campania, Calabria and the island of Sicily itself.

Irsina was chosen as the funerary venue because, excluding the two dead from Mancanzano, whose bodies were still being dissected and studied by the *medico legale*, its dead teenagers were in the best condition. Much of the bodies of the two Montescaglioso dead was camouflaged by planks of maple, but the mortician's success with the Irsinesi was particularly stirring. Those corpses were dressed nattily in their Sunday best. Their shoes were polished. Their hair was combed. Their fingernails had even been manicured. In fact, they looked so good you'd never have believed there was a latticework of stitches under their clothes. Or that a few scattered body parts still sat in a forensics lab in Potenza.

After a bell tolled four times, once for each of the dead being mourned this day (and then another six times for the rest), a priest spoke, but briefly. He'd been asked to keep his prayers and benediction short, in order to leave more time for Dr Biaggi's own address. So the cleric sped through Mass, burned incense with all of the fanfare of someone spraying canned freshener into the air, and then delivered a few compact remarks with the indignation of an envoy who's made to wait on the other side of the door.

'God help us,' he told the mourners. 'And God help you all.'

Then when the priest had finished, and the requisite amens had followed too, it was the first time I ever heard anything approaching applause at a funeral. Linda and I had traveled the hour from Mancanzano to Irsina in one of the beat-up Fiats we'd initially used for our trip from Bari, and we'd had to park it far from the church because of the sprawling crowds. Counting family and friends of the dead, plus scattered others who had heard about the event on the street, in newspapers, or even on Radio Maria, there were close to four hundred people in attendance.

Still, news travels fast (especially when caught in the same winds that normally carry gossip). As we were parking the car just beyond the town's central square, an elderly woman with a tight bun, black dress and even darker demeanor stopped us on the street and shook her head with disdain.

'A car like yours should be washed before you drive it,' she hissed. 'A car like yours isn't fit for driving to something as important as this! Shame on you! I have an old car too, but the taillights are out. So I walked a full quarter-kilometer to get here, just so I wouldn't show any disrespect.'

When we told her that our trip had taken us some fifty kilometers and over ample hills, the woman shook her head again and said, still scowling, 'That just sounds like an excuse for you to be lazy. All you young people are lazy! That's what gets you killed! So, I wonder if it's even what you deserve! Look at me. I'm seventy-four years old! I'm not lazy. I'm going to live for ever!'

'For ever?' we asked her.

'Yes, for ever,' she clucked. 'Or at least longer than the people I don't like!'

Then we watched her shove her way into the church, forcing a parishioner from one of the last seats in a pew with the hard edge of her purse.

But when the priest sat down, it was finally time for Dr Biaggi to address the mourners. Some people stood at the back of the nave, holding hastily made placards. Teenagers from each of the towns mobbed together, their eyes looking as sunken as Mancanzano's craters. They joined those clamoring like activists protesting the repentance in Nineveh until Dr Biaggi motioned for them to hush.

'We are here to pray,' Dr Biaggi said softly, and the priest looked relieved. 'We are here to mourn,' he continued, and the congregants nodded their heads bravely. 'But while the spirits of our children have already ascended into the sky – like the sweet aroma of the most savory spiedini di salsicce – today we are here to return their mortal remains to where we found them. Now, where's that?' he asked the crowd.

The audience gasped.

'Into the welcoming womb of the earth,' Dr Biaggi said.

'*Nel ventre accogliente della terra,*' the congregants repeated.

'Where the children sought the nourishment that they lacked.'

'*Dove i nostri figli non soffriranno più,*' the congregants said.

'Where our children won't suffer any longer,' Dr Biaggi repeated.

Linda nudged me with the soft edge of her own bag, and whispered, 'Into the earth, where there are always the essential minerals in your food.'

176

'Into the earth,' I recited back, 'where Count Tramontano still rules over Hades, and where he waters the flowers in his own particular way.'

'Where the children so desperately wanted to be while they were living!' Dr Biaggi intoned. 'But they couldn't find peace!'

'No!' the audience shrieked. The teenagers, particularly.

'They were desperate!'

'*Disperati!*' the audience echoed. '*Dolenti. Malinconici!*'

'They were as miserable as a former patient of mine who was so afraid of gaining weight that when bones protruded from her ribs and hips, and people asked if she had a disease, only then would she rejoice. Because only then did she believe she was thin enough!'

'Say it's not true, Dr Biaggi! *Ci dica che non è vero, Dottor Biaggi!*'

'I have treated patients so afraid of gaining weight that they have even developed cuisines around their own secretions. So they could limit the introduction of new calories into their bodies!'

'*Dottore, dottore, rimetti i nostri peccati.* Pardon us for our sins!'

'But I've also had patients who understood that the freshest breads go stale, and, likewise, the choicest meats rot. And thus life slips away if you don't swallow what God sets before you! Eat, drink and be merry! That's in Ecclesiastes, and also in Luke! So, mourn the dead, I tell you. But celebrate yourselves! And when your cup runneth over, may it be with the very best reds you can get! Today we say goodbye to our beloved teenagers by burying their bodies, but not to their spirits, because we will relish them inside us for ever.'

'*Signore, pietà!*' the congregants chanted. '*Dottore, pietà!*'

I'm not sure if we were the only ones having trouble taking Dr Biaggi seriously that day, but I do know that somehow he'd nudged his followers into beatifying him even while he stood before them. The teenagers in church were ready to throw their full weight behind him, and I couldn't help but notice Filippa Grossoglio in the crowd, her tears now replaced with nervous energy. Her knees bounced up and down, and she looked into Dr Biaggi's eyes, rapt.

Yet while the souls of the four dead fueled the doctor's rhetoric, his transition from savorer to saint wasn't all that unexpected. This part of the world has always been home to ascetics – the Benedictines certainly saw to that. So if any more canonizations were going to occur, the right man for a feast day was Dr Biaggi. I almost expected him to invite a few anorexics up to the pulpit, just so that he could cure them miraculously. He'd shout hallelujah, and let the wine flow copiously from his cup. Then he'd lick it from the floor once everyone had left.

Needless to say, at the end of the Mass, the four checkerboard coffins were lowered into the earth. The priest was invited to say a few more words and almost refused. But finally he gathered the enthusiasm and patience to finish the sacraments, and the coffins were covered in a blanket of dirt. Filippa and the others threw pieces of tufa in the graves, burying the four just as if they were Mancanzani. She dropped some leftover shards. I picked one up and threw it in, too. Then, for the rest of the day, people cried when Dr Biaggi told them to, and ate when he told them to. And shook his hand seriously when given a chance. And for the rest of the day, even the parents of the four dead teenagers were able to achieve flashes of understanding and peace that came upon them unexpectedly, like waves of warm air, whenever Dr Biaggi walked past.

One more thing: these funerals occurred exactly eight days before Dr Biaggi's own body was discovered wedged in a crevice, back in Mancanzano. Friends went to look for him when he didn't show up for dinner, and his body was found two mornings after that, once anxious companies of townsfolk took to the streets and then into the hillsides. From all of the evidence, Dr Biaggi had slipped into a small fissure on the far side of the canyon, in the vicinity of the Cimitero Santa Maria della

Palomba. He had struggled a full day to get himself out, and then suffered a heart attack as the second evening arrived, just when everyone else in Mancanzano would have been preparing to eat.

There was a note in Dr Biaggi's shirt pocket that he'd written himself, apparently once he'd considered the inevitability of his own demise. It merely said, '*Per favore*, send my body back to Messina. No funerals for me in Mancanzano.'

People all over the city were disappointed (it was hard to discount how convenient their local cemetery would have been!); but the doctor's wishes were too dear to the townsfolk not to be respected. So back to Messina he went. In a truck. Just the way he'd arrived, picked up by a rig on its way to deliver furniture to Reggio di Calabria.

I didn't attend that funeral, but I heard it was a majestic affair, with enough food to feed half of the city. People devoured. It didn't matter if they were hungry. They just ate. And ate and ate. Afterwards, it was easy to imagine a squadron of bulimics lining up outside the bathrooms to make a final tribute to the man who hadn't quite cured them, but had always been their friend.

Dr Stoppani attended the ceremony. He returned to Mancanzano looking as though he'd been to a Roman orgy, the kind where at least a dozen Christians were slaughtered. His shirt was badly stained, but for a full day he refused to wash it. He merely trudged around town, mouthing the words, 'Benedetto, *benedetto*.'

# Chapter 13
# Simmer, Sweat

'Some *deus ex machina*!' is how Major Martella put it. 'I didn't invite Dr Biaggi to Mancanzano for him to die, just like everyone else! *Che rottura di palle!* What a ball-breaker!'

Dr Biaggi's demise now greatly complicated life for the major. Now there were new excuses and explanations for him to make; and not just to the Mancanzani and Messinesi (who'd lost their favorite son, the soon-to-be canonized Santo Plumpino), but to the Irsinesi and Montescagliosi alike: a new brood of mourners from all over Lucania who were similarly convinced that the only things constant in Mancanzano were bad omens, a bad diet and bad luck.

'What nerve of Dr Biaggi to walk around here like he was practically immortal, and then go ahead and die! At least the kids in those caves didn't have any pretensions,' Major Martella griped. 'But Dr Biaggi wasn't even willing to be buried in our hills. So talk about a new kind of inconsiderate!'

But Major Luigi Martella's problems went far beyond coping with Dr Biaggi's death. There were still his pesky anthropometric studies to finish, along with the various calls to animal rightists in northern and central Italy, who Major Martella still hoped might add their money and support to his investigation. And then, as everyone in town acknowledged, there were those ten unexplained deaths that needed solving too. Which was just another way of saying that Dr Biaggi's boorish demise left the major busier than ever. Which created another problem all by itself. Because no matter how much Major Martella hustled around the city, his mother still lived those hundred and thirty kilometers away in Moliterno, and she kept reminding him that *she* wasn't dead yet. There'd be no end to her grousing if Friday arrived and her prodigal police officer son wasn't attending to his most precious assignment: care for the woman who breast-fed him for the first three years of his life, not to mention an additional four months later on.

Briefly, Major Martella considered redeputizing our crew, and asking if we might complete the doctor's calibrations. He even made the trip to our quarters to raise the subject with us personally. But there was something about walking into our space, and hearing so much English spoken at once, that moved him immediately to reconsider. From the moment the first out-of-control syllables spun into his ears, it was clear he was glad our passports were locked up in his desk.

For a second time, it was my good fortune to be the one who greeted Major Martella at our door. A scowl seeped from his mouth the moment he saw me. Then it mushroomed into a full-fledged grimace.

'You're not from around here,' the major conceded, as soon as he walked in. 'You're not Italian. So how can I know you'd even get me the results I want?'

'What kind of results did you have in mind?' I asked him cautiously.

He slouched in a chair at our kitchen table. Then he sighed: 'A miracle.'

'Aren't those hard to come by?' I wondered aloud. I sat down beside him.

'No, they aren't!' the major snapped back. 'The only hard part is coping with the fact you English-speakers are always so negative from the start! Maybe miracles are scarce in the places you come from, but here you can practically buy them in stores.'

'So how much do they cost? Should I ask Bishop Pascoli?'

'No, ask *me*!' the major barked. 'Bishop Pascoli's market is indulgences. I don't have anything to do with that.'

'So, how much then?' I asked him again.

But this time the major only stared forward blankly, as if calculating prices in his head. Then, as his gaze focused on me, he came to the point. 'It's hard to be certain with the fluctuating exchange rates, you understand. But I'd think that a miracle would go for roughly the same price as your getting your passports back, or as someone figuring out why teenagers keep dying in town.'

'*Maggiore*, I think most people here would be willing to solve the murders for free. I would. Linda would. Wouldn't you?'

'Well, fortunately, we don't have to worry about me,' he replied hastily, 'because I get a salary. But in any case, I'm glad to hear what you're saying about *you*. Because that means I don't have to bother with your passports at all.' Now a bona fide smile emerged on the major's face. (I watched for a while to see if it was going to decay into anything gloomier.) Then, when the expression remained fixed, Major Martella leaned toward me and said evenly, 'So, here's what I want. I want you to pick up the measurements where Dr Biaggi left off. Because those measurements are going to point me in the right direction.'

'But your measurements won't tell you anything,' I told him. Again.

'Of course, they will!' he cautioned me quickly. 'Because the measurements can say whatever I want. That's the part that makes it a miracle.'

'You want us to make the data up?'

'Yes, but I want you to decide to do it on your own.'

'If you want fake numbers, why not just devise them yourself?'

'I would,' Major Martella answered, 'but I'm not a scientist. So how can I be sure I could trust my results?'

From our brief conversation it was soon obvious that our group of Anglophone scientists (the Amsterdam art restorer included) would never be up to the clinically rococo mission that

182

Major Martella envisioned. No matter the things that I said – or how the major tried to refashion his own grimaces and snarls into smiles and smirks – ultimately, it didn't take anything more than Winston Fortune entering the room in his underclothes, with an ale in one hand and the lines of a rugby song at his lip, for the major to savvy that he had ventured into the wrong place. From his own homegrown perspective, our quarters could have been the foreign embassy of an enemy state – one where not even the floorboards were to be trusted.

But as the major sat in our kitchen (perhaps now eyeing a sinkful of dishes for signs of subversive activity), I kept recalling something the Scottish novelist Norman Douglas wrote of his own travels in Italy just before the First World War: 'Southerners are not yet pressed for time; and when people are not pressed for time, they do not learn the time-saving value of honesty.' In Italy, Douglas met people who claimed that eating puppies cooked in a saucepan had cured them of rickets; and he watched others cast pictures of saints into ditches for failing to keep misfortune away. Sure, many in the south here are religious (and for reasons that have nothing to do with what Montefalcone said), but the ones Douglas met all seemed to pray to a God they were ready to swindle.

Now, in our kitchen, the major stood up from his chair. He tugged on his shirt cuffs, carefully pulling them past his jacket's sleeves.

'The purpose of science is to serve people,' Major Martella told me forthrightly.

'I agree. Everyone here agrees. Linda, Middelhoek, Fortune and I agree.'

'But you think I do nothing!' the major continued. 'And you think that makes me a bad police officer,' he said.

'We don't think that,' I answered him. 'I don't think that, at all.'

'Yes, you do. *Of course, you do*,' the major insisted. 'You're much too obvious when you're lying.' Now he extended his grooming to adjusting his collar and fixing the knot of his tie. 'You realize I could arrest you for lying to a carabiniere,' he reprimanded. 'Maybe I should. I *would*, actually, if I thought that it mattered. But what really matters is that at the end of my investigation, someone will sit in prison.'

I looked at him dolefully. 'The longer it takes, the more people die.'

'That's sad and it's true,' Major Martella acknowledged, 'but that's not my problem. Because the more people who die here, the greater a hero I'll be at the end. In the meantime,' he snarled, 'each time someone dies, it means I'm eliminating suspects.'

Then Major Martella turned on his heels and headed toward our door. But with his hand on the knob, he turned to face me and warned: 'The problem with you all is you're obsessed with honesty. You stink of the truth. But when you live like that, one little slip-up brings permanent repercussions.' He pulled the door open. 'So try worrying less about telling a few lies. Then your mistake won't ever be worse than blabbing the truth. It's your way that sounds dangerous,' he reproved. 'So maybe you *are* someone for me to keep my eye on.'

Then Major Martella disappeared from our quarters, heading back toward Via Stigliano. But once he was gone I thought about what he'd told me about honesty and truth, and about lies and deceit, and also I thought about danger. There still weren't any suspects in Mancanzano for the murders. And in a city of recluses, that meant anyone could be a killer. Even my own psychological profile made me a possible culprit: a loner sick of not fitting in. Mancanzano was a capital city for digging in different directions. Catching whoever was responsible for the deaths might not have much to do with honesty or lies, just as the major argued. But it was still going to require the impossible, which was teaming together, and that was the real reason I couldn't imagine Major Martella's force standing a chance.

If the major left our quarters that afternoon self-righteous and threatening, for the most part the rest of us were just left alone. Middelhoek had already been barred further access to the frescoes, and now Fortune was equally hobbled, since any drilling or hammering would be plain for Major Martella's carabinieri to see.

Initially, Linda and I had been able to keep to our ethnographies, as long as we posed our questions cautiously and didn't take notes. But now that Dr Biaggi's death had hoisted the metropolitan death tally to eleven (casting Dr Stoppani into a peculiarly solipsistic world of grieving; he kept mouthing the names, 'Benedetto, Monica, Benedetto . . . Anna'), our interviews similarly turned brief and grim, before fizzling out altogether.

Now the Vedova La Calamita would tell me: 'Maybe it isn't so bad being blind. Because I don't think I'd like what I saw if I were able to see.'

And Linda would come back to our quarters, equally frustrated. She'd grumble, 'The men in town all smirk at me, and say, "You're not allowed to ask us any questions. So it's too bad you're not finishing the major's calibrations, because then I'd let you measure *me*."'

As our obstacles mounted, Fortune and Middelhoek tried appealing to the high deputy. But all Dottoressa Donabuoni would do was exhort them to wait. So Fortune would mope around our quarters, brooding, 'My mistake was thinking that Mancanzano's badlands were just on the outskirts of the city.' And Middelhoek wasn't any better off: with most of the Calabrians gone home, he'd gone back to pining for Mathilde. Now, in the slow wake of policework that trailed after our discovery of the teenagers like geriatric sharks, the rest of us merely occupied our time by trying to decide what to do with it. Naturally, it was a sore spot for us all that I'd refused Major Martella's one offer to return to work.

So with no place else to go, we returned to the creek. As April set in, the weather in Mancanzano had continued to warm, and somehow it now doubled the vengeance of spring's arrival. It was as if the sweltering days that once made Lucania their home were furious at being banished for the few anemic months that passed here for winter, and now they weren't going to let anyone forget what they could do. So we returned to the creek, amid the southern Italian broil. We'd go to the creek, to escape the burning air that could solder your veins and arteries shut. Two or three times a day, we'd take Via d'Addozio, walk down the hillside, past the mosaic of broken stones and metal scraps, and head to the creek to splash our way toward some satisfactory illusion of solace. Because as the days grew emptier and longer and hotter – and ennui attacked each of us like an infection – the only way to relieve our animosity and tedium was to walk out into the ferocity of the sun. We'd been kicked out of the caves. So now there was no place to go but into the heat.

In the days that followed the major's visit to our quarters, each of us talked about leaving. We considered packing up our bags and trunks, just as so many townsfolk had done since we'd arrived here, and driving the beat-up Fiats back to Bari, or onwards to Naples or Rome: wherever we could go to get to the places we'd left behind. Wherever we could go to be finished with Mancanzano.

It wouldn't matter if we didn't have passports. There were always other options: letters and phone calls, visits to consulates and embassies. There could even be forays over Italy's borders – to Switzerland, Austria, or to France – always in the dead of the night, past weary frontier guards who couldn't be bothered to check anyone's papers, much less argue with anyone who claimed not to understand a word of Italian. So the way we figured it, we were free to leave, despite what anyone from the carabinieri had said. We didn't need passports. We could leave the country whenever we wanted, because no one in it would make us stay.

That was our thinking. That gave us freedom. And, then, because we didn't feel trapped, we chose to remain.

This was the sort of discussion that would take place among us at the creek:

FORTUNE: I'm only staying here as long as I feel like it.
MIDDELHOEK: I'm not leaving my frescoes in the care of Italians.
LINDA: I'm not leaving my research unfinished. (She'd look at me skeptically, and then sometimes add, 'For you to finish it.')

But prodded along by Mancanzano's hot sun, the truth was that none of us wanted to leave the city if anyone else in our group was going to remain. That was true most of all for Linda and me, because we'd both come to Mancanzano as cultural anthropologists with the same goal before us. There wasn't much teamwork fueling our present unanimity. Even more than not feeling caught, it was professional jealousy that made us stay. We each wanted to finish the work we'd begun, and none of us wanted to see someone else publish his or her work alone. I felt this as strongly as anyone else on our team. I wanted to return to New York with research other anthropologists would debate. I certainly didn't want to come home fending off requests for extradition from the Republic of Italy. Or reading about the extraordinary successes of the other industrious members of our group.

So each of us secretly blamed one another for the fact that we stayed. It was Fortune's fault, or Linda's, or Middelhoek's – or mine now, especially – that we were hanging around Mancanzano with so little to do.

But how many mistakes did we have to make? Breaking down the cave wall had been our first. Not contacting Rome once we did was our second. Remaining in Mancanzano was now our third. But all of them paled beside the error of envy. Because none of them was significant compared to the resentment that crept upon us like the most seasoned spy.

So that's how the creek quickly became a second, better home. It was a littoral retreat, if you didn't mind the explosions of dung, or infestations of frogs and flies. Still, it was also a place where I might find succor with my head submerged – where I'd be able to fantasize about being someplace else – and then still look up from the base of the canyon and see the magnificent cave homes embedded into Mancanzano's two bluffs. But the best thing about the creek was that, with a little good luck, it could also be a place where the current would block out everything but its own motion. Then all that would be left, as I approximated floating, would be an impression of progress (and it wouldn't matter anymore if I knew there was none).

So mostly the creek became a place to forget; it was a place for lotus eaters. When I'd go to the creek, I'd like to imagine that memories and impressions tumbled together at the mouth of the stream, cresting on top of each other with the power of waves, somewhere beyond the sputtering boundaries of Mancanzano. Then, as I'd lie in the water, trying to ignore my team members quietly ignoring me, I'd imagine that Mancanzano's tiny creek picked up speed and volume somewhere outside of the city, and that by the time it reached the Ionian coast, the tributary had all the power of the whirlpools of Charybdis, and that everything I wanted to forget – mixed, perhaps, with some of the things I didn't or shouldn't – bounced around there like the flotsam of a pulverized ship. Then, the one way of recapturing those memories would be to stop the flow of the water, to erect a dam. Because that would be the only way of locking the water, of shunting the stream, and shuttling its contents back into my memory.

When we're down at the creek and Fortune lets fly with something malicious, I pretend I can't hear him and I let the creek's gurgle enter my brain. Then, when I try to think of my life before I got to this city – and of the world that existed when crying was only a reflection of sadness, and my anthropology was a tool for gauging responses to my flesh and my bones – all that I picture of you are your legs spread before me, like the banks of this decrepit creek; and I know that I want to be fucking you with the force of its water, fucking my way back inside you, fucking myself into a place where Mancanzano is only a memory, and skyscrapers aren't just mounds of tufa heaped until they are thirty feet tall.

So our child is growing, and we're far apart. I'm here in Mancanzano, and I've made the promise to be home by June. But if I leave the city now, there won't be any point to my having come, at all. I've got to salvage this city if I want to do the same for you and me. So I'm going to keep to my work, and I don't care what the major says. Here's one more ethnographic note just to prove Martella's an ass, and that, as far as my work goes, I'm still able.

When a body's buried in plain view, there's a direct route for the mourners to confront their loss. In southern Italy, howling and tearing your hair are signs of honoring the dead. The Synod of Potenza banned these forms of lament in 1606, but the clergy today know better than to insist on the impossible. Despair can be channeled by religion, but never absorbed by it like a sponge. Occasionally, what the heart can't handle, the eyes and mouth can; and mourners in Italy's south will throw themselves into the graves, to cover the caskets with kisses.

But when a body's ferried away to a distant setting, there are too many factors and fantasies of what may occur. There's too much to fathom without any anchoring of place. Christ's draw wouldn't be the same if we still had his coffin and bones. Likewise, there were people in Mancanzano who wouldn't believe that their dear Dr Biaggi was gone for forever. 'He *could* come back!' they'd argue stubbornly. 'He hasn't been away from us for forever yet!'

Only the barber-surgeons in town were convinced he'd vanished for good. Antonio Montefalcone got word for me to come to his sasso in the melancholy days following the doctor's

189

funeral, and he told me, 'It's no secret I didn't trust Dr Biaggi when he was alive. But now that he's gone, the things that he said have started to make sense. So tell me, does your skin still itch?'

'Sometimes,' I answered hesitantly, thinking it was probably the sunburns from all the time I'd spent down at the creek.

'Then you're in luck!' Montefalcone told me. 'Because I have a handkerchief that belonged to the late doctor. Rub it on your skin while you recite a Hail Mary. That will cure it.'

He handed me the cloth.

'How do I know this really belonged to Dr Biaggi?'

'That's why it's essential that you recite the prayer. The cure only works if you have faith!'

I estimated what I thought he'd say the scrap was worth, then handed Montefalcone some money. Why not?

He frowned. 'If you don't give me more, the itching may spread.'

'I'm not going to give you more,' I told him.

'No?' he threatened. 'Do you realize if you don't give me more, there's a good chance the cloth may become infectious?'

'If I don't give you more money, do you really think you'll be able to sell it to anyone else?'

'If you don't give me more money, then you're going to be responsible for an epidemic. And if you let that happen,' he cautioned, 'not even I will be able to cure it.'

# Chapter 14
# Cave Canem

Then when the dogs started piling up in Piazza Ridola, everything went from bad to worse. Their carcasses were eviscerated, their throats crudely slit. The animals' bodies were drained of blood, although there was still enough of it to mat their fur and splatter the stone tiles where the bodies were dumped. One by one, the dogs landed in the piazza as a pile of pelts, and the tiles that were tufa soaked up the blood greedily.

Major Martella took the slaughter personally. He saw a connection between the dead dogs and his calls to the animal rightists. He now understood the process of calling and killing as one of cause and effect – and one where he'd strayed into the role of unwitting catalyst. Ultimately, Major Martella was so incensed by the slayings that he ordered his officers to stand guard over the piazza during the night, and before a single day passed Mancanzano slipped a half-century back in time.

Suddenly it was as if the Fascist troops of the thirties had once again laid siege to the city. The carabinieri who had been stationed along Via Annunziatella and other arterial routes to the town were recalled from their posts and redeployed in Piazza Ridola. But for the first time, these officers were equipped with automatic weapons: submachine guns that they slung from their shoulders from frayed canvas straps. When pedestrians wandered into their range leading dogs (always live ones, but now always leashed), the Berettas would be raised to their eyes, and they'd target the dog owners in their sights. It was enough to empty the piazza like a whirling centrifuge, one that hurled any pedestrians to its farthest edge. Within days, the open-air market for fruits and vegetables moved from the square to Corso Umberto II, now that there was a real possibility of the sky opening up and starting to rain bullets.

But better dead dogs than more dead children, people reasoned. Five carcasses had been dumped around the city, in all: three in Piazza Ridola, and another two on narrow streets in the neighborhood of the sassi. All five of the dogs had been German shepherds – wild ones as far as anyone could tell – and, like the teenagers, their exteriors had been blanketed in powdered tufa.

Those Mancanzani who owned dogs as pets now kept them at home, and watched over them carefully, like precious jewels. Dogs that had gamboled around Mancanzano with absolute freedom now pawed with frustration at the insides of doors, and their barks and their scratches could be heard all over the city, no matter the hour. This was especially true in the dead of the night, when you closed your eyes and sought out a silence that you only remembered from the days before so much mysterious dying, whimpering and yelping.

We had been used to seeing one or two dogs at the creek, pouncing on frogs in the stream, or trying to rid themselves of the buzzing of flies. Beside the skeletal cattle grazing on the grasses and weeds, the dogs had been a sign of Mancanzano's vitality. But now the creek had become a sullen place, a languorous locale for moping and forgetting. It was where you came to soak your despair, since you realized you couldn't ever wash it away. But as the stream ran low in Mancanzano's springtime heat, we found it took more time in the water if you wanted to feel buoyant – and then, longer still, if you hoped for the surge of an actual smile.

But, still, we converged on the creek. It's where we'd come by day in our swimsuits, as we tried to figure out what to do in the city. And it's where we'd come to shut our eyes, and try to remember our lives before we got to this place – where my mind might recall the trembling temperature of your skin. Where there was the heat of your jawline. The hard soft satin, where your teeth were buried in pink. And the hard soft slipperiness where my teeth always buried in pink.

But what I also want to say by the banks of the creek – as I try to recall how it felt not to be so alone – is that no one has ever existed in a vacuum. Not the Wild Boy of Aveyron (the French kid found among wolves, then taught to drink *café au lait*). Not Franz Boas's Kwakiutl. Not the Neanderthals. Not even Adam and Eve. So I don't care what the geologist Winston Fortune says about the awesome immutability of the laws of the universe. The people inhabiting this planet change every place they go; and their personalities change too each time they speak a new language. The world only makes sense because of its cultures. That's the essence of anthropology: figuring out how custom and language shape the man. But now I was learning in Mancanzano that desolation could be a kind of idiom too. Because the deeper I dug through the city, the better I understood how digging through tufa – and then through each other – was the one thing holding these people together, even as many of their bodies were drifting apart.

And so, what I want to say most about this hollowed-out hill town, and about the life we explored and then escaped at the creek, is that it wasn't long before they finally congealed into a single world of calm violent succulence – where Calypso herself lolled in her cave, while the loyal warrior Odysseus forswore immortality but went along with the sex. Because soon Mancanzano's creek became a place for a less brawny ethnologist to pose an epistemological question, viz., does faithfulness reside in the heart or the hard-on? And because I want you to know that my actions there weren't ever meant as ones of betrayal, but of heat, desperation and of the thirst for sensation – I can even call it a 'surrender to local customs', if you like. And, given the chance, I swear I'd blame everything on Middelhoek if I could, because *he*'s the one who once showed me a passel of photographs, and then asked if he debased his love, would that help him stop missing Mathilde so much?

So blame it on the creek. Blame it on death. Or blame it on this stone-cold city, where even passionate people can suffer so much they forget how to feel. But remember this: if I only had cheated, that wouldn't have mattered. Because *that* kind of trauma people get past. Maybe I'd never have told you, or maybe I'd have come with my head bowed in regret. But while infidelity erodes trust, more or less, the damage stops there. And what I'm talking about requires infinitely more understanding.

You asked me long before I left for Mancanzano if I would have an affair with Linda. 'It's her eyes,' you worried. 'She has better eyes than I do.' Somehow, you admired the curve of her retina. Somehow, you thought the blue of her iris was a color that even nature needed to awe. So, when you invited her to our home, I couldn't shake the idea it was for you to gauge your competition. Because no matter the things that I said, when your shoulders shook in the kitchen, saturated by tears, there was no way to claim that happiness resembled the things we'd created.

You knew that Linda and I had dated in the past, even if the times that we slept together are mostly recollections of the next morning's hangovers. But if it's true that Linda still flirted with me, and true that every once in a while I'd feel a hand at the small of my back, flirting alone would never have done it. Because I always preferred your eyes to hers. Or to anyone else's. The only problem now was just that I couldn't see them.

Linda was the first of our group (not counting Dr Stoppani, who had given in long before any of us met him) to succumb to the lassitude, displacement and expatriation of being for so long in Mancanzano, particularly now that we had so little to do. 'Succumb' is the right word, I think. Because, somehow, it carries with it the hint of a succubus, and I hope that, in turn, will shift away some of the responsibility. Maybe that will even connect what happened here to the awful and wonderful images of the lovers and demons in Middelhoek's underground frescoes. Because where sex was concerned, it was the time on our hands that did us in. That, and the inevitability of our being human (and the inevitable 'custom' of blaming everything on it).

Then Linda pulled me aside one day and said, 'I want you to hear it from me directly. You know the art student with the beard? The Calabrian, Riccardo? The red-haired one Fortune calls 'the orangutan'? The one who hasn't gone home even though there's nothing to do here? Well, we're having an affair. We're fucking. What Riccardo's doing is me.'

She looked at me restlessly, and opened the top few buttons of her blouse, revealing a melee of hickeys careening across her breast.

'You see these?' Linda said, running a finger across them, as if she were reading Braille. 'That's what I am now. A chomping bit for a mule. But I shouldn't complain. Because it *does* keep me occupied. You know what Oscar Wilde said about resisting everything but temptation? I'll go a step further: I can resist everything but boredom. Because when I get bored, I become a slut.' Linda pushed one half of her blouse far enough down to display the fringe of her bra. Then she said, 'You see, our problem is that you've only known me when life was interesting.'

Then Linda explained how Riccardo hadn't even been persistent in trying to seduce her; he'd just been glancing at her one afternoon at a café in Piazza Ridola, in the days before the Berettas and dogs, when suddenly she felt so listless she couldn't think of anything to do but respond.

'The marks run down my stomach, my thighs,' Linda recounted, casually. 'They cover my ass. The first time I saw myself naked in a mirror, I asked Riccardo if he was trying to mark out his territory.'

But the imprint of the hickeys reached far beyond Linda's skin. The three brothers who had invited her to their home for Christmas dinner, the other men in town, the Mancanzani – the ones who called her 'Sirena' at the bars and the creek, and made lewd references to the fun they could have with measuring tapes – they all regarded Linda's new romance with a combination of confusion, envy, curiosity and indignation. Linda was supposed to be *theirs*, after all. Something for *them* to play with, especially if the local women weren't going to accommodate. They reasoned that Linda was a gift to them from the United States, just like France had presented the Statue of Liberty.

One of them remarked, 'I spend most of my time at cafés, so it really should have been me Linda selected. But if our *sirena* wants a Calabrian, a filthy Calabrian from all the way in Africa, then she's got to be as infected as he is. So she'd better not dare come back to the creek. Because we don't want that *fica* – that cunt – contaminating our water.'

But Linda couldn't go back to the creek now, anyway. Not on account of the bruises that covered her body like a medieval pox.

Then Fortune disappeared for a few days, and he returned to town saying, 'I had some business to take care of in Montescaglioso. I mean, to *really* take care of. You can ask Dr Stoppani to explain it, if you want. Then you can ask him why he's not seeing Anna anymore.'

From what we understood, there had been a radical transfer of affections. Apparently, Fortune had tired of watching everyone else's affairs from Mancanzano's canyon, and, as part of his geotechnical mapping of the terrain, he'd already identified Anna as someone who readily gave in. So he rode the bus back to Montescaglioso with her one evening after work, solemnly visited the parents who'd lost their teenage children, and made such an impression of goodness and kindness on Anna, that the next morning in Mancanzano she offered him a cappuccino for free. Then, two days later, Fortune returned to

Montescaglioso as Anna's guest, and he spent the night on her family's couch, much of it with Anna beneath him.

'But what about Dr Stoppani?' I couldn't help asking.

'What about him?' Fortune replied. 'I gave him his chance. So as far as I'm concerned, he should have thanked me. Just because I started screwing his girlfriend, that didn't mean he couldn't have had something to say. Dr Stoppani could have *fought* me for Anna. Or he could have asked to watch. But since he didn't do anything, that means the stakes weren't high enough for him to care. He was lucky to have me show him that.'

Here, Fortune paused for a moment, closing his eyes as if lost in computations of vectors and torque. Then he looked at me wide-eyed, and asked: 'Do you think my mistake wasn't trying to sleep with his wife? Do you think *that* would have provoked him?'

'It sounds like the kind of thing that would have really burned into his skin.'

Fortune laughed. 'When I sleep with Anna, she clasps her hands overhead and cries out, *"Mamma mia!"* That's not something a fellow like me should have to miss! You see, I'm learning a bit of anthropology over here too. Each time I screw Anna, I become that more of an expert.'

'I assume you're telling me this to put into an ethnography?'

'Just make sure I get a proper footnote.'

'Of course,' I tell him. 'The pursuit of science is my one true motivation.'

Then, one more thing: on yet another blistering day, I leave our quarters, and head into the sassi. I go into town.

I pass Signora Bitonto's bakery on Via Pentolame, where her industrial ovens buttress the day's already unbroken heat; and I walk past the piazzetta by Fedelina Soppresa's home, where the laundry bodies are now only fabric phantasms – inanimate blouses, slips, dresses and skirts – and it is impossible to look at them and not feel you are missing something important.

197

Then I take Via Lucana, and pass Tonio Archimede's studio, where I watch him meticulously crushing failed figurines over an anvil through his shop's window, hammering at the heads and the torsos and the misshapen limbs.

Then I go past the tables of produce now stationed along Corso Umberto II, where the filmy skins of the plums have torn in the heat, and the purple flesh of the fruit oozes past each curling lip.

I stop by Via Bradano, where Antonio Montefalcone's new racket appears to be charging patients for shade. I pass Signor Federico Freccero, the roué earring-explainer, who yells out to me, 'I can tell you what every woman wants. To be missed when it's over! Am I right?' And I pass Via Sant'Isaia, where Gianluca Porfiri still bemoans the modern conveniences he doesn't have, has read about, but has never seen. '*Aria condizionata!*' he shouts. 'The air isn't just cooler. It's reconditioned!'

And then I pass all this, and take Via d'Addozio from the sprawl of the sassi, and I head out of town, down Mancanzano's bluffs, and into the canyon. As I descend the hill, I go past the clutter of metal and glass scraps that, along with the scarred fragments of calcified rock, are the multiform tiles flagging my path, and now against the quiet squelch of the heat, the flies in the air buzz by my head like the carabinieri's automatic artillery. Here, as I follow Via d'Addozio down to the creek, the bushy trees of the scrub are practically broiling, and my shirt is already coated with powdered tufa (and yet still somehow soaking with sweat), and I think how the swelter's so fierce in this part of the canyon that – forget the sun overhead! – I can feel it seeping from the ground and into my shoes, before it runs the full length of my legs and into the rest of my body, where the tingling is so unmistakable and perhaps criminologically atavistic that not even Cesare Lombroso could expect me to mind it.

And so when I finally reach the banks of the creek – this miserable stream that has always relied on imagination to swell it into what it is not – before I can even get my own wet, powdery shirt off of my chest, I see Filippa Grossoglio reclining across the rock. She lies on her back, under the sun; her breasts are hillocks saluting the sky. Droplets of sweat gather between them. They're as perilous to passers-by as Scylla and Charybdis. Today there aren't any tears, and the tips of her fingers dangle in real water. Toes wiggle lazily in the open air, and toggle the sky. Every once in a while, she sighs. Bare stone, bare skin; a surface forthrightness. I think to say something. I'm sure to say something. Of course, I'll say something.

But I don't say a word.

Because language is weaker than desperation. And it only pays attention to acts.

'*Antropologo*,' she mumbles, catching sight of my shadow, 'is it true you collect bones?'

That, and everything covering them. I sit down beside her and finish removing my shirt.

## Chapter 15
# Twenty Thousand and One

There is a phrase here in Italy: '*Chi abbisogna, non abbia vergogna.*' Whoever has need has no shame.

Sometimes, I imagine a meeting on the Via del Riscatto. Like the two teenagers I spotted there when I first got to town, I'll intrigue her by saying, 'I want to hunt you inside your clothes.' Then when I have her attention, I'll threaten again, 'I'm going to devour you.' And now she'll respond, 'Please, take your time.' Which I will. Because what is good is better if you make it last – but best if you can make time stop *entirely*.

Have need, then have no shame. Maybe this explains Fortune's new affair. To use his own jargon, there aren't trace elements of embarrassment anywhere in him, no matter how far you dig. He's a mother lode of brashness, equipped with his own hammer and pickax. He even admits, 'The trick with Anna is I don't play her daddy. Instead, I treat her exactly as though she were a real live *adult*.'

But Linda's romance with Riccardo is simple to understand this way too. She tells me, 'What works best is if I try to forget he's all grown up. So, my new thing is trying to convince him to shave more than his face. Because the more this resembles a fantasy, then the less any of it exists.'

Somehow, I picture Linda and Fortune and Anna and Riccardo in an endless round robin of age-defying antics, in

200

which they grope one another to keep from groping themselves.

But there's another phrase I've learned here too: '*Cento volte misurare e una volta tagliare.*' Measure a hundred times, but cut only once. Keep your blade sharp, and your hand steady; because you only get one chance to change everything for ever.

Dr Stoppani, the expert, says that's the way to manage affairs: 'Play them out in your head a few times before you do it. Figure out if she's going to call in the middle of the night. Imagine how you're going to react the next time your wife kisses you. And write out your excuses long before anything happens. Then cheat with a woman who's married, if at all possible. To maintain hegemony. In the interest of detente. In short, do everything I've done, except having your wife leave you.'

Then Dr Stoppani's voice trails off into inaudible whispers, far too faint to convey any conviction.

'But you've gotten your wife back,' I say to him, hopefully.

He sighs. 'It's not going to last. Especially not now. Monica was only willing to be with me as long as Dr Biaggi was in the picture. She wanted him there. That amused her.' Dr Stoppani smiles, but the look is unconvincing. Both lips tremble, like taut rubber bands that have just been snapped. Then he says, 'Do you know how I got my wife back? Do you want to know? You cannot guess. It is inconceivable.'

'How?' I ask.

Dr Stoppani fidgets, grinding a heel. 'When I traveled to Bari with Dr Biaggi,' he says, 'I found that Monica had changed the locks. But I could hear her moving around inside the apartment. So I got on my knees, and I begged her to let me in.'

I look at him skeptically. This is Dr Stoppani. I ask, 'You begged?'

'I begged. That part was Benedetto's idea. But I got down on my knees, and I begged. Just like in church, although at least there they put cushions in the pews. But finally Monica opened the door, and she glared at me with a look that said, 'Gaetano, you didn't even get down on your knees the night you proposed marriage.' Of course, back then I knew I didn't have to.

'But now, don't forget,' Dr Stoppani continues, 'Benedetto was on his knees on the floor beside me. He'd been adding his voice to mine during my apologies and declarations of love. And all the time that I'd been promising Monica I was ready to change, he'd been saying to her, "Signora Stoppani, your husband has changed already." But now it was obvious to me that Monica had changed too. Maybe I'd cheated on her once too often. Or maybe she'd just watched all those times without making me pay. But now my wife looked at Benedetto and me on our knees on the floor, and she said, "If you want me, Gaetano, your friend gets you first." Benedetto didn't say anything initially. But then he glanced at me, and offered obligingly, "It's up to you."'

It is six o'clock in the early evening, and Dr Stoppani and I are standing at the overlook by Via della Vergine, where we first came as a group the day Dr Biaggi arrived in town. This evening, with the dusk already upon us, the lights of the sassi are burning tight holes into the night air, and I can imagine the town's two slopes sloughing the sassi down to their base, in a last-ditch effort finally to be rid of them. Then the lights from the homes would be the only things left in the sky, and, in time, the night could even fix a patch over them too. Then it might be as if none of this had ever happened.

Now it is faith and obstinacy that make me look at Dr Stoppani head-on to see if he is joking. But I can tell from his grip on the railing that everything he has said is the truth. So instead, I ask him tenderly: 'Gaetano, why are you telling me this?'

He smiles back at me timidly, loosening his grip on the bar, just long enough for the blood in his hands to re-establish its flow. Then he answers, 'Because I want you to know why you're never going to see me again. None of you are. I'm telling you because I'm not going to tell the others. So please be kind when you talk to them. You could even make something up.'

'Where are you going?' I ask him, now starting to feel equally unnerved.

But the only answer he offers is, 'There are twenty thousand towns in Italy. I'm leaving tonight.'

'And there's no chance with Anna?' I ask, although I already know there is not. But I am looking for something, anything to moor Dr Stoppani to this place. So that he will stay with us here.

Dr Stoppani sighs, and then for a brief second there is even a flicker of his witty self, the flicker of the candle not completely extinguished. 'I thought there was some body language between Anna and me,' he says softly. 'But as it turned out, I was just talking to myself. Maybe it was just that she was young, and her vocabulary's not good. Or maybe I wasn't the right man for her. Anyway, I know about Winston, and I wish him luck. I really do. He'll be happy with her. At least for another month. But I can't think about Anna anymore,' he says. 'Not now. Not after Monica.'

'You want your wife that badly?'

'No, I don't.' He surprises me. 'I don't want her at all.'

'Then what is it?' I ask him.

He looks so uncomfortable, but I am curious.

'Tell me,' I tell him, 'especially if you're disappearing.' I half-expect to hear that he had found what he'd been looking for all along in Dr Biaggi. It would be funny to hear that – to hear now how Dr Benedetto Biaggi was his sexual salvation.

But Dr Stoppani says, 'Monica wanted to disgrace me. And she succeeded. But what we discovered by accident was that I didn't dislike it. Not the sex with a man, which was painful and filthy and I tore up the sheets afterwards because of how they smelled, even if Benedetto was willing to do it again. But the debasement. The anguish. And Monica's scorn. How it felt in the rest of me to have a man inside me while she watched. There was something pure in the brutality of it that moved my heart. And then both Monica and I knew we weren't talking only about my heart. Because like I told you at Christmas, you always have to know the source of your swelling. And of your excitation.' Now Dr Stoppani pauses, his face flushed and packed with apprehension. 'I didn't mind the way Monica made me feel that night. But I'm not ready to face that again in myself.'

'But maybe that's the kind of thing you don't face alone.'

'There are things I would do now that I can't imagine. But my wife will make me do them, I think. Did you know there are people in this world who actually eat their lovers' stools? I understand they do this as expressions of their sexuality. I'm not saying this to be specific, I mean it only as something Benedetto mentioned to me once. But my point is things like that do exist. And my wife will take pleasure in discovering them. She will still wear her jewelry and makeup, and the dresses I have bought, but she will research these things. Then she will make it her mission to force my heart to a different beat. This is my same wife who knows, by her own heart, how to quote the great Marxist, Gramsci.'

'And you know you don't want that? You said that there were things you liked.'

'No, I can't,' he answers quickly. 'I'm not ready. I need to explore those things first in myself. Especially before I let someone else do it.'

Now Dr Stoppani smiles nervously, which I immediately recognize as the smile he brought back with him from his trip to Bari. 'I'm weak. I don't have a lot of experience exploring myself,' he says.

'So tell Monica you want what the two of you had once.'

'But I don't. Neither does she. We had nothing.'

'So you're really leaving?'

'Yes.'

'Where will you go?'

But now Dr Stoppani doesn't say a word. He distances his hands on the railing, until they are perpendicular to his body.

Then he uses the bar to raise himself over the cliff. His arms are straight, and his elbows are locked against his sides. He rocks forward until his chest is extended over the slope, like the figurehead at the prow of a ship – and now I think how easy it would be for him to launch his whole body into the darkness. For a few moments, Dr Stoppani lifts his weight completely from his feet. He wavers, and I think of the teenager's dog those months before. I imagine limbs in the air, both animal and human, and I picture them so vividly that I think now that I almost can see them. But now I also picture the flailing arms and legs from the underground frescoes. And against the bullet-hole perforations that the cave homes' lights make in the black, I see both real and painted limbs tumbling through the sky.

Then Dr Stoppani groans, and lets his weight sag back onto his feet. He tells me, 'Like I said, there are some twenty thousand towns in Italy. This is an enormous country, even if it still manages to look small. But there are places inside Italy to get lost. Places of worship. Places of God. There are monasteries in some of the towns. St Francis wasn't the only one to recognize he needed that.' Dr Stoppani looks at me wearily, as his hands now slip from the railing and drop to his sides. 'I think the Benedictines found a thousand years ago that they wanted that too.'

'I think we still have to discover what they wanted,' I say to him earnestly. 'We could use your help.'

'No, not mine,' he replies. 'I need whatever there is for me. But I hope you succeed. Yes, I really do. Because after the last frescoes you found, you'll have to decide for yourselves if the monks wanted disgrace or absolution.' He looks at me warily. 'Now I have to ask the same question of myself. Do you know which one it is that you want?'

But I don't answer him now; maybe I'm not even sure.

'You won't see me again after today,' Dr Stoppani repeats.

And he is right; by morning he's gone. This is the last anyone hears of him, this day. Within hours, Dr Stoppani has pulled away in one of the broken-down Fiats, skulking, slow, with the headlights off.

Since Major Martella's carabinieri had been transferred to Piazza Ridola in recent weeks, there weren't any officers left on Via Annunziatella to record the doctor's starting direction. So we weren't afforded any more of an idea where Dr Stoppani had gone than he'd had those months before, while he was searching the country for his wife. But once Dr Stoppani disappeared from town, one thing became clear: somehow we knew that our connection to the nation beyond this stone city, and to the exterior world beyond this narrow peninsula – the lands from which we'd made our own pilgrimages once – had grown far more fragile and less absolute. In Dr Stoppani's absence, we felt more stranded in Mancanzano than ever before, and the severed connections to our places of origin cut all the way to our hearts and heads.

Dr Stoppani quit Mancanzano to explore his own disgrace, but he didn't know that he was abandoning the rest of us to confront the full force of our own.

—

And the other part of it is this: here, in Mancanzano, where there's nothing to root us, no stanchions and no ties, the ground is dusty. The air is dusty. Everything flies up in the hot wind. If there's a moment of stillness as you head down Via d'Addozio, the powdery ground clings to your shoes, transforming the brown leather into a brown-speckled beige. But if there's a breeze, then you cough as you go, as you try to remember the last time it rained, and you wonder if one day it will ever rain again. Then, as you look at the powder covering your shoes, you wonder how your lungs look these days, and you wipe your mouth to get out the grit, and you arrive at the creek tired and sweaty, thinking only: I really need to be wet.

So what I want to express is how, when you get there, it doesn't matter how low the water is running, or how crowded it is, or anything else. What matters only is that you strip off your clothes and enter the water as quickly as possible. Because that's what matters. And what I try to do.

And Filippa Grossoglio is there. She is there again. So it doesn't matter to me now that there are dogs, and they're the first dogs I've seen since people started locking them up in their homes. Filippa is there, and she is waiting in the water, and today it is deep: it is up to her knees. She is kicking the water into the air. And it splashes. And it feels good when it lands on my skin, and I say something about that to her now, about what is obvious.

And it is true – as I've suspected the times that I saw her, especially that time while she lay on her back – that I am taller. Because now the water is at my shins. Her chin is at my shoulders. And her hand is below mine, even if my arm extends farther. So what I want to be saying is that she has to reach up. She does. She takes my hand, and she leads me from the creek, back across the canyon, and to the foot of the bluffs, to the mouth of a cave. Neither one of us talks now. It is spring, I have said. A time for fertility.

We go in, and it only takes a second or two to feel the change in temperature and humidity. It is cooler here and it is damp, and this forces our bodies together, so that we'll each be warm. We were sticky and hot, but now we're sticking to each other and cold. I kiss her.

It has been a long time since I have kissed, and now I am finding out that I am hungry. Her saliva is sweet, and it is a kind of sustenance. It is in my mouth, with her teeth and her tongue, and we are kissing each other; and while I am thinking how the soft inside of her mouth is such a fine place for my tongue, our hands have moved up from our sides, to each other's sides, and I am moving my hands into her bathing suit, and her nipples are like stones. They are as hard as stones.

Then her hands are moving across my back. She is nineteen years old, perhaps. Do I care? Her hands are moving, and they are giving me shocks and I feel it between my legs. And I am hard. She holds me hard.

And now I have moved my mouth away from hers, and I am tasting the sweat and also the powder on her skin, and I am licking it away, and leaving the same marks I saw on Linda's body, which maybe I would have liked to have left myself. Maybe I'm even jealous that Linda went to someone else, when I'd have been happy to make those marks on her, if only there had been the possibility of discretion and absolute secrecy.

Which there is here. There is now. Filippa Grossoglio yells out when I bite – and I think for a second to look for tears – but I can tell that she is not angry, even if now she is suddenly trying to bite me too. Although I stop her. Because the fundamental principle of secrecy is it leaves marks only on others.

And now my hands are moving across her chest, and her bathing suit is coming down. The straps are loose and dangling beside her arms, and I am pulling the nylon down to her stomach and to her feet, and then I am taking the swimsuit off of her entirely. And in an act of graciousness, she should see it as graciousness, I hand it to her to put under her head.

I push my own bathing suit down my thighs, and I am pressed against her. Our bodies are damp because of the coolness of the cave, but also because of the sweat and our saliva, and I am pretty sure because of the wetness between her legs. And when I touch her, she calls out again, and I am right. She is wet enough that I don't have to be careful. My fingers slip inside easily.

Our teeth are against each other's when I push myself into her body, and this place where I am is a place I have not been for a long time, a world of satin and caverns and hidden seas, and a world that is soft and wet and surrendering.

I am fucking Filippa Grossoglio. In this Mancanzano cave, I am fucking her. By the creek. And at nineteen years of age, Filippa Grossoglio is fucking me too.

Now, it is true, I am thinking I wish that I were older, in my forties maybe, because then I could be fucking a woman who wasn't even born when I first learned to fuck. I could be fucking an infant. And that's what I'm thinking as I press my body against hers and the top of her head is against the cave wall, protected by the sheer nylon of a bathing suit I have taken away from her.

She is not a virgin. This is not new. She has done this before. She is pushing herself up to meet me, and both of us are breathing hard. And both of us are loving this, this love without love, this yielding and plunging. This succumbing.

I am inside of Filippa Grossoglio, and now she is starting to shake. She is beginning to shatter like a pane of glass, and I know I am giving her an orgasm, because I know she would not fake it for me, because she doesn't know me any better than anything else that's American. But this soft wet plush place has become all stubborn and goose bumps, and it is trembling where her body ends, and where mine disappears, and she is biting down on my shoulder again.

Now I let her. There will be bruises to cover. But I let her. Because I am starting to feel the tightening in myself. I was hard before. But now I am harder.

I am a cock. I have not been a cock since I came to this city so long ago, and I am glad finally to lose all those anthropologist trappings, and go back to being what I am. I am a cock with a body, and you can throw out the brain because right now it is as useless as shit, and as boring as shit. Leave the rest alone, because I am using the only part that matters to me now.

I am inside Filippa Grossoglio, and she is coming, and now I am ready to be coming too. I am an earthworm on amphetamines, the root of a maple, stretching myself to where it is wet. I'm back to being who I am. For the first time since. For much too long. With all that longing. For the first time since I've been back inside. Since coming, *that's it* – because now in this cave I am going to come.

So I start to pull out of her, so that I will come on her stomach, or maybe I will come on her face. She has beautiful eyes, and I want to tell her that I'm going to come by her beautiful eyes – the eyes that not so long ago I watched flooding her face. But now this is when she takes her hands from my ribs and places them along the sides of my neck, with her thumbs to the front. Now this is when she squeezes with the full force of her body. A body that's in the middle of an orgasm, and that is making me harder. That is harder than anyone's heart. And as I am pulling myself out of her *fica* to come on her face, those hands at my throat are squeezing and the thumbs are pushing, and the palms are pressed against where the blood is rapids. Not anything at all like Mancanzano's one trickling creek. Because I am hard. And I am a balloon. And I am filling. And then what I know is that I am breathing. And I don't even know if she is there. Filippa Grossoglio. Filippa Grossoglio? Because everything is black, and the only thing there is is the breathing. And the recollection of it. And the breathing. And faintly I hear the whining and yelping of a dog.

And I am opening my eyes to a new place even before I can see it.

# Chapter 16
# Target Practice

I am here in Mancanzano, breathing harder than I ever have, and I am wondering about the parts of me that are with two different women. In two different cities, countries and continents.

I am here in our quarters, where outside our windows all I can see is stone, and I am thinking of flowers. Blooming, dying and distracted.

———

We are in our quarters, and Joost Middelhoek tells us a story about Mathilde (a.k.a. Mathilde the Terrible).

'OK, this is when I really wanted to make the relationship work. So I'd tell her we needed to spend more time together. But she'd answer, "I spend seven hours in bed beside you every night. So find other times to sleep if you think that isn't enough." Or on evenings when both of us got home from work early, she'd look at me slyly, and suggest, "Hey, Joost, let's take a nap." But it wasn't a way of moving us to bed for something more intimate. It was just that the way she liked to spend her time with me was asleep.'

Middelhoek says, 'I read somewhere that zinc will make you virile. As potent as the demons we found in the frescoes. But the capsules I took in Amsterdam only made me expel gas.'

I can picture him popping fifty, and then a hundred milligrams a day. 'What do you mean, this doesn't do anything positive for our love life?' he'd ask Mathilde, perplexed, after filling the room with his own powerful stench.

Middelhoek says, 'Once I even concocted a dish of aphrodisiacs to woo her. But I was limited by the ingredients I could find. Still, I tried bananas, asparagus, cucumbers, squash, a couple of yams, figs, melons and some nicely rounded peaches. I even got a mandrake root from an Indonesian specialty shop that had opened in the Leidseplein. Then I spread everything over a plate, garnishing it all with candied ginger. And I put the dish in front of Mathilde, making my intentions known. But she roared, "You must be kidding. Are you kidding me?" I asked, "Will it help if I dribble some coconut shavings over it?" She suggested, "Try vodka." Then she drank it straight.'

Middelhoek says, 'But even after I served the plate to her, we still got into a fight. We yelled. She yelled. Mathilde threw glasses. Then once the mood had calmed, Mathilde said, "We still can eat together, but then you're going to have to sleep on the couch." And then she told me, "You know what would be a real turn-on, darling?" And I was excited. And I was hopeful. And she said, "If you'd wash the dishes."'

Middelhoek says, 'I couldn't find a camel hump, sea slugs, dove brain, hyena eyes or hippopotamus snout. Do you think if I had, that would have made a difference?'

What Middelhoek doesn't know is that I may become the father of two children I may never see. That I'll have a baby in New York, and now maybe I'll have one here, and that I wish I could fuck myself back inside their mothers, with all the tenacity of a salmon sprinting upstream. Because what Middelhoek doesn't know is that if I could find an aphrodisiac that induced violent convulsions – ones where the spasms and shudders might also mean a woman couldn't help but lose her baby – then I'd order a gross, plan out a banquet, and extend invitations to a terrific Mancanzano meal. Because what Middelhoek doesn't know is all of the things that I will keep secret, that inside my heart I want to deny.

Then Middelhoek says, 'So what happened to Dr Stoppani, anyway? *There*'s a man who really knows how to woo a woman!'

—

Betrayal is a liberating force. So it's exactly as Middelhoek argued when he returned from Amsterdam those months ago: if you betray someone you love, then you can't be worthy of her. And then you can't miss her. And then you won't want her, and it won't matter what you have done.

Hoc est purgatorio. Hoc est inferno. *Hoc est* a cave. Or a chamber, like Sartre said, without any exits. Hoc est a tomb for Count Giancarlo Tramontano, filled up with stones. And with bones. And with regret.

I want to talk to Filippa Grossoglio. I want this badly. This is what happened. When I got back to my senses, Filippa was walking away from me, heading toward the mouth of the cave. Her bathing suit was back on and when she turned to look at me, I saw the suit was wet at the crotch, where I imagined the fabric was holding my semen inside her. I got to my knees, breathing again, and then, as she disappeared into the open air, there was the sound of the dogs again in my ears. I heard barking and growling from just beyond the cave.

When I was able to stand, I found my own bathing suit at my ankles, and I pulled it up. Then I stumbled to the cave's mouth. It was about two o'clock in the afternoon. The sun was blazing overhead, and its glare was excruciating after I'd just spent moments unconscious in the shadowy cavern. So I put a hand to my eyes, and when I did, a half-dozen forms eased into focus. They were three large dogs, on leashes, guided by three kids. The boys approached. I recognized them immediately.

The first was Flavio, the teenager who'd lost his dog those months ago when it leaped from the battlements overlooking the

Church of the Madonna della Virtù. The other two boys I'd seen around town, not necessarily malingering; I think I'd even seen one on a pre-kestrel stroll with his parents. They were Maurizio and Giorgio, evening regulars on the Via del Riscatto. All three looked about eighteen or nineteen, about the same age as Filippa. The dogs were all wild, mongrel German shepherds.

Filippa was already ascending the hill. I was still leaning against rock, and I knew I'd have to gather all of my energy fast if I wanted to say something to her. So I pushed myself off the rock and into her direction, centering my weight on my feet. But when I sprung forward, one of the dogs lunged back. I remember its teeth, because you always remember the teeth. A snarl is an expression we human beings can't mimic with the same ready viciousness. Because no matter how ruthless we are, our worst grotesquery usually reeks of sarcasm and parody. Then, over time, our mercilessness becomes burlesque.

But right now the dog was barking.

'*Scusa! Scusa!*' the dog's master was saying to me, but his voice was bereft of any particular emotion. It was the one named Maurizio, restraining the German shepherd, half-heartedly at best.

I wondered immediately what the teenagers knew. And what they had seen.

I mumbled to them that I needed to pass. I pointed to Filippa with the hand that had been shielding my eyes.

Then Maurizio pointed to her too. 'Oh, do you know her?' he asked me playfully, intent on securing a role for himself in the intrigue.

Then Giorgio advanced, with another mongrel shepherd. He laughed, and then asked, 'Yes, do you know her *well*?'

'Well enough to know that –' I started to tell them. But then I stopped; I knew I didn't have to explain anything. '*Scusate*,' I said now. '*Fatemi passare*. Please let me by.'

I moved away from the dogs. They started to bark. Then both the boys and dogs followed me.

'I'd like to talk to her too,' Maurizio told me, grinning.

All three of the teenagers started to laugh.

Then Flavio approached, and asked, '*Antropologo*, is it true you study people?'

'*Sì*, he studies people,' Giorgio piped in. 'But only certain people.'

'Certain parts of certain people,' Maurizio added, giggling now with true adolescent delight.

Then the three teenagers kept laughing. Except for their dogs, which kept to their barking.

But now Flavio pulled at his dog's leash, drawing the animal backwards. He handled the animal more confidently now. Perhaps he was mindful of what might fly through the air when given the leeway. This dog wore a choke collar, and, as Flavio jerked on the leash, the collar tightened and the dog let out a few tiny yelps; I recognized them immediately as the ones I'd heard inside the cave, when Filippa Grossoglio was choking me herself. Then another of the dogs pressed forward, and started sniffing at my groin. I pushed its nose away, risking its teeth. But even after I'd done this, the dog growled and returned its attention. The boys laughed again. A second dog joined in the game. I covered myself with my hand.

'*Che c'è?*' Flavio asked the dogs. 'What's there? Is there something you like?' The teenager looked at me derisively. 'Do you have something for our dogs in your pants?'

'Listen, I'm going to go now,' I repeated to them, even while the third dog began growling. 'I don't have anything for your dogs,' I said. 'Not even a stick. So move your dogs away. Please make this easy, and do it now.'

The boys did nothing.

'Move your dogs. Please.'

Flavio dug his heel haphazardly into the stone.

'Move them,' I repeated. 'Please move them now.'

'Maybe you should ask the dogs,' Flavio said to me finally. Then he repeated: 'You should ask them. They're dogs. With sharp teeth. And you are a man. And we're only teenagers. Three little boys who live with their mamas.' The dogs kept growling. And sniffing. 'So ask them,' he said again.

Maurizio and Giorgio laughed.

'No, I am asking you,' I answered him now, and as I did I felt the insides of my body roil in a way that suddenly made me feel I understood animals. Because now I knew the difference between exasperation and contempt: contempt has a physical consistency, taste and smell. It is a weapon of acid.

So then I said, 'Your dogs will get locked up if you don't pull them away. The carabinieri will do that. That much we know. But if you really want me to talk to your dogs, I'll do it in their language. I'll do it with a stick. Or with a rock. I can bash their heads in for them, if that's what they want. I can take a large stone and smash it down on their skulls, if that's what you want. I can mangle their snouts.' I was almost out of breath. 'I can rip off their tails. Is that what you want me to do to your dogs?'

Now the boys briefly considered the options. 'OK, OK,' they answered after a pause. 'We didn't mean anything.'

'Yes, you did,' I said.

'OK, yes, we did.' They laughed again. Then added, 'We still do.'

But finally the boys relented and pulled on the leashes, and restrained the animals so that I could pass by. But by then Filippa Grossoglio was already up the hill, and too far away for me to shout. And much too far for me to chase her. There was only a last glimpse of her swathed in the flimsy, wet layer of nylon, and striding up a hulking staircase before she disappeared into the opening of a cave.

Now, as I walked back up the bluff in the sun, I felt sick to my stomach. My heart was pounding, but I could feel it circulating bad blood throughout my body. Heading uphill, I passed chunks of stone and discarded pieces of metal, and I looked around them for a hefty stick, something to use in case the dogs reappeared. But I knew this was only a ruse, and that it was only designed for fooling *me*. Because it was easy to know what the dogs had smelled. In the dry air, I could smell the scent of Filippa on my skin too. Outside the cave, I had covered myself in front of the teenagers because I hadn't wanted them to see what my own body was doing to my suit. And what Filippa was doing to me. I'm not talking about soiling myself from nerves, or about my own body caving in. I mean the hard breathing that had stayed with me until this last moment, and the swelling that had spread into my groin with the obduracy of an idea that has become a conviction.

So, as I trudged up the slope, my heart beat a coronary elegy to everything I'd loved and had now ceased to be, and the tattoo of my heart instantly made me think of Dr Stoppani. Because of his own stirring, he'd realized ten years ago that he wanted his wife, and then when it returned, as startling as thunder, that no one he knew would ever see him again.

—

Mancanzano, city of stone, what have I done to deserve this? What have you done?

Filippa arrived at our quarters two days later. I'd looked for her in town without any success, and my only other strategy for finding her had been to return to the creek, which I no longer wanted to visit. (As far as the creek went, our bathing corps had suddenly dwindled to Middelhoek alone. He'd come to the door wearing his swimsuit, with a towel draped across his arm, and ask, 'Who wants to join me for a dip? The creek's still the most peaceful place in Mancanzano.')

It was late morning when Filippa knocked at our door. Linda, Fortune and I were in the living room. They weren't due to see Riccardo or Anna for a few hours. The timing was horrible. It complicated everything that they were here.

Linda smiled playfully when Fortune let Filippa inside.

'Who's your new friend, Winston?' she asked, running a

217

finger over a hickey that was peeking out of her shirt like the wet, crumpled nose of a small creature.

Fortune laughed. 'I hope she *is* my new friend.' For now, they were both sticking to English so Filippa wouldn't understand.

Then he told Linda, 'You know who she is. We've seen her at the creek.'

Fortune looked at me coyly, and then back to Linda again. Then he whispered to Linda, 'She's one of Mancanzano's finest. She even has Anna beat. This bird's been endowed with the mother of all arses. And, mind you, that's even counting the kestrels.'

'I thought I had the mother of all arses!' Linda cooed, with mock indignation.

'I don't look at your arse,' Fortune countered. 'I'm an Englishman, a poet, and I take tea.'

Then he turned to me, and asked me straight out, now not even bothering to whisper, 'Do you look at Linda's arse?'

'We all do,' I said, keeping cool. 'The whole town looks at Linda's arse. And also her ass. Except when she's sitting on it, of course.'

Linda huffed histrionically, and then she stood up. 'Well, they should study it,' she pronounced. 'And they should teach it at school! As far as I'm concerned, everyone should treat my derriere like it is royalty, because it's queen of the whole Western Hemisphere.'

'Actually, it's *two* little hemispheres!' Fortune suggested.

'That's right!' Linda said. 'But look at it without the proper respect, and I'll have all naughty knights deprived of their lances!'

By now Linda was laughing, and Fortune had joined her. Then Linda spun on her heel, and switched into Italian.

'*Buon giornissimo*,' she said to Filippa. She greeted our guest, and offered her a seat.

Filippa Grossoglio walked into the room. She was dressed in Capri pants and a loose blouse, both of which appeared sewn at home. Her hair was down, across her shoulders. She wore sandals, and carried a purse. She still looked unmistakably nineteen.

'Yes, have a seat,' Fortune repeated, a moment after Filippa already had.

I hoped Linda and Fortune wouldn't lose interest in their banter. They could go on between themselves as long as they wanted, especially if that kept Filippa herself from talking. Besides, what they said to each other didn't matter, because the truth is that I barely heard them. I was only listening to Filippa, who so far hadn't said a thing. I had a hundred things to say to her myself, but I wanted to say them all elsewhere.

Then Fortune stood up from his chair and walked over to Filippa's. He pushed her chair toward the table, with a chivalrous sweep of his arms.

Filippa looked at me skeptically, then she looked back at Fortune. '*Lei è molto gentile*,' she told him sweetly. 'You're very kind.'

Fortune murmured, 'I've learned this attention to detail from our very good friend, the talented art restorer Joost Middelhoek, from Amsterdam, Holland. Now, Middelhoek's a real lady's man. We know that because that's what he tells us. If you're going to the creek, perhaps you'll even run into him there. He'll be the one with the red shoulders, and the zinc oxide on his nose.'

Then Fortune pointed to me, changing his tone once he saw my grimace. 'Middelhoek may be a twit,' he said, 'but that one's no fun. Not even once you get to know him. Supposedly, there's a "girlfriend" back home.'

Filippa's glance chilled. She adjusted her blouse, and pulled back her hair. The marks that I'd left two days before were every bit as obvious as Linda's. They were burgundy welts along the sides of her neck.

Linda saw them immediately, and smirked. 'I'd like to meet that boyfriend of yours!' she laughed.

'Oh, some day you will,' Filippa answered quickly. 'But don't think less of me if I admit that he's quite a bit older.'

'Older than I am?' Fortune asked, piqued.

Filippa pointed to me. 'More like his age,' she said to us all.

'Well, is he handsome?' Linda asked.

'I never think men are handsome,' Filippa replied. 'I think they are all animals.' Now Filippa pointed to the paisleys on her neck with the tip of her finger. Linda nodded appreciatively, and then Filippa smiled. 'But sometimes they can be useful,' she said.

'Oh, they can, they can!' Linda agreed. 'Present company excepted, of course!'

'You never can tell,' Filippa answered. She looked at me ambivalently.

Fortune spoke up. 'I'm bloody useful. I'm more useful than Philip Mountbatten and T. E. Lawrence combined.' He turned to Filippa. 'So, tell me, how can I be of use?'

Filippa smiled politely, if perhaps momentarily confused. But then she leaned in toward the center of our table. She was nineteen years old, with a nineteen-year-old's physique, with the same body I'd been drawn to at the creek. She brushed her hair away from her cleavage. For a second, we were back in the cave, and my hands were exploring the convexities of flesh only now revealed. Then Filippa spoke up. 'I'm sorry for barging in here when I don't really know any of you,' she said. 'But I came here because I wanted to hear about America.'

I looked at her warily. Fortune was crestfallen. He offered, hopefully, 'I can tell you about England. The entire United Kingdom.'

'No,' Filippa said. 'The United States. I want to know about America. Because I've heard it's a place of great ambition.' She smiled. 'Is this true?'

Linda looked at me. I shrugged. I wasn't saying a word. Then Linda said, as if trying to joke, 'America's a place where anthropologists come from, ambitious anthropologists, who come to Italy to advance their careers. To make themselves

220

famous. To make their lives better.' She turned to Filippa, and said, 'But, of course, that may not be what you meant.'

'But that's interesting,' Filippa said. 'Especially the part about making lives better. About making life.'

Still, Fortune wasn't to be excluded from the conversation, at least not so easily. He cleared his throat deliberately to attract everyone's attention. 'At our most eloquent, we English say that Caesar was ambitious. Although look where it got him.' Fortune rubbed his forehead, and then stood up from the table. 'Actually, ambition has a bad history in Italy,' he observed. 'But forgive me for saying that.'

'Oh, I'm very forgiving,' Filippa said. 'But only up to a point. But what I really mean is this: what would you do in America if a man gets a woman pregnant and doesn't want to be the father. Of course, I'm talking hypothetically. Not because there isn't a baby, but just because I haven't told the father yet. But let's just say the father has all kinds of dreams, and he thinks that being a father is going to destroy them. That's what I mean by his being "ambitious". So, if he wants to run away, can he do that in America? Because here in Italy, people will chase him and hunt him like he is a wild animal.'

Linda sighed. 'Men run away all the time in the United States. *Especially* in the United States.' She looked at Filippa sympathetically. Then she said, 'I'm glad you came to us to talk, if you didn't have anywhere else to go. I don't have any experience with being a mother myself. But look at our friend over here.' Now she pointed to me. 'Our friend has a girlfriend in New York who is going to have a baby. So he is the father, even if he's not a full-fledged husband yet. But at least he's made the promise to be home with her before their baby is due. So even if our friend *is* an ass – and a real one, I mean – for leaving his pregnant girlfriend at home while he comes here to make his investigations, we know he's going to make a wonderful father.'

'Yes, I can tell he's going to make a good father,' Filippa said.

'But, of course, he's going to have to learn to talk first,' Linda laughed, still wondering no doubt why I was so mysteriously silent.

'Oh, I bet he can talk,' Filippa said. 'If you ask me, it's more like he's speechless. Or maybe he's sick. What's the matter?' she said to me. 'Do you have a sore throat?'

'I always have a sore throat!' Fortune intoned. 'I need loving kindness!'

'My throat is fine,' I answered. 'It's just that the story you're telling leaves a bad taste in my mouth.'

'Oh, he's not telling anyone in Mancanzano about the baby back home because he's worried that if it gets out, then people here won't trust him,' Linda explained to Filippa. 'But now I've told you. So you'll have to keep it secret.'

'What kind of father will you be?' Filippa persevered, looking right at me.

I looked at her coolly. 'I will be a sensible father,' I said.

'Sensible!' Linda screamed. 'Ugh! Sensible? Be more fun than that!'

'See what I mean? See what I mean?' Fortune screeched. 'My God, he's boring!' Now Fortune was laughing so hard that he was holding his stomach exactly where I would have liked to have kicked him.

'I hope you are sensible,' Filippa said to me. 'This is a sensible town even if people in it are dying.'

'No, this is a disastrous town,' I told her, 'and it's just getting more disastrous.'

As cryptic as Filippa was, she did not cross the line that morning. I barely knew her, but I learned then that she did have an inclination toward restraint. Knowing that made me feel peculiarly grateful. But was I grateful to *her*? I think it was merely the first time I'd felt grateful to anything since I'd raised myself to my knees inside the cave and realized that I was still breathing. Given the circumstances, I wasn't feeling especially choosy. Still, I know I'd have appreciated the sense of relief more

222

if I'd had any faith that everything set in motion might now somehow work out for the best.

I rushed after Filippa as soon as she left our quarters. Linda and Fortune had already gone to their rooms to ready themselves for their afternoon trysts, so neither of them noticed when I ducked outside. Filippa stopped when I called her. Then we made a plan to meet.

She kept to her promise, and showed up at three o'clock that afternoon in Piazza Ridola. She had selected the place and the hour, and both were good choices because the piazza was empty, except for the carabinieri, who were still on the lookout for dead dogs. Since the officers had nothing else to practice training their guns on, they trained them on us. Occasionally, as if to make the greatest possible joke, one would pretend to pull his trigger, make the sound of his weapon firing through his mouth, and then jerk the gun skywards, as if it were recoiling. This was a prank that one of them would repeat every few minutes. Every once in a while, a pedestrian would wander into the square, see a carabiniere pretending to fire, and run off in terror.

Filippa and I walked side by side.

'Of course, you know what you've done,' I said to her evenly. I didn't know how else to begin.

'I know what *you* have,' she answered. 'And I know what *we* did, too. Of course – since that's the way you put it – the only part I didn't know about was the woman in America. Do you miss her?'

'I miss her,' I said.

'I bet she misses you too.'

'I know she does.'

'*Of course* she does.' Filippa smiled back at me. 'I bet you can feel her missing you, inside of you, this very second.'

'Inside of me, if that's what you're asking about, I miss her more than I like you. I miss her more than I even know you, Filippa.'

'Still, I bet you were missing me a lot yesterday when you looked for me in town. Maybe you even missed me until I showed up at your door.'

'I hoped I'd never find you, that you'd disappear.'

'That's not true.'

'No, it isn't.'

'No,' she repeated. 'You asked me to meet you. And from the way you're looking at me, maybe you haven't even stopped missing me that little bit yet.'

But as we paced Piazza Ridola, with the hail of imaginary bullets firing and ricocheting around us, both Filippa and I knew what she said was the truth. I'd never wanted to know her, except for a thought by the creek, and a moment without thought inside a cave, where the thick walls of stone blocked out reason just as they blocked out heat. But somehow Filippa understood how to encroach upon my emotions, even as she so deliberately intruded on my life. Before, in the cave, Filippa had squeezed and she'd taken. Yes, she had fucked. But now, in the open, she was as steadfast as the sassi around us. And she was constructing on top of them, just as people had done here for thousands of years.

But wasn't I the anthropologist? It was my role to study and probe – not hers. So what bothered me most as we circled the square, still not daring to touch, was that if I wanted to blame her I couldn't: because I wasn't even sure I wanted to reject her. Right now, I couldn't keep my eyes off of Filippa as we paced. In the three o'clock sun, sweat dripped from her skin, and it made her blouse cling to her like a wet sail. And my own anger toward her felt forced, like something I owed and had been called upon to deliver.

We walked. If she got ahead of me, my eyes automatically slipped to her waist.

'Of course, I'm sure I'm pregnant,' Filippa said idly. 'But if I'm not, will you do it again?'

'No, you know that I won't. Especially not now.'

224

'Of course, I won't know for sure for a month. But tell me you'll do it,' she repeated. 'Tell me you will.'

'I don't want you to be pregnant, Filippa!'

'But I've been careful,' she answered. 'So I have to have conceived!'

'Look, you had no right!' I whispered to her. But not as softly as I had thought. A carabiniere cocked his head toward us, and raised the foregrip of his gun. The tip of the barrel followed our bodies around the piazza, bouncing after us in the air. Then, once we'd moved out of earshot, I repeated, 'You had no right to take from me! You stole.'

'Stole?' Filippa scoffed. 'Stole what?'

But I didn't answer until I was sure how to say it, because to use the wrong words would be worse than keeping silent. Then finally I said: 'My sperm. My seed. You stole *me*!' I looked at her with what I hoped would be contempt. 'You know, Filippa, everything Linda said in our quarters is true. In America, the land of ambition, in New York, the capital city of ambition, I have a girlfriend I will marry and who will be the mother of my child.'

'Then we have a lot in common,' Filippa answered hastily. 'So maybe us girls should correspond. Receiving postcards from a foreign country makes everyone happy.' She paused for a moment, as a smile crept onto her face. 'I read that in a magazine once. But I'm not so sure it's true. Because I guess people in other countries can decide to write nasty things too.'

'Not just write. But also say and do those things. And not just in other countries, Filippa.'

'Do you think?'

'Yes, I think. I don't understand why you're doing this.'

'Because I want to be pregnant. That's what I keep telling you.'

'I hope you're dead inside you.'

'Funny,' she answered me. 'I hope you're full of life.'

But as Filippa and I walked the perimeter of Piazza Ridola this afternoon in the squalid Mancanzano heat, it didn't take long for a carabiniere to have mercy and shoot us dead in the eyes. I placated myself by imagining us bloodied and sprawled on the ground. Then I wondered if our prostrated forms could possibly rise like innocent angels. But they were gone from the frescoes. And now they wouldn't come here.

Then I said again, 'Look, Filippa, you can't know for sure yet if you're pregnant!'

'Then how come when I asked what you felt in your body, you didn't ask what I felt in mine?'

But the answer, of course, was that men don't know what women feel in their bodies, because we don't feel the same subtle changes in ours. So when women suggest that they are pregnant, we always believe them. For men, the certainty of pregnancy is more convincing than the existence of God, and that's equally true among the religious. This afternoon, as we circled Piazza Ridola, I wasn't asking her because I still wanted the luxury of doubt.

'Filippa,' I tried saying now, 'I didn't want to come inside you!'

'But you came inside the cave.'

'I followed you there. I followed you in. But that doesn't mean I'd agreed to more.'

'You mean, *more* than sex? *More* than pulling my suit off? More than leaving marks all over my body? You don't like risks? You didn't even wear a condom! You can find them all over the floors of the caves in this city. The guys I know even keep them in their wallets.'

'There were no condoms! This is serious. And now you're making a joke!' Inside my body, if that's what she really wanted to know, I could feel the volume of my blood doubling, tripling, and becoming oceans. No doubt it was surging, looking for where I was weak. But I was weak all over. 'Look, I don't have a disease,' I spat at her, 'but I wish I did. Something that would make a part of you die for ever. Or I could choke you, Filippa.

The way you choked me.'

But now she only smiled. 'You could not choke me like that with these carabinieri and their guns,' she said. 'You know you could not do that here. But answer me this, if you're really so upset. What you did those times we weren't together, before we met – weren't they as good? Didn't you like me choking you? I know you did. Because you were as hard as stone. You were a stone inside me.'

Now Filippa was looking right at me. And as my own eyes fixed upon her, I could feel the muscles and tendons making them move. 'So if I am not pregnant,' she said now, 'you can be a stone again. You can be inside me again. Would you like that?'

I wanted to hate her, and couldn't. And I wanted to accuse her.

'I'm not going to do it again, even if I would like it.'

'Then you are selfish. Not only to your girlfriend, but to yourself.'

'I've done enough harm already. You have too. You've done more. You've done it on purpose.'

'Why? It makes you feel better to think it wasn't an accident?'

'You're old enough to know the damage you're doing.'

'You are old enough too. To take responsibility. To be a man. You come from a city of skyscrapers. I thought that might mean you'd have perspective. But you don't even have a view from the ground. Listen, if the only way you can grasp what we did is to think of a trade, you'd better try that. I gave you something that makes your heart pulse. You gave me what I wanted too.'

'Filippa, I believe you when you say you think men are animals. But we're not.'

'No, you're not.'

'No.'

'No?'

'What you're doing is killing me.'

'You're not dead yet. You shouldn't joke about that. I know

227

people who are. That's why I go to the funerals. What about you?'

'I hope you lose the child. If there is one.'

'That is something I am sure your girlfriend in New York would not like to hear you say.'

'She is the mother of my child. Only her.'

'Then she doesn't know the father as well as she thinks.'

Then we said goodbye to each other because there wasn't anything more to say, even if a hundred thoughts now whizzed through my head like a sudden discharge of shrapnel.

What had happened? And what had I allowed? I hated that I'd opened myself to this accountability. I hated that now there were these new seeds of responsibility, when there was so much depending on me in New York. But mostly I hated that Filippa Grossoglio, whom I'd wanted to fuck inside a cave, was so intent on introducing me to something more. And something far more enduring than pounding and stone: elements akin to what Dr Stoppani had found with Monica, to which his dear fat dead friend had only been peripheral. So, now, as Filippa and I parted, ours was the kind of goodbye where we each kept turning our heads, wondering if we should begin to shout angrily. Or if it finally made sense to try to keep silent. Because silence could also be a weapon that smothered.

Then Filippa was gone. She disappeared in the direction of Corso Umberto II. I stayed in the square, finally letting some distance fall between us. Then I headed to a bar on the edge of the piazza. It was the only one there that the carabinieri's target practice hadn't forced out of business. The barman eyed me appreciatively as I entered. I was probably the first customer he'd had in hours. He offered coffee.

Then he said, 'Do you know that girl well?' He pointed through the window, to where we'd been standing. 'In fact, didn't I see you interviewing her great-grandfather the other day? He told me he took you to see the old Madonna in the fields.'

228

'If that's who he is, and that's what he said, then we both know you didn't have to ask.'

'Still . . .' he told me.

'Yes, still,' I answered.

'The girl you were with. His great-granddaughter. She is a fine girl. Everyone says that one day she will make a fine mother.' Now the barman gestured toward me directly. 'So imagine the shame of anything getting in the way of that. Look, all of us in Mancanzano realize how ideas from abroad can exert a dangerous influence on the way a young girl thinks. But I'm sure nobody wants that. Least of all you.'

'No, I don't want the coffee,' I told him as he placed the cup on the counter before me.

Then I continued past the bar, and headed into the bathroom. It's where I'd meant to go as soon as I'd entered. The bathroom in the bar was a typical public one for Italy: no actual toilet, just a hole in the ground with a white porcelain finish, with treads on either side showing you where to put your feet. I considered it for a moment, then I put my back to the door. I could feel the metal against my shoulders and spine, and the coldness of the slab through my shirt. My heart was racing, as it had those days before when I'd ascended the hill. But now it was as if hundreds of red blood cells were popping under my skin, like a full cartridge from one of the carabinieri's Berettas.

So, then, just as the old man – her great-grandfather – had done with me outside the rock churches, long before I'd gotten into this trouble, I slid down my pants. I thought of the old man whacking his penis and lamenting to me that it wouldn't work. This afternoon, my own hands felt clammy as I worked them into the elastic. But then I took hold of my own body, and I thought about Filippa Grossoglio, the fine girl, the bad girl, the eventual mother, Filippa Grossoglio stealing her way into being a mother, stealing from me, kissing me, grabbing me as I was hard as a stone, making me as hard as stone, and touching my neck, especially touching my neck. I touched myself like that in

229

the bathroom until I'd done what I'd come there to do, and when I did it I did not think of you. My love. The tears by my eyes weren't for you.

Mancanzano, city of tufa, city of stone, what have I done to deserve this? What have you done?

## Chapter 17
# Foundations

The caves where the frescoes were found were reopened provisionally. Middelhoek was the first in our group permitted back inside them, but now only under the wary supervision of an expanded detail of carabinieri from Potenza. Now that the body count in Mancanzano had risen to ten – including the lives of four *non*-Mancanzani – and renewed talk in Italy of the sassi as national monuments, Rome extended a curious, but shaky, hand into the investigation.

With the additional deaths, the entire region of Basilicata was now involved, and the prosecuting magistrate (based in Potenza, with offices just across from the *medico legale*'s), faced pressures from the Eternal City to pursue the mysterious crimes in this rocky hill town with all his conceivable energy and force.

So the magistrate telephoned Major Martella to funnel those pressures further down the line, and as we later understood from the high deputy's reports, it couldn't be said their conversation went well.

The magistrate told Major Martella: 'Every time someone dies in Mancanzano, it makes the rest of us all over the republic look bad. That isn't good.'

'No, sir, it isn't,' Major Martella answered unequivocally.

'Every day that goes by without these crimes being solved is a day you treat the country you love with disrespect. Is that what you want?'

'No, sir, it isn't.'

'Are you standing when you talk to me, *Maggiore?*'

'No, sir. I'm not.'

'Then this would be a good time to start,' the magistrate told him abruptly. 'Now, listen. Every time that I have to explain to my higher-ups in Rome why the tiny region of Basilicata has ten unexplained deaths, while the regions of Calabria, Campania and Apulia only have homicides that are completely understandable, it makes me feel like you have something against me personally.'

'I'm sorry to give you that impression,' Major Martella answered.

'*Maggiore*, is it possible I'm projecting my feelings of revulsion for you back on myself?'

'You'd certainly be justified in doing so,' Major Martella tried appeasing the magistrate. 'Sir, it's all right to dislike me, if you feel that's what's appropriate. But please don't think I have anything but the greatest esteem for you.'

'Oh, listen here, *Maggiore!*' the magistrate warned. 'Don't get cheeky and start telling me what to do! Because we both know that if you really respected me, and you respected yourself, then you'd do something about solving these crimes in Mancanzano.'

'Of course, I'm making real progress,' Major Martella lied.

'Well, that isn't good enough,' the magistrate shot back. 'Talking about progress is like boasting about not succeeding. I can't see any reason to do that.'

'No, sir, me neither,' Major Martella answered resolutely. 'I'm with you on everything, a full one hundred percent. Still, I can't help wondering just the tiniest bit: isn't promising people that I'm making progress a little like assuring them that I'm doing my best?'

'No, it isn't,' the magistrate told him flatly.

'No?' Major Martella asked.

'That's what I said. No. No, no, no. Look, it's already too late to replace you on the investigation, that much is painfully clear.

Because if I admit to the newspapers that you're inept – let's say, for example, that I send out a press release that says your thumb's stuck all the way up your ass and into your small intestines – then people will start asking why I didn't realize you were incompetent before now. And that's also not good, because it makes me look bad.'

'I wouldn't want that,' Major Martella reasoned.

'I wouldn't want that either,' the magistrate replied. 'So I don't have any choice but to let you stay on the case. And hope that you solve the crimes as quickly as possible. Or, actually, a little bit quicker than that.'

'That would make me look good too,' Major Martella suggested.

'Yes, you can look good too,' the magistrate told him, 'but that's not the point. The point is you're going to have to stay focused if you want to make my life any easier. So for the present, don't worry that I think you've got the brains of a donkey. Because that's my problem, not yours, and I don't want there to be anything more sapping your attention. So now I'll tell you what I'm going to do: I'm going to send you a little help. Just a few experienced officers to assist around the edges. Just a little something so you won't forget the importance of solving this quickly. Just a man or two so you won't forget about me, *Maggiore*.'

'Don't worry, sir,' Major Martella said. 'I'm not going to forget about you.'

The following day, two dozen carabinieri arrived from Potenza in a caravan of souped-up sedans equipped with caterwauling sirens and an entire overhead discotheque of flashing lights. They screeched into town like bulls into Pamplona, spraying dust with their wheels and revving their engines in authoritative displays of automotive bravado, until they'd lined up along both sides of Via Annunziatella. Then it wasn't more than an hour or two before the Potenza officers began relieving their Mancanzano counterparts of many of their duties in a befuddling *pas de deux* of investigative jurisdictions. Virtually ignoring the major's officers, these Potenza carabinieri descended into the sassi with carts of equipment and began examining the false walls that had hidden the latest crop of deceased youths. Then they also began recombing those caverns, and others, for any missed clues.

Still, to appease the local folk, the prosecuting magistrate ruled that while the Potenza carabinieri would lead the investigations inside the caves, Major Martella's force could rightfully maintain its authority everywhere else in the city, namely in Mancanzano's piazzas and on its winding streets. For Major Martella, this meant his men could remain in Piazza Ridola and focus their energies on the lookout for dogs. For the Potenza carabinieri, this meant they could pursue their investigation with a minimum of local interference. In regional newspapers, the jurisdictional ruling was nicknamed 'The Decree of Direct Sunlight'. But in Mancanzano papers, and on Radio Maria, the town's inhabitants once again began grousing about a history-repeating eviction from their caves.

None of us was really very surprised to see that once the Potenza police arrived in Mancanzano, a feeling of aloofness swelled among the local inhabitants like a carnival balloon whose *raison d'être* was simply to pop. A sense of detachment from the rest of the country distended easily into resentment and rage, and some inhabitants of the city now argued that as long as the killings didn't extend to their own children (and, here, the childless felt particularly at ease), it might actually be better for the crimes to go unsolved than to have a new crop of outsiders interfering in them.

As purveyors of reason, the parents of the dead teenagers held a different view, but there were few of them, compared to the rest of the population. On Radio Maria, and in some of the daily newspapers, editorialists reminded everyone that Jesus had gotten along fine before meddling Romans and Jews stood in his way, and that, even more recently, it had been the Neapolitans who installed the curmudgeonly Count Giancarlo Tramontano in their city, and Mussolini's Fascisti who ripped down the town's trees, many caves, and at least the same number of people.

True, in the last eight months six Mancanzani had come to mysterious ends. (The additional four dead Irsinesi and Montescagliosi didn't count in these local calculations, nor did the bonus deaths of Dr Biaggi and several unidentified canines.) But as far as the still-grieving parents were concerned, many residents of Mancanzano now argued, 'Why should the parents care so much? They've already lost their children. So it's not as if they're going to lose them again.'

The last word on this was uttered by a clothesline-slinging Fedelina Soppresa outside her home, as she busily suspended a tangle of socks: 'You mean we're supposed to let more people come into our city and tell us what to do? They're the same people who called us a national embarrassment in the thirties! And the same ones who tried to kick us out of the caves. So look who's embarrassed all over again! I tell you, I'd sacrifice my own life for a quick trip to Heaven if I thought it would humiliate Rome in front of the rest of the world!'

Eventually, it took Padre Caduta to calm her. 'The living owe it to the dead to continue on earth,' he cautioned her piously. 'And we owe it to God to honor His life-giving handiwork. But if you really want to send a message to Rome, I suggest you write a letter to Pope Paul VI.'

'What should I tell him?'

'Say you support his opposition to artificial contraception.'

'I do, I do!' Fedelina shouted. 'I'm completely against people getting rich because others want to have sex! That's just one more thing I've noticed our so-called "legislators" in Rome allowing to happen!'

But as more non-Mancanzani kept entering the city (and more Mancanzani packed up their bags and left), the ratio of long-time residents to outsiders was starting to shift. The narrow lanes of Via Annunziatella were hardly enough to contain the new convoys of traffic, especially with both sides lined with cars from Potenza.

To many stalwarts of the sassi, this influx and outflux of Mancanzano's population was the first stage of a phenomenon they'd forecasted and feared, and which the older ones had already experienced forty years before: the dismantling of a city and culture, and the vanishing of local traditions. Dottoressa Donabuoni had counted herself among this group of concerned citizens back when the death toll in Mancanzano was only at two, and she'd spearheaded the effort to get us to the city. But now everything had begun to change. A strain of xenophobia had accompanied the Potenza carabinieri into Mancanzano, and it was every bit as dangerous as the one which kept Italy from unifying until a hundred years ago. So maybe Dr Stoppani was right to leave town when he still could be remembered thoughtfully and missed. Because where xenophobia was concerned, no one was more of an outsider than we were. If this had been India, we'd have been cast from society right alongside the untouchables.

Now it didn't win Middelhoek any favors with the people of Mancanzano that he was participating with the Potenza police, and consequently with Rome. He briefly considered refusing to work with the new officers as a show of his solidarity, but he recognized right away that wouldn't get him far. Middelhoek wasn't going to be accepted by the people of Mancanzano no matter what he did, and this had never been truer than now. So the only thing left for him would be to keep to his business, finish the job accurately, and then head home.

After all, the concordance between the inscription on the underpainting of the first fresco, where it read HOC EST PURGATORIO, and the HOC EST INFERNO that had been scrawled in dust beside the six bodies was too great for either squad of officers to chalk up to chance. So despite protests from the

Istituto Centrale del Restauro (which neither wanted to get involved in a series of bad-press slayings nor cede authority over the frescoes to anyone willing to handle the flak), the Potenza carabinieri instructed Middelhoek to return to work. They wanted to know what else he might uncover as he stripped away more layers of paint. But as we watched Middelhoek return to his restorations, what Linda, Fortune and I felt most of all was envy. Having our hands full was something we all missed. Especially me, since that was the one thing that would have gotten my mind off of Filippa.

Then Fortune was given the go-ahead to return to work too. The high deputy knew better than to succumb to the furor sweeping the city, and she made a special case for Fortune to Major Martella, who could hardly be a hard-core xenophobe himself, since he *did* have a mother living those one hundred and thirty kilometers away in Moliterno. So whether it was the magistrate's insistence that the major take immediate action, his own common sense, or a feeling of competitiveness with the Potenza carabinieri, Major Martella consented. And soon Fortune was permitted to return to his geological surveys of the terrain, with the single proviso that he stay outside of the sassi, and thus in plain sight of Mancanzano's heavy artillery-toting carabinieri.

For the last several months, Fortune had been studying the geological strata along Mancanzano's periphery. He'd been examining the natural folds and buckles that had formed the city's canyons, and the tension gashes and scars that had helped turn the landscape into a crosshatching of crevices, cliffs and cicatrized plateaux. But Fortune had also been gauging the structural consequences of generations of earthquakes. He'd analyzed the fault lines running across the canyon, and he'd looked at the erosion that had occurred closer to town where the city had been stripped of its forest, and then just plain strip-mined. Fortune's studies had taken him from Mancanzano's farthest fields, through the creek, and to the foot of the two bluffs. He'd drill boreholes into the earth, and insert stress meters inside to gauge the deformations and forces beneath us. This was work Fortune seemed born to do.

Then it didn't take much more urging from the high deputy for Major Martella to give up on his hardline further, and for Linda to return to work. After almost a month of accomplishing nothing, she was bursting with energy, and in a race to fill up her remaining tapes with oral histories (although from my perspective, it felt like she was in a race against *me*). Still, while Linda would hurry to her interviews, she'd return to our quarters in the late afternoon a picture of anger and frustration. If it had been difficult for Linda conducting interviews when she wasn't supposed to, the quality of her exchanges had plummeted now that she and her informants communicated freely. As Linda recounted, sometimes all that would come out of her interviewees' mouths were a string of obscenities, attacks in which she'd be called a prostitute and slut for carrying on with the Calabrian art student Riccardo.

'All these months here, and I'm supposed to be as chaste as Santa Lucia!' Linda would complain, now in a state of complete agitation. 'Obviously, the men by the creek used to call me "*sirena*" because a mermaid's anatomy doesn't include a pussy and ass!'

As an anthropologist pursuing her fieldwork, Linda tried everything she could to win back the locals' favor. She started wearing long dresses. She began wearing white. She even tried presenting her informants with small gifts of appreciation. But none of this made any difference, because the townspeople of Mancanzano had already decided that Linda was a woman they preferred to shun. If not for the recent deluge of interlopers from Potenza, perhaps they might have overlooked Linda's affair as something that didn't concern them, but now that there was an exponentially expanding number of outsiders in town, the crisis of intruders couldn't be stanched by displaying leniency. The way Linda figured it, it wouldn't even matter now if she stopped seeing Riccardo. Their affair had been etched in people's minds as indelibly as the frescoes covering their walls. So the only thing she could do now by way of *a secco* activity, would be to start up with a man from Mancanzano, marry him, bear a few children, and then raise them in town as orthodox followers of the tufa cult.

'I know, I'll let some guy fall in love with me, have his baby and then I'll leave him!' Linda would scoff, even as she tried, most of all, to mask how deeply she felt hurt. 'Then the people of Mancanzano will find out what happens if you fuck with a *sirena*!'

But as far as fucking with sirens went, I'd already found out about that for myself, via the lure of Filippa Grossoglio. In the pit of my stomach, I could still feel the slipperiness of her skin against my own, as her nylon-clad butt twitched in ways I wouldn't resist. But as I stewed in our quarters, reviewing everything that had happened between us this last week, what didn't make any sense was why Filippa could behave as she liked in Mancanzano without becoming the *puttana* that Linda had in everyone's eyes. Shouldn't Filippa have been scrutinized more closely under the loupe of southern Italian community standards? So I figured it must be that no one knew Filippa's real behavior. She must have choked that part of herself off to everyone else too.

At first, I wondered if this realization meant an escape from Filippa's pressures. Could I go to her great-grandfather? Could I threaten her with something as simple as revealing the truth? Or would Filippa finally agree to keep quiet if I promised I'd keep her secret quiet too? Of course, that strategy would only work as long as there wasn't a baby, since she'd have to say *something* when the townsfolk noticed she'd begun gaining weight. But then how would Filippa explain to them that *I* was the one who'd fathered her child? And how would I?

As far as my own work as an anthropologist was concerned, I still wasn't going to be permitted to conduct any more interviews

239

since I'd been the one who broke into the cavern and disturbed the decaying bodies. On this last matter, Major Martella was sticking steadfast, and there would be no use importuning the high deputy, Mayor Taciuto or the Potenza police.

'You've got to learn respect for my office!' Major Martella lectured me one afternoon on Via Stigliano. 'Only elected and appointed officials can conduct themselves with immunity. That's the law!'

Then, in the days following his call from the prosecuting magistrate, Major Martella informed me that he was stepping up his investigation and placing me under official scrutiny for upsetting a crime site. I probably should have begun worrying how this would impact my legal status in town, but at least I knew that my ethnographies wouldn't be directly affected. It wouldn't mean anything to me now if I received permission to return to work. I'd already been around too many dead in Mancanzano for the people to want to talk to me about life.

—

The last applications of AB57 were conducted under the closest of scrutiny, from mixing the ingredients to spreading the corrosive mash over the frescoes. Once again, the caverns filled with the heady stench of ammonia. It was a pungency that cleaved straight to the membranes of your throat, and then felt like it was ripping them out from the inside, layer by layer. If there was any joking to be done, it was that Middelhoek seemed to be drawn ineluctably to bad smells, now that we'd all heard his tales of taking zinc. But the truth is the burn of ammonia in the caverns was nothing compared to the stench that had preceded it, and no one in town knew the smell of putrefaction better than I did. Its memory was the memory of death.

The AB57 was applied again and again, in a ceaseless rotation. Given the strained state of affairs, Middelhoek couldn't be sure how much longer he'd have access to the caves, and now he didn't want to lose his chance to finish the restorations he'd once so reluctantly begun. So the AB57 would be applied for three minutes, and then quickly removed. The remaining members of the team from Calabria would aerate the surfaces with hand-held blow dryers (and not over twenty-four hours as the Istituto insisted), and then the mixture would be spread over the frescoes again.

Layers of paint came off the wall as handfuls of pigmented goo. It was as though a few hundred years of the frescoes' history were reduced to a colorful goulash. At the direction of the Potenza carabinieri, the wood pulp was slopped into plastic containers for possible later analysis by the Soprintendenza per i Beni Culturali ed Artistici della Basilicata in Potenza. To differentiate among them, the bins would be marked either by the colors they held, or the names of the body parts and outdoor scenes the AB57 removed.

For four days straight, Middelhoek made his way from our quarters to the caves to apply the AB57 to the frescoes. His time was tight: as soon as he finished spreading the mix onto a few inches of *a secco* paint, and then onto the next, he'd proceed to a new wall altogether. But Middelhoek took comfort in the deadline. With his time now ordered, he began to feel order in his own life too, and the moment his team had finished covering the frescoes with AB57, it was time for them to remove it, dry the walls, and start again. This went on with breaks only for meals and sleep.

This went on day after day.

In fact, this went on without a single interruption to Middelhoek's routine until Fortune came to the caves one afternoon with the news that his stress tests had revealed an instability along this bank of caves, not far from where the frescoes stood. With the right jolts, he warned, there was a risk of slides along the escarpment.

Fortune suggested that the town hire a full outfit of geologists to examine the sassi and gauge what effects the seeping rainwater, chimneyless fires and recurring earthquakes had had on the cave homes' stability. He also suggested that the town reinforce the structural integrity of any abandoned caves by inserting concrete linings or buttressing them with a framework of I-beams and arches.

But the Potenza carabinieri, who'd been granted authority inside the caves, answered him perfunctorily: 'All of that can wait until we finish gathering evidence. Because in case it's not clear, we're trying to solve murders. You talk about saving caves. We want to save lives.'

Meanwhile, Middelhoek would mutter, 'If anyone's interested, I'd like to save frescoes.' And Linda would complain, 'How come nobody wants to save me?' And Fortune would say, 'If that's really the way things are going to be around here, then I'm better off buggering Anna in Montescaglioso.'

—

A real shot rang out the afternoon of April 30. It was one month after Easter, and seven since I'd arrived in Mancanzano. The report was heard all over the city. It was as if its echo bounced back and forth, from wall to roof to canyon and to piazza, ricocheting that way until everyone in Mancanzano heard it.

The gun was fired by one of Major Martella's carabinieri. Their siege of Piazza Ridola had gone on long enough for the last functioning bar (where I'd enjoyed my brief conversation with the barman) to padlock its doors, so this day two officers had left their posts in the square, and wandered into the sassi in search of a three o'clock coffee.

But now it wasn't caffeine that provided the carabinieri with a jolt. On Via del Riscatto, two teenagers were dumping the body of a wild German shepherd onto the street. The remains of the animal were a matted mess. Its shell was covered with blood, and the fluid was smeared across the boys' shirts. At first, both officers thought the teenagers were merely discarding a sack of garbage, and that their bag had developed an unfortunate tear. But since the tear was, more precisely, an incision running the

242

length of the dog's abdomen, the boys chose to run when the carabinieri came into view. Rather than chase them, one officer had decided it would be that much easier to fire. After all, he'd spent two weeks in Piazza Ridola practicing the motions.

They were Flavio and Maurizio. Maurizio stopped dead in his tracks.

'I think you've hurt me,' the teenager announced, amazed. He steadied himself against a wall. Then Flavio looked at his friend and stopped running too.

When the carabinieri caught up with the boys, the officers were impressed at their aim. A fleshy red chunk had been gouged out of Maurizio's upper arm, but he wasn't injured beyond that. So the officers cuffed the teenagers' wrists behind their backs amid Maurizio's moans, and then radioed for a backup team to recover the dead dog's carcass.

'Tell the Potenza carabinieri they're welcome to come get it,' the two Mancanzano carabinieri said.

At the station house on Via Stigliano, the teens were brought before Major Martella directly. Flavio wore the dog's blood emblazoned on his chest, while Maurizio's own fluids trickled down his sleeve. Both of them stuck to the same story: they'd found the animal's body by the creek, and rather than leave it there to rot, they'd decided to bring it with them to town.

But why were they dumping it on Via del Riscatto without saying anything? And why had they run when they saw the officers approach?

Maurizio pointed to the carabiniere who'd kindly provided the bullet hole in his arm, and said, 'We ran because we could tell he was about to open fire. If we hadn't run, this guy would have blown off my head!'

'Or he'd have shot me!' Flavio offered defiantly. 'If we hadn't run, we'd be as dead as the dog.'

'Which we found, like we told you. Without any organs,' Maurizio said.

'Just sitting there. Like a rock,' Flavio added.

'A furry rock.'

'No, a *mossy* rock.' The boys looked at each other, and nodded their heads in satisfied agreement.

'You expect me to believe you?' Major Martella asked the boys skeptically. He was standing before them holding a large cardboard box, grazing its lid lightly with the tips of his fingers.

The boys looked at each other again, and then back at Major Martella. Then they answered, 'Yes.'

Later that afternoon, the two officers were questioned about having applied an excessive use of force. It wasn't a formal inquiry, as might occur in the United States. Rather, it was a fifty-year-old woman wailing outside the headquarters where her son was being held, venting the full force of her motherly wrath.

A few passers-by said, 'Your son's barely hurt. So what's the big deal?'

The mother answered, 'I suffer along with all the mothers who have suffered these cruel months in Mancanzano.' She tore at her hair. She tore at her dress. The others walked on.

Under advice from his union, the officer who'd fired his gun didn't say anything, but his partner avowed, 'We made the right decision to shoot. Kids like these need to learn a fear of God. So if my safety hadn't been on, I might have hit the other kid too. But, look, there are enough dead in Mancanzano, so we're glad this pair isn't dead too. Because then we'd have to put up with another investigation. And the one we have now is already a pain in the ass.'

But Maurizio's mother kept wailing outside the police headquarters. Even after Maurizio was escorted outside and asked her to stop. Even after he whispered to her, 'Look, *Mamma*, you might want to hush. Because the way I see it, I've gotten into a little bit of trouble.'

Elsewhere in Mancanzano, Middelhoek was hard at work. He barely looked up when he heard the gunshot. His world was one of caves, AB57 and the stench of ammonia, and he was captivated by the new images on the wall before him.

Once the rest of the *a secco* paint had been stripped from the frescoes, the images were all the same. So it didn't matter whether the pictures were of madonnas, saints, cherubim, monks or even lay people. Once the *a secco* paint was gone a quadrant of each fresco contained the same illustration: living penitents interred inside a cave.

Along the caves' floors, the penitents' feet were buried in rubble, or waist-high boulders pinned their whole bodies to the walls. At the tops of these quadrants, demons stood over the caverns, peering in, while they resealed the cavities with giant rocks. And in each of these pictures, the men and women of the city stood with their hands at their throats, as they exhausted the air around them.

Inside the caverns, the penitents were naked, and their skin was pale. They were suffocating slowly, and they were dying. In these underground frescoes – masked a millennium ago by the monks – the charcoal demons watched from above, while their own monstrous organs shook and bulldozed the earth. They watched while their quarry stared back at them in awe. Because buried beneath the piles of rubble, the people of Mancanzano had been captured in caves – and underneath countless layers of paint. But little had changed now that the paint was removed. On the wall before us, their anguishing eyes were again beginning to shut.

Filippa came to our quarters the afternoon we all heard the gunshot, and I met her outside. The sun was overhead, and bearing down hard. She wore a loose dress. It hung limply around her.

'So let me guess,' I suggested bluntly. 'You've come here to tell me that you are pregnant.'

'Oh, it's still too early to know for sure. But if it gives you any comfort, I should know almost any day.'

'I haven't felt any comfort since I met you,' I told her now.

'That's nothing,' she said. 'I'm not going to feel comfortable for close to nine months.'

'No one knows what happened between us, do they?'

She shook her head, no.

'No one knows this thing you have done?'

'No.'

'When are you going to say something?' I asked.

'I'm not going to tell people that you forced me inside a cave, and raped me, until I'm sure that I'm pregnant.'

'That's what you're going to tell people?'

'Yes,' she said. 'Wouldn't you?'

'Don't do it,' I told her. 'Don't do it, Filippa.'

She looked at me, smirking. 'Why not? Would you give up everything in your other world if I didn't? Would you give up that woman and that baby to stay here with me?'

I looked at her callously. 'I'll never be with you.'

'Or me with you. Especially if you're going to be so inflexible about it. But tell me this then, do I at least still make you hard?'

'No,' I told her.

'Then you're of less use than ever!' But she looked at me still, and her expression was serious. 'But what if I offered you the chance to forget everything?' she asked. 'Would you take it?'

I didn't know if her question was meant in earnest, but it jarred my indifference and knocked the wind out of my lungs. Once more with Filippa, I felt at the end of my breath.

But before I could answer, Filippa smiled at me, turned the corner and left.

I thought about chasing her now, but the streets were full of carabinieri and the last thing I needed was to draw their attention. So I merely watched as Filippa threaded past them and disappeared. But now I thought about home, the life I'd had, and all I'd do to return there. Because if Filippa's question were serious, I would answer yes. Then wouldn't anyone forgive my determination?

# Chapter 18
# Measure the Man

What makes desperation? Hope in the face of an infinite black hole?

1. I look at the old women here huddled in black. Always in spite of the brutality of the season. Their misery's immeasurable, but they know not to expect anything better. Dreams are what cause the most serious trouble.

2. I ask a teenager in town what he thinks about all the kids dying. He tells me, 'It's all right with me. When a mother loses her child, she doesn't yell at the other ones so much.'

'You lose a brother?' I ask him.

'Yes,' he says, beaming. 'Now nobody beats the crap out of me.'

3. The parents of the dead teens know their children aren't coming back. So they're resigned to their desolation, and immune to despair. Freud said that psychoanalysis cured neurotic miseries to make way for the miseries of daily life. He understood that there's no desperation without ambition, just as there's no real suffering unless you expect your suffering to end.

4. I walk through these tired sassi. These are playing-card houses, with powerful walls. I think this whole place is a rarefied ghettopolis, but people who are miserable choose to be. They thrive on it. It's a form of monstrosity. They're too busy with their misery to intuit what's beyond their reach. Among them, the

anthropologist learns it doesn't mean anything to say, 'Live your life to the fullest.'

But desperation is what I feel. So I suppose this means I still feel hope. Because I look at myself and the snare I've slipped into, and I want to pull my organs out. I can picture my hands ripping my intestines up through my mouth. My stomach and liver and pancreas will come out with it too, thanks to all the internal stitching. But that's OK because I want to flip myself inside out, like a pillowcase, or like a body on the *medico legale*'s table. Because then I'll dismantle everything, and put it back together. I can't really say if things will be better then, but I know they'll be different. And different's not bad if you hold on to hope.

And that's what desperation is, I think. Knowing that if you can't change your environment, you have to change yourself within your environment. Because if all I am doing is trying to get to a place where I can come back home – to arrive at a state that's as safe and comforting as a womb – then what does it matter if I use a hatchet to get there?

Desperation is ruthless and reckless. And it is dark. But it lets you do anything, and so,

5. sometimes, it's creative.


Another feature of desperation is it requires desperate measures. Whatever you do, it's got to be more than talk.

Major Luigi Martella lifted the cover from the cardboard box he was holding, and put both pieces on the table. A strip of tape on the lid had been marked 'Lombroso'. The major reached into the box and pulled out a tightly coiled tape measure. He placed it on the table next to the cover. The teenagers looked at him warily. The major was smiling.

'Stand up,' Major Martella said.

A carabiniere nudged the teenagers to their feet. Then the major unfurled the yellow tape measure as dexterously as an experienced tailor.

He approached.

A second officer was seated beside the table, and Major Martella said to him, '*You*, write.' Then Major Martella began barking out measurements, as he held the tape to the teenagers' forearms, trunks, chests and outstretched arms.

'Thirty centimeters . . . Sixty-eight centimeters . . . One hundred and six . . . One hundred and seventy-eight.'

Next, the major raised the measuring tape to the teenagers' faces, and recited the lengths and diameters of their ears; then the lengths, breadths and circumferences of each of their heads. The officer jotted the numbers down dutifully.

Major Martella returned the tape measure to the table, placing it beside the box. The bright yellow strip, loosely spiraled and twisted, looked like a streamer left over from a New Year's Eve celebration, though perhaps one where a component of common sense had been chucked aside.

Then the officer handed the major the pad with the various figures scrawled across it, and Major Martella scanned the pages intently.

He said to the boys, 'I know you are guilty. I just don't know how much yet.' He looked back at the pad, and again at the teenagers.

'We haven't done anything!' Flavio insisted.

'Except move a dog,' Maurizio added obligingly. 'And normally a dog will move all by itself.'

'This one only needed help because it was dead,' Flavio rejoined.

'Did you kill the dog?' the seated carabiniere asked. Now that he'd put down his pen, his hands were free and he could gesticulate however he liked. Soon, each of his fingers conveyed the airborne menace of the thongs of a whip.

Major Martella glared at his deputy. He clearly preferred a softer approach to interrogations. So he turned to the boys, and bent his mouth into a slow, creaking smile. Then he repeated the officer's question: 'Did you kill the dog?'

Maurizio answered languidly, 'The dog killed itself.'

The seated carabiniere reached for Maurizio's arm, clasping it just above the bandage. He squeezed. Maurizio's features squeezed themselves. As the wound sent spikes up and down the length of his arm, the teenager's face assumed the appearance of a lemon slowly being crushed into juice.

Then, when the carabiniere relaxed his hold and the teenager's arm finally stopped throbbing, Maurizio added, 'Yes, maybe we helped.'

Major Martella pointed out, ' "Maybe" is what we defenders of the republic consider an outright admission of guilt.'

But Flavio shook his head violently from his chair, and interjected, ' "Maybe" is what I tell my mother if she asks if I've taken out the garbage. "Maybe" is how I answer my girlfriends when they ask if I love them.'

The carabiniere suggested, ' "Maybe" is how I should answer when you ask if I'm going to shoot you.'

'As long as you're joking,' Flavio suggested.

'*Maybe* I'm not joking,' the carabiniere told him flatly.

' "Maybe",' the major offered now, 'is how I should answer the prosecuting magistrate the next time he calls to ask if I've got a break in the case. Or a suspect.'

Then Maurizio put a hand to the hole in his arm, where it was screaming for the return of its missing flesh, and he said to them all, soberly, 'What I explained to my mother is that it was euthanasia. We were quick.'

'Besides, the dog was sickly,' Flavio reasoned. 'It wasn't anyone's pet.'

'So you did everyone a favor?' Major Martella asked the boys evenly.

'Particularly the dog,' Flavio answered. 'When I looked in its eyes, I saw a call for help.'

From what we understood from the high deputy's reports, Major Martella didn't say anything else to the teenagers at first. Perhaps he was still intent on taking a coaxing approach to his questioning, and trying to gauge if there was any way this might be possible with this pair of particularly smart-mouthed suspects. For a few minutes, he busied himself with his cardboard box, recoiling the tape measure and placing it in his pocket, then returning the pad to the box and replacing its lid. No doubt he was considering his strategy. It wouldn't be long before the Lombroso measurements fit together in his head. Then all that would remain would be to graph those numbers over the hilly terrain to show how ten teenagers in Mancanzano had died. That appeared to be the major's theory.

The carabiniere, on the other hand, was itching to take immediate action: maybe smack Flavio or Maurizio across their mouths, maybe fire a second shot that would also attract Flavio's mother, and set both women bitching and wailing outside the station house like a couple of wing-clipped harpies.

Finally Major Martella spoke up, articulating his words slowly. 'How many other dogs have you killed?' he asked the boys.

The carabiniere's eyebrows perked up in sheer interrogational delight.

'No other dogs,' Maurizio answered uneasily.

'No, none,' Flavio said, with the unlikely conviction of a mercenary claiming he's never fired a gun.

'Do you know what I'd do to you if I found out you were lying?' Major Martella said to the two boys.

'Arrest us and bring us back to the station house for questioning?' Flavio suggested haphazardly.

Major Martella smiled at the two teenagers sympathetically. Then he suggested, 'No, I would handcuff you to a dog that was in far better shape than the one you were found with. Living, for sure. Also, hungry. Definitely hungry. Especially hungry.'

He paused for a second as he fished through his desk for a stick of gum, which he folded against his tongue as edible origami. Then, he continued, 'Now, how long do you think a dog could go without eating? I mean, before the animal turned on you out of sheer starvation? Hours? No. Days? *No.* But a week? A week? No. Definitely no. You couldn't last a week with a half-starving dog. Not one that realized that just one chunk of a thigh would help keep it alive. So now what I want to make sure you boys know is this: there are places in Sardinia, inland villages around the city of Nuoro, where this very sort of experimentation takes place. There are facilities there for this kind of torture. Institutes where methods are researched, and continually improved. And the fees are low. That makes it accessible.'

Flavio and Maurizio eyed each other uneasily. Then Flavio said, 'You think we believe you? You think we're convinced? You don't know what you're talking about.'

'You think I'm lying?' Major Martella asked the teenagers lazily. 'You mean, you don't like it when you think I'm not sticking to the absolute truth?'

'Well, maybe, yes,' Flavio told him.

'That's funny,' Major Martella said. 'Because I'm not even asking you to tell me the hundred percent truth. Eighty percent would be good enough for everyone here.'

'I'd hold out for eighty-five,' the carabiniere recommended.

'But why should we tell you anything more?' Flavio asked the major. 'What are you going to do? Shoot poor Maurizio again?' He smiled at his friend. 'Maybe get him this time in a vital organ?'

'No,' Major Martella replied. 'I have something in mind that's much better.' He nodded to the seated carabiniere, who began to grin broadly. Then the officer stood up, and left the room.

While the carabiniere was gone, Major Martella studied the boys intently. Their reflections were distorted in the window's glass. Only their brightest garments showed up in the pane, making the pair of teenagers seem as elusive as ghosts.

But when the carabiniere returned to Major Martella's office a few minutes later, he was leading eight large dogs by their

252

leashes. These dogs were growling and barking; they were snarling and vicious. As soon as they spotted the boys – in fact, just as soon as they were able to smell them – these eight brawny animals began pulling at their leashes with enough raw force that a second, and then a third, officer was needed to prevent them from mauling the boys. Soon, the animals were barking so loudly inside the station house that you could no longer hear Maurizio's mother wailing from beyond the walls. The dogs kept barking and snapping their jaws.

'I think these dogs know you,' Major Martella said to the teenagers, smiling. He couldn't help but take pleasure in the change in the two boys' expressions. A ruddiness had spread to their faces, glimmering now in the window's glass. 'If you co-operate with these dogs, I may be in a position to help you myself,' he told the teenagers. 'You see, in the best of all worlds, there would be someone else in this city who is guiltier than you two. Even someone who has killed all ten teenagers. So I have to ask, who wouldn't like to find somebody like that? I think even the dogs here can taste how I would like it!'

Major Martella paused, as his carabiniere's fingers wrapped and rewrapped themselves around the leashes. 'But I would like that person to be older than you are,' the major allowed, 'because I would like to hold that person up as an example. You two are not good examples, no matter what your mothers will say, because your crania have the wrong diameters. And your trunk and arm lengths show that while you are bad, you are not really bad enough – not for everything that has been happening in our little town. So co-operate with me.'

The dogs kept snarling. The officers could now barely restrain them.

'You see,' said Major Martella, 'it's a lovely day for co-operation. A day like today makes you glad to be alive in Mancanzano.'

'I'm glad to be alive every day,' Flavio quipped, 'although sometimes I think I'd be happier if I lived in another city, where

253

I didn't have to live with my parents inside a cave, and where movie stars like Brigitte Bardot and Sophia Loren sometimes came for a visit.'

'So will you co-operate with me?' Major Martella asked again.

Maurizio rubbed his arm, just below his wound, and then nodded his head yes.

Flavio said, 'OK, we'll co-operate, sure. But no homosexual stuff! Because if my mother finds out about *that*, then I know she's going to kill me!'

Major Martella and a phalanx of carabinieri followed the teenagers down the side of the bluffs. The corps brought the full complement of dogs with them: they were animals that had been picked up over the last several days from the countryside by a special detail of Mancanzano carabinieri (funded, in part, by sympathetic animal rightists across the country's north, who thought of Mancanzano in the same patronizing ways they thought of Italy's former colonies in Ethiopia and Somalia: backwater, poor and in desperate need of paternal assistance) so that the wild dogs' lives might be safeguarded in a way that the citizens' never would because the people of Mancanzano wouldn't ever matter as much. Now, as the animals strode through the streets, it was the first time that many had been outdoors in days. The dogs would interrupt their bounds to sniff at the earth and defecate in the open air. Afterwards, they'd redouble their efforts at pulling their leashes and nipping at the teenagers' heels whenever they grew close.

Now both the boys and the dogs led the carabinieri in the same direction. The corps took Via del Riscatto, past Mancanzano's cathedral, past Piazza Ridola, past the Potenza carabinieri, and then down the hill until they reached the overlook at Via della Vergine. Then the group wove through the sassi, swelling, compressing and surging along with the varying widths of the streets. Townsfolk watched the frantic herd from the sidewalks, and jumped out of the way as the wild pack passed them. Occasionally, a bystander would find himself with his back pressed against a wall – perhaps holding a grocery bag in one hand and a child in the other – and hope the group would go by without knocking him down. As these wild animals rumbled through half-burrowed streets, other dogs that were indoors added their barks to those they heard outside, and soon the clutter of howling, yelping, pawing and barking grew to such cacophonous proportions that the sound of the carabiniere's single gunshot earlier that morning now seemed muted, trivial and even idyllic.

Then the group worked its way down the rest of the hillside along Via d'Addozio, and past the uninhabited sassi, the rock churches and the abandoned and partially collapsed caves, until it emerged into the dusty open space of Mancanzano's flatland periphery. They passed flowers, broken glass, broken stones and aluminum cans, and the sheets of tufa that spread across the ground as smoothly as ice. Here, the terrain was green, brown, black, orange and rust – nearly the same colors we'd seen when our group arrived in this city so many months ago. But now that spring had arrived in Lucania, the region was furiously full of life.

Wherever you looked, the ground was aswarm with darting lizards, snails and myriad insects. But if the dogs tried to catch one, their intended prey would disappear fast into crevices, and even down the many boreholes that now pricked the rough-hewn landscape. After all, Fortune's drills had dug deeper than any animal could go, and the dogs inevitably lost interest in any prey they couldn't catch. That was how Dottoressa Donabuoni later related the story of how everything happened – focusing on the colors and smells, and the picayune anecdotes that distracted the listener from the abject reality of the tale, because the story itself sputtered from one grim event to the next.

The group forged on. The air was dry, it smelled of thyme, and, above all, the air was hot. The corps crossed the creek, and then headed, still farther, across the broad canyon. But when the sound of rushing water had receded into the distance – and the only sounds were the buzzing of flies, the barking of dogs, everyone's huffing and the shifting of pebbles and branches beneath their feet – this motley corps finally ground to a halt.

The dogs began sniffing at the air frantically. The boys simply shrugged and said, 'Here.' Then Maurizio extended a hand, and pointed to the mouth of a cave.

Major Martella motioned for the boys to come with him. Two of his officers came too. The remaining carabinieri stayed outside with the dogs.

The opening gave way to a corridor that gradually sloped into the inside of a hill. The entrance was about a meter and a half wide, and it maintained the same low height as it descended. The group hunched their shoulders slightly as they walked, and Major Martella kept a hand on the chiseled ceiling just to make sure he didn't bump his head.

'How far do we go?' he asked the teenagers, after threading twenty meters into the hillside. The barks of the dogs were now barely audible.

'Only to here, I think,' Flavio said uneasily.

'Just don't turn around,' Maurizio added now. 'Or your eyes won't adjust.'

But once everyone's had, what the group saw through the dusky shadows was that the body of a dog lay stretched across a black plastic tarpaulin. The animal's body was stiff, evidently still tight-muscled from rigor mortis. Through the darkness, Major Martella could make out a length of a rope strung from the dog's neck to one of the walls. One end of the cord had been looped through an iron piton embedded in stone. The other end of the cord had been looped through itself, so that the rope transformed into a crude choke collar. The dog's head, in turn, had been slipped through the noose. The rope was as taut as the dog's muscular body, forming a hypotenuse with the wall and the slick black tarpaulin. Depending on how you surveyed the scene, the animal's death could be expressed as a gruesome lark or the miserable result of geometric certainty.

'You will explain what happened here,' Major Martella said, as he stared at the dog. 'And you will kindly explain it in a way that makes you seem contrite. You will do this for me.'

Flavio kneeled by the animal, and loosened the rope from around its neck. Slowly, he slid the noose from the dead dog's head. Then he said, 'It's just like you told us about in Sardinia, *Maggiore*. A hungry dog will lunge at anything it can eat.'

'I was making that stuff up about Sardinia,' Major Martella said.

'This dog in particular hadn't eaten in two days,' Flavio offered. 'So you can imagine how hard it pulled forward when all of a sudden it sensed a piece of meat.'

'Thanks to you, I don't have to imagine,' Major Martella replied.

Flavio nudged the dead animal with his hand, and the rigid form slid slowly across the tarpaulin. It moved with a slip, like a throw rug across a cold tile floor. Then Flavio said, 'But what you can imagine, *Maggiore* – and thanks to us – is how badly an animal can want something that's just out of reach. That's what I think about all the time. That part is interesting. Because *me?* I've never wanted anything that much.'

'You've never been starving,' Major Martella answered. 'Also, you've never been a dog. Although people might say you act like something lower.'

'Well, it's true I've never had a noose around my neck,' Flavio reasoned. 'But that doesn't mean I'd strangle myself if I did.'

'We'd have let the dogs go back into the wild if they hadn't choked themselves,' Maurizio now spoke up. He pointed to the dead dog, still on its side, sprawled across the plastic tarpaulin. 'Do you think we could have done that to the animal with our own hands?'

'I think you would. And I think you'd do worse,' Major Martella told the boys steadily. 'But I'm still giving you a chance to tell me what happened to the animals after they died. Understand, I'm giving you this opportunity because if I had my officer shoot you again here, then we all know your mothers would really start to complain. And then you can imagine what tactics would be necessary to shut them up. So this is your chance.'

'It's quite a chance,' the carabiniere remarked. 'It's almost a gift.'

'Well, afterwards we did what anyone would do,' Maurizio explained. 'We let the animal go, just as we were going to do here.'

'Of course, by then it was dead,' the major said.

'Uh, yes, it was dead,' Maurizio confirmed. 'Although I'd say it looked kind of peaceful.'

'By that point the dog had ended its suffering,' Flavio added casually. He leaned forward on his hands and knees, beside the animal, stretching his own body before he stood up. Then brushing some tufa powder from the tarpaulin that clung to his pants, he looked at the animal, and shook his head. He sighed. 'Fleas. Scaly skin. Bad breath. Starvation. That's a dog's life. And that's no way to live.'

'So, we were bringing the dog with us to town,' Maurizio explained. 'Because that's where we'd found it, when it was still alive. Of course, that's also when you stopped us.'

'Right after you sliced its gut open,' the carabiniere prompted.

'After we unzipped it a little,' Flavio said. 'Like the *medico legale* in Potenza.'

'But we left the parts inside,' Maurizio specified. 'All of them. The lungs. The bones. The sweetbreads too. You can check if you want.'

'That's true,' Major Martella reckoned. 'The other dogs we found in Piazza Ridola all had their innards removed.'

'Because that's how the *other* kids do it!' Maurizio said. 'It's like they're emptying their stockings on Christmas. Except that none of them gets shot.'

'At least not yet,' the carabiniere offered.

'You want us to believe there are other kids involved?' Major Martella asked them.

'You know, just because we've been experimenting a little, it doesn't mean we're the only ones to do it,' Flavio answered.

'What do you mean?' Major Martella probed.

'When you catch someone screwing your wife,' Maurizio said, 'what makes you think he's the only one doing it? There could be others.'

'There usually are,' Flavio theorized.

'So who are they?' Martella asked the teenagers.

'Kids from town,' Flavio offered. 'Kids from other towns too.'

'Will you show us?' Major Martella asked the teenagers.

They looked at each other. Then they said, 'I think we'd rather not.'

'No, I think you will show us,' Major Martella told the two boys. 'I'm confident of it. You will show us where to find the kids who have cut the dogs open. And then Italy will be a better place. Because then it will be a kind of America. A country where teenagers don't disappear into caves after they've been shot.'

'They were wild dogs,' Maurizio reminded. 'We never took anyone's pet.'

'And I told you already,' Flavio said, 'the particular dogs we're talking about were already ill. But our way was more humane. What those other kids did, now *that* was sick.'

'Sick, sick, sick!' Maurizio affirmed. 'Really sick!'

'Then maybe you should have run some ropes around their necks too,' the carabiniere suggested.

Flavio coughed uneasily and rubbed his hands on his shirt. Then he said, 'Just so that you know, *Maggiore*, we cut up the one dog, but we're no butchers. And we're not involved with the dead kids in Mancanzano, either. At least not in the sense of making them dead.'

'We're opposed to death,' Maurizio offered weakly, clutching his arm.

'Yes,' Flavio said. 'We're anti-death.'

'So, show me the other kids,' Major Martella said. 'If they're sick like you say, maybe that will even make you seem wholesome.'

'We can show you their cave,' Flavio offered.

'I'll bring my gun,' the carabiniere suggested.

'Yes, you will,' Major Martella said. Then he looked at the two teenagers. 'Of course, he will,' Major Martella assured them.

Then the officers and boys emerged from the cave. The leashed dogs had remained quiet while they were inside, but once they saw the teenagers again they opened their jaws and began to bark. They barked the same way a single gunshot can start an entire war, or the way a single collapsed wall can upset the balance of a whole building: sporadically, surprisingly and then inevitably.

The dogs kept barking until one of the carabinieri went back inside to retrieve the German shepherd. Then, when he returned into the open with their cousin stiff in his arms, the dogs straightened their necks, and their barks turned into howls.

The other cave wasn't far away. It took the convoy of carabinieri, dogs and boys no more than ten minutes to reach it by foot. A large ash tree, dangling winged samaras, stood outside the cave's mouth, partially obscuring the opening into the side of the hill. In the breeze, the seed pods shook like the tentacles of a great green sea anemone, wild and gyroscopic, promising an almost mythological threat. Two of the officers accompanied Major Martella and the boys past the tree and into the cave, while three other carabinieri remained outside with the baying dogs.

The entrance to this cavern sloped downward, as had the one before it, but it also continued twice as far into the interior of the hill. In this cave, however, there was no waiting for your eyes to adjust to the light: about five meters in, the entranceway veered to the right, before angling once more sharply, and entirely blocking out the sun. No one in the group had thought to bring flashlights, or even something as old-fashioned and useful as a kerosene lamp. So the two carabinieri fished through their pockets for boxes of matches. One of them managed to pull out a cigarette lighter. He would keep the button depressed for as long as he could without burning his thumb; then he'd screech out an obscenity, and the crew would once again be engulfed by the dark.

'How far do we have to go?' Major Martella asked the teenagers a second time now. It was bad enough kowtowing to the prosecuting magistrate and to the Potenza police. But the major clearly didn't like having to rely on Flavio and Maurizio.

'I really couldn't tell you,' Maurizio wavered. 'I've only been here this once.'

'I've been here twice,' Flavio admitted, 'but who's counting? Anyway, we're almost there. It's not much farther. But I'm pretty sure this is going to be a lot like visiting a nest. Because as soon as the bird realizes someone else has been there, it's "*Buona sera*, pal", and "*Arrivederci*". Then the mother bird abandons her chicks and finds a new place to settle. So, if you ask me, this reminds me of when we had all those kestrels.'

'Not me,' said Maurizio, clutching his arm. 'It reminds me of when I got shot.'

'Not me,' said Major Martella. 'It's reminding me right now of breaking open this case.'

Once the corps reached the end of the tunnel, they were at least fifteen meters into the interior of the earth. Great hulking walls of tufa enclosed the cadre on their remaining sides. The officer with the lighter struggled to keep it lit amidst his curses. He circled the chamber, trying to find whatever he could. First, he looked for the bodies of more wild dogs. Then, he searched for leashes of rope, or even pitons or hooks that had been driven into the walls. But the walls were smooth wherever he probed.

However, the officer found great deposits of powdered tufa and pebbles at the base of the walls. Loose mounds had been shoveled against them. He squatted slowly to inspect the heaps, and, in the soft illumination of the flame, he saw that a trail of pulverized tufa led toward the middle of the chamber. The trail was a haphazard sprinkling, as spangled and irregular as the flicker of light beside his thumb. On his knees, with the cigarette lighter only inches from the cavern's floor, the carabiniere followed the trail of the powder to see where it led. When he did, Major Martella, the other officer, and the two boys remained virtually in the dark. To them, the motion of the lighter resembled the taunting sizzle of an explosive's fuse.

The carabiniere stopped after he'd crawled several meters. He'd come to a patch on the floor of soft, compacted and powdered stone. When the lighter stopped moving, Major Martella called out to him, 'What do you see?'

The carabiniere answered uncertainly, 'I'm not sure.' So now, with his free hand, he began to dig. The work was halting. First, he carefully pushed away some pebbles, some powder and stones. Then, he put down the cigarette lighter and started digging with both of his hands in the dark.

Against the lone sound of the carabiniere clawing in the charcoal-black cave, Maurizio and Flavio started to giggle.

Flavio cooed nervously, 'It's just like the guy's digging all the way to Pompeii!'

Except that what the carabiniere's fingertips touched underground had the unmistakable feel of an animal's hide. So, the officer now grabbed handfuls of powdered tufa and tossed them away. Then he brought the cigarette lighter to the rim of the hole, and illuminated the body of a German shepherd.

The dog had been buried alive. That much was clear once the rest of the tufa had been removed from the hole, a lantern was brought to the site, and the only thing found in the cavity was the dog with its legs bound together, tightly enough so that once it fell into the hole, it would never get out.

'Why would someone do this to an animal?' Major Martella lamented. 'Isn't it bad enough to do it to your own kind?'

262

Maurizio said, 'The kids who did this are really barbarians!'

Flavio asked giddily, 'Can you imagine the torture of being buried alive? I bet it's like drowning without getting wet!' He crouched next to the hole, his fingers dangling inside it, like lures.

'So explain what happened here,' Major Martella told the teenagers, seething. 'They dig up the animal and then remove its organs?'

'It's like I said,' Flavio told them, 'the sickness of these kids is incredibly sick. They chop up the animals like plates of polenta.'

Major Martella turned to Maurizio. 'So, do you know who the teenagers are who buried this dog? Who maybe killed other dogs too?'

'You want someone to blame?' Maurizio asked the major.

'Yes, I do,' the major replied.

'But you want someone other than us. Just like you said, back at the station house. In front of my sweet, suffering mother.'

'I want people who are guilty,' the major said. 'I want people who don't understand that everything I said about Sardinia was only a joke.'

'Then that's easy,' Maurizio answered. 'You don't want Flavio, and you don't want me. Because we're so innocent and young and naïve that it's not even believable. But I'll tell you who's guilty, *Maggiore*, if that's all you want.'

'That's what I want.'

'Then when you know who's guilty,' Flavio added, 'you'll really be a hero. It's going to be sick how much of a hero!'

'So tell me,' Major Martella answered, 'before the suspense kills me. Or one of my carabinieri's guns slips, and it kills you.'

'OK,' Flavio replied. 'The answer is this: the one who's guilty in Mancanzano is you. Because teenagers keep dying in town. Ten dead so far. And I could be next. Or poor Maurizio over here could be next, even while he recovers from his life-threatening wound. So the answer is you, *Maggiore*. You're the worst of the worst. A regular Adolf Mussolini. Because all this police commotion comes from you. So protect us, please! I mean, if you like. Because nobody has to be guilty if nobody else dies.'

'And find someone else to blame,' Maurizio told the major evenly, 'that way, you won't have to blame yourself.' He smiled, and managed to swing his wounded arm a little. 'That's what I do,' he told them, 'and I find it works all right.' Then he knocked his fist against the cave wall. 'After all, we're all victims of our environment.'

'Of course,' Major Martella told them, 'people are dead already. That's why I have a job. And it's why I've received so many wonderful gifts. So I agree with you both that nobody has to be guilty – that's even the sort of thing I'd be willing to sweep under the tarpaulin! But that's only as long as you teenagers keep dying. Because once you stop, if I don't find a killer, the townspeople may start to think they don't need me.'

'So, which is it?' the carabiniere asked the boys. 'Which of you wants to be the reason we prolong the investigation?'

Flavio and Maurizio remained silent.

'No, I didn't think either of you did,' Major Martella told the boys swiftly.

'I didn't either,' the carabiniere added. 'And I'm not even that much of a thinker.'

~

Desperation is a kind of sarcasm, too. Vaudevillian wit at the cost of generosity. Anxiety instead of integrity. Recognition of retroactive deceit.

But maybe that's what the Benedictines figured out long ago too: that they needed painting and panting, and copious regrets, to mortify their flesh in Mancanzano. Maybe they painted the frescoes of lovers so they could *really* repent. So they could feel the desperation of promises made to God and not kept, and then surround themselves with the very elements they rejected.

Too long ago, I came here to do something worthwhile. But I succumbed to the squalor – and then to my own astonishment. Once I came here like Leakey or Geertz, and then I caved myself in. But if the last fragments of love rely only on hope, I've also learned that betrayal is built out of the tiniest pieces. Love's already desperate. So why should anyone want to fuck it up further? Now I am my own generation's Count Giancarlo Tramontano. Reviled in a piazza, far from the safety and succor of his castle. And far from you. Farther than I ever thought.

Forgive me, my love. I didn't intend this. I didn't mean to take this direction.

But at least I don't have to travel any farther than to our door for a beginning for answers. Filippa is there. She is waiting outside. Now she tells me, 'I hear they found the dog that I buried.'

'You killed the animal? Why you?'

'You know how the simplest answer is usually the right one?' she asks. 'Well, that's not how it works here. Maybe it's like that in other places.'

'Where people erect buildings, instead of digging them out of the ground?'

'I guess our way could make a person feel uneasy.'

'You have no idea. You can't imagine.'

'Well, if you want more insight, maybe you should ask some of the people you've been interviewing. You like to talk. They like to talk. You talked to my great-grandfather.'

'I did,' I say. 'Maybe, I should talk to him again. I can be more forthcoming.'

'If that's what you want to do, go ahead. But understand that I'm standing here now, offering you a way to forget everything. To put aside what's happened between us.' Filippa smiles. 'All my great-grandfather's going to give you is crap.'

I think of the old man on the outskirts of the city. All he ever needed was a faded titty popping out of the immaculate virgin's blouse to feel complete. I should have left a lump of my own fieldwork at his feet.

'So, which of us do you want?' she asks. 'Because you have to choose.'

But before I can say anything, Filippa reaches toward me. She places a hand on my chest, just below my shoulder. I'm sure she can feel my heart beating. I know *I* can feel it.

It will be up to me now to decide what's beyond her reach.

'So, which one of us?' she asks me again.

I nod to her soberly. 'You.'

'But are you *certain*?' she pries. And she lowers her hand until it's resting over my heart. 'Because the way your heart's beating, it makes me worry that you might be sick. So maybe you're not ready to discuss our child. Or even the body right next to you it's going to come out of. So maybe we should talk about something less important. Something fun. Like dogs.' She giggles, unabashed. 'We can consider it foreplay.'

And now I watch her hand fall through the air. It separates from my body, frozen in time, as I pull myself back.

'You spread trouble –'

'I try to.'

'Like it's nothing more than a slab of cheese.'

'So which is it?' she asks. 'Curds or whey? Me or *me*? Dead dogs or live babies?'

'Dogs for now,' I tell her. 'That is, if you don't mind. Maybe I'll find it less upsetting.'

'Oh, don't worry,' Filippa answers. 'I'll still find a way to describe it that makes you feel sick.'

'Then I'm going to hope like an idiot you're going to surprise me.'

'No, the wonderful thing is you don't have to hope. Because I'm not going to surprise you the tiniest bit. Still, if you're worried you're not going to remember everything, go get your tape recorder first. Then you can listen to what I say over and over.'

'So if I'm ever in a good mood, the sound of your voice can spoil it immediately? No thanks.'

'But maybe that's what it's going to take,' Filippa says. She takes a step closer; and I can feel her blouse touching my skin. 'Because I'm still not convinced that you don't want me. And I don't think you believe that, at all. So, go get your tape recorder. Go get it now. At least this way you can hear the sound of your own voice on the tape rejecting me. Because maybe that's what you need. That can be your support.'

'I don't want your support.'

'That's not what I hoped to give you. And it's not what you took.'

'Yes, I'm going to get the tape recorder,' I tell her.

Then, as I head inside, I hear Filippa telling me her period still hasn't come.

<hr />

One final thing from those caverns, where they spread across Mancanzano's outskirts like the rectilinear illusions of an Escher print: Major Martella didn't let the boys go. At least not yet. After the second dog was exhumed, after the tarpaulin was taken as evidence, and the pulverized tufa, the pitons, the ropes, the shovels too – after all that had been carted away, and brought up the face of the bluff to Via Stigliano. After the carabinieri stood outside the caves, holding the leashes of the living dogs, wondering what to do with them now. After the officers had removed the collars from the animals and let them slink back into the canyon. After those carabinieri had turned on their heels and begun the slow walk back up the bluffs, with their bodies getting smaller and smaller as they receded into the fragmentary contours of the rock. After all that.

After these things, Major Martella lingered in the last of the caves with Flavio and Maurizio, and three of his officers, including the one who had fired the shot.

Maurizio asked, 'So what's going on? We told you everything. And showed you everything. Even more than you asked for.' The blood from his arm had seeped through his bandage, forming a wet blotch on his biceps. Flavio was silent.

Major Martella said, 'Yes, you have. You've been most agreeable. And you're right, you've been of such great and generous help that in just a few minutes we can all head uphill and back into town.' Major Martella held the lantern to his wrist and looked at the face of his watch in the dark. Then the major said, 'You know, it's not even late. It's only five o'clock. In an hour, we can all get some coffee.'

'Why not now?' Maurizio asked.

Major Martella answered, 'Because of due process.'

'What's that?' Maurizio wondered aloud.

'Citizens getting what they deserve,' the major answered. 'My understanding is that it's an American concept. Thanks to our visitors, I've been reading up.' He dug a heel into the ground, just beside the hollow where the German shepherd had been buried. Then he said to Maurizio, 'Now, I want you to remember what you see here. And when we get up the hill, and you find your mother wailing outside our headquarters, I want you to tell her everything that happened here. Forget nothing. Can I trust you to do that?'

'I have an excellent memory,' Maurizio said. 'Like an elephant's. Plus my teachers at school say I'm verbal too.'

'Good,' Major Martella replied. 'I'm happy to hear it. I'm glad that I know it.'

Then one carabiniere grabbed Maurizio's arm just under his wound, and the other two carabinieri took hold of Flavio by his armpits. Major Martella reached into his pocket and brought out the measuring tape he'd used before. He unfurled it a full two meters, folded it in half to be sure that it wouldn't break, and then wrapped the plastic strip around Flavio's neck. The teenager struggled, but the two officers held him against the cavern wall. Maurizio tried to struggle too, but the carabiniere holding his arm squeezed at his wound, and then the teenager didn't budge.

Then Major Martella told Flavio, 'The circumference of your neck is thirty-nine centimeters.'

He pulled on both ends of the tape. 'Now it is less.' He pulled again. 'Now, it is only thirty-three.'

Then, holding the boy there, so that he couldn't breathe, Major Martella of the Mancanzano carabinieri raised his knee and brought it heavily into Flavio's stomach. Then into his ribs. Then into his groin, relaxing his grip on the tape every few seconds so that Flavio could gasp and be able to stay alert and enjoy the whole thing. And then Major Martella would pummel the teenager again, first with one knee, and then with the other, hitting him as though his knee were a piston, a pile-driver, even a giant dozer from the tufa quarry. He did this until the officers finally decided to let the teenager drop to the ground, and Flavio was spitting up blood and curled on his side in a way that made him look not entirely well. Perhaps he looked like the young chicks that had sat in their nests at the tops of trees while Mussolini's men had gunned down the trunks. That was certainly the romantic way you could see it.

Then Major Martella said, 'That's for the dogs. And the truth is I've always thought they were pests. But if they're man's best friend, I've got to wonder where that leaves you.' Then Major Martella looked at Maurizio, who was staring at Flavio and wondering when his own turn was going to begin, and he reminded the teenager, 'Now, I'm counting on you to remember everything. Tell everyone what you saw here. Spread the word. Or next time it's going to be you, and we'll see if your friend has a better memory.'

Then the officers hoisted Flavio up from the cave floor, carried him with them to the top of the bluffs, and brought him to the hospital on Corso Umberto II. Next, they released Maurizio into his mother's care.

'What happened to Flavio? Did he get hurt?' Maurizio's mother asked her son.

'Yes, he got hurt,' Maurizio answered. 'And I'll tell you what happened. Whatever you ask. But do you think we could just go home first?'

'I'll make you some dinner,' Maurizio's mother said.

'Oh, no, I don't want to eat,' Maurizio answered.

'Not even my lamb?'

He shook his head. His mother cried. Then Maurizio cried too. Their tears followed after them as they walked, dropping to the parched ground.

As the pair walked away, the carabiniere said, 'I guess this means he doesn't want to meet us for coffee.'

Major Martella answered, 'Truth be told, he never said that he did. But he could always have ordered a soda, or a cup of tea. Now that really would have been polite. But that's the problem with youths today. No sense of manners.' Major Martella sighed, and he wiped at his forehead with a handkerchief. 'But I bet that's true wherever you are. Not only in Mancanzano.'

'Actually, I've always thought things were quite good in Mancanzano,' the carabiniere told him.

'Yes,' Major Martella said. 'They certainly are getting that way.' Then he folded the handkerchief back into a square, and carefully returned it to his pocket.

## Chapter 19
# The Count in the Caves

What is an anthropologist doing in Italy looking for truth? This is a culture of generosity and duty and friendship and honor, but not one of truth. Here, truth is a whore who tells you she loves you. Here, truth is logic strung together from suppositions and rumors. Both may be true. Truth is opacities, ambiguities, and spaces of darkness and blinding sun. Here, the truth is that Count Giancarlo Tramontano never wanted to come to Mancanzano. He lent money to Re Federico, the Aragonese king of the Two Sicilies, who then transferred him here to relieve himself of the debt. Tramontano, cheated, vituperative and later insane, was himself a casualty of politics, vengeance, fecklessness and deceit.

—

Filippa is waiting for me outside our quarters. It is one day after Maurizio and Flavio were found with the German shepherd's lifeless body, and just hours since they accompanied the carabinieri to the town's farthest outskirts to find a second dog, and then a third. Now, just beyond the warren of sassi – where Mussolini's engineers jerrybuilt a neighborhood out of a framework of social estrangement – I return inside our quarters.

In the last weeks, they've assumed an even more squalid veneer. Empty glasses fill the sink. Piles of newspapers are the ruins of columns, collapsed into loose pages beside the door. In

271

none of the rooms does anyone feel like emptying the garbage. Our quarters remind me of the steel drums out by Via Annunziatella, long filled past their capacities and spilling empty bottles all around them, always while bearing the same bold-face admonitions: *LA PULIZIA È UNA PROVA DI CIVILTÀ. USA I CESTELLI* – 'Cleanliness is a proof of civilization. Use the trash cans.' This is the home, and the comfort, to which I return.

Linda is sprawled across the sofa, watching Middelhoek's TV. She lifts her eyes lazily from the screen to watch me pass as I head into my room for the tape recorder.

'I thought you weren't allowed to do any more interviews,' she remarks, when I come out with the device in my hand. 'I thought only *I* could interview the people. You know, *me*, *sirena*, the slut.'

'I don't think any carabiniere is going to arrest me for having a cassette recorder,' I tell her.

'When I hold one, the people wait till it's on before they start calling me "*puttana*". That's because they plan ahead.'

'Fuck this city,' I tell her.

'Yeah, fuck this city,' Linda repeats. 'And take a crap on it too. All in the name of science.'

Then Linda goes back to watching Middelhoek's TV, even if the reception's so bad that the images on the screen are barely discernible: black and white shadows against a refraction of more shadows, until the picture's just a faint chiaroscuro of human existence, no more meaningful than a cluster of stick figures compared to the explosion of bodies that Middelhoek has restored in the caves.

'Science,' Linda repeats, as the images blur across the screen. 'Science is why I became an anthropologist. And science is why I became a slut. Most importantly, science is why I'm here in Mancanzano. To interact with the people, for the whole fucking world's scholarly benefit. Well, enjoy your day. It's sunny outside, no?' She pushes an empty water bottle off of the couch.

'Yes, it's sunny,' I tell her.

'Good,' she says. 'That makes it a good day for sluts.'

Outside our quarters, Filippa is waiting for me, and there's no question she's riled. She leans one shoulder against the wall of our building while she grinds her toe into the ground.

'You were in there a long time!' she gripes. 'What were you doing? Don't tell me you were having sex with that other one too!'

Now Filippa steps away from the wall, and the hem of her dress clings to it from static electricity: I figure the spikes keeping it there are the physical manifestations of our own mistrust. 'But I suppose that shouldn't surprise me,' Filippa reasons aloud. 'You cheat on everyone, don't you? So now you're even cheating on me!'

I hold the tape recorder in my hand, menacing it at her like I'm holding a mallet.

'I went in to get this. You know I went in to get this.'

'Once a girl's hormones start acting up, it's so hard to know anything, of course.'

'The idea of having a baby with you still makes me feel sick.'

'Having a baby with you will make me feel sick sometimes too, just like I've said. So that much we'll have in common. That, and our little, wonderful secret.'

'You mean the one that you choked me?'

'Or that you seduced me, or raped me, or fell in love with me, or that you just had some fun one sunny afternoon inside a cave. It doesn't matter.' She shrugs. 'I don't think your woman friend in New York will care which one it is either. Because by the time she'll find out, she'll be too busy having her baby.'

'Not yet,' I tell her. 'And *my* baby too.'

'OK, maybe. Your baby too. But that will bother her, anyway. That you left her to find me, and fuck me, and have a baby with me in Mancanzano. Because your baby with her wasn't enough.'

'I didn't come here to find you and fuck you, Filippa. Right now, I wish you were lost.'

Now we walk from my quarters, following Via Argia and Via

273

Cererie, into the ancient neighborhood of the sassi. Once we're surrounded by cave homes, the walls of the houses and the mammoth stone doorjambs framing their entrances loom as ferociously as any skyscraper in any city I've seen. I was wrong to think of these streets as tenebrous and eerie when I first arrived in Mancanzano. Because the sassi are much more stridently grotesque. Nothing in this city is as it should be.

Filippa, meanwhile, practically skips.

'What do you know about cheating, anyway?' I ask her, feeling every unmanageable provocation as she prances beside me. 'What do you know about my girlfriend? What do you know about me?'

'That's just it,' Filippa answers. 'I don't know anything. *Niente. Meno di niente.* Because you're the only who does! *You* are the expert. Isn't that why you came to Mancanzano? Because you are the expert. You and your friends. Including the slut. You didn't think we could look after ourselves, did you?'

Filippa stops in her gait.

'So is it time to turn this thing on?' I ask her, raising the tape recorder again in my hand.

'Yes, switch it on,' she says. 'Whenever you like. Because I'm only trying to make it easier for you to reject me. In fact, why not send a copy of the tape to your girlfriend back home? Then she can play it to herself and your child. That might make it easier for them to reject you too.'

The hulking walls of the sassi box us in as we further descend the face of the bluffs, weaving past homes, wandering past caves, and treading the streets that the carabinieri and the boys, and especially the dogs, took to confront everything that has been happening in this town. As we thread down the slope, the cathedral's tower is swallowed up by the sprawl of the sassi, and I see us disappearing, Filippa and me, and now even the blur of the sun, into the very city I came here to study.

The tape recorder is on. 'You killed the dog in the cave,' I tell her.

'I tied its hind legs together. While I was petting it. Then I tied the front ones too.'

'The dog let you do that?'

'The dog was preoccupied. There are ways to preoccupy an animal. I'm not talking about food. You know Flavio? I *know* you know Flavio. His dog committed suicide after what I am talking about. So maybe my dog would have jumped too – that is, if its legs hadn't been tied together. I can't know for sure, but I *do* know that I got its attention. There's no questioning that. Because you should have heard the dog wail. Its moans are different from a human being's.'

'I know what a dog sounds like.'

'Well, these howls were more like sounds of betrayal. But without any unnecessary words. And so then I stood up. And the dog whimpered. It licked my shoe. And then I kicked it into the ditch. How do you like that?'

'I don't like that very much.'

'But you haven't asked me the most important question?'

'What is the question?'

'Did I make the dog come?'

'You want me to ask that. You're dying to hear me ask you that.'

She motions to the tape recorder. 'No, I only want to make sure you get it on tape. Because I'm really starting to like the idea of your hearing everything over and over. Everyone says the best romances are timeless.'

'I'm not going to ask you, Filippa.'

'No, I guess you're not. That's probably what holds you back as an anthropologist too.'

'This isn't anyone's romance.'

'You're just saying that to play hard to get.'

'I'm not playing, Filippa.'

'Well, the answer's the same, anyway. I only made *you*. And I know you remember. So don't start thinking that I treated you like an animal.'

But even as Filippa is telling me this – even as she's trying to convince me that I don't have it so bad – I can't help thinking about Major Martella's carabinieri. Bolstered by animal rightists, they've combed through the countryside like a cell of the Resistance, so that someone might finally come to the local dogs' rescue. At least, those dogs are free again. They're back in the wild, where they can open their jaws and bark. But in this desolate hill town, I am wondering about me. Because who will come to my rescue in Mancanzano, when I'm five thousand miles from where I've promised to be? And where there's a woman waiting, with our baby inside her, kicking and squirming and also trying to set itself free.

The Potenza carabinieri say they want to safeguard lives. So how do I begin to tell them about me?

⸺

Last night at dinner, Fortune told us about Anna. He said he went to Montescaglioso. Then he said he went crazy. He pulled a cigarette out of his mouth, lifted her skirt, bent her face down over the kitchen table, and then made little burns across her tush. First, she hollered. Then, he held her. 'A guy gets ideas scrambling around town with a drill,' he tried to explain. He swore that the burns wouldn't leave permanent marks.

'What did that poor woman do to deserve that?' Linda demanded.

'Deserve it?' Fortune marveled. 'She didn't deserve it!'

At dinner, Middelhoek told us about burning his shoulders, and transforming the skin into a fresco of peaches and reds, until the sun started peeling off layer after layer. Then Middelhoek told us he knew he wouldn't need any more AB57 in his life. The sun was already equipped to accomplish more than enough, and the ingredients would always be available whenever there weren't clouds. Middelhoek told us that back in the Netherlands he'd try inviting Mathilde to the beach, and see if the sun could wipe away their mistakes. It was wishful thinking, like

276

Napoleon believing he could take Waterloo, and the consequences would have to be disastrous.

That same evening, Linda metamorphosed into her own sinkhole: she hardly emitted a sound other than to berate Fortune. She leaned on an elbow, and fished through a plate of pasta distractedly; but the prongs of the fork barely got past the cracked rim of her lips. Watching her eat/not eat made me think of Dr Biaggi: the leviathan from the Straits of Messina, who like the dogs here had died in a ditch. Now *there* was a man who knew how to enjoy a meal, and who'd have strangled himself for a last savory morsel!

But watching Linda at dinner also reminded me of something the doctor had told us during his ravenous, garrulous prime: that the term 'anorexia' comes from the Greek word for longing. Now, it wasn't hard to imagine Linda longing for a place and a time when she wasn't a *puttana*, Middelhoek for Mathilde, or Fortune for a world where he could behave however he liked, free from rebuke. But it was strange to be comparing myself with them in the first place, since I was the one in our group who supposedly had the things he wanted. To use Dr Biaggi's parlance, my focus right now was on watching them get flushed away.

So, I can't help but wonder here, what is my theory of life in the sassi? Where is the sense in murder and isolation? And like all good ethnography, where is the confession?

This afternoon, I held the tape recorder in my hand as Filippa and I descended into the sassi.

FILIPPA (INFORMANT): I stood over the hole.
ETHNOGRAPHER: Which you dug?
INFORMANT: With a shovel.
ETHNOGRAPHER: And then you watched the dog?
INFORMANT: I watched it try to get out. But it couldn't get out. It couldn't get to its feet. It tried to, of course. Of

277

course, it tried. But then do you know what? This dog forgot all about leaving the hole. And it started pushing its pelvis against the side of the ground. Do you want me to show you?

ETHNOGRAPHER: No, I think I can picture it.

INFORMANT: Besides you'd never successfully get that part on tape. You'd need something louder for your recording. To make it convincing. Like the sound of you hitting me.

ETHNOGRAPHER: I haven't hit you, Filippa. At least I haven't yet.

INFORMANT: That's the one part of the story I can't figure out. Because if I told any of this to someone from Mancanzano – like to my great-grandfather, for instance – I'm not sure you realize the beating he'd give me. But that's not your way, is it? No, your style of abuse is fancier. More refined. Still, I bet it's going to hurt your girlfriend back home worse than any bruises.

ETHNOGRAPHER: How about we stick to the dogs?

INFORMANT: Why? You think it's a safer subject to discuss? It's not.

ETHNOGRAPHER: Then what about the foreplay?

INFORMANT: This *is* the foreplay – do you mean you're not enjoying it yet? Well, the rest of the story is this: the dog wanted to come. It wanted to ejaculate. Because that's how an animal thinks. It's trapped in a hole. It may even die. No, it's going to die. But, fortunately, it doesn't have any stupid human hang-ups about satisfaction or pleasure. So the dog's happy to come, whenever there's the chance. So, you know what? I'm sorry I didn't have any food with me in the cave. Maybe even some of Giandomenico's mother's cavatelli. Because I'd have liked to have thrown something delicious down to the dog. Because that dog in the hole, with its legs tied together, would have really appreciated the food.

Particularly after the sex.

ETHNOGRAPHER: If I took you to another country, where it was legal, would you have an abortion?

INFORMANT: If you took me to another country, then it would be kidnapping, and you'd go to prison. Is that what you want?

We are walking past the little piazzas and tiny, nameless neighborhoods – the *vicinati* of homes and roofs and streets and stairs – the agglomerations of ancient homes that couldn't have known they'd first become wombs and then living crypts. We are passing Padre Caduta's Church of the Madonna della Virtù, where a dog's lifeless body once landed before I knew what to suspect. Now we are coming to the sassi on Mancanzano's farthest edge, just beyond the panorama at Via della Vergine, and we are approaching the caves where the first frescoes were found: the peach-mottled murals I once also believed to be a marvelous thing. But this is also where the first two teenagers died. And not far, either, from where Filippa tells me a new life has been squeezed into existence.

From deep in the hills, there is the sound of a dog barking, and the burst of it sets Filippa off. She says, 'The other thing I can't figure out is why you don't ask if I hate you.'

'I've done nothing to you.'

'What does that matter?'

I say to her, 'I'm still trying to understand you. But I will say you are young. And you're not very careful about me. And your body is finding out what it can do to other bodies.'

'That's what you'll say?'

'It's what I keep telling myself.'

'Then you study people, but you still don't understand them.'

'I've learned not to judge them.'

'Yes, I've heard that's what older people do.'

'I came here as an anthropologist.'

'What were you planning to leave as?' she laughs. Then

279

Filippa quickens her gait, and I have to catch up. 'You know, you really should have started hating me when you saw me on my roof. Or at the funeral in Irsina, or back at the creek. Back then, you still had the chance.'

'My fantasy is that at the creek, you'd slipped on some pebbles in the water and drowned.'

'The water wasn't very deep.'

'No, but that's all it takes if you're on your back.'

'Then your other mistake was fucking me standing up. Not very romantic. But don't worry. I don't hate you either.'

'No?'

'Not yet. Because I'm still getting to know you. But give me more time. Then I will.'

And, meanwhile, the dog keeps barking. And Filippa and I keep walking. As we head down the hill, the caves all around us are gritty and gravelly chunks of Lucanian Swiss cheese. The sassi are a thousand handfuls of dice, all of them offering terrible odds. They are Pandora's boxes, constructed of tufa, wafting evils, and dribbling all kinds of ills. But maybe what Filippa says is right: I should have started hating her long ago, because what matters in this town isn't the present or future, but the past.

'So then what happened to the dog after you kicked it into the hole?' I ask her. 'I mean, in the past.'

'Do you mean, was the dog able to come after I stopped touching it?'

'No, I mean what did you do to the animal after you'd trapped it in the ground?'

'Well, I shoveled the stones back into the hole, in the past. The stones that were big enough, I dropped on the dog's head, in the past. The smaller ones, I poured into the hole like they were a fine powder. But I kept filling the hole up until the dog disappeared, and the ground was as smooth as the one we are walking on. Then I patted it down with the back of the shovel. That gets us to now.'

'That's it?'

'Yes. It. And, also, I left fingerprints. Lots of them. Like little kisses.'

'I don't think anyone will think of your fingerprints as little kisses.'

'No, but maybe when I patted the ground with the shovel, that can be the closest I got to giving the whimpering little animal anything resembling hugs.'

'And am I right that you feel no remorse?'

'You're old,' she says. 'So you don't realize the things a teenager has to do to be popular.'

Filippa and I have followed the trickling course of the creek along Mancanzano's outskirts, and combated the broken terrain, the heat and the flies, and now we have entered the cave with Middelhoek's frescoes. 'Mancanzano's frescoes' you also could call them, although that's not what Joost Middelhoek would say. At the flanks of the paintings are the images of cherubim: the fat little outriders of God, filling their gullets and smearing their faces with the blood of the penitents. But at the feet of these angels, there are now also the more recently revealed depictions of demons, the images the AB57 brought to light. These grand excavators – the phallo-destroyers of mortal flesh – tower over the illustrated caverns, while below them are the men and women of Mancanzano, all of them buried alive in the ancient, malleable, gougeable ground.

Now Filippa says: 'I was going to dig up the dog, once I was sure it was dead. Then I was going to slit open its throat, and gulp down some of its blood, like your friend showed with the cherubim after he stripped off the first layer of paint. So don't be cute and say, "Like a vampire." Because that only trivializes what we wanted to do here.' She points to the fresco. 'Because what I'm talking about now is what you see in the picture.'

'I wouldn't dream of trivializing you, Filippa. OK, I'd dream about, fantasize about it, maybe even pray about it happening. But with everything going on, I don't think that would work.'

'See, it's just like with the angels and demons in the fresco,' she continues. 'And also' – she pauses, snickering – 'with their . . .'

'Having trouble with the word?'

'No.' She smiles well-meaningly. 'With their cocks.'

'But those images have only just been discovered.'

She looks at me wryly. 'That doesn't mean they were lost. Just because you're in our city today, that doesn't mean we don't know our own history.'

'But no one told us anything.'

'So, who'd you ask?'

And now I think that maybe for a second time Filippa is right. Because where did we go? To a Dutch restorer? A sinecure from Bari? Graduate students from Calabria? A gold-bricking police chief mainly interested in accumulating gifts and keeping others at bay, while he measures out how best to cut a *bella figura*? And finally to a bunch of carabinieri from two hours away in Potenza? Not the best study sample, on reflection. Definitely not enough for a margin for error, unless what's happening now is exactly that error. But what about Dottoressa Donabuoni? The city's High Deputy for Public Works? She's from Mancanzano. So shouldn't she have known something, said something? She's the one who brought us here.

'We asked the high deputy,' I tell her.

'You can't ask people like Dottoressa Donabuoni!' Filippa laughs, loud enough for her roars to echo through the cavern. 'The high deputy's fifty or sixty years old, and she hasn't ever even had a child! In Italy, that makes a woman unreliable. In this country, that barely makes her a real woman! So, you should have asked me! Because I'm only nineteen, but I've already gotten pregnant.'

'I wouldn't have asked you.'

'But once we were so terribly close!'

'You're not someone I trust, Filippa.'

'*Of course* you can trust me,' she answers quickly. 'But that's exactly my point! You've just got to stop expecting me to say the things you want to hear. I don't know why you do that. From my perspective, it *is* kind of weird. But maybe you know better. Because you are the anthropologist.' She points to the frescoes. 'You know everything better.' And now she sweeps her hand before her as if to indicate the entire city of Mancanzano. 'Yes,' she tells me, 'you definitely know everything best.'

But from my own perspective, I am wondering when anthropologists are finally allowed to admit that things are weird. Is it when those patterns of behavior start to make sense? Or, perhaps, when the spirals of understanding weave together, not into simple braids (as I once imagined, when aspects of Mancanzano still seemed fanciful and appealing), but into the nucleic acids and double helixes that started us all – and are still supposed to explain how we human beings behave. Because, if Count Tramontano arrived here from Naples, took a look at this city, and beheld his own complicity, I'm beginning to understand why he kept trying to urinate beyond his castle's walls.

'Cock, cock, cock!' Filippa screeches at me now, from inside the cavern. 'Cock, cock, cock! See? No problem saying it, at all!'

The tape recorder is in my hand, and I am watching the two small sprockets in its insides turn – two little gears following the same perfect course in my grip, while everything else in my life comes unhinged.

But for the first time now since I have known her, there is something new about Filippa. It is altogether different from what I felt in Piazza Ridola, when I couldn't resist the memory of her hands upon me. Sometimes understanding slips into the woodwork like an army of termites: insidiously at first, but then with enough force to make the floorboards crack.

So when I think of Count Tramontano, I understand how torrents of acid are better than tears for rinsing away obstacles. And how they are better for burning through tufa too. Because now I don't have to ask what Filippa was planning to do after she'd gulped the animal's blood. And I don't have to ask why she wasn't afraid about leaving fingerprints on the shovel or getting caught. It's the same reason why she's not even worried about the tape recorder capturing everything in my hand. Because now I can guess that Filippa was also going to end up dead in a cave. Except that maybe she was also going to do it with the baby I never wanted. And since the dead in this city have always come in pairs, maybe the rest of the equation was that she was going to do it with me. So was that her offer? Was that it? The one way I could forget everything I'd done and created with her in Mancanzano?

Then Filippa asks: 'Did you hear about the tarpaulin the carabinieri found in the cave?'

'I did,' I tell her. 'Along with the tale of a dog, and some food, and a choke collar around its neck. But I don't suppose you find any of that surprising.'

'Of course I do. It's always surprising when an animal dies. Even more than with human beings. Because the animals are innocent.'

But now Filippa looks at me, and I swear there is something akin to compassion on her face; and the expression on her is strange and revolting, unexpected yet natural, like the face of a sinewy ballerina regurgitating her dinner. And somehow I am glad to see this expression, because it reminds me that we don't always have to have the things we want. Because maybe desperation can be a kind of resistance too.

Then Filippa repeats to me, 'Of course it's surprising. The dogs were innocent. And so were you.'

But that isn't right. Because I know I'm not innocent, not now, not here. Not with the thoughts and the things I have wanted in these caves, so far from the woman and life that I once thought would make me feel right. Especially not now, on the eve of the birth of our creation. And absolutely not here, while Filippa and I stand in this cave, and I know that deep down inside me (as deep as these caverns, and even deeper), I'm still going to want her, even if I don't let myself look.

And so this is why I keep my eyes fixed on the small rotating gears in my palm, and on the tiny red light beside the microphone that cravenly blinks to her inflection. Because when I look at Filippa, I see her mouth and her tongue, and the split amaretti of ass. I see the parts of her body, the sun and her hole. And I think the parts of her body are the sum of her, whole. And I think that maybe *this* is why I came to Mancanzano: to feel what it's like, finally, to be out of control.

So she's right to say I'm not ready to reject her. Because even while Filippa is telling me that I should hate her, and she is describing to me the things she has done and enjoyed – and I know I should be imagining *my* hands squeezing her neck – it's still her ten curlable fingers that I wish were holding *me*. (So, as far as the core of my ethnography goes, here is my confession: I am focusing right now, in this particular cave, on how easy it is to push away the thin straps of a dress with a finger, a palm, a tongue, a chin, or even an *elbow*. And I am thinking that the number of ways to bare a breast is equal to the variety of ways that you can devour it. And I know that neither one of those things makes me any objectively identifiable kind of innocent.)

Then Filippa says, 'The tarpaulins were for sealing the caves. They were for sealing the caves' mouths.'

As she says this, she reaches for my hand, and pushes both flesh and mechanism out of the way. Then Filippa Grossoglio kisses me on the mouth, and I let her. It is a deep kiss, and I really let her. Filippa's mouth is hot and wet like the mineral springs of Montecatini. It is bubbly, and, I should joke, it's even vaguely sulfurous. Then Filippa says to me, 'One mouth fits another better than a tarpaulin.'

I wipe my mouth with my sleeve.

'I wanted us to be alone,' Filippa tells me. 'No. I wanted a baby too. A baby of stone. I wanted to be inside a cave with a baby inside me, and I wanted to feel the draw of using every last breath, and I wanted to fall asleep inside the earth, inside a cave. That's what I wanted. Is that so wrong?'

I am looking at Filippa Grossoglio, and I am wondering about wrong.

'Giandomenico and Lucia,' she says, 'the first two who died, it was all they could talk about before they did it. They went on and on about Count Tramontano being buried in a cave. And they went on and on about burying into each other. That's how Giandomenico described it.

'Now, Giando and Lucia were crazy to watch. Crazy and beautiful. She liked to have fingers inside her, sure – all of us do; you have to know that. But Lucia also liked those fingers around her neck. Which is an acquired taste, even if it's one you have acquired. But it's difficult to do without leaving marks. And marks can be much worse than death, especially in a chatterbox city like this one. So what's a girl supposed to do?'

Filippa is looking at me intently, but it's clear that the narration of her friends' death doesn't evoke in her anything like sadness. So maybe it's true that Filippa is sadder about the innocent dog, or about events from Italian history, like the death of Garibaldi or the spray of bullets that pockmarked the sassi here decades later than she is about her two friends dying. And probably about other friends too.

'But strangulation is violent,' she continues. 'There's no way around that. Wearing fingers at your neck isn't like wearing a necklace. There's a much heavier clasp. So I don't like what those two, Flavio and Maurizio, did with those dogs any more than you do.'

I flip the tape over, fumblingly.

'So there had to be another way,' Filippa says. 'And there was. You know the tarpaulin? The mouths of the caves were small. The cave where Giando and Lucia died – and also Pierino and Angela – was small. So it wasn't hard to fit a tarpaulin over the openings. And it wasn't hard to let a few charcoals smolder inside with them. Because charcoal is so easy to come by, and

286

also to light. So picture the romance. Yes, it was romantic. The glow of briquettes in a tar-black cave. A man. A woman. They don't need clothes. They don't want them, anyhow. Who wants clothes?

'So the coals smolder, eating up oxygen, just like the monster from that Greek story in school who could gulp down the sea. But the coals also add carbon monoxide, so you can only use a few. You see, a dog died for science last year. Funny, huh – the idea of us being scientists, just like you? Well, you should have heard that dog retching and coughing and wheezing pathetically when we tried sealing it up in a cave with great heaps of coals. So that's when we realized carbon monoxide poisoning was no way to die. Because to hear an animal in pain like that was to question your humanity. And death should be silent if you're going to respect it.' Filippa pauses, and smiles, and puts a hand to her womb. 'Now, do you want to know what is the right way to die?'

'Tell me, Filippa. Tell me so that I can know it, and so that it can be on this tape.'

'*Asfissia*. Suffocation,' she tells me. 'Just using up what air there is in a cave. It is so easy. And it doesn't hurt. You don't even cough. This is a kind death. And it is restful. Right after it turns you on. Plus, if you're careful about the way you do it, you can make sure there are enough coals to speed everything along, and then act as a night-light so you don't even get frightened by the dark.'

'So you do this. Why do this?'

She points again to the fresco on the wall, and to its depiction of penitents caught in a cave. 'People in Mancanzano have always been doing this. Since long before they put pictures of it onto the walls,' she says. 'Because that's what this city is, even if you cover it up with paint. The paint comes off. Isn't that what your restorer showed? Eventually, the paint has to come off. Because it's not a part of the wall.'

'That's what you see in the frescoes? Burrowing into the earth?'

287

'And burying yourself.'

'And that's why the teenagers were naked? To die the same way they came into the earth? To die like they're painted here on the wall?'

'No,' she says, 'the teenagers were naked because teenagers' clothes always come off. For the same reason you took off mine a month and a half ago in the cave. In order to *scopare*. So that we could *fuck*. For the same reason you liked it when I had my hands at your throat. Because –'

Here Filippa pauses; she takes the hand that was pressed to her abdomen, and she moves it, like a planchette grazing a Ouija board, to the outline of her breasts. Now she brushes her body where it is hardest beneath her dress, and I am watching her finger it as though it were some kind of polished and precious stone: something earthen and rock hard that was sculpted by a millennium of grinding pressure. Now I am looking at her in the cave, and remembering the salty, mineral taste of her skin, and the stony tufa enticements of where we are all soft and hard, and strong and weak. And, as I'm listening to her, I am imagining Filippa's body still pressed against mine and kissing me hard in this cave, and telling me everything that she is doing and that she has done, and when I think of her words, and the weight and the shape and taste of them in my mouth, if I found out they were poison, I don't even know now that I would spit them out.

Then Filippa says: 'Giandomenico and Lucia and Pierino and Angela took off their clothes and fucked each other in the cave, without enough air, barely being able to breathe, because it is better. You know that. You know it is better. That is the reason. Because coming that way is the only way that completely and totally, and absolutely consumes you.'

'I know that,' I hear myself whispering back. 'Yes, I know that,' I say to her now, even as I am trying to picture myself lying in bed, being in love with you, and being with you. Even as I am trying to visualize a baby gasping its first breaths in a hospital room that I know now I'll never see. Because Filippa is right. I know that she is right. She is still touching her breast, and I am trying to picture myself touching your breast. But it doesn't matter anymore if I try, because now I am not able to see it.

'There,' Filippa says to me. 'That is the story. Now do you understand us? Do you have what you wanted when you came to Mancanzano?'

Filippa and I are walking through the caves where the last teenagers were found. Where a wall was constructed from powdered stone. Middelhoek has finished his work inside them, and the carabinieri from Potenza have sealed these caverns off. Fortune has warned us that he thinks they might be ready to collapse, and that the broken-down walls, already weakened by a century of aftershocks and tremors, already strained by the scatttershot of Fascist gunfire, already crumbling from their own weight (although probably not from the gnawing of suffocating teens), could come tumbling down like a massive row of dominoes. But that's where Filippa and I go. We climb over a single plastic yellow barrier that the Potenza carabinieri have strung across the cavern's mouth.

'That's what Giando and Lucia and Pierino and Angela did,' she says, although I'm not sure I want to hear more. 'They made love in the caves with their last breaths,' Filippa says. 'Giandomenico was crazy. Incredibly crazy! The way he bit at the walls! I'd like to think he knew what he was doing. Maybe he did. Because he found the frescoes. And they are beautiful frescoes! After he found them, it was impossible to think about letting yourself go without a mouthful of stone.'

'So you could swallow the city that was going to swallow you?'

'Blood and tufa, that's what this whole city is,' she tells me.

But Filippa is wrong, just as she was wrong about my being innocent. Because this city is more. It is bodies and caverns and kestrels and wailing parents and decaying flesh, and I think of all the tears that I have seen here; and then I think of the ones that I left behind, and of what's been found and also lost, and what is now decaying inside of me. Because now I know that Mancanzano is a city of so much more than blood and stone, because it is also a city of loss and of appetites that can't be filled, a city that swells beyond its own borders, to Montescaglioso, Irsina, Messina – and then across the ocean, all the way to New York – before reversing itself, and shooting back here. And so now maybe I'm finally ready to ask, because I'm beginning to understand what Filippa's telling me the same way I understand how powdered tufa can clot to itself until it forms a wall. And if I mouth the words it's also my chance to hear them.

'So is that what you were planning to do? To die in a cave. Like the others. Beside a lover?'

'No,' Filippa answers me. 'My lover lived. You know that, because you're the proof.'

'You mean, you couldn't find anyone to put the tarpaulin up? You always found someone to pull them away!'

'It wasn't me all the time,' Filippa replies sharply. 'There were ten people before me. There would have been more.'

'But this time Flavio and those other kids with dogs – they just decided not to help you? Are you telling me I should thank them?'

She smiles. 'You'd like to think that, wouldn't you? You'd like to think I was trying to kill you.'

'No, I like the part about your not being able to. And about other people not wanting to help. Somehow, it makes me feel strangely alive.'

But Filippa says, 'No, of course they would have helped, if only I'd asked. Flavio's friend Maurizio would even have taken your place in the cave. But that's not what I wanted. I wanted something better.'

'You mean, better than death?'

'I wanted a baby.'

'I know,' I tell her. 'You wanted mine. But why mine when there was an entire city of men here who would have offered?'

'I didn't want offers,' she says. 'I wanted to take. And you were perfect. Because you are American, and that's what you do in your superior country, where you are the experts, where you see things you want, and you take. Besides, your things weren't hard to identify. They were different from everyone else's. Like I told you, more ambitious. That made them closer to mine.'

'Filippa, I want them back.'

But as she stands before me, I see that her hand has returned to her abdomen. It is back over the part of her where a baby is growing.

'You want answers?' Filippa asks me. 'You want things *back*? And you think that I care?' Now, Filippa's voice is rising and pounding and shuddering, and for a second it even occurs to me to laugh, because I think how she's been saying she wants me to hear her words over and over and how, as they fill up this chamber, they're bouncing at me off the walls.

'You think I strangled you, but that I still care?' Filippa says to me now. 'You think that I care about you, and about the things you want? I am having this baby, this baby of stone! Because it feels right to have this child, this creature inside me, as insignificant as a dog, and maybe as ugly, or as beautiful, or as stupid as its father. I wanted your baby because women, and even men, sometimes want babies! I wanted this child because I wanted it to feel every bit as lonely as everyone else I know, and even before this child was born and before it had grown, I wanted it to find itself back in a cave, back in a womb, and stuck like the rest of us in Mancanzano. And maybe, one day, I thought a cherub could even come off the walls and gargle its blood, or even watch as it died with its mother. I wanted this baby because it isn't enough to be swallowed up inside a cave! I wanted this baby so that instead of giving it life, I could finally do the opposite, and take it away! You see, I wanted this baby

291

so that I could teach it, and myself, and anyone who happened to care, what it means to be in Mancanzano. And to live here with something as misplaced inside you as hope. Something so misplaced and awkward that your only choice is to hate it.'

I am looking at Filippa and my conscience has the weight of stone.

Today Filippa and I are walking in the caves, and I am holding the tape recorder in my hand. We are walking where we are not supposed to be. We are walking where Fortune has told us not to go. We are walking, Filippa and I, and the baby inside her. Now it is so easy to knock into a wall. It is so easy to take a piece of metal and force it where it does not go, where it can do the most amount of damage, where it can break something and everything, and fill up a cave, which I have finally understood is a three-dimensional expression of longing. I know now that a cave is a petrified vacuum that needs to be filled.

So we go where we're not supposed to, where we have gone already, and for the first time Filippa Grossoglio follows. We walk into the interior of the mountain where it is dark and deep. We walk past the beams that have been added to give support, and I take a stanchion that is lying on the ground – a meter-long section of metal pipe – and I have to admit I even consider hitting Filippa with it. I can imagine the pipe moving through the air, and the breeze that that motion would make as it unsettled the air, and I can picture the piece of metal traveling through empty space, and into the province of Filippa's head, where it would crackle the bone, first bending and then bursting it, just as the broom handle I held with Fortune so effortlessly pierced, sank and then writhed inside a wall.

Now Filippa looks at me, and it is comforting to see a look of fear on her face. It is an expression of honesty, contempt and doubt, so different from the expressions I knew and I saw when I had a life, and a woman I loved, and a city, and the promise of another baby, and promises I intended to keep. But I don't hit

Filippa. No. I have the stanchion in my hand, and she is afraid, and she is smiling, and for now that is enough. So I do not hit her. Because now it is like we are at a monster movie, a horror movie, and she is smiling, and she is laughing, and I am the creature, the golem, the monster rampaging through the country-side, because it is ugly and unloved, and because it has been betrayed.

So now I take the stanchion, and how marvelous it feels in my grip! And how wonderful to find, with this meter-long piece of pipe in my hands, that it works all right to have my heart pump into my spleen, while I use my intestines to strangle the parts of my body I might otherwise deny. So now I take the stanchion, and I hit it hard against one of the supports. I hit it again. The clanging echoes in the cave until the sound of the ringing is all around me. So I hit the support. Then I hit another. And why not even a third? In moments of desperation, you can do a third. Then I am walking back toward the light, toward the mouth of the cave, and I am hitting the struts, I am banging the supports, I am hitting the pipe against the soft tufa walls, and hitting whatever I can that doesn't breathe. And the clanging is enormous, the banging is violent, and I can breathe the fresh air and see the sun, and I know soon I'll be back in the open if I can keep banging whatever is in my way.

The afternoon sun in Mancanzano is strongest at three o'clock. It is an hour when people stay home. Because at three in the afternoon, the sun is too hot, the sun is too bright. It is too stifling, and the day is no good. You feel these things especially when you're escaping a cave. You feel them acutely when you walk out into the sun. Under the sun's blasting rays, I remember Filippa telling me, 'Yes, the dog did come. The dog came, because it is an animal.' And while it's true that I know this delight – and the only truth which counts is that I like it – mostly I hear the sound of my clanging, clarion and shrill, and I know that it's welcoming me back to the open because it rings in a new day.

# Chapter 20
# *Hoc Est*

First, I ran. There was the canyon, the creek, the caves I'd never visited, the ones that I had. There was Via d'Addozio, with its upwards spiral across the bluffs. Via delle Belle Pietre, Via Bradano, Via Ginosa, Via Palata, Via Folletto. So many others, each maybe a thousand years old. Each a guardian of secrets. Some of them now also purveyors.

On Via Argia, Fedelina Soppresa was emptying sweepings from her home into the piazzetta. On Via Sant'Isaia, Gianluca Porfiri was calling to anyone, 'I've read that Chrysler's new Imperial LeBaron is a hundred and twenty-four inches long! I need someone to tell me what that is in metric!' On Via Lucana, Diego Gattini was hawking recordings of Adriano Celentano's *'Impazzivo per te'* ('I Was Crazy for You'), blasting the rock-ballad from his shop like a muezzin summoning worshipers to prayer. And on Via Pentolame, Signora Bitonto was baking breads so heavy and solid that just handling them threatened to give you bruises.

But who was I going to talk to? What was I going to do?

So, first I ran. And then I stopped. Then I came home. Now I needed to find a place inside myself.

It took no time to apprehend me. Major Martella was finally able to assume the role of a man of action, for which he seemed inordinately grateful. The prosecuting magistrate would finally get off his case. Perhaps, like his father, the major would even become a *colonnello*.

Three Mancanzano carabinieri, accompanied by a member of the Potenza corps, arrived at our quarters and led me outside to the street through the newspapers, the garbage, the half-filled glasses and the rattling sounds of Middelhoek's TV. Linda was still on the couch, wearing a sweaty tank top and athletic shorts: she looked exactly as others assumed she would, a whore in her boudoir, lounging around in discolored, second-rate under-things. She fixed the officers with a curious gaze that quickly transformed into a glare once she was fed up with having her view of the television blocked. But then, as the carabinieri led me away, she curled her hand into a snug fist and warned, 'Don't let on to anything. Tell them you were interviewing the wind. Or tell them the tape recorder wasn't loaded.'

Before Filippa's body was brought to the mortuary (this time, both the 'cause' and the 'mechanism' of her death were so plainly apparent that the *medico legale*'s sleuthing wouldn't be needed), Major Martella arrived on the scene with his Cesare Lombroso cardboard box and measuring tape. First, he shooed the busybody carabinieri away, then he lifted the clear plastic wrap that had been laid over Filippa's body, and folded it down as if he were preparing a bed. Then Major Martella unfurled the bright yellow tape and placed it to the dead girl's cranium and ears.

He beamed.

In fact, the major was so impressed by the numbers inching across the strip like escalating ticker prices that he actually two-stepped as he circled the corpse. Giddily, he lowered the tape measure to Filippa's midsection and pelvis, and he read those numbers aloud to the assembled officers.

'I'd never have thought she'd be so wide here!' Major Martella marveled, still lost in his mirth. 'But we all know a measuring tape never lies!'

—

The trial did not take long. Here in Italy, when you're suspected of crimes, you sit in the courtroom in an iron cage, like you are a wild animal. Except for a single hard bench, the cage is empty, and – dressed in your street clothes, with your wrists uncuffed – you're left to grab at the bars, either anxiously or angrily. If you're fortunate enough to be a Mafioso, sometimes you can sneak out through a hole in the floor and disappear into a small town in Sicily. But if you're someone like me, with fewer outright connections, then no one arrives to offer any help, and the thick vertical bars of the cage provide your only support.

In so far as it mattered, my crime was destroying national treasures; that is, deliberately demolishing Mancanzano's sassi. I'd knocked down girders, and ceilings had fallen. So had walls. The tape recorder with everything Filippa had told me was lost under falling stones. So was Filippa. Her body was broken, sandwiched, squeezed. A large stone fell on her chest and forced out her final breath.

There were additional manslaughter charges involved with her death, of course. But the fact that a foreigner was responsible for even one of the problems that had been plaguing Mancanzano for almost a year was more than anyone expected the townsfolk to bear. So it wasn't hard to imagine that my court-assessed guilt would have been the same if Filippa had skipped away from the caves unscathed.

A couple of newspapers covered the trial. There were reporters from Amsterdam's *De Telegraaf*, and both the *Guardian* and *Independent* of London. *Il Messaggero* and *Corriere della Sera* dispatched reporters from Naples. Someone from Turin's *La Stampa* even came down for a lark. The Mancanzano newspapers and Radio Maria, of course, sent their entire reporting staffs, and then editorialized for weeks about the proven dangers to their town from outside involvement.

With all the national publicity, representatives from the Milan-based industrial firm Chemitalia traveled to Mancanzano, and overcame local resistance among their fellow Italians by distributing appealing sums of Italian money. Then Chemitalia purchased all rights to Mancanzano's tufa quarry, and also to the spare stone from where one particular – and now famous – cave had collapsed. A statue of Filippa was erected on the spot. In turn, the additional publicity that this act generated throughout the republic was enough for the company to secure hefty governmental subsidies (the likes of which are unknown in the U.S.), and erect two new fertilizer plants in Basilicata, just outside of Moliterno.

It wasn't long after this that Tonio Archimede finally picked up his tools with a newly restored vigor, and launched a successful enterprise selling miniaturized copies of the statue of Filippa. There was an expensive version carved from a single block of tufa, and another made of compacted tufa dust. But collectors familiar with everything that happened here generally wanted to own both.

In a press release issued around the same time, the *medico legale* in Potenza explained how he wasn't going to accept any blame for failing to identify the causes of the teenagers' deaths. He argued that 'environmental suffocation' never produces any specific findings in an autopsy, and other *medici legali* across the peninsula corroborated his assessment. When the oxygen content of air drops from a naturally occurring twenty-one percent to somewhere below five – as would have occurred in the sealed-off caverns – loss of consciousness and death typically take place within a handful of minutes. For many people, sleep comes naturally after sex. But in these caverns, the teenagers' heavy breathing soon made it irresistible.

Then once the tarpaulins were removed from the mouths of the caverns by other teenagers (each awaiting their turns at this last ardent thrill), outside air would immediately rush back inside the caves, purging all indications of oxygen depletion. Likewise, the coals that were burned inside the closed spaces never led to any significant amounts of carbon monoxide in the teenagers' blood, and by the time anyone had discovered the corpses, the briquettes' ashes had been carted away too. Then nothing else was left in the caves, save for the bodies, a fresco or two, and the townspeople's memories. When practiced alone, self-strangulation during sex is called 'autoerotic asphyxiation'. But there isn't a term in the medical dictionaries for what these teenagers discovered they could do to themselves and to each other in Mancanzano.

After the trial, many townspeople expected a final comment from a local official to wrap up the troubles and suffering of the past year, and provide a salve to their still-tender wounds. To this end, the *medico legale* published a notice in regional papers, stating: 'Only three days ago, on June 2, an accidental decapitation occurred at a machine parts factory in Bernalda. That young man's body was brought to our offices at 10:47 a.m., and the correct cause of death was firmly established by noon. A death certificate for this man was also issued the same day. So citizens of the republic should not worry. The Region of Basilicata is still a safe place to die.'

But in the city of Mancanzano, Mayor Luciano Taciuto had nothing to say. He merely came to Via Annunziatella as the Potenza carabinieri were taking off – whirring their sirens and flashing their lights in a final show of constabulary bravado – pulled out his handkerchief, and waved.

—

A visitor came to my cell yesterday. *'Mille grazie,'* he told me. 'You gave us what we always wanted. And you did it with a terrific bang!'

'You're welcome,' I answered. But I wondered aloud about Filippa.

'Her body's been buried,' he told me. 'They dug her up from the collapsed cave. Then they placed her body back under some stones at the Cimitero Santa Maria della Palomba. So now we're all very happy for her.'

I told him, 'That makes me happy for Filippa too.'

In so many places, in so many cultures, people try to transcend a corrupt, modern world by reaching a higher state. They strive for the heavens, even if it's rare that they actually get there. But these Mancanzani, and the other teenagers they converted from neighboring towns, sought out a lower state with the same tenacity. The difference was that with their goals closer to home, they succeeded.

The visitor told me, 'Filippa makes us proud. There are those of us who don't think of you as a murderer.'

He could just as easily have written that in the dust.

The one tiny window in my cell looks away from the sassi. The only thing I see is Count Tramontano's castle, bricks of tufa used to construct up. Maybe if I look at it enough I can forget about caves (the conceit of interment is that I have plenty of time on my hands). I can stare at the castle and pretend that I am in it, promenading the battlements, with my bladder full and my whang hanging out. But I know now that not even the Neapolitan count could evade the caves. So, better to concentrate on the teenagers found, entwined, enamored, albeit dead, but slumbering together after a final exclamation.

The greater the number the people who died in this city, the less each one of their lives and their deaths mattered. But, I have to figure, at least these teenagers were trying to turn Mancanzano into a place where they could have an effect on their own futures, and do something tangible with their ambitions. (Filippa, then, took this a step further, and wrought her own effects on *me*.) But maybe those were the only two choices Mancanzano would ever offer: huddle inside your cave, digging until you can't go any deeper; or search out in the open for an airborne Madonna, while your eyeballs soft-boil in their sockets. Either way, one final thrill is more than most people get to experience in their lives at all. So, I can't be too sorry I caused a cave-in, even if I'll never know for sure whether Filippa meant to kill me. Because, once we get to the end, we're all reduced to the same fine tufa powder.

The things I saw here, the things I did, these are what you read about in societies that exist far away, and in spaces and times that exist only in books. This is not me. These are Clifford Geertz's Balinese, Margaret Mead's Samoans, Claude Lévi-Strauss's Tupi-Kawahib. Sometimes, I think I should still be in class, with a notepad in my hand and a bookbag at my feet, debating the true nature of ethnography. But then my mind lands on the parents in this town who remember their children as they wanted them to be, and I know that I am among them, and I am equally present and equally lost.

Sometimes, it is enough to lick my fingers and run them down the lengths of the walls, and taste what I can now only begin to fathom. I put my hands to my neck and feel the stubble growing from the skin, and when I press the soft pads of my fingers against the prickly hairs, I recollect everything that once happened to me inside caves.

The truth is there were never any murders in Mancanzano, other than the one I happened to commit. Now, when I think of what happens to people in deep, damp, small spaces, there's a desperation inside me to hold my breath. Sometimes I sit here reminding myself, over and over, how a hero's journey is supposed to be one of return.

So, yes, I will tell Antonio Montefalcone the next time I see him, the itching has spread. The one benefit of incarceration is that from here on in, the rest of his visits are going to come out of the Italian government's pockets . . .

—

Middelhoek headed back to the Netherlands. Fortune practically fled to London. Linda left for the United States. She will come to talk to you. She will tell you things you want to hear. And others, certainly, that you won't. She will tell you I love you, and you will decide which one of those that is.

Middelhoek has promised that he will write to me about marvelous, inescapable Mathilde. Maybe one day he will write to tell me that she is having a baby.

Dottoressa Donabuoni visits. Her expression is invariably grim, with all the gravitas of a mother unable to forgive her kin. She tells me, 'I'll visit you periodically because I live here.'

No one hears word of Dr Stoppani, but I figure he must have come across me in newspapers or seen me on TV. When I think of the doctor, I remember his translations for us at his home in Bari, as we watched the fisherman's wife on the evening news, the one whose husband died from eating a bowl of bad mussels.

If I picture Dr Stoppani as I first met him, then I can try to forget everything that followed. But I still wonder what happened to Monica, her airs, her jewelry, and the Geiger-counter clicking of her heels. Then, as always, I picture you wrapped in the netting of fresh cotton sheets, and I hear the sound of you laughing as powerfully as falling stones.

I still have my eyes. Otherwise, I could hope to break out of here like Samson.

With those eyes, I like to picture you giving birth during my trial. Operating-room lights that are stronger and hotter than the sun. You, on your back, with your knees raised by your sides, and a doctor easing a child from your womb and into the pregnant possibilities of the open air.

When you sit in a prison, you wonder how often you should masturbate. What do the monks do, you wonder, having made vows to God of a lifetime of celibacy? Sitting in a prison cell, what else is there to do? Locked alone in a cave, without the touch of another, how do you decide how often you should touch yourself?

Twenty years. Hoc Est Purgatorio. *Questo tribunale condanna l'imputato a vent'anni di carcere.* This court sentences the accused to twenty years of imprisonment. I think it sounds better in Italian.

But does anyone know that a prison only mimics what it's like to be in a cave? Do they know that in Rome? Does the prosecuting magistrate have any idea of it in Potenza? I'm pretty sure people suspect in Mancanzano. A cell is damp. It is tight. The air is stale. The air is fungus. Prison is like wearing a damp wool sweater all the time. You shiver inside, even when you are hot.

Occasionally, the smell of cigarettes wafts through the corridor, and it is remarkable enough that I pretend I am smelling the sweet fragrance of lilacs. Or the exhaust of a car will claw its way up the prison's exterior walls, and in through my cell's one window, and then there will be the odorless gust of carbon monoxide in the cocktail of fumes, and, along with it, the hint of charcoal slow-smoldering in a cave. Afterwards, at night, in this cell, there is always the darkness. The light from stars never reaches this far. The stars flicker in the sky, and I can see them, but I do not think they are particularly interested in me. The hallowed and hollowed exist in different places, on different planes.

A cave and a prison exist on the inside, and they are every bit as undeniable and dangerous as a thought, and they are every bit as real as an action.


Padre Caduta comes to visit. Just the other day, he wanted to know if I'd join him in reciting any Hail Marys.

'Are there any Jews you can send me?' I asked serenely.

'Not who will recite Ave Maria,' he answered me, honestly.

'Then you're the one.'

But as he stood before me, clutching a worn missal in his hands, I realized that his face now had the same eerie chalkiness of Dottoressa Donabuoni's breast. Padre Caduta smiled wanly. But who could blame him?

So we chanted: '*Ave Maria, Madre di Gesù e Madre mia, difendimi dalle insidie del Maligno in vita e particolarmente nell'ora della morte, per il Potere che ti ha concesso l'Eterno Padre . . .*'

But as we stood in my prison cell, reciting the verses aloud – the priest and I and the holy-moly meandering spirit – another version of the prayer tumbled like loose stones in my head:

*Donna Giulia della Vagina, Donna Filippa dell'Irresistibile Culo*, forgive me my weaknesses, my errors, my sin. Would you take hold of my map, and show me your churches? I'm down on my knees, and I need to pray!

*Difendimi dalle insidie.* Protect me from snares, especially if I'm going to be my own *Eterno Padre*. But don't unravel whatever it is you're knitting. It will keep you warm, particularly in winter. Will you cover yourself, and our baby, and another man with it?

Padre Caduta looked worried. He said, 'Young man, perhaps you're distracted.' Then he lowered his book, and asked, 'Do you think you've been sentenced for so long because you are American? Do you think it is because you are a Jew? That's not so bad. You might have been Protestant.'

'Lucky me,' I told him. 'A gift of birth. Admittedly more common where I was born than it is here.'

'My point is, do you think a real Italian, one who understands all the saints properly, would have been treated more leniently?'

Now I could tell he was worried I'd have a bad impression of his country.

'No, Padre,' I assured him. 'I love it here. Really. Everything's been very fair. And, in court, the bars of my cage had a genuine spit shine. But, do you think, since you're visiting, we could talk a little about the saints? Tell me about Lucia. I hear she was pretty, immovable and inflammable too.'

'She is the patroness of eye disease,' he answered uneasily. 'Perhaps you have been to her Feast?'

'Been there. Done that. I hear she has a great ass.'

'We think of other things,' he told me, looking for an appropriate adage to recite from his book.

303

'I'm in no rush,' I answered him idly. 'Take your time. Right now, I'm happy to consider all my options.' I smiled. 'What are they?'

He shook his head. 'I don't know. Try prayer. But if that's no good, you can ask the guard for a chisel.'

I looked at him.

'No, of course not,' he said. 'But you might try humor. Think of the opportunity you'll have over the years to work on your timing.'

*A joke*: let's suppose Dr Stoppani killed Dr Biaggi. Now, when the big man tells the little one, 'Honey, you're finally satisfying all of my appetites!' the little one can answer him, with the steely premonition of death in his eyes, 'Just because you have me now, it doesn't mean you're going to get to keep me! There are a lot of holes around here, Benedetto. Not only my own!'

*Or, a joke*: Dr Stoppani is moping around, kicking his heels, dejected after his latest amorous failure. He gave a woman a bottle of perfume – which he figured would get him into the sack – but she poured the entire bottle's contents over her body at once. She was young and eager, and splashed herself like she was christening a ship. Awash in perfume, she kept wanting to retire to Dr Stoppani's room. But now the doctor didn't want to go. Because he was afraid he might suffocate.

Fuck me in this cage. Fuck me in this cave. Fuck – I hear birds from beyond the walls calling me; are they kestrels? The sorrow of stone is its heaviness on the ground. I want to float up and disappear into powder. So do not forget.

Or have you forgotten already?

Once upon a time, I wrote my name on the wall. I inscribed it in stone. I scratched my name in the dust. I did everything but put my arms around you, and use them to keep me by your side. Instead, I traveled here. To Mancanzano. As I too long ago told you, to get lost in the sassi.

My darling (can I still think to call you that?), I picture you with our child in New York City, in a city that is also composed of cells, and I hope, one day, that you escape them. That is my wish for you and for me, and for the child who may one day ask about the country called Italy, and a tiny southern hill town in it named Mancanzano. Wherever you go, kids can be rough. That's a fact. One day, at a playground, our child may pick up a rock and hurl it at a bully, and in that moment of hitting him squarely between the eyes, suddenly understand the power of stone. And I hope, for that moment, you will prepare him.

# Acknowledgments

The city of Mancanzano does not appear on every map. But at the same coordinates (40° 40' N, 16° 37' E), you can generally find the town of Matera. Both towns share a good deal of history, and Matera is equally famous in Italy for its sassi.

In Matera, I have many to thank. Their generosity on my trips to the city was only surpassed by their knowledge of their hometown, and both helped make this book possible. Giovanni Moliterni's tours of the landscape and academic expertise in his bookshop were indispensable. Rita Padula gave me access to her restorations of the facade of Matera's cathedral – that is, when she wasn't otherwise offering delicious meals. Silvia Padula and Tonio Acito provided insight into the local architecture, past and present. Dorothy Zinn supplied her doctoral thesis on life in Lucania – and the best reading list any would-be anthropologist could hope for. Italians *ex situ* Giovanni Padula and Carlo Monticelli provided corrections, clues and copious suggestions, both where I knew that I needed them and where they came as a sobering surprise.

Several books were particularly useful to me in addition to those already named in the text. The Lombroso passages would have been impossible without Mary Gibson's essay 'Biology or Environment? Race and Southern "Deviancy" in the Writings of Italian Criminologists, 1880–1920', in *Italy's "Southern Question,"* Jane Schneider, ed. What I know of the decomposition of human beings and wall paintings relies chiefly on *Forensic Pathology,* by Dominick J. DiMaio and Vincent J. M. DiMaio, and *Art Restoration,* by James Beck and Michael Daley. Respectively, of course.

In New York, thanks go to those who read drafts: Lev Dassin, Lynn Harris, Veerendra Lele, Jeremy Mindich, John Rousakis, Jon Rubin, and Elizabeth and Herbert Sturz. I also want to thank Suzanne Gluck and Caroline Sparrow and my London editor, Kate Elton, for their insights and energy. Beyond this, love and gratitude go to my parents, Robert and Beverly, for their tireless enthusiasm, even past death, and to Paula, who teaches me about life, and without whose shrewdness and support the road would have been twice as daunting and one-third as fun.